Cowboy

Avonelle Kelsey

Hot Springs, South Dakota

ISBN: 978-0-9816116-0-0

Cover design by Nola L. Kelsey

Printed in the United States of America

www.AvonelleKelsey.com

Contents

The Diary   1

The Horse Thieves   7

Night Raiders   17

Healing & Memories   35

Life of a Gambler   57

The Bennett Family & Ms. Melissa   77

Evil Twins & First Loves   89

Rules for Teachers in 1872   101

Growing Up   103

The Homestead   115

Move 'em out   123

Letters & Poems   149

The Recovery   159

Return to Vermillion   195

Melissa & Rod   205

Home Again   249

Claudette   267

Deadwood Gulch   273

Two Bears, One Bear & Fawn   289

A Ghost from The Past   327

Fate-Twisted Lovers   379

Annabelle & Sheldon   413

Secrets and the Twins   427

Weddings & Surprises   461

Dedicated to:

The O.K. & Edith Anderson Family and their descendants.

The Diary

The sun rose as my estranged father and I parked on the hill above the old family homestead. My heart beat wildly in anticipation; as though I shared some secret knowledge with the caved-in, sod hut on this desolate prairie.

Fragmented signs of life on the weathered hillside must have triggered memory genes in my body, I thought later. My father, whom I had met for the first time in many years at the reading of Grandpa's will, got out of the truck and led the way to the ruins of the Soddy. We peered into the cool, dark interior.

The front of the Soddy had collapsed but a mammoth fireplace stood intact. A light breeze rustled tall buffalo grass growing on the roof. I jumped back, startled as a stray lamb 'baaaaed' and ran past me from dark shadows inside the ruins, down the slope to its mother.

Avonelle Kelsey

The stranger beside me chuckled and said, "Your great-grandfather, Rod Anderson lived here. He was a sheep man. He built this sod house just after the discovery of Gold in the Black Hills, about the time Custer was killed. This was still called Dakota Territory. Buffalo and Native Americans roamed the prairie. It took a brave man to carve a home in this wilderness," he paused thoughtfully.

I was certain he was remembering Mother and wondering if I would hate the land as much as she. Mother was dead now. Both of us were alone, but . . . I nodded, my imagination running back in time as we cautiously made our way inside. Colorful bits of wallpaper curled on the walls. Sunbeams filtered through a hole in the roof, flooding the room with dusty light.

"This fireplace is probably as useable now as when he built it, or Fawn, Two Bears and One Bear used it," Father continued to recollect as we poked among the debris.

I remembered an old, brown-toned photograph of a tall, kindly-looking, broad-shouldered cowboy leaning against this very fireplace. A shepherd's staff with a crook at the top hung on the wall where he might have placed it many years before.

I explored aimlessly the tunnel leading through the side of the Soddy to the sheep fold and returned full circle to the front porch and to the smoke-blackened fireplace. An old pot hung in the corner and there were Native American relics above the fireplace.

Shelf-like niches had been dug into the walls behind an old picture frame with a torn photo. I reached into each one, pulling out dirt and rusty objects. There was a hole in the bottom of the largest opening. I put my hand into it, drawing out papers and a small book. Father and I looked at the book and then one another. A question hung in the air between us. Should we invade the privacy of an ancestor?

"I don't reckon he'd mind his namesake knowing about his private life. Let's go outside in the sunlight and take a look." We sat on the hill beside the remains of the old sod house and looked at the age-stained pages.

There was a copy of the Homestead Act, old letters, photographs, poems, sketches and the diary. I hesitated, and then opened the book. The diary read like a story I already knew but had refused to remember.

Rod Anderson, after whom I was named, suddenly became very real to me. I read of the hardships and adventures he encountered during those wild homesteading, gold rush days, of Native Americans, about his handsome gambler-father, the talented, eccentric Bennett family who adopted him, as well as the twists and unexpected paths their young lives took when love and ambition conflicted. The land I had inherited took on a new meaning.

The strange man, my father, sat beside me reading over my shoulder. When we finished, the sun had cast long shadows across the land.

I sighed, closed the diary and rolled over on my stomach to watch a blazing, orange sun slide behind a barricade of prairie cottonwoods. I heard bird calls and smelled the sweet scent of a nursing lamb. Soft breezes curled around my face and lips. In a stream nearby ducks floated under ancient trees. Beside me, the massive figure of my father threw a cooling shadow across my face.

He brushed away a tear. I pretended not to see, not knowing just how to react. My own sight blurred.

Mother, an actress, had taken me back east when I was a child. I seldom saw Father, knowing him only as the tall, handsome stranger who visited us once a year until she died. For the first time I felt comfortable with our silent communion.

I turned to look at him. Then, reached out to touch his arm. Is he thinking of Mother, too, I wondered.

Father and I had come here today, two lonely people. Now, I had fallen in love, in love with this man, my father, and in love with this strange quiet land. My life seemed enriched by the words I'd read, yet they filled me with a nebulous brooding. It was as though reading the diary had given me a cushion for my lonely life.

I tried to speak of this. "The words in the book, they . . . they help me to understand a little better, how you feel about the land. Why you stayed here instead of living with us in the east."

"It is not often one has the opportunity to see into the heart and mind of a wise human being," he answered simply.

I laid the book aside, reached out and took his hand. Together our spirits soared back through time . . .

Avonelle Kelsey

The Horse Thieves

Three outlaws, in love with hate, pushed their horses toward Anderson's Springs in spite of the roan's limp. Two Bears, their guide, lagged behind hoping to slow them down for the sake of the tired animal.

The sheepherders had said, "Rod Anderson is a good man. He shoots with the swiftness of an arrow. To us he is known as Smoking Wind."

Two Bears passed along the warning, but the outlaws laughed. "We need horses. If'n he won't trade, we'll take 'em," Sam bragged.

Rod Anderson sat on the porch in front of his Soddy, drinking coffee and enjoying the beauty of a Dakota prairie morning, unaware of the four unsavory-looking horsemen approaching his homestead. The coffee was his recipe, made from dried dandelion roots and chicory. The joy of being, the kiss of spring in the air and thoughts of sharing the future with Annabelle, coiled in his mind, lighting his face with a smile.

A flaming sunrise gave an orange cast to the tall cottonwoods, the sheep going down the draw, horses, pond and cows. His dog, Nellie, faithful companion for many years, raced up onto the porch, licked her puppy and snuggled against Rod's buckskin jacket. Rod absent-mindedly scratched her ears and pushed his battered cowboy hat further down on his thick curly hair. A strong, chilling wind swirled from the north attempting to whip it away.

"Ah, Nellie," he said to the collie, "the morning's near to perfect, but I can smell a storm in the air. We've work to do before it snows."

For two years Rod had worked from daylight till dark 'proving up' his homestead, and the land he had purchased when still too young to stake out a claim. The young man felt a satisfying kinship with this rolling land. For a moment his pleasure wavered as he wondered about Annabelle. Would she feel the same way? He watched his Arabian mare and her yearling trot around the corral and smiled as he thought of presenting the colt to Annabelle as an engagement present. The mare was old. His father had won her in a race in another land.

"I'm twenty-one today, Nellie. Glad I was able to buy this homestead cheap, or I'd have had to wait to get it in my name. Gonna' bake me a cake?"

He scratched Nellie's ears. She gave a little yip and tried to lick his face. Her puppy stumbled over his knees and fell off the steps. Rod laughed, leaned over and picked her up, placing the puppy by its mother.

Suddenly, Nellie tensed and growled. Rod leaned forward, listening for unusual sounds. The dog stood tail and ears taut. A low growl issued from her throat.

Rod touched her shoulder. "Hush," he commanded softly, getting swiftly to his feet.

Horses in the corral snorted and pricked up their ears. The ground vibrated even before the sound of hooves rang on the crisp air.

Nellie growled again. Rod motioned her down, picked up the excited puppy and thrust her inside the door. His interior light of joy was replaced by a feeling of uttermost cold. Anxiety flashed through his body. Before pulling the door closed, he placed a loaded rifle against the outside wall and adjusted the pistol on his hip. He waited quietly on the porch, hand hovering near the gun as he and Nellie watched the bend on the wagon road.

Three white men and a Native American rode up to the barn yard. One of their horses limped. They stopped, studied the horses in the corral, and then looked around, cautiously. Rod pushed his leather jacket aside in order to free his pistol. He had learned how to use his gun from his father. So far, a man had never been the target.

The white men sat on their horses with an air of belligerent arrogance. They caught his movement and swung around. Their horses snorted, tugging at the reins; they smelled the water and fresh hay nearby. Leather saddles squeaked and moaned when the men shifted their weight. After a long silence the broad, bearded leader nodded his head. They rode up to the hitching rail by the porch where Rod stood waiting. Smells of dust, tired horses and sweaty men filled Rod's nostrils.

"Howdy. Name's Sam Smith. This here's Brent and Rafe." He ignored the Native American. The men showed blackened teeth for a moment, nodded and sat in silence, eyeing Rod's gun.

Rod lifted his left hand in greeting. His right hand continued to hover near his pistol. "Howdy. Rod Anderson. What can I do for you?"

"We're heading fir the gold strike in the Black Hills. Brent's horse is limpin'. How much fir the black?" Sam asked.

"Sorry, he's not for sale," Rod said. "I'll be needin' them all. If you was to set for a spell, I'd take a look at the roan's leg and give you some grub." Lonesome as Rod was for news; he hoped these mean looking sons-of-guns would move on. Nellie stood beside him, her lips curled back, low growls issuing from her throat. Both of them sensed evil in the men.

"You can't ride but one, boy," Sam, the big hulk, snarled. His hand strayed near his pistol.

Rod felt his body tense. He had worked too hard to build up his homestead stock to let a bunch of greedy wanderers steal it.

To shoot a man went against his grain, but these three would make tempting targets. Could he possibly take them all at once, and would the Native American enter the fight? Rod took a step backward toward the door, balancing on the balls of his feet, ready for action.

The three continued to watch the young man and his gun. He did not flinch. A thousand words in eye language filled the silence between them. Finally, Sam nodded and waved his hand for the crew to dismount.

"Reckon we could use some grub."

"Take a seat on the porch. I'll bring coffee and biscuits." After they were seated, Rod picked up the rifle, stepped inside and spoke softly to Nellie where she stood defiantly in the doorway, "Set."

The puppy rushed out onto the porch and began to dance around the men. Brent reached out to it and Nellie growled. The man quickly withdrew his hand and swore at the dog, "Mean little bitch."

Rod watched the men from the doorway as they made themselves comfortable on the porch. The Native American guide sat off to one side looking in the direction of the Black Hills as the morning sun rose higher, taking the chill off the day. Gusty wind continued whipping around the hill which entombed the Soddy.

Pioneer hospitality required no pilgrim be turned away hungry. Rod normally enjoyed company, but this was the worst crew to stumble into his place so far. He reckoned there'd be more before the gold rush to the Black Hills was over and done with.

Going into the cave behind the main room of the Soddy, he cut four slabs of steak from the antelope haunch stored there and returned to the fireplace.

His eyes didn't leave the door for long and he listened for a warning from Nellie. She never let anyone over the door sill without his permission.

Rod added water and a handful of chicory coffee to the pot, pushing it to the hot side of the iron slab in the fireplace he used for a cooking surface.

While the meat cooked, he paused in the doorway and suggested they let the horses rest for a couple of days. "There's a storm in the making. Probably just a spring snow. Won't last long, but they can be violent. You can bunk in the barn. There's fresh clean hay."

"Not on your life," Sam turned, looked up and grinned wickedly. "We've outwitted soldiers and Injuns and aim to get to the Black Hills 'fore the spring floods and other miners who'll come with warm weather. A bit of snow or lame horse ain't gonna' stop us, now," he sneered. The rasping laughter of the men seemed to contain more threat than humor.

Rod suspected they were running from the law.

Custer and his men had discovered gold in the Black Hills of the Dakotas. Recently, he and his soldiers had been killed by Native Americans in Montana Territory, as though fate had pronounced judgment on their discovery. The gold strike had led to a boomtown called Deadwood Gulch. In spite of anything the government or Native Americans could do, miners, fortune seekers, outlaws and settlers flocked across the prairies and into the sacred hills. Soldiers often deserted and joined miners in their search for gold.

Native American reservations were divided and more land was opened for homesteading; a railroad was being built. Many homesteads, like Rods, had already been staked out and abandoned. The Dakota Democrat News had advertised the land for fifty dollars. It was near the marks Custer had checked on Rod's map. Rod thought about this as he cooked breakfast and carried it to the men on the porch. His serving plates were slabs of polished wood and the forks he'd carved from cottonwood boles.

Each man carried a knife and used it for eating.

Nellie lay on the porch, watching the clumsy puppy. With a low growl Nellie subdued it, then rose, taking it to the barnyard where it could play and she could keep an eye on the men.

Rod returned with a plate of cold biscuits and filled the tin mugs each man carried on his belt. "According to treaties, the Black Hills don't belong to white men. It's the sacred hunting ground of Native Americans."

The three men laughed at him. Brent answered contemptuously, "An animal can't own land."

Rod glanced toward the guide. A glaze of pain passed over his face. There was fire in his ice-gray eyes, but he lowered his head.

The young Indian was probably a half breed, Rod thought, brought up in town by a 'do-gooder' and blown like a seed in the wind when he found white men would not accept him as a human being. Rod bit his lip to keep back the anger gathering inside. "My grandmother was a Native American and I'm proud of it," he glared at Brent who sneered, but lowered his eyes.

Why was this young man with them? There was dignity and pride in his bearing. He was not one of the local tribes and would be safer alone than with these men. "I'll throw out some hay for the horses and take a look at the mare's leg while you eat."

Rod closed the door, picked up his rifle and took the bridle of the limping mare. Keeping the horse between himself and the men, he led her to the barn where his salves and liniments were stored. Nellie lay on the ground, watching the porch.

Rod paused outside to scratch the dog's ears. "Stay here and keep an eye on them, girl." She sat on her haunches by the barn watching the men on the porch, as alert as though guarding sheep from a coyote.

The Indian followed him inside the barn. He helped Rod throw hay out of the loft to the horses. As they examined the mare's leg he said, "I'm Two Bears."

Often Native Americans didn't tell their real name. Rod wondered what Two Bear's other name might be. He's almost as white as I am, he thought, smiling, reaching out to shake his hand.

"I'm Rod Anderson."

The barn was warm, smelling of clean hay and animal flesh. They worked in comfortable silence.

"Have you seen General Meade?" Two Bears asked. His English was as good as Rod's. There were urgency and passion just under the surface of his words.

I hope I'm not around when that tension bursts lose, Rod thought. "Well, let's see." Rod pushed his hat back and thought for a minute. So many groups stopped at the old watering hole, it was hard to keep track.

"Last summer Meade camped down by the creek and in January a scout sheltered here during a storm. He said the general was farther south this winter but would probably head for the Dakota Territory and the Black Hills come spring." Rod tried to fathom his reason for the inquiry. "He's foxy and doesn't let his where-a-bouts be known ahead of time. Maybe he'll headquarters at the new fort that's being built at the foot of the Black Hills. Some call it Meade."

Rod held the leg of the horse while Two Bears applied the salve and bound the lame ankle. His movements were skillful. The horse would be all right with a couple of days rest.

"You're pretty good with animals."

"Our mother was a medicine woman."

Rod noted the plural instead of my or me. The young man said no more.

They fed and brushed the horses while the three men lounged on the porch. The morning was getting colder, the wind stronger. They went back inside to check on the lame horse.

"Two Bears, you're welcome to stay on here if you like. I don't trust the crew you're riding with."

"Thanks, but I must get to the Black Hills and find a man. These renegades are nasty but I'm not afraid of them. People talk to them and not to an Indian. They move fast. When I reach the Black Hills, I'll leave them."

Nellie began to bark.

"Git your butt movin' and saddle them horses," Sam yelled to the young man from the yard.

Rod and Two Bears shook hands and led the horses back to the porch of the Soddy. As they approached the lounging men, Rod again kept the horses between them. He quickly stepped to the doorway, standing in it as the four men mounted, turned and rode away.

The burly crew left without saying, thanks. They stopped by the spring near the bend in the wagon road and filled their canteens. Two Bears raised a hand in farewell.

Rod was relieved to see the backs of the men as they rode over the hill and out of sight.

Night Raid

The storm moved in quickly from the Southwest. Rod saddled his horse and went out to meet the returning shepherds. "We're in for a heavy, wet one," he shouted into the wind. "Shouldn't last too long. Leave the sheep in the fold and head on home. I'll round up the cows."

"Saw some wolves stalking a herd of buffalo just over the ridge," one shepherd warned.

He'd best bring the cows in from the far pasture, Rod decided, facing into the stinging storm which had turned to sleet. The cows were reluctant to move from their shelter in a draw beneath a group of cedars. Rod had planned on raising cattle, but agreed with Mackenzie, the prairie was ideal for sheep and buffalo. He kept a few cows for milk, meat and some experimental breeding. Sometimes Rod often smiled and thought he could make more money selling butter, cheese and milk to the many miners and homesteaders who passed the place than he could on the sheep.

Mackenzie had said, "Now, take them Rambouillet French sheep; they're made for the prairie. Cows need too much hay and pasture." He'd been right. Rod decided to trail a few head to Deadwood Gulch next fall. They should fetch a good price. With all the miners coming past the place on the way west to Deadwood Gulch, he doubted he'd have to leave the ranch to sell them but he was curious about Deadwood. It might not hurt to take a look at the Black Hills sometime. Maybe Annabelle would enjoy taking the trip with him. He smiled with pleasure as he remembered her racing across the green meadow on a horse and her curls tumbling wildly in the wind. Wet snow slapped him in the face bringing him out of his reverie. The sleet had turned to snow.

"Nellie, go after them. Take them home, girl." He whistled. The old collie raced around the cows, nipping at their heels and barking. Rod fumbled with cold-numbed fingers at the drawstring of his hat, the brim fell down across his ears from the weight of icy snow. When they neared home, the cows broke into a trot and headed for the shelter of the barn. Several would be calving soon. The Native American shepherds and dogs had put the sheep into their pen and returned to their own Soddy.

With Nellie to guard the fold and Rod on the other side of the tunnel, they should be safe enough. He latched the gate securely, bowed his head against the wind and raced for the warmth of the barn, glad the wives of the shepherds had taken on the chore of the milk cows, making cheese and butter. When he assured himself all the animals were safe in their pens and barn, Rod breathed a sigh of relief, turned into the wind and headed for his Soddy.

The sleet gave way to swirling snow. Rod carried extra wood inside, banked the fire with a large cottonwood log, roasted a potato and a skewer of antelope over the flames and sat down at his hand-built cottonwood table by the fire to eat. He glanced at the shelf of books above the fireplace. Melissa, his school teacher in Vermillion, had sent him a copy of Jules Verne's book, *Journey To The Center of the Earth* . . . He already had copies of Verne's other books. I reckon I miss my talks with Mary and Melissa more than anything else, he thought, except maybe Annabelle and her brother, Dan.

After clearing the table, he sat down to write in his diary. With it was a packet of letters. Before going to bed he pulled out the last letters from the Bennett family, Melissa and Annabelle, reading them for the hundredth time.

He held Annabelle's letter to his nose and took a deep breath from the lavender scented pages. Before sleeping he tucked the book and letters into a secret niche he had dug in the wall.

During the cold months of the year, Rod kept a treated, scraped antelope hide tacked over the window by his bed. Its translucent, amber glow let soft light into the cozy room during the day. The room was orderly, except for the corner he used for making furniture. Indian relics sat by several books on the mantle of the fireplace. A shepherd's staff hung alongside. By the door his shaving mug and mirror were surrounded by scraps of paper, photos of the Bennett family, poetry and dried flowers.

One poem was Poe's *Annabelle Lee*. Another, *The Sunflower Woman* written by his mother so many years ago, had turned yellow from age.

That night, Rod tossed restlessly upon his handmade bunk. He shivered under the buffalo robes covering his long frame. The hides usually kept him warm. The room was lit by flickering flames from the cottonwood log burning in the fireplace. Rolling over onto his back, he listened for unusual sounds in the night. Was the chill a premonition, he wondered? But of what? He dozed fretfully. His nightmares usually came back when something was about to go wrong.

Outside, a March blizzard raged across the prairie. Its roar covered the violent scene which had just taken place in the stormy corral, leaving the body of Nellie lying across a path of footprints in the snow. Her puppy whimpered and licked scarlet blood as it dripped onto the soft white blanket beneath her. Its whines were lost to the ears of the dead mother.

Ill tempered wind slammed icy snow against the unlatched gate of the sheep fold, causing it to bang with each gust.

Rod sat up. Were there strange Indians outside? He waited for the wind to quiet down, ears straining for the familiar sounds. Things were too quiet.

But Nellie would bark if anything was wrong he told himself. What had wakened him from a sound sleep? Perhaps it was a dream. He lay back pulling the robes up to his chin, listening and alert.

Rod checked the time by the logs on the fire. They were only half burned away so it must be shortly after midnight. Instead of the comfortable warmth he usually felt when he gazed into the fire, the restless flames sent sinister shadows around the room.

Once again he wondered if this humble place would be good enough for his beloved Annabelle, Annabelle Lee. Rod loved the poem and her name, as well as her lovely, blue-eyed, dimpled face with its mischievous smile. He thought of the black curly hair which danced around her shoulders when she walked, as though it had a life of its own.

For a moment Rod permitted himself the luxury of thinking about her and the words of the poem. Then, he laughed at himself. Poe, in the middle of the night in a prairie 'nowhere,' surrounded by snow, sheep, and Indians. He felt lonely for the people he loved.

Rod's dream-like state came to an abrupt end as another gust of wind set the gate banging. "Oh my Lord," he said aloud. "The sheep-fold gate. The wind must have blown it open."

With a sweep of his hand he threw back the covers and reached for his pants. Quickly he pulled them on, grabbing his sweater and boots. He buckled his pistol around his waist, dropped a handful of shells into his coat pocket, swooping the rifle from above the fireplace. Opening the door into the storage area between the hut and sheep fold, cautiously, he slipped through the darkness and pushed open the outside door. The cold, blowing snow stung his lips and face, where beard failed to cover it.

A three-quarter moon ducked in and out of retreating storm clouds. Most of the snow in the air was coming from drifts which were being gathered up by gusts and stacked against sheds or fences, Rod realized.

The storm was over, except for the strong shifting wind. Deep shadows moved restlessly as snow sparkled and swirled in their ebony depths. He propped the banging gate open, looked inside and listened for Nellie. In spite of her age, she was a good sheep dog. Her eyes and ears had saved him a great deal of time and energy during the past two years. His glance darted about the snow-filled darkness.

The animals were loose, but the sheep wouldn't scatter too far away at night. The shepherds who lived over the ridge would not have taken the sheep. "Nellie," he called softly.

Rod slipped quietly toward the barn. The puppy's whining reached his ears. He turned and went to the puppy.

His beloved Nellie lay across the path. Rod knelt beside her. Wind had swept snow across her cold body. Blood was frozen around the wound on her shoulder. The puppy snuggled against Rod for warmth when he picked it up and held it close. It licked at the tears running down his face before they could freeze in his beard.

Lifting Nellie, he carried her to the empty barn. Putting the puppy inside a stall he used for baby lambs, he closed the door saying softly, "It's all right girl, you'll stay warm until I return."

The corral was empty as well as the barn and sheep fold. Breathing deeply, Rod smelled the cows and heard their restless tinkling bells and shuffling down by the pond. Apparently, the thieves had driven them off but were too slow to take very far in the blizzard.

Rod returned to the house to put some beef jerky and a biscuit in the pocket of his buckskin jacket, along with extra shells for the rifle. As he prepared for the trail, he thought about his situation, trying to eliminate possibilities that might send him off on the wrong track. Native Americans would take the cows as well as the horses, unless they were in a hurry.

Standing for a moment outside the door he let his eyes adjust. The spring wind shifted, now coming from the Northwest, a Chinook, the Indians called the sudden warm moist air which often swept from the coast even in the winter. It could change the weather in a few hours, melting all traces of tracks within a short time. He must hurry.

The local Indians were his friends and wouldn't disturb his animals. More than once they had brought back strays. He returned the favor with food and a night's shelter in the barn.

Sheep huddled against the fence near the backside of the barn. He nudged the leader until he entered the fold and shelter in the cave at the back of the Soddy. The rest of the flock stumbled through the entrance. He checked the catch and wire hoop. Who had opened the gates, he wondered? Without horses, how could he run a ranch? Guess he'd run like his ancestors from back east, the Iroquois.

Rod picked up a bit of the trail. Blowing snow had erased most of the tracks. He went out of the corral and down toward the creek away from the house. The cows huddled under cottonwood trees by the icy stream. They would wander back home in time for hay.

Stealing more than they needed and driving off his stock was the act of evil men. He paused again to look more closely at the tracks.

The moon came out from behind a cloud and turned the dancing snow into a silvery, fairyland. For a moment Rod gazed in wonder. He pulled his gaze away from the glittering beauty of nature. It calmed his body and mind as he returned to the job at hand.

The wind which had brought the blizzard, died down. Clouds retreated leaving moonlight and long purple shadows on the snow. The Chinook blew gently from the coast, across the Black Hills, and out over the prairie. When he crossed the creek, the ice under his feet was already getting soft and slushy. Tallow on his boots kept his feet dry. Their horses wore shoes he noted, so it wasn't Indians after all.

The faces of Sam, Rafe and Brent flickered through Rod's mind as he followed the path up through the cedars, across the prairie and on toward another draw. "Why those shifty bastards," he muttered to himself.

He smelled an animal and heard it blow warm air to clear its nostrils. "Developing your sense of smell is a Native American tracking trick," his half-breed father had told Rod when they had gone trapping back in New Salem, Illinois. Rod stepped silently off the trail, blending in with the landscape as much as possible. It was the limping horse belonging to the man named Brent. The horse came to Rod, nuzzling him as though asking for help. He scratched its ears, speaking softly to it, promising to come back.

I must be getting nearer, he thought. Running lightly through snow drifts, Rod covered the ground swiftly. It was near dawn. When the sun came out, it would be a lovely spring day as often happened with a Chinook, even in the middle of winter. By evening there would be very little snow and a great deal of mud.

Apparently, they'd waited to resaddle until they were out of sight and hadn't expected him to follow them until morning. His Arabian mare would be fresh and easy to control. It would also be easy to spot, should they take it into a town to sell. Annabelle's horse was barely 'green broke.' The plow horses would be good pack horses, but were not very fast. Each had a yearling at her side and would be dropping another foal soon.

The men knew this and must have taken them along out of spite, Rod decided. The horses would bring a good price in the boomtown of Deadwood Gulch, if they ever reached the Black Hills. His O over K brand would not be easy to alter.

It was hard for Rod to understand men like the outlaws who had visited his place, accepted his hospitality and then, not only stole from him, but tried to destroy his animals. His father had understood people well and tried to teach Rod to read men as well as nature, but Rod had remained too trusting, until now.

The small creeks were narrow and deep in spots. If they broke through the ice they would freeze, or have to build a fire to thaw out. There were soft shoulders along the deep gullies that would cave in. Cedar trees lined the sides of these passages, their smell was fresh and clean.

A buffalo or cow path was the safest way to go, even though it looked farther. In the event the horse thieves headed west, they would have to go north or south along the bank of the larger stream to find a safe crossing.

Rod guessed they would ride north since the bank sloped in that direction. However, the tracks led south. Two Bears was good. He might try to slow them down until Rod caught up. Would he fight for those men?

Would they give up without a fight when he demanded his stock back? Rod's stomach lurched as he thought of killing. It was hard enough for him to kill an animal for food.

"I'll do what I have to do," he said to himself grimly. In the distance he saw the sunlit top of Bear Butte, the sacred Native American mountain. "Git to it and you're purty near Deadwood Gulch and them Black Hills," several people had told him. He sighed and pushed a thought aside; perhaps I'll never see the hills.

Around him, drifts stacked up for several feet in places, bare spots shown in others. He pushed on. Climbing another ridge, he slid down the other side. Snow slipped under the neck of his jacket, melting on his sweating back.

Voices on the wind. His ears picked up sounds of snorting horses as well. He paused, smelling the wind for odors, listening intently.

There were faint traces of smoke and animals in the air. He had often camped in the gully where they were located. It was surrounded by a large clump of cottonwood trees, out of the wind. There would be some grass for hobbled horses, if the snow wasn't too deep.

The men must have been very confident he wouldn't be able to follow them and claim his animals. Anger rose like bile in Rod's throat. Never had he been so full of rage.

"They'll find Rod Anderson is man enough to protect what's his," he muttered. Then paused, breathed deeply, calming his mind and body. Rod remembered his father's words, "Never enter a fight with anger in your heart. Anger tends to give a false burst of courage which will abandon you, leaving you trembling and helpless."

In his mind he visualized the area. The horses were staked in a clearing with a lasso fencing tied between cottonwood trees near the creek. Knowing his horses would recognize his scent, he stayed down wind.

Creeping from tree to tree until he was behind the one where Rafe, the guard sat, Rod looked into the camp. Rafe was catching a nap. He leaned against a cottonwood with a rifle across his lap. A whiskey bottle lay nearby.

Brent was drinking coffee by the fire. Sam was holding a skillet over the flames attempting to fry bacon. He yelled at Two Bears, "Git them damn horses saddled, 'fore that young punk comes lookin' fir his stock."

The body of the Indian tensed. He flicked a glance in Rod's direction, got up, pulled his jacket tighter around himself and ambled off toward the horses.

Rod unbuttoned his coat and freed the pistol in its holster. Holding his rifle in front of him at waist level, he quietly moved up behind Rafe. With his gun leveled at big Sam and Brent, he kicked the rifle off the lap of the guard.

"Put your hands up. Now. All of you."

Rod would never completely rid himself of the scene which followed. Everything seemed to move in slow motion and burn a picture into Rod's mind.

Sam looked up from the fire, shouted an oath, dropped the skillet and leaped to his feet, drawing his gun. He was fast, but Rod was faster. Clutching his shoulder, Sam fell backward into the fire, screaming. Rod stepped around the tree, dropped the old, single- shot rifle and drew his double-action revolver.

Brent and he both fired. Brent toppled forward. Rod felt the bullet rip into his shoulder and was thrown sideways against the tree.

He heard a shout and turned in time to see Two Bears lunging toward the guard with a knife. Rafe had retrieved his rifle and was pointing it at Rod. Rod fired hurriedly and saw the top of Rafe's head fly into the air as the young man hurdled toward him. They went down together. Two Bears rolled away from Rafe and came to his feet gazing around in amazement; blood from Rafe covered his clothing. He and Rod looked at one another in surprise.

Blood gushed from Rod's shoulder. He could feel it running hot inside his clothing. Sam still lay in the fire. The smell of burning flesh filled Rod's nostrils. The guard's brains ran out on the snow. Brent lay with his hand outstretched toward Rod, sightless eyes gazing into the morning sun.

Rod began to cough, and then vomit. He sank slowly to his knees and fell forward onto the snow-covered ground.

Only the snorting horses were heard in the sudden silence.

Two Bears sheathed his knife, wiped his hands on the snow, shook his head in Rod's direction and went back to the horses. He took his own horse, Rafe's and Sam's. As he paused to pick up their gear, he heard Rod moan.

Rod's book of poetry had slipped out of his pocket. The wind blew it open to the much worn pages of Poe's, Annabelle Lee.

A couple of loose sheets of Rod's own poetry slipped out, face up, as if waiting for the open eyes of death to read them in appreciation. Rod had written a poem each time a new season rolled around.

Two Bears bent over and picked them up. He read:

(The printing was in a neat hand. Annabelle always wrote with a flourish, like she lived . . . Rod had thought fondly when he compared their handwritings.)

Rainbows

The Opposite Of That Vast Gray
Which Drenches Me,
There Are No Raincoats For Mankind's Soul
Unless It Is A Rainbow Lifting Up The Eyes,
Warming Up The Heart.

Rain, Rain,

Noisy, Wetly, Rattling Like
Jungle Drums On My Tin Roof.
My Feather Bed Is Warm And Dry,
I Cuddle Down Beside Grandma
Feeling, Oh, So Safe.
Glad You're Outside, In Me.

Snowflakes

Leaping Out Of Nothingness,
A Vapor Molds Itself,
From That Mysterious Shadow Which
Orchestrates And Sculptures,
Universes--You And Me.

Two Bears read the poems and sighed. He could not leave a man who loved nature like this to die. Bending over Rod's body, he put the poetry back into the little book and placed it in Rod's pocket. Then, turning him over, he sprinkled herbs from a package carried in his saddle bag and packed snow against the wound, mumbling an ancient healing chant. From one of the dead men he cut off a shirt, packed the wound again with icy snow to stop the bleeding, tied the arm and shoulder across the cowboy's chest. The bullet had gone through the flesh above the heart and out the other side.

Two Bears could not be certain what damage the bullet had done inside. A great deal of blood was being lost. Leaning over Rod's chest, he could hear a faint heart beat. The young man made a travois from tree branches and bed rolls, attached them to Rod's horse with leather thongs from the harness of Brent's horse and pulled Rod through the snow, back to the ranch. He was doubtful Rod would live long enough to see his home again.

Two Bears was just outside the corral when a voice yelled in broken English and Sioux, "Leave the friend of Sioux and turn around."

Two Bears dropped the reins and looked into the face of five bedraggled looking renegade Indians, two Native American shepherds and several snarling sheep dogs.

Two Bears raised his hand and replied, "Rod Anderson is my friend as well. He has been shot by bad white men. I am bringing him home, perhaps to die."

The shepherds rushed forward to look at Rod while the renegades Indians disarmed Two Bears. Dogs circled and nipped at his heels. In the barn the puppy whined and barked.

"Mr. Rod is dead," one announced after pulling back the blanket, exposing the blood-soaked shirt. Another tried to set him up.

"Stop," Two Bears shouted. "I am a Medicine Man. You will kill him."

The leader of the five Indians drew the knife he had taken from Two Bears and approached him, smiling wickedly. "You do not tell Spotted Pony what to do."

The shepherds turned, grabbing his arms as he raised the knife. "No. This man is of my woman's tribe. We need his medicine."

Spotted Pony shrugged, turned away and climbed onto his horse. "If Mr. Rod dies, you die," he shouted as they rode away.

Avonelle Kelsey

Nightmares and Healing Memories

Rod lay on the bed in his Soddy, his body racked with pain. Time seemed to twist and turn back upon itself as he tossed and moaned. He dreamed of men looming out of the darkness with guns and knives while he tried to run away, but his feet would not move. Sometimes he lived in the past with his mother and father. Native Americans both chased and came to his aid.

Mary held him in her arms like a baby and sang to him. Then Rod, Dan, and Annabelle would be racing horses over a cliff. He built a grand house for Annabelle and it fell down before she could go inside. He felt hot and then his teeth chattered in icy coldness.

In his delirium Rod relived the death of his pregnant Mother and his eleventh birthday. It was a sad birthday memory.

Avonelle Kelsey

He kept repeating the poem:

"She was a child and I was a child,
In that kingdom by the sea,
And we loved with a love that was more than love,
I and my Annabelle Lee . . ."

In his nightmares he saw his mother's face. She had her arm around him as he proudly recited the poem. She was a teacher and had presented him with a book about the Civil War and Lincoln's death.

His mother's curly blonde hair and blue eyes shone with pride as she sat in the light of a kerosene lamp and listened to his school lessons.

John, Rod's father, sat by the fireplace smoking his pipe watching the two of them. Suddenly, Rod's mother clutched her rounded stomach and moaned, her head fell forward and she slumped against him. Rod stepped backward in astonishment as she slid to the floor.

John dropped his pipe and ran across the room. He lifted his wife in his arms, carrying her into the bedroom. The baby was not due for another two months. At the door he paused long enough to shout, "Rod, take your horse. Get Mrs. Johnson. Bring her back with you. Have Mr. Johnson ride as fast as he can to get Doctor Massan. Hurry!"

The urgency in his tone set Rod into action. His fingers felt numb as he fumbled with the bridle. The pony was young and swift. As they raced through the night, long shadowed thoughts of death kept pace with the pounding hoofs. His eyes were blinded by tears.

He kept looking behind him, remembering the mid-wife's tale about coming home late one night in the winter and feeling something jump up behind her on the horse, the horse trembled but ran on until they came to her house. The thing jumped off. She called Mr. Johnson who ran out of the house with a lantern. Mrs. Johnston slide off the horse as it collapsed. The rump of the horse had been eaten by a mountain lion.

Rod pounded on the door of the midwife's house. "Please, please. Open the door."

Mr. Johnson stood in his underwear and peered out a crack in the doorway. Seeing Rod, he opened it and pulled him inside. "What ye be doin' out so late at night, lad?"

Mrs. Johnson came into the room, pulling on her bonnet and cloak as if she already knew his errand.

"Come quick, Mrs. Johnson. My mother's hurtin' bad. Father wants Mr. Johnson to go to town for the doctor, quick as he can."

Mr. Johnson saddled two horses. He headed for town while she and Rod raced down the old wagon road to the Anderson place. Over the years she had birthed many children and willingly came to the aid of the sick. Rod's mother was both daughter and friend to the Johnsons. She had lived with them during the years she taught school before marrying John Anderson.

That night Rod tossed in his bed, clamping his hands over his ears to block out his mother's screams of pain. Finally, he got up and went into the large kitchen which served as a living room as well.

Mr. Johnson sat in a rocking chair before the fireplace. "Come here lad and set a spell with me. Reckon we could both use a mite of comforting."

"Why doesn't the doctor help her? I thought he was supposed to help people."

"Some things a doctor can help, some things only the good Lord can put out his hand ter give 'er take." He rocked Rod as his mother had rocked him when he was a small child. The screams gradually weakened and quit. Rod dozed.

When he woke it was a cold, gray dawn. All was quiet. The doctor had gone. Mrs. Johnson opened the door to his parent's bedroom.

The silence was louder than the screaming. Fear clutched at him as he hesitated just inside the doorway. His father was holding his mother's body in his arms, rocking back and forth, moaning and mourning in the way of a Native American.

Rod ran to the bed. His mother looked as though she was asleep, but when he climbed onto the bed and touched her hand, it was cold. Rod had seen enough of death to realize his mother was no longer alive. He threw his arms across his father's shoulders and mourned along with him.

The midwife left them to go home for a few hours and prepare for the funeral while her husband passed the word of her death on to nearby homesteaders whose children remembered her as their beloved teacher. Toward noon, neighbors came and took the body from their arms.

The Sunflower Woman, as his Father called Mrs. Johnson the hard working midwife, was the only grandmother the boy knew. When the grave had been dug, and a wooden coffin was built by Mr. Johnson, the neighbors gathered with food and words of comfort outside the house.

Mrs. Johnson insisted Rod bathe and dress. John Anderson looked like a defeated man. He sat staring with unseeing eyes into space. Rod pulled at his father's shirtsleeve before the funeral, but his father only shook his head and passed a hand across dazed eyes. John stood and followed the casket, standing outside the fenced cemetery when the neighbors carried his wife to the graveyard. He looked across the Illinois landscape with unseeing eyes.

Since John had been their only local minister, Mr. Johnson stammered through a ceremony: "Our beloved daughter, your teacher, our songbird, has left us in body but not in spirit. She'll be with us in our hearts and in the learnin' she done give many of you. Mind what she taught you, follow the fine example she set fer all of us . . ." He began to sob. He, Rod and Mrs. Johnson clung together while the school children and their parents sang, 'Shall we gather at the river . . .'

Rod felt her tears dampen his hair. Before the neighbors filled in the grave, they took him home.

John stood in the hot sun long after the funeral procession departed. Mr. Johnson finally led him away from the graveside and walked with him back to the house. He sat on the porch as though in a trance.

Mrs. Johnson put food in the cupboard and taking Rod aside, admonished him to, "Take care of your Pa, Son. He be a mighty fine man, but he don't know how to stop himself once he gets started on a thing, whether it be fightin', preachin', gamblin', or lovin'. Sure glad you take after your maw."

She folded her apron and went to John. Placing her hand on his rigid shoulder she said, "John Anderson, I reckon as how the world has had a great loss, but you're more fortunate than most. You still have one youngen. Take care of him, you hear?"

Rod wanted to chase after her, but he knew his father needed him and vowed silently he would never leave his side.

For two days Rod fed the chickens, watered the stock and milked the cow. His father sat on the porch without talking, seeing only the fresh grave on the hillside. How long he would have set in that fashion, Rod often wondered, if it hadn't been for the snakebite.

One day Rod rushed barefooted into the hen house to gather eggs. He didn't notice a big rattler coiled just behind the open door. His flashing bare legs nearly brushed it as he reached into the nests.

Too late, he heard a rattle, whirled and screamed. The fangs of the rattlesnake grazed his leg. He dropped the basket of eggs and jumped up onto the roost. The snake coiled to strike again. Rod's piercing screams broke through his father's silence as nothing else could have.

In a flash John was across the yard, stomped the snake to death with his boots and picked Rod up in his arms.

"It bit me, Father. It bit me," he sobbed holding his leg.

Taking a knife, John cut a slash across the marks. Laying Rod on the porch, he shot a chicken, tore open the warm breast and wrapped it against the bite. All day and night he kept his arms about Rod, rocking him in Grandmother's old rocking chair.

To keep Rod from passing out, John bathed his fevered body and held cold cloths to his brow. For the next two days he held Rod or sat by his bed holding his hand, telling him stories about his Mother and Grandmother and their life together. It was a healing time for both.

"When I was a boy about your age, I lived for a summer in a teepee with my Indian mother and Irish father. Your grandfather had been a priest until he fell in love with your grandmother."

John would pause and shake Rod gently to make certain he was alive. "As a young Native American girl, Grandmother came to the church. She asked the young priest, "How can you condemn an Indians as a heathen until you have lived in his

Avonelle Kelsey

home?" The priest agreed with her and went to live with her tribe.

"He was cast out of the church in disgrace. Grandmother's tribe gave them land when they married. He build this house for her and the gambling hall in town for himself. On Sunday he preached in it. During the week it had a dining room; the gambling saloon was upstairs. Father kept a place where even women could go with their husbands to have dinner, listen to music or see plays. Women served the food and acted on the stage. Upstairs were hotel rooms and a gambling casino, but he didn't allow prostitution or blacksmithing as some call it.

"What is prostitution, Father?" Rod mumbled when John became quiet. Through the haze of pain and remembrance, he did not want his father to retire into silence again. Rod looked at him with large, fever-ridden, dark blue eyes, so much like his mothers. The face of his father seemed blurred and he blinked, brushing his hand across his brow.

"There are many forms of prostitution. Women with no other way to earn food for their children or themselves are just one of them. Slavery is another."

John continued to talk throughout the day about anything that came to his mind, pausing often to bathe the flushed body of Rod, put another cold cloth on his forehead and silently pray Rod would not die, too. He hoped stories about the family would keep Rod from sinking into a sleep from which he would not return.

Even when Rod dozed, John continued to talked, as though reliving his own past.

"Native American women solve the problem by taking extra wives for their husbands so that each woman has a home and hunter to provide meat. In return she helps with the children, raises and gathers food and makes clothing.

John paused, thinking Rod slept, but he opened his eyes again and asked, "Jim said Grandpa was shot. Why did someone shoot Grandpa?" He had wondered about it for several months, after a bully at school taunted him and called him an 'injun'.

"Your grandfather was shot while protecting a woman from a drunken soldier. The army hung the soldier. Your grandmother sold the gambling hall in New Salem and went back to her tribe to live a great deal of the time. I was fourteen, called a half-breed and the only thing I knew how to do was preach, gamble, and shoot a pistol.

"Mother was afraid for me. When I told her I'd go to war if I could figure which side was right, she said, 'Johnny, I didn't raise you to be cannon fodder for white men or a hopeless sacrifice for my people.'"

"Even though she didn't believe in the white man's religion, she saw the clergy as a way for me to escape war."

"Didn't you help Abraham Lincoln?" Rod asked weakly.

"Mr. Lincoln was father's friend. I was young at the time and didn't know him well. He agreed with grandmother that I should go to college back east."

Rod woke in the dark. A woman stood by the fireplace. His vision blurred. He felt so hot. His father was speaking with someone. Was it Mother?

Mrs. Johnson held her hand on his forehead. "He'll be lucky if he don't loose that leg. The doctor's way 'tother side of the river. T'was me I'd do a lot of prayin'. The skin's about to bust, unless you cut it."

"Your leg is black and swollen Rod," his father whispered. "I'm going to give you a couple of sips of whiskey so you won't feel the pain as much. We have to cut the skin."

Rod felt the sting of whiskey in his throat more than the sharp razor blade which slit his skin for several inches. It saved his leg but he carried the scar the rest of his life.

When his fever broke his father continued to sit by his side, feed him broth, and tell stories.

"Tell me about Abraham Lincoln, Father."

"Abe Lincoln was an older neighbor and came to our house often before his presidency. He and Father would spend hours on Sunday afternoon discussing the Bible, politics, church vs. Native American philosophy and the slave issue. Abe eventually chose politics for himself.

"Mother chose the pulpit for me." John Anderson stared into space. Then he continued talking as though trying to sort out his own life. Rod would close his eyes and listen. Years later he could still hear his father's deep melodic voice and see the long tapered fingers with which he played the violin or dealt cards equally well.

"My parent's religion was more of a questioning philosophy than a set of rules," he said thoughtfully. "The white man often believes everything is either black or white. Whereas the Indian's beliefs are more earthy and flexible. There are many ways to deserve a happy hunting ground, Rod.

"The white man sees straight ahead. His past is what he can stand to remember and his future plans are based on social patterns, not what he has reasoned out for himself. Only in becoming rich and powerful does he think he can be free to decide his own actions."

His hand moved to the pulse on Rod's neck, then up to his forehead. Rod stirred and looked at him with deep blue eyes. John's body shook with a dry sob. He bit his lip until it bled.

Through tears he stammered on, hugging Rod closer for comfort. "The Native American is a seeker. His wise men and women see visions and other possibilities besides the physical." He laughed at himself. "There I go preaching again."

"Why did you quit preaching, Father?"

"I tried it for awhile, but there was too much conflict in my mind and heart. Like my father, I was always torn between the Indian's and white man's point of view. It takes a great many years to develop the wisdom to be a true teacher about the nature of life. Your mother suggested I farm and write until I could sort out things in my own mind."

"When Father died I had been packed to attend a college back east. Mother insisted I go, even though the loss was almost more than either of us could bear."

"What will you do, Mother," I asked hoping she would let me stay.

"I will attend to the needs of our people, son. You must prepare yourself for the merging of both our worlds."

John realized the pain of his memories would be unbearable without Rod in his arms. Which of us is really comforting the other, he asked himself and smiled sadly. Rod moved restlessly.

"Mother went back to her people for awhile. When I came home in the summers, she had the house cleaned and aired. We spent part of the time here but often went to her teepee, if our tribe was nearby.

"There was a great deal of unrest among slaves, Native Americans and conflicting ideas between Northern and Southerner. Our farm here is between New Salem and Springfield. It was the road walked by Abraham Lincoln. We saw him go by often in his carriage before the war."

Like with most school children, Abraham Lincoln was a hero to Rod. "Was he like they tell us in the history books?"

"Your grandfather said Abe was a strange figure in his tall black hat as he walked to work reading a book. At first people made fun of him, but soon everyone knew him. Housewives often stopped him to talk and ask him to bring back a spool of thread, or some necessity. Mr. Lincoln helped firm up Mother's claim to our farm when Father was killed.

"I guess the history books never know what's in a man's heart except by the way he chooses to life his or her life. A great deal of Lincoln's charm came from his droll sense of humor. If Douglas hadn't under estimated him, he would have been president." John could see Rod trying to figure out what he meant and tried to talk more simply.

"The slave issue would eventually have had to be settled in our country. Abe was the first person honest enough to face up to the issues and risk his career for his fellowman. The Civil War and slavery were in the debating stage and heating up when I was not much older than you, Rod. At first Mr. Lincoln tried the impossible, to reconcile both the north and south. Mother and I went to hear some of the debates."

"Is Mother here?" Rod tried to sit up.

"No, Son."

He continued, "I was telling you about Abe Lincoln and the Civil War. I stayed on the farm. Both he and mother said the soldiers needed food more than another body for cannon fodder. I was torn between so many ideologies, not certain if my loyalty lay with any one group.

"Abe told me she was right, and asked me to organize farmers and natives in the state to raise extra food and the women to make clothing and bandages for soldiers. My pulpit became more

Avonelle Kelsey

of a support group for the north than a church. In this way I salved my conscious."

John paused and watched Rod closely. When the boy stirred, he would continue talking softly.

Rod's leg ached and burned. His vision seemed blurred and voices receded, then came booming into his ears. Mr. and Mrs. Johnson and neighbors stopped to inquire about his health and left food.

"I wish I had known Grandmother," Rod said weakly. "Where . . . where is she?"

"Mother was killed by renegade soldiers who came across her village while I was on a trip. The war had ended, but for men with evil in their hearts, it continued."

Rod felt the hot tears of his father fall on his face.

"After her death I organized a group of braves. We made some raids on small bands of renegade soldiers, but the war was over. "

"Where did you meet Mother?" Rod knew, but he wanted to keep his father talking.

Rod felt his father's body shudder with a silent sob.

John Anderson had sworn himself to a life of chastity after watching the painful experience of a premature birth and long recovery of his beloved wife, Rod's mother, during her second pregnancy. It was she who made him break the vowel. As a result of his weakness, she was dead, John believed.

Rod tightened his grip on his father's hand as though sensing his pain.

After a long time John continued, "My parents are both dead, Abraham Lincoln has been shot, your mother is . . . gone. You're the only person I have left, Rod," he said sadly.

By this time Rod was able to sit up. His leg was still swollen and red where the skin had been slit, but he could stand on it and walk a bit more each day. Something within him made him want to remain an invalid and continue to receive his father's attention.

"After Mother's death I wandered around the country for time trying to decide what to do with my life. One beautiful fall I was riding through the woods enjoying the golden sun which fell on my face, and I remembered the scarlet maple in the yard. I seemed to hear a voice calling, "Come home, John."

"Just before Christmas, Mrs. Johnson rode over with a Christmas cake. They had brought the farm next to ours years ago. She insisted I come to the Christmas Program at school and then to her house for dinner on Christmas Day."

"You know how hard it is to refuse the Sunflower Woman." Rod nodded and smiled.

"I finally agreed, although I hadn't been in the old schoolhouse for years. She had sized me up and decided I was just right for the school teacher who lived at her house during the school year.

"That night an angel sang. She became your mother, Rod."

He paused for a long time. Rod could imagine his beautiful mother as an angel. When he closed his eyes and listened to his memories at night, he often imagined he could hear her clear voice singing him to sleep.

"What happened after you met her, Father?" Rod enjoyed hearing it over and over.

"You know that we were married in the church and Mr. Johnson gave the bride away, but what we never told you Rod, was about your mother's parents. When her father heard I was part Indian, he canceled the wedding plans and wrote to her saying he would disown her if she married an Indian."

"Why, Father?"

"Her parents were plantation owners. Any thinking Native American is against slavery and, if forced to fight, would be on the side of the north. Their oldest son had been in a battle and was killed by an arrow. That was many years before the Civil War, but they never forgave the Indians.

"Now I must write to them about the death of their daughter and their little granddaughter, Annabelle Lee. Your mother said Annabelle Lee was to be her name because you had been saying the poem when she died. She wanted me to tell you she was named in your honor because she was so proud to have you as a son."

His voice broke and their tears intermingled. He held Rod tightly as the bereft boy buried his head against his father's shoulder and sobbed.

Out of necessity to talk or to quiet Rod, he began again. "Because I look more Indian than white, I'm not accepted by many white men. It's a tough world out there, Rod. With your mother's lighter skin, deep blue eyes and curly hair, you'll have little trouble passing as a white man. As much as your mother enjoyed the poetic differences between the Native American and white man, she could not understand completely.

"Why did they take our country?"

"Because the Native American had few tools and no material wealth, the white man believed he was poor. Whereas, each Indian feels he owns the whole country and white men are satisfied with only a tiny farm. That is why they didn't mind the first settlers using a bit of land here and there for a house and garden.

"Each is uneducated in the ways of the other; therefore, they each think the other is ignorant. It never occurred to Native Americans that people could own the land any more than they could the wind and the sky, or that there were people in Europe who would swarm like flies over their hunting grounds, devouring it as vultures with no thought for anyone or anything other than their own selfish greed."

John paused for a moment and laughed harshly. "I'll be darned if I don't sound more like Father every day. You've just had another sermon, Son. I'm starving, how about some of Mrs. Johnson's chili and pie?"

Rod's recovery from the bullet wound and loss of blood made his recovery a long one. Often he seemed to be over the fever only to have it return. Each time he tossed and turned only to go off into another time and place.

Two Bears was anxious to be off looking for the father who'd caused his own mother's death.

Gradually, the shepherds and neighbors accepted him as one of them.

Although the neighbors lived far away, once a week one or another would stop to check on Rod and give Two Bears help and advice on the running of the ranch.

After a month or more, two Bears realized it was beginning to feel like home. However, each time travelers stopped by the spring he managed to bring General Howe's name into the conversation. He'd promised his twin, One Bear that he would continue to pursue their hated father.

Rod continued to live in the past. Being held in the dream-arms of a loved father seemed to bring relief from the pain. Still, he felt as though there was something urgent he should be doing. Often he called out strange names: "Annabelle, Mary, Joe and sometimes laughed and said, "Dan, you wouldn't dare . . .."

After Rod recovered from the snakebite, restlessness settled on his father's spirit. Day after day he would watch him walk to the cemetery and stand gazing out over the lush Illinois farmland, talk to his wife's grave, then come home and pace the floor until morning. It was almost worse than the quiet withdrawal.

One day he called Rod to him. "Rod, you're nearly ready to become a man. I cannot bear to stay here without your mother. The Sunflower Woman wants you live with her. You can go to school and be her son. She needs you and would be good to you, like she was to your mother."

"No, No! I won't stay with her. I want to be with you. I'll run away." He threw his arms around his father's waist and held on tightly.

"I would like to take you with me. But gambling is a hard life."

Rod sobbed and would not release him. Finally, John relented.

"You can go with me for awhile. Anytime you want a home, you can come back. I'll travel and gamble. We'll sleep in a tent or the open when we can't afford a hotel. If my fortunes are lucky, we'll eat, if not, we'll hunt or go hungry."

They picked an armful of flowers and spent the last evening by his mother's grave. The Johnson's agreed to take over the farm and keep it until Rod returned, or grew up.

Rod waved to the Sunflower Woman and her husband as they rode away. His father never looked back.

Rod's mother had written several poems about the women of the prairie. The first night he sat by the campfire and read the one about Mrs. Johnson, the Sunflower Woman. Then, he carefully tucked the poems inside her Bible.

Avonelle Kelsey

Rod carried a copy of his Mother's poem with him until he moved into the sod hut. Then he hung it on the wall beside his small mirror. Loving hands must have placed it in the niche.

The Sunflower Woman

Looks blindly past a dusty mound, seeing faces
gone before her, friends and family gathered round,
disappearing in the nightmare of her life.
She sees a young man come a ridin', on a wild,
half broken mare. His Sunday shirt is stiffly starched
and crackles with his care,
to see a lovely lady, just nearing sweet sixteen.
She lowers eyes and giggles sweetly,
runs her fingers through her hair.

"Come with me my darlin, we'll follow wagon trails,
where land and people all are free,
I'll build a house for thee."
She goes to tell her Mother, who says,
"No, my little one, don't do it," sighing, "God bless thee.
Take with you this bonnet, my shawl to keep you warm.
Till you return my baby, a candle I will light,
keep it in the window if you return at night.
Life is hard my daughter, be careful, do what's right."

The wagon trip was long and cold, heading
into the vast unknown.
They spent the winter in a cave,
worked harder than a purchased slave.
Children came and died unknown.
Parent's hearts were wrenched and torn.
The man-child drank when things went wrong,
hit, cursed, forgot the love he'd known.
Both grew old so very young.

She planted sunflowers round the door,
and on his grave when Indians came.
He's there beneath the flowered mound,
along with children and the rain.
Day after day she sits and stares,
as windy sand-dogs take the ground.
Lonely memories still surround,
even though she's moved to town.

Avonelle Kelsey

Life of a Gambler

To a young boy, it seemed like an ideal life. Rod left home with his mother's Bible, and a couple of her favorite books of poetry, a geometry book his father insisted he take, a bedroll, a winter coat, two changes of clothing and a beaded shirt made by his grandmother for John when he was a boy. A pack horse carried their small tent, rain gear and a few hand tools. On his saddle was a small rifle. Rod felt very proud and happy for the first time since his mother's death.

As they rode along, or camped at night, his father taught him to use his senses like a Native American. "Do you hear anything, Rod? Look at that grass, something large has passed this way." They'd get down on their knees and follow until they found a cave where a wild animal hid or a meadow where a herd of animals fed. "Smell the distinct odor of each animal. It may save your life.

"See that shadow in the cliff? The mother is nearby watching."
Two coyote cubs played in and out of a cave.

Sometimes they saw buffalo or bear in the woods but the
railroad crews had wiped out most of them.

Smelling, tracking animals and guessing which kind became
a game. Often a serious one. Rod's hearing, sense of smell and
seeing became more acute. Green was no longer green. Each
clump of trees or bush held a dozen shades of greens, blue's, and
brown's.

"Did grandfather teach you these things?" Rod asked.

John Anderson laughed his slightly cynical laugh; dark eyes
flashed under heavy brows. His features and coloring were those
of the tall, gaunt, high cheek-boned, north-eastern Iroquois. His
hair held a glint of red like that of his Irish grandfather and
tended to wave, falling forward across his forehead when he
removed his gambler's hat.

"Father was a priest. Maybe when he fell in love with Mother,
he had to fall in love with the out of doors as well. She was my
teacher. 'The spirits of grass and water are clean. Only when
they're trapped inside or by people, do they become diseased,'
she told me.

Rod nodded. He looked at the clean blue sky and smelled the
acrid smell of Autumn's decaying leaves and understood. "I wish
I could have lived in a teepee in her village."

"The old villages were like small towns and her ancestors
lived in long houses," his father said. With the coming of white

people they were destroyed. The white men of today see only a straggling spirit of a people who have already died. Teepees were for traveling, not permanent homes."

When they moved from town to town they rode up into hills and spent time hunting, reading, talking and thinking. Rod often wore the beaded, leather jacket his Indian Grandmother had made and carried a bow and arrows across his shoulders, Native American fashion.

His father laughed and said, "You look like an Indian dressed for church or a parade, Rod."

He blushed and smiled. Each thing he carried and wore had a special meaning to him. He could not leave any of it behind. His father patted his shoulder in understanding and his laughter died.

John Anderson wore buckskin pants and jacket when they were in the woods. His pistol was always under the flap of the jacket and became a part of his daily dress. He carried a rifle on his saddle.

In the evening when he went forth to gamble, John dressed elegantly in a brightly embroidered vest of satin, a black jacket, pants, boots and hat. His pistol was always the latest design and slung low over his hip, hidden by the long tails of the suit jacket. Rod's quick eye could never catch his draw, the movement was so swift. Each day they practiced before breakfast; but Rod was never allowed to carry his gun in town.

"Guns or bows are for protection, not aggression or circus stunts. In the days when a brave became a warrior and destroyed an enemy, it didn't count as a fair fight if he did not touch his opponent before killing him. Even the life of an enemy is sacred. Never strike first unless you're out numbered and evil exists in the men before you."

Both John and Rod enjoyed their outdoor life. Often they followed the weather and headed south in the fall. In the winter, they camped near towns by a creek in a fur lined tent. Rod was taught by his father how to gather most of their food.

"Look here son, see this root? Boil it up and take off the skin. Tastes like a sweet potato. Or, I see you found some duck eggs."

"There's a whole bunch of nests down in the corner of the pond, but I remembered you said just take a single egg from each nest that has one or two eggs in them."

"Sounds as though some ducks are about to become mothers. Their eggs will have chicks in them or taste spoiled. Keep watch and let me know when they hatch. There's something special about seeing baby chicks and ducks emerge from shells and face the world for the first time," he would say, or, "About time for thistle hearts to be ready. We'll rustle up some for lunch and maybe pick some dandelion greens."

These hunting trips and afternoons or early evenings when Rod was not in school were his favorite part of the day. His father seemed determined to give his son an Indian education as well as that of a white man.

On Sunday's and afternoon's Rod had lessons in philosophy, geography and math, unless he was in a town where he could go to school. Sometimes they used cards for arithmetic.

"I don't want you to be a gambler son, but if you do feel the call, I want you to know what it's about. Now, tell me, how many jacks are left in the deck?"

"Three," Rod said without hesitation. His father smiled and nodded.

On Sunday, John Anderson never entered the gambling halls. The two often attended church and then went fishing until night time. They'd study the stars and Rod would listen to the ancient tales of Gods and stars. Sometimes he looked at his father in amazement and wondered how he remembered so many stories.

John would buy books or borrow them as often as possible. He listened to Rod's reading, spelling, and science, talked with him about plays, and took him to cultural things when they were in a town that offered any sort of culture.

Usually, they were in new mining towns on the edge of the wilderness. Sometimes they stayed in cities like Denver, or took a paddle boat on the Mississippi.

"Who's that funny man dressed in white that always carries a pencil and paper with him?" Rod asked.

"Oh, you mean Mark Twain. He's going to do a reading tonight in the Saloon. Would you like to hear him?"

"Sure, but that's a strange name. Same as they call when they measure the depth of the river."

"Samuel Clemens is his real name. He used Mark Twain for some of his lighter things. His sense of humor has caught the eye of the public and he's known better by his pen name than his given name. Says he's writing some books."

Rod didn't realize until many years later how famous the man became, or that he was seeing the end of the great steamboat traffic which crowded the Mississippi. There were many debates about whether or not the railroad would be able to take over the hauling the river barges had been doing for many years.

River men said, "Never," but by this time, the tone held a note of anxiety. Roustabouts still unloaded boats and repackaged merchandise for wagons which hauled overland freight. More often though, trains waited for the cargo and carried it to distant new cities inland.

Rod loved the smell of the water and the camaraderie of the river people.

When they were on the river, John Anderson often took out his violin and Rod his mouth harp. The boat people would gather round and join in. They clapped and stamped their feet, sang or looked wistfully into a distance, remembering. Sometimes a dozen or more steamboats and flatboats would pull over for the night and join in with drums, voices or hand-made instruments such as flutes and willow whistles. Rod enjoyed the elaborate shows on the gambling boats.

Black people often sang at dusk as they finished their tasks. He wondered why their beautiful voices were not heard in the show houses. The Civil War was over and emancipation declared. But freedom, laws and day to day equality were not the same things, he realized.

"How'd you like to go to Europe, son? Here. Let me show you on the map."

"That's a long way, Father."

"We won't swim," John flashed his charming smile. "I won a poker pot last night and two tickets on a boat to Europe. 'Course if you don't want to go . . . ?"

Rod laughed. Father liked to tease him. He picked up his saddle bag, threw it over his horse and said, "I'm ready."

New York seemed like an endless forest of brick and buildings. The ocean and ship were a relief until Rod became seasick for several days. By the time he felt better; his father had made new friends and joined a group of gamblers or went dancing each night. The women with the gamblers loved to drink, dance and play card games as much as the men.

Rod tried not to feel resentful at being left alone. He sat reading on the deck nearly every day, until a young, red-haired girl close to his own age sat down beside him. They glanced shyly at one another.

"I'm Claudia." She held out her hand and he hesitated, wondering if he should kiss it as gentlemen often did the hand of an attractive woman.

"I'm Rod Anderson," he said touching her hand briefly.

"What are you reading?"

"Just some of Poe's books."

"I get scared when I read him, don't you?"

"Well, maybe a little."

"Want to go to the game room and play some games? I'm pretty good at chess."

Rod had been about to go back to his book but the challenge was inviting so he went along. He'd met girls in school. The last couple of years they had traveled so much he never made the acquaintance of one for very long. At thirteen, he was beginning to stretch in height, his body, thin and wiry; his blue eyes were inquisitive and his brown, curly hair was so thick it almost looked like a wig.

"Why aren't you in school?" he asked, during the chess game.

Claudia was good at chess, but held back to keep Rod with her for awhile, until she found out he was her equal or better at the game. "Checkmate."

Other kids her age were in school and the long ship voyages were often lonely. "We're actors. Mamma and Papa are staring in plays in London and Paris. I play the guitar and sing between acts. Sometimes I dance. Want to dance tonight?

"Check." I . . . I'm afraid I don't know how," he mumbled."

"Oh, it's easy. I'll teach you." With that she made a move, checked his king again, went over, put a record on the victrola and held out her hands.

With Claudia, dancing was a riotous game. Rod ended up out of breath and sat down laughing. She continued to dance creative, innovative steps, while he rested. What a graceful swan, he thought; I never realized how beautiful a dance could be.

When the record finished, he pulled out his mouth harp and began to play. She continued to dance, then ran out of the room and returned in a few minutes with a guitar. On the last night when the ship sat in the harbor in England, she stood on her tiptoes and kissed him. Neither of them had a permanent address so it was doubtful if a letter would find either of them. The trip became a memorable event in his life because of Claudia. Her parents presented John with two tickets to their theater performance. John and her parents became friends while in London and their friendship continued.

After going to several plays and seeing the sights of London, they rented horses and went sight-seeing along the coast of England.

"We must go to Ireland and look up our ancestors," John said. Ireland was cold and rainy. The people were cool, until John told them who his father and grandparents were. They became even more impressed when they found out he was half Native American. They brought neighbors from miles around to look at him and shake his hand.

"Perhaps we should stay in a country where our people are appreciated," John chuckled.

Rod pulled his coat around him. Even though it was July, he found the dampness chilling. "Let's find a country that's warmer."

His father felt his cheek, "Maybe you had more than a touch of sea sickness on the boat. We'll head for France tomorrow."

Claudia came to the boat and again kissed him goodbye. He blushed when he saw his father's knowing smile across her shoulder. John patted his shoulder and led him on the boat. "Kissing is all a part of growing up, Son. No need to be embarrassed."

They crossed the channel with some friends from the ship, saw Paris, went south to Spain and caught a boat on the Mediterranean to Italy and Greece, even took a boat on the Nile, rode camels, and went to the pyramids.

John gambled with a group of Arabs by an oasis. They had been admiring the Arabian horses. When one man wanted to bet his horses, John looked at Rod and winked. "Guess my son could use a good horse. He's outgrown his pony." Before the evening was over, John had won two horses.

They looked over the horses, each trying to decide which one to choose. John liked the large, sleek, black stallion. "If you get a filly, Rod, we might make some money breeding the two in the states."

John saw how pleased Rod was, patted his back and said, "Come on. Let's look at their teeth and legs."

The mare Rod chose was only green broke, but she was sleek, lively and beautiful. He knew it was a horse he would be proud of for many years to come.

Both John and Rod had enjoyed the new sights but agreed it was time to go home. They shipped the horses on the same boat and sailed for America. It was summer. There were several young people on the crossing; none were as much fun as Claudia.

New York was just another large city to them by this time. They went straight to the train station, loaded their Arabian horses as well as the three which had been boarded at a livery, and headed west.

Never had the soft grass and smell of trees seemed so wonderful to Rod, when they went hunting again. They sold two horses and kept the pack horse. Rod hated to give up his boyhood pony, but he had begun to feel ridiculous with long legs dangling half way to the ground. The mare was a pleasure to ride with her swift long strides. John's stallion was a terror for anyone else to ride. He spent a part of every day talking with him until he become docile and seemed lonesome when John was gone for any length of time.

"That horse sure likes you," Rod commented. The horse tolerated Rod only because he was with John.

"A good horse and a good woman need a kind, loving hand. You gentle them any other way and they aren't worth their weight in chili beans. If they can't accept tenderness and love, abandon them."

"What about the saloon girls who fall in love with you? Are they good women?"

"Mostly. Usually they work in a saloon because they can't find another way to feed themselves and their children. Fate often deals people a hard hand, Son. That's no reason to condemn them."

"You every think about getting married again, Father? The women on the ship seemed to like you. Some of them were real purty."

"I've loved many women, Rod. Your mother's the only one I cared enough about to change my way of living. Marriage is a big compromise, Son. Make sure you're willing to pay the price for a soft body in bed. Guess I was born to be a wanderer."

"I remember how pretty Mother always looked and how nice she smelled. She sang better than most of the women on the show boat. What was so special about her that you quit traveling and settled down?"

They were riding by a stream and the horses seemed thirsty.

John hesitated, threw a leg over the saddle, and dropped the reins. He washed his face and took off his moccasins, letting his feet cool in the water. Rod followed suit, deciding his father would not answer him. They lay back on the bank in the cool grace.

John closed his eyes. "I'm trying to give you an answer to your question, Son, but damned if I can find one. The night I heard her sing in church, her eyes, so like your eyes, met mine and something clicked inside. I tried to tell myself it was just her beauty and I was lonely.

"Every thing about your mother enchanted me. Her intelligence, her voice, and the nearness of her body were overwhelming. When I was away from her, I counted the hours until we could meet again. The feeling never went away."

"But . . . you like women. Sometimes you stay away nearly all night."

His father leaned on an elbow and smiled at Rod. "Sexual desire is one thing; love and sexual desire are not always one and the same. Some men say women have little sexual desire. Don't you believe them? Women have more self control and may not be so easily intimidated because they can become mothers in one encounter. It's a disgrace if a girl becomes pregnant, even if it wasn't her fault. A man does not have any responsibility to the mother and child unless he chooses to take it on."

"Why not?"

"Indians care for all children. All children belong to the tribe and family of the mother. White man's religion seems to have distorted the natural desires of men and women. A virgin birth is worshipped and seems to indicate there is something bad about the natural way a man and woman get a child." He paused.

"It's a wonderful thing to become a parent to a child borne of love between a married couple who want the child."

"Just as it's pitiful to see a woman with child who does not want it or a man who goes from woman to woman scattering his seed anyplace it falls."

They lay in silence looking at the setting sun. The horses munched on sweet smelling grass. A light breeze cooled their sun-drenched bodies.

"I sometimes sleep with a woman because she attracts me and my bodily needs become almost uncontrollable. When I do, I try to protect her from becoming pregnant by not letting my seed enter her body. It is frustrating, but not as much as never feeling the warmth and softness of a woman's body. Women invite me to share their beds. It's awkward when I turn them down. Sometimes it helps her build self esteem when a man she admires treats her like a lady. There are times when two people just need to be held and flesh touch flesh."

Rod blushed in the darkness as his mind flashed to Claudia. Although his father talked easily about relationships between men and women, he seldom talked about himself.

"If you plant a seed, carelessly, there are plants Native American women use to wash it from their bodies. I will show it to you. Egyptian women even used cow dung inside their vaginas to keep from getting pregnant."

"Oh, lord," Rod moaned.

John laughed. "I almost envy you and the experience of your first love." He sat up. "We're pretty close to a town called Vermillion. Beyond it are miles and miles of green, grassy farm lands and the great Missouri river. On the other side I hear there's prairie, free land, wild Native Americans who've never seen a white man and hills full of gold."

Rod thought. Here we go again.

"We'll camp for the night and ride in, look over the town tomorrow. Might even visit the school. Heard there's a woman trying to get a high school and college going way out here."

Vermillion looked prosperous. One old timer was telling some travelers on the steps of the Bennett Dry Goods Store, "The prairie on the other side of the great Missouri is Injun land. Them Sioux don't hanker to explorers and such. Custer says them Injuns know there's gold in the hills out yonder and they want it fir themselves. The government wants people to stay on the east side of the river until reservations and treaties be signed."

He squinted up at John, suddenly realizing the man listening was a half breed. He spit over the rail, got up and walked away. John chuckled, tipped his hat to a woman and entered the store to buy camping supplies. Their money was running low.

When Rod first set out on the gambling trail with his father, John had said, "It's probably wrong for me to try to educate you myself, Rod. But a great part of my education was a waste of time. As long as you co-operate and study when I'm gambling, you can stay with me. I do expect you to enter school in whatever town we stop. I'll teach you to shoot, but only with me. I don't ever want you in a saloon until you're eighteen. Is that understood?" Rod nodded, even though he didn't understand completely.

Rod liked school. Sometimes he enrolled for a week, or month, until John Anderson was on a losing streak or invited to leave, because he won too often. Sometimes a jealous lover, poor loser, the local preacher or Marshall helped them on their way. There were times when Rod wanted to cry out and beg his father to go back home to New Salem where it was safe, but he never did.

Often Rod day-dreamed of a home and family. What did his father dream of, he wondered? Would he ever fall in love and marry again? Rod's feelings about this were a combination of hope and dread. No one could take his mother's place, but he worried about his father and knew he was playing with death each time he entered a gambling hall.

John dressed like a white man, kept to himself and was always polite. There was a silent strength in his walk and his piercing eyes warned off many would-be opponents. Problems were most often the result of women who found him extremely attractive or sore losers. Sometimes a cocky youngster with too much to drink challenged John. When his pistol covered the youngster before his gun cleared the holster, the astonished challenger would drop his gun or turn tail and run.

When Rod went to school and it was cold outside, John spent the afternoon in a saloon, playing the piano and talking with the women, if no card game was available. The saloon belles soon learned to ask for his advice and help as well as what the women wore in New York or Paris, and they loved his stories. He sympathized with their tales of woe and usually advised them to save their money as a way out of their present occupation.

His Father slept after Rod left for school in the mornings. He was usually waiting for Rod when he came home. Sometimes they'd go fishing but he never failed to review the day's lessons and often added extra insight. If Rod had a problem with math, he'd patiently work through it with him. Due to John's coaching he was often so far ahead of his classmates he was asked to help the teacher with lower grade students. After finding his peers were envious of his knowledge, he learned to keep quiet. A good teacher silently gave him advanced work after having a discussion with John.

They'd eat by their tent or in a hotel in the evening. As usual, John Anderson donned a brightly colored vest and black jacket, polished his black boots and brushed his hat before leaving for the evening.. His father never failed to touch or hug him before going to work at a gambling hall. Rod would watch him as he threw back his shoulders, combed his hair, placed his hat carefully over it and walked with long strides toward the best poker game in town.

Rod hoped he would be handsome when he grew up. John was over six feet tall, with a reddish cast to his black hair, snapping brown eyes, olive skin, and thin of face and body. Even thought half Indian he was no darker than the average white man who worked out of doors.

If he wore a beard, Rod thought he would look like Abraham Lincoln, except much more handsome and elegant.

When entering a saloon for the first time in a new town, John would order one drink. If the bartender was alone, he'd give him a generous tip and say, "Keep my glass filled with sarsaparilla the rest of the time I'm in town." If anyone commented, he'd give him a steely expression and say, "Whisky and poker don't mix, or boys, you might not like the spirit whiskey calls into my body; something between a mad tiger and a rogue elephant." Sometimes he'd just do a lightning draw with his pistol, twirl, it and do a couple of tricks, place it back in the holster and go to the poker table.

John's expression was somber and remote, until he smiled. When he gave his flashing smile, it was as though the sun came out from behind a cloud. Rod and women saw it often, white men seldom. Women usually fell in love with him the first time he directed its warmth toward them. He never failed to be a gentleman, kind and thoughtful to old and young alike. He would talk with the saloon women about fashions, the world, their problems, and treat them as equal. Sometimes he taught a reading and writing class in a saloon.

Some of the women attempted little business ventures in which he invested and supervised until it succeeded. Often he encouraged them to start a new life in another town; many married and became good wives and business women as soon as they developed a feeling of self-worth.

Women loved him, but men were envious. Cruel, ignorant men often took advantage of the corner society had backed women into. When a woman asked for his help, John never refused. Sometimes, there was trouble.

Avonelle Kelsey

The Bennett Family & Miss Melissa

Rod and his father rode up to the new Vermilion middle school. Two girls looked at him from the window. One giggled. The other met his eyes with a flashing spark, tossed her curls and turned away.

Soon Rod met Melissa, Annabelle and Mary, the three women who would change his life.

Rod's teacher was an amazingly, intelligent young woman, Miss Melissa. Rod loved her classes from the moment he heard her speak. In spite of her high collar, granny glasses, and tight hair bun, he thought she was beautiful and not more than a few years older than he. When she laughed and became excited about a subject, she removed her glasses and tiny wisps of red-gold hair curled about her face. She smelled good, too.

One of his classmates was a boy his own age, Daniel Bennett. Dan had red hair and freckles. He enjoyed teasing the teacher by leaving secret messages in her books to make her blush, funny pictures on the board, or bouquets of wild flowers with a lizard in the bottom of the vase.

"Come on down to our store after school," he invited Rod the first day. "You can help me unload some freight and then we'll go huntin'."

They unloaded the freight. By the time they finished it was too late to go hunting. Rod felt a bit like a character in Mark Twain's book about Tom Sawyers and Huck Finn. He suspected Dan had read it, too, and was using him.

After he met Dan's sister, Annabelle, he didn't care. That same night he walked down the alley behind the store and stopped to listen and watch as Annabelle played the piano, sang like an angel and deliberately ignored Rod when their glance met once again through an open window.

The Bennett family was always busy at the store or helping Melissa with fund raising for school by having box socials, spelling bees and plays; yet they were close knit. Mary, Dan's mother, and Melissa were good friends. They often talked of the gambler's son and his good-natured intelligence.

When a 'part-time help needed' sign was placed in their store window, Rod asked Joseph Bennett if he could try doing the work.

"Sure son,' Joe said. "Need someone two evenings a week to load freight and on Saturday in the store to give Mary and the girls some time off."

A late supper was included with the job. Melissa often joined them. The family banter at a meal was fun, even when the twin girls, Nettie and Bettie made snide remarks to Annabelle. This was the first time Rod had been inside a family home and he listened in amazement.

"Dan, will you be an actor in our new play?" Annabelle asked.

"Only if you let me kiss a pretty gal. Last time I had to kiss you."

"Well, in this one you can be my Tom-cattin' brother."

"Annabelle," Mary frowned. "I think all this acting is making you vulgar. Maybe you'd better give it a rest."

"Yeah. She's a sinner all right," Bettie said. "Yeah and people all over town are talkin' about her," Nettie added. The identical twins always spoke in tandem.

Melissa looked at the girls severely. "Sounds to me like a little green imp called jealousy is speaking and not the two lovely creatures you wrote parts for in the play, Annabelle."

"Did you Annabelle? Can we be in the play?" Both girls quit eating and stood up.

"Sit down girls. You're ruining my appetite," Dan said. "Hope you don't expect me to kiss them, too."

"No. That's Rod's part," Annabelle laughed peering at him from lowered lashes.

Rod looked from one face to the other to see if they were kidding. He blushed when Dan teased, "You get to kiss Annabelle. That let's me off the hook."

Joe came in, washed his hands, kissed Mary's cheek and gave her a gentle pat. "How's Dan getting off the hook? What are you up to now?"

Little Willie climbed over on Joe's lap, smearing him with gravy. "We're all gonna' be in Annabelle's play."

"Well . . . I didn't write a part for you, Willie." Annabelle stammered and then brightened; I do need you to help sell tickets." No one could resist Little Willie's sales pitch.

"You take the money when I sell tickets. I wanna be in the play."

"What would you like to do?"

"Buy and sell candy."

Rod had an idea." Why not let Little Willie keep a penny from every ticket he sells?"

"A penny buys too much candy and is a lot of money out of a dime," Mary said. "We're raising money for the school fund."

Joe solved the problem. "I'll give Little Willie a piece of candy for each ticket he sells. That OK, Willie?"

The boy nodded, gave a contented sigh, leaned his food smeared face against his father and went to sleep.

Rod was excited. Annabelle was finally noticing him. That night he dreamed about kissing her. She had given him the lead part in the play.

In the play summary, the two friends, Becky and Annabelle, were in love with the same man. He and Dan were trying to decide which would make the best wife for Rod who was going off to homestead and needed a wife. The ultimate test was a kiss, but when Dan caught him kissing Becky, he realized he loved her and knocked Rod down. Annabelle rushed to his side and kissed him. He knew his choice was made. End of play.

That is if Dan didn't pull one of his shenanigans again. Last time he'd pinned a tale on the best man and turned the serious play into a comedy. Annabelle had been angry but so many people told her they enjoyed having something to laugh at for a change that she overlooked it and decided to ask him for some comic suggestions.

Rod looked forward to rehearsal. This was the first town they both seemed to enjoy. Just maybe his father would let them hang around for a whole school term.

Usually they went south for the winter.

"Now son," Rod's father would start off with those words and that special tone when it was time to make another move.

Vermilion was the largest town on the edge of the Dakota Territory.

Rod wondered if it was the rumors of a gold discovery by General Custer and opening up the territory that had kept them in this small western town for three months, or his new teacher.

Then, John Anderson began talking about going to California.

"Now, Son, we could take the new railroad to Denver and as far as it's completed, go on west. These little towns on the edge of the wilderness will be cities one day but it may take some time."

"Are you thinking of looking for gold, come spring, Father?"

John pushed his hat back from his eyes, peered at the setting sun, smiled and answered, "I'm thinking."

Rod cringed inside. He liked it here in Vermillion and hated to think of leaving. "Father, couldn't we wait until spring?"

John looked at his son. He'd caught a couple of the scenes in the play and saw how Rod looked at Annabelle. He laughed knowingly, "I'll think about it." This was the first time Rod had tried to hold back from a trip.

Later he said, "Maybe you're right Rod. If we waited until spring we wouldn't have to rush to beat winter. There's a lot of country between here and California." He looked pensively into space as though trying to picture the trip. After a time he stood up and walked off into the woods alone.

Rod suspected they were also low on money. He was proud of the little money he earned, hoping if John went broke, they could use it for a winter room at a boarding house. It was beginning to get cold in the tent. Rod also had the money from a colt and the Johnsons sent a small check each Christmas. His Arabian mare would have another colt in the spring.

"I have the money for a boarding house," he offered. Maybe Europe had spoiled them for outdoor living and they'd have to get used to it again.

"The money from the mare's colts is to be kept in the bank for your future education and the money from the Bennett store should go for a suit and new shoes. You're beginning to look a bit shabby. Nothing impresses people more than good clothes, Son, until they get to know you. When you live in a white man's world and have the taint of mixed blood, good clothing is doubly important."

By November John said, "Winter is settin' in. The school marm seems to take a great deal of interest in you. She thinks I should keep you in school here. Even offered to take you in herself."

"You seem to like her, too," Rod grinned. He had noticed his father stopped by the school often and talked with Melissa longer than seemed necessary.

"The Bennett gal you're rolling your eyes at is full of talent and mischief. You and her brother Dan seem to be hitting it off pretty well. Would you like to spend the winter here?"

"Oh, Father, could we?" For a moment Rod forgot he was fifteen and nearly grown up. He hugged his father and turned a handspring in excitement.

They stood laughing together. "Mrs. Bordensky sets a mighty fine table at her boarding house. Reckon we'd best move in before the next storm."

Happily, Rod watched as his father got ready to leave. Suddenly, underlying his happiness, he felt a foreboding of dread. "Maybe we should celebrate here tonight," Rod suggested.

"I promised to help one of the women this evening. She wants to leave the saloon and marry a cowboy, but's afraid of the owner. When we get it settled, I'll come back."

Rod sat by the fire to wait.

A chill wind blew across the rich, grassy flat-lands from the prairie in the west. The sunset was blood red on heavy clouds. In spite of his happiness at the thought of staying near the Bennett family and his beloved school teacher, Rod shivered and threw another log on the fire. Even the creek chattered excitedly. Usually, the sounds of water and nature comforted the young boy. He listened intently to the surroundings as he laid waiting on his bedroll.

In the direction of the town he heard shots.

"Father," he shouted, sat up, pulled on his boots and raced toward Main Street.

Sally Bryson's face was pale as she stood beside the young cowboy. They were facing her boss, the owner of the West wind Saloon. His hard-faced, gun-slinging bartender stood behind the bar, grinning.

"Sally ain't goin' no where," he told the young man. "Now git out and don't come around here no more."

"You have no right to keep her here," the young man croaked and stepped backward against the bar, his hand hovering close to his gun.

When John entered the saloon, he saw the owner take Sally by the arm and nod to the bartender.

Men in the saloon moved quietly out of the way; some lay down their cards and began to shuffle toward the door.

John walked to Sally, removed the hand from her arm, and ducked as her boss swore and swung a whisky bottle at the gambler. Behind him, the bartender reached over the bar, grabbing the cowboy's pistol. The owner cursed and called John names, then drew his gun. John shot him and swung around when Sally screamed a warning, pointing to the bartender. The bartender shot John in the back. Sally's cowboy had tried to hit his hand, but was too late.

The Marshall rushed into the saloon and found John Anderson on the floor beside the owner. Several cowboys from H-Bar Ranch had the bartender pinned against the wall. Sally was sobbing in the arms of another saloon girl.

"He's all yours, Marshall," the owner of the ranch said. "If he don't hang, we'll tear this town apart. Judd, have Sally get her things and bring her home. Reckon Ma can use a helping hand."

When Rod reached the West wind Saloon, they were carrying the body of his father to the undertaker's home.

A man who recognized Rod said, "Your Pa told that dead polecat bar-owner yonder to leave one of the saloon gals alone and he got his dander up. He called John a 'Cheatin' Injun and pulled his gun. Your Pa shot him. The skunk bartending' shot yer Pa in the back. Marshall has him now and you can bet your boots there's gonna' be a hangin'."

He kept talking to Rod, thinking to comfort him, but Rod followed the body of his father without answering. They had scooped the gambling money off the table and given it to the undertaker to bury John Anderson in the nearby cemetery.

Rod sat by the body all night and followed when they carried the wooden casket to the graveyard.

The Bennett family, Melissa, and half the town, many of them women, turned out for the funeral. In the little time John Anderson had been in Vermillion, he had become known as a straight shooter.

Dan and Annabelle sat outside the cemetery until dark watching their friend mourn his father. For a week Rod did not go to school. He sat by the grave during the day and rolled up beside it in his bedroll at night, knowing he'd not only lost a father but the best friend he'd ever have.

Maybe I should go back home to New Salem, he thought. A chill wind blew, covering the grave with white, sparkling snowflakes. The Johnsons wrote once a year, inviting him home. But he'd found a home in Vermillion. Melissa was the first teacher to challenge his mind. His thirst for knowledge matched that of hers.

Rod remembered Claudia from the ship on the way to England. She had been the first real friend he'd made during his travels. Now he had Melissa and the Bennett family. He pulled his blankets tighter around him and lay with his head on John Anderson's grave.

Dan and Annabelle came for him one morning, insisting he eat a sandwich Mary had made. They put their arms around him and walked with him to school. Only Melissa seemed to notice his gaze often wandered from his studies to the snowy landscape outside the window. She wondered if he would stay. After school she asked if he would help her with the stove, then insisted he eat supper with her. Dan had invited Rod to stay with him but he felt the need to be alone.

The owner of the stables let Rod keep his horse in the pasture nearby and sleep in the loft over the barn. It was like parting with a dear friend when he sold his father's stallion.

One day the gruff stable master said, "I brung you a present. Hit were the first to bark so thought you might find it a comfort you." He hugged the Collie to his chest and for the first time slept the night through. Rod was fifteen; too old to be an orphan and too young to be a man.

Avonelle Kelsey

Evil Twin & First Love

Rod was a hard worker, neat, and well liked. He was good at bookkeeping, a job which both of the Bennett brothers, Joe and Uncle Mark, hated and tried to avoid as much as possible.

Sometimes he missed a week of school when they went on a supply trip. Melissa didn't approve. She helped him catch up on weekends. In many courses such as ancient history and geography, he knew more about the subjects than she.

"Your father was a wise, intelligent instructor," Melissa nodded approvingly, a curl falling loose from the coil piled high on her head. "Can you tell the class what it was like to actually visit the great pyramids of Egypt? " Her questions broke through the ice of grief.

"Well, first he had to catch a camel," Dan interrupted and got his usual giggles and laughs, I'd like to hear about that. How do you keep from falling off the humps?"

"We actually took a boat on the Nile and hiked to the pyramids. It was pretty hot. I still have some of the sand in my shoes."

"Weren't you afraid of the Arabs?" Annabelle asked.

"They seemed to like Father. He gambled with the leaders of a caravan and won our two horses. They did give us a ride on a camel. Not much different than a horse after you got used to a different gait."

"How about the gals?" the banker's son asked. He looked away as Becky frowned in his direction, then tossed her braids and looked out the window.

"Couldn't see much of them. They wore veils over their faces and long dresses."

"How did they eat?"

"Don't know. They never ate with the men. The men ate with their right hand. The left hand is used for toilet functions and is thought of as unclean. Father said it was sanitation for them because they have so little water." Once again Rod realized his frankness was shocking to many people.

"The women were too good to eat with the men," Annabelle commented and the girls laughed.

Melissa smiled. She agreed with Annabelle, but remembered to bring the subject back to a learning situation. "Tell us about the food they ate, Rod, and where it was grown."

Since Rod had been the only one who had ever gone to Europe as well as traveled the length and breath of the Eastern part of America, he was often used as a reference. Sometimes Melissa would have him write about an area, at other times give an oral report.

She'd invite him to supper often and talked with him about the Mississippi river boats, the ship on which he crossed the Atlantic, the plays in England and Paris.

Philosophy and human relationships were other subjects seldom talked about in public or by the average person even in the privacy of their homes. Melissa and Rod probed, theorized and talked openly as they contrasted the way of living and social expectations of various people around the world.

When they were alone, she'd take off her glasses, unbutton her collar and sit leaning back in a chair listening to his rich full voice. He's going to be a handsome man, she thought. Annabelle's lucky he's so in love with her he can't see anyone else, but then she's always been lucky.

Rod watched her glowing face and intense eyes and thought, if I was a man, I'd fall in love with her. Then worry, if she did get married, would she go away and not be his teacher.

In his mind he'd hear his father's quick laugh saying, she's here now Rod, enjoy the day. He often helped her with dishes after supper and brought in a load of wood. Anytime the boys in town cut wood for the winter each carried a load to the school and teacher's small house nearby. It was part of her pay, like eating at their houses when she'd first arrived in town.

Melissa was the only one Dan studied with willingly.

"I'm gonna' marry her one of these days," he told Rod. If you see any other men hanging around, let me know, I'll get rid of them."

"Don't you think we're too young for her, Dan?"

"Speak for yourself. I see past her glasses and teacher act."

"But, she'll probably marry before you're the marrying age."

"I intend to ask her to wait for me."

Rod didn't laugh. He knew Dan was serious. He shook his hand and said, "If I can't have her, I wish you luck."

"You know you don't have eyes for anyone but Annabelle. You going to ask her to marry you?"

"I'm only seventeen, Dan. Annabelle's just turned sixteen. Your mother would skin me alive if I approached the subject."

"Becky's engaged to marry that banker's son-of-a-gun and she's the same age."

"That's different. Annabelle wants to have a musical career on the stage. That will take awhile. I'm keeping my eye on things."

"Better keep an eye on Annabelle and not spend so many evenings with Melissa."

"Anytime you feel like studying you can join us."

Rod and Dan were of the same age but had very different dispositions. They had become good friends, going hunting and fishing together as often as they could slip away. The Bennetts felt sorry for the lonesome boy and often invited him to supper, giving him extra work when possible.

It was obvious to Mary. Rod was in love with Annabelle. She was a tomboy and often rode with Rod and Dan.

"I can shoot as well as Dan," she bragged to her friends.

Annabelle's figure was trim, her mind and body nimble. The boys at school admired her music as well as beauty, but they were awed by her relaxed manner and commanding ways. "Seth, if you want to be in my band you're going to have to set up straight and practice more. No more mice in my piano. Dan does so many stupid tricks; a little mouse doesn't impress me at all."

Seth blushed and stammered, "Just because Rod's been to Europe don't make him any better than me. Beside, he's a redskin. Everybody knows that." He sat up, looked around at Rod and smirked.

"He knows when not to say 'don't'," Annabelle snipped back, stuck her nose in the air and seated herself at the piano. With a 1, 2, 3 and 4, they began play practice for her latest musical.

Melissa and Mary took Rod 'under their wings'. When he missed school to earn extra money, Melissa saw that he made the work up at night or on the weekend. She enjoyed the boy's thirst for knowledge, quiet good humor, and philosophic insight. Sometimes he was a bit too intense, but it was also a relief from the farm boys who came because their family insisted, or they had nothing else to do in the winter time. Mary often fed Rod and mended his clothing.

He was six feet tall. He could do a man's job. Both women told Rod he was too thin. His large, thoughtful, deep blue eyes and mop of dark curly hair belied the fact that he was one-fourth Native American, even though his olive skin tanned deeply.

Like his father, John, and grandfather before him, he was courteous and thoughtful, especially to the ladies. If Mary wasn't available, the women always sought out Rod to wait on them in the store.

At night when the very lonely young man couldn't sleep, he often waited until after dark, and then put his bedroll by the back door of the Bennett's store. They were the closest thing to family he had. He listened hungrily to the sounds of Annabelle's piano music, family singing, the twins squabbling, laughter, and family voices. His nose twitched when he smelled Mary's home baked pies and good cooking. Sometimes it was the only place he could go to sleep.

One night he had a nightmare and began to shout. Mary was up with one of the sick children and rushed to the back door to see what was wrong.

At first she though it was a drunk in the alley, until she saw Rod. "Rod Anderson. You come in here this instance," she insisted.

He reluctantly came inside.

"Now. Have you been sleeping by our back door?" When he nodded, she said. "I won't have that young man." She placed some milk, and a piece of pie before him. "You eat this. Then, take your things up to the attic. You can sleep in Dan's room."

Both he and Dan were delighted. After that, Rod lived with them. In their home he seemed to counter-balance Dan's disposition.

Dan was impulsive. Rod was a planner. Where Dan chatted, laughed and shouted, Rod smiled quietly, told long tales of adventure, often with a funny twist at the end. He taught Dan to draw a pistol from the hip while riding, to ride barebacked and on the side, Indian style. Often Annabelle insisted on joining them. Dan objected, but like his father, Rod always welcomed her and went out of his way to help her learn.

At first Mary was a bit reluctant to trust the children to him, until she found that he was very protective of the whole family. She was busy and began to rely on his help more and more.

Rod was diplomatic; however, he would not be bullied. After Mary had spent long hours in the store and Annabelle or Dan had gone off to more important things, Rod helped Mary with the dishes and house chores in the evening. It became a time of friendly exchange to which both of them looked forward. They gossiped about the children, school, and church socials. Eventually, he even confided in Mary about his mother's death and that of his baby sister, Annabelle Lee.

Mary put her arm around him and hugged him in sympathy. "You aren't alone, Rod. You have many friends here in Vermillion and we'll always be your family."

Mary encouraged Rod to talk of his past. "Tell me about the different parts of the country you and your dad visited, or, your Native American grandmother and Irish grandfather," she would say, "they must have really been in love for him to give up the priesthood."

Joe often came in from the store, sat down to listen or join in with stories of his own adventures. Dan and Annabelle might wander into the cozy kitchen. It was Rod's favorite time of day. The twins and little Willie were in bed. Annabelle would watch him with shining eyes while Dan made wisecracks. Except for missing his father, Rod was happy.

One day Dan found an Indian asleep behind the store and gave him a hot foot. As Dan doubled over with laughter at the dancing brave, two other's who had been snoozing behind a stack of barrels, sat up. They took in the situation and stole stealthy up behind Dan, put a hand over his month and stuffed a rag into it. They quickly tied a leather thong across his mouth, and then bound his wrists and ankles.

Rod came out just as they picked him up and trotted away down the alley. Knowing he couldn't overcome them by himself, Rod began yelling, chasing them, and throwing rocks.

People came out of the backdoors of nearby stores and houses to join in the chase. Realizing they were outnumbered, they dropped Dan and ran away as fast as they could. Several men rode out to look for them, but they were never found. The family was grateful to Rod for this and for other protective episodes.

But Dan never seemed to learn his lesson. He tormented his teachers, teased Annabelle and the twins and said he was too old for school. Mary was firm, even when Joe might have relented.

"You'll stay in school until you pass High School, Dan, if you're fifty when you graduate. After that, if you don't like law, you can become a doctor or engineer. Your minds too good to waste in foolishness." When Mary got that tone in her voice every member of her family listened with respect.

At night Rod coached Dan in math and they poured over his law books together. The young teacher, Melissa, helped both of them prepare for written exams. Even though Dan could study with a lawyer and didn't have to go to college to become one, he had to pass his high school exams and study with a practicing attorney.

Melissa said, "Rod since you haven't chosen what you want to do and are learning along with Dan, you might as well take the same tests." She wanted Rod to become a teacher. It was her dream to found a college in Vermillion.

Teachers in Vermillion were paid very little. They often had a room in the schoolhouse or in a home and ate one meal each day in the home of a student. On Sunday morning they were required to go to church, couldn't drink, and the women could not be courted. Melissa hid behind high collars, severe hair arrangements, and glasses, but both students and the men around town were aware of her attractions. She ignored them,

Avonelle Kelsey

knowing even a glance on her part would cause gossip and lead to the end of her career.

After church on Sunday, Melissa often came to the house and had both lunch and the evening meal with the Bennett family. She had continued the practice even after her aunt left her money for a tiny house and her salary increased. In summer. after church they went on picnics by the river or in the woods. It was a pleasant way to spend the day and was the only time the Bennett clan seemed to get together as a group.

The twins, Nettie and Bettie, were jealous of attention given to anyone besides themselves. The rest of the family seemed to get along well, but the twins agitated, spied and tattled. Their speech was broken; one began a sentence and the other finished it. They especially seemed to envy Annabelle her talent, although both were musical themselves.

One Sunday a revival preacher stood in the pulpit and shouted hell and damnation. Joe rose and walked out. Rod and Dan followed him. That afternoon they had a picnic by the creek and talked about the sermon.

"You heard what the preacher said, Annabelle," Nettie began. "Stage actors and actresses are no better than saloon gals and will go straight to hell," Bettie finished.

"Hey Mom. Bettie cussed." Little Willie had just gotten his mouth washed out with soap the week before and was very conscious of swear words.

"I did not," Bettie reached over and pinched him. Willie yelled and rolled out of her reach. Mary looked at her with a frown.

"She's just sayin' what the preacher said," Nettie looked at Annabelle accusingly.

"You two are trying to cause trouble again," Annabelle flipped her long black curls over her shoulders and looked at her parents for help.

"Why would they want to do that?" Mary asked.

"Melissa asked her to sing the lead in the operetta and they're burning with envy," Dan winked at Rod. He nodded. "Let's cool them down."

They each picked up a squealing twelve year old girl and threw her into the creek. Little Willie pushed Dan in after them. Rod tossed Willie in and turned in time to grab Annabelle as she slipped up behind him. They tumbled over the bank together making a huge splash. Melissa bent over the edge laughing, trying to retain her dignity and give Willie a hand up. Very casually, Joe lifted a foot and pushed her in after the rest.

"Joe!" Mary smothered a laugh behind her hand. Joe continued to act lazy with his hat over his face. His light skin burned easily in the sun. Dan's red hair and the twin's strawberry blond hair came from his side of the family. Annabelle's dark curls and smooth skin looked like Mary's.

"She's still just a kid under all them schoolmarm trappings," he mumbled to Mary. His slow southern draw was filled with chuckles as he looked at the churning mass of young people, giggling and splashing in the creek.

"And people wonder where Dan gets his mischievous streak," Mary wiped away a trickle of sweat from her smooth brow. "Oh, heck. Let's not let them have all the fun." She stripped off her skirt and blouse, jumping into the midst of the fun in her bodice and bloomers.

"Hey, Dad. Come on in."

Joe pretended to be asleep. Suddenly, from the creek bed, eight sets of hands began to splash. Soon he, too, shed his soaked trousers, boots, and shirt and joined swimmers.

Rules for Teachers in1872

1. Teachers each day will fill lamps, clean chimneys.

2. Each teacher will bring a bucket of water and a scuttle of coal for the day's session.

3. Make your pens carefully. You may whittle nibs to the individual taste of the pupils.

4. Men teachers may take one evening each week for courting purposes, or two evenings a week if they go to church regularly.

5. After ten hours in school, the teachers may spend the remaining time reading the Bible or other good books.

6. Women teachers who marry or engage in unseemly conduct will be dismissed.

7. Every teacher should lay aside from each pay a goodly sum of his earnings for his benefit during his declining years so that he will not become a burden on society.

8. Any teacher who smokes, uses liquor in any form, frequents pool or public halls, or gets shaved in a barber shop will give good reason to suspect his worth, intention, integrity and honesty.

9. The teacher who performs his labor faithfully and without fault for five years will be given an increase of twenty-five cents per week in his pay, providing the Board of Education approves.

Growing Up

Law was the only subject that interested Dan. Rod wondered if his interest was more in winning arguments than love of the law. It was as though the two boys had been born into the wrong families. Rod took the High School exam with Dan, upon Mary's insistence, and made one of the highest scores to date.

Dan rebelled when they tried to send him back east to college. The family compromised when he promised to read for the law with a local lawyer and long time friend of the family.

Rod had assumed more and more responsibility at the store, especially after Uncle Matt joined the army for a couple of years.

Even though Rod was not eighteen, he was usually consulted when an opinion was needed. The wages were not large and he saved very little money. Each year he received a bit of rent from his parent's old farm back near New Salem and a letter from Mrs. Johnson inviting him to come live with them; but New Salem

Avonelle Kelsey

seemed long ago and far away. Remembering his father's insistence he put the checks in the bank along with the colt money and forgot about it. Did he want to go to college?

After passing his exam and watching Dan begin his life in the field of law, Rod began to think about his own life. He realized he wanted to be out of doors. The indoor work of the dry goods store was too confining. He remembered the life he and his father led as a young boy. Could I be a gambler at heart, he wondered? He decided to talk to Melissa about it.

"You're not cut out to be a gambler, Rod. You're a thinker, a teacher. I've told you often enough," she stood close to Rod, looking up at him seriously, removing her glasses as though they were a barrier between them.

Rod smelled her womanly fragrance, felt the warmth of her nearness and suddenly wanted to take her in his arms. He blushed and stepped back. "'I'll think about it," he murmured and hurried out the door. I love Annabelle, he told himself and wondered at the strange attraction he felt for both women. Am I like Father after all? He kicked a stone and hurried to work.

Mac, an Irish sheep man from over near the Missouri, came into the store often and began telling Rod and Joe about the prairie and what a great place it was to raise sheep. "That buffalo grass is waist high during a wet year. All you have to do is turn the sheep out, get a shepherd and a couple of good dogs, the land's free and you're in business."

That night Rod took his bedroll down by the creek to look at the stars and think. By morning he had decided to give homesteading a try. But what about Annabelle, he wondered?

Rod never knew where he stood with Annabelle. She seemed to resent him at first and later took him for granted. She used him to run errands, escort her places her parents would not let her go alone, such as the circus, plays, dancing or to a friends house after dark. She was angry, friendly, loving; whatever she felt at the moment was on the surface.

"Rod's going to walk me to the Church for choir practice, or over to Laura's house," she would announce without asking him before hand.

Annabelle played the piano, danced, sang and wrote endless plays. She often conned Rod and Dan into being both audience and actors.

She scorned most girls her age and preferred the company of Dan and Rod. Whatever her whim, Rod never complained. Just to be in her company was enough.

Rod both taught Annabelle and encouraged her independence. But in spite of him, she was a bit on the selfish side. Very gifted and lovely with a stubborn persistent nature, she usually managed to get her way. Instead of helping Mary, she spent hours at the piano and playing the violin after Rod placed his father's battered case on top of the piano.

When Mary insisted she learn to cook and sew, Melissa took Mary aside and said, "I know Annabelle's spoiled, Mary, but she's a child prodigy. For God's sake, anyone can cook, sew and have a passel of kids. Help her talent grow."

Melissa was young, but Mary respected her opinion. After that, the twins resented Annabelle even more and took every opportunity to torment her. One day Mary overheard them scheming to spoil Annabelle's new dress for the operetta. She kept them home from school every day for a week and separated them. One worked in the store and one in the house or garden. At night one had to sleep in Willie's room. By the end of the week, both girls had lost weight and turned pale and listless.

"You'd better let them get back together, Mary," Joe whispered one night. "Do you think they'd die if they were separated for a year?"

"I don't know," Mary answered softly. "Sometimes they scare me. They can be such monsters. Where did I go wrong, Joe?"

"Some people are just bad seeds, Mary. Maybe they've learned their lesson and will grow out of it."

Within a month they were back to their normal, tormenting tricks. People laughed at Dan's tricks but often cried at the tricks of the twins.

Rod seemed to have a steadying influence on them. They loved to swim and after work on long summer evenings, he often chaperoned them when they wanted to go to the creek, listening patiently to their complaints about Annabelle and their mother.

"She likes Annabelle best," Bettie would say and Nettie continues, "Yeah, we're just slaves to do Annabelle's work while she becomes a big star." "She's a sinner. We hate her . . ."

"You know girls; I had a baby sister named Annabelle Lee once.'

"What happened?" Nettie asked. "Where is she?" Bettie finished.

"She's dead," he answered somberly.

"Oh, no!" "We don't want Annabelle to die."

"I'm sure you don't, girls. But sometimes people we love die unexpectedly. It's too late to be kind after people are dead."

"Your whole family died." "Your dad was shot."

"We're glad you're our brother, Rod." They each took a hand and skipped along beside him. Rod stopped and hugged them. They eased off on Annabelle for awhile.

Mary felt guilty about giving Annabelle free time and not the twins, but didn't know what to do about it. "Sometimes it's more bother to supervise Annabelle than to do the thing myself," she told Rod. "Her mind just isn't on household duties; but she does play the piano beautifully and sings like an angel."

Rod could play the violin but not as well as his father or Annabelle. He preferred the mouth harp or reed flutes made of willow. Annabelle had written a new version of the Pied Piper when he made willow flutes for the whole class.

Melissa, Joe and Dan played guitars. In family sing-a-longs Melissa high soprano voice, Joe's deep bass and Mary's alto

joined Annabelle's strong soprano. Rod often played the mouth
harp while the twins improvised on the piano. For laughs, Dan
rigged a combination wash tub and broom bass instrument for
himself and for Rod, an old saw with a violin bow. They made
Little Willie a set of drums from wooden barrels and hides so he
wouldn't feel left out. The group spent many winter Sunday
evenings gathered around the piano making wild music.

Annabelle was usually the center of entertainment for parties.
There were few other things she enjoyed doing besides music and
acting. Horseback riding was one exception. She rode horses as
free as a Native American as soon as she was out of sight of her
parents. A wagon horse was not good enough for her. With the
help of Rod, she talked Joe into buying her a feisty, young mare.

During High School, Rod, Dan and Annabelle rode with
reckless abandon across the rich black soil of the eastern Dakota
Territory. Rod was happy watching her grow and mature not
realizing how much he, too, was changing.

Then, suddenly he and Dan were eighteen, Annabelle was
sixteen. Many young ladies were married by this age. He began
to worry. What had he to offer a 'fair young damsel' of the town's
elite? Mac's homesteading stories came at the right time. A ranch.
Annabelle loved to ride. With his savings, he could outfit a small
place. He'd have to buy a homestead since he needed to be
twenty-one to settle on land and claim it for his own.

"You not be needin' to worry. I know some places that can be
bought, cheap. People make the mistake of trying to farm or run

cattle on the prairie. Just plum wears the land out in a hurry. They git unhappy and up and walk out on everything. Mostly huntin' phantom gold mines and gittin' themselves killed. With the right use, the land will come back. If you have half the grit I think you have, you'll make out fine."

"I'd appreciate all the help I can get, Mr. Mackenzie."

Joe overhead the exchange. Later he called the young man into the back room. "Just between you and me, Rod, if you need a partner in some land or a grub stake, let me know. Until you leave, you can work full time in the store and you'll get an extra bonus when you fix to go." He shook hands with Rod and waved away his protest of thanks. "I should a given you a raise long ago, but you keep the books and it just plum slipped my mind."

Mary, Melissa, Annabelle and the twins decided to give a combination birthday and farewell party for Rod. Annabelle was in charge of the music, the twin's decorations, Mary the food and Melissa invitations. At first it was to be held in a large classroom. So many people wanted to come they decided to hold it in the combination school auditorium and community meeting hall.

The widow Cleanbeck said to Mary in the store, "It appears to me a heap of folks be wanting to bid Rod Anderson their good wishes. Him and Dan come by last winter and chopped wood a couple times after Clarence died. Later he brung me a blanket and some calico fir the kid's shirts."

Milt Roeman dropped by the school, "You need any help with the Anderson boy's party? He pulled me out of a snow bank, took me home and thawed my feet and hands slow-like. Be a regular medicine man, if'n he lived like an injun."

Finally, Melissa simply posted notices at the store and post office.

"A farewell party will be given for Rod Anderson next Saturday night at the school auditorium. His friends are invited. Bring a pot, plate, lantern, an instrument if you play one, and eating utensils. Wear your dancing shoes."

A week before the party General Custer arrived with a large entourage and camped near the river just outside of town while he waited for scouts to return from across the Missouri. Melissa knew one of the soldiers and invited the Custers to the party.

Annabelle had organized a band when she was thirteen for her plays. A large number of members in the community attended her Saturday afternoon orchestra practices. She chose a dozen people to play for the dance. Nettie and Bettie spelled her at the piano. They loved the attention. Their duets were loud, lusty and lively.

Mary had to slow them down. "Girls. It's time to quit showing off. Play dance music." She danced with Little Willie, Rod, Dan and several others.

"Mind if I dance with my wife?" Joe cut in on Rod. He had closed the store early. "You're still the most beautiful woman in the room," he whispered. Mary smiled at him. Over his shoulder she watched Dan and Melissa dancing together. She was surprised when one of the young soldiers with General Custer cut in. Melissa seemed to know him. Mary frowned. He was looking at Melissa like a man in love and she was returning his gaze.

There was a commotion at the door. Melissa and the soldier went to greet General Custer and his wife, Elizabeth. She was dressed in such an elegant gown the other women in the room seemed dowdy.

It was a party no one was likely to forget. The men seemed reluctant to ask the fine Elizabeth to dance until Rod, at Melissa's urging, broke the ice. Dan and Joe followed suit. Soon the Custers became one of the town's people as they laughed and danced the evening away . . .

Annabelle felt jealous and asked Rod, "Does the famous Elizabeth Custer dance as well as me?"

"No one dances as well as you, Annabelle, and you know it."

She put he head on his shoulder, surprised to find he was a head taller than she. "Why must you go away?" She whispered, pulling back and looking up at him.

The passion he saw in the depth of her blue eyes startled him.

She felt his body tremble with desire, smiled and lowered her long lashes to hide her own response. It was the first time they had both acknowledged the depth of their feelings for one another.

Dancing beside them, Mary saw the look and nudged Joe. "Ask your daughter to dance. Now."

Joe released her, looking surprised, but knew Mary had a reason when her voice held that tone.

Rod stood as though in a daze, watching Annabelle turn slowly to her father. He felt Mary's hand on his arm.

"Mary. I'd ask you to dance but I need a breath of fresh air." He did not say he needed to get control of his emotions, but Mary sensed it.

"Sounds like a good idea. Mind if I walk along?" Outside they stood looking at the stars. Nearby Custer's horses were staked out. Three of their dogs were tied to a tree and a guard waited by the door.

"Rod. Since you don't have a mother, can you pretend for a minute I'm yours?"

"Of course. You're the only one I have."

She squeezed his arm and they walked to the gate by the school house. "I saw the way you and Annabelle looked at one another. It's hard to be young, in love and have to wait when passion is gushing through one's body."

He nodded, stopped and waited. As usual, her voice soothed him.

"Both you and Annabelle need time. You don't want to marry until you have a home. Annabelle is a lovely young girl, but she is not only talented, she's ambitious. She would probably run away with you tonight. Knowing my daughter, she would make you pay for her lost career the rest of your life."

Rod lifted his eyes to the heavens and closed them as if asking for strength.

The moonlight shining on his upturned face reminded Mary of his gambler father. His hair and eyes were lighter. The Native American blood showed only in the high cheek bones and the shadowed mystery of his large eyes. She caught her breath. Rod was turning into a handsome young man. Someday he would look like his father. Would he, too, get the gambling spirit of his father and grandfather?

Turning to her, he reached out to touch her face. "You're right, Mary. The spirit of the night and your wisdom has given me strength. Will two years be long enough?"

As they turned to go in, Mary saw Melissa and her soldier walking under the stars.

Many people left tools and gifts for Rod. The family stood with him by the doorway saying goodnight to the well-wishers. Melissa had not returned, Mary realized.

The Custers seemed reluctant to leave. "It's not often I get to dance with my husband," Elizabeth said looking at him fondly as he stood shaking hands with Rod.

"Stop by the camp 'fore we leave tomorrow, young man, and I'll tell you where to head for a good homestead. It'll be in the path of Black Hills travelers. You raise animals and you'll have a market for them going by your ranch nine months out of the year."

"I'll do that," Rod said as they shook hands. He kissed Elizabeth's gloved hand, remembering the small hand of a girl named Claudia in London.

She laughed and patted his cheek. "Perhaps we'll meet on the prairie." It was well known she had an elegant wagon and several dogs. She followed Custer, staying at the nearest fort while he rode out to fight Indians.

Mary wondered later if that night was last time Custer and his wife danced together. He was killed a few months later.

The Homestead

Each week wagon trains went through Vermillion. Men and women came in talking about free land. People died but even that did not slow people who dreamed of a better life 'goin' west'.

Free gold and land lying around for the taking, according to greedy spreader of tall tales, was a bright banner, blinding people to the reality of their real needs and the possibility of sharing with Native Americans. "One hundred and sixty acres for the taking," said Joe with longing in his eyes. A kingdom."

Melissa had suggested to Dan and Rod, "Perhaps it's not one hundred and sixty acres men need but a sense of adventure, some excitement." In school she often suggested that politics, building better schools and more open minds were really needed. She hated wars but her students couldn't seem to wait to get into a uniform. When she dared suggest that the Civil War had been a waste of so many young lives it seemed that each student was either firmly for the north or south. The school board warned her to keep politics out of her classroom, if she wanted to keep her job.

Rod hated to leave the Bennetts. Family life with the Bennett's had given him the warmth and comfort he needed after his father's death, but it was time to try life on his own.

He received a small salary, plus room and board and used the small store salary for day to day expenses. The money he had been paid from the farm rental continued to go into a savings account for his education as he father had recommended.

Like Joe, Rod felt the call of wide open spaces. The reality is that I can only be out of doors by ranching. Each friend and family member gave their opinion without being asked.

"Melissa, I know you want Dan go into politics and me to become a teacher, but for awhile at least, I feel the need to try my muscles, carve something in the wilderness." He grinned a bit self consciously; yet wondering if his longing was Indian blood calling him or his father's words.

"Perhaps I need to live a bit first, my dear friend."

She laughed. "All right, Daniel Boone. I give up for the moment, but minds like yours should be shared. Perhaps you do need to expand your horizons. Maybe that's why I moved away from home." Her glasses had fallen off her nose. Her bright eyes twinkled as she looked into his.

"Thanks Melissa." On impulse he leaned over and kissed the tip of her nose, turned on his heel and walked out the door, whistling.

Melissa stood in the school house window watching him. Tears rolled down her cheeks. She felt as though she was loosing her best friend. There had been no letters from her soldier.

Rod decided he could not ask Annabelle to marry him until he had a place of his own. He had collected every bit of information he could about the Homestead Act. He would build a house with his own hands and use his money to buy stock, he decided.

The dilemma was, should he speak to Annabelle before he left or when he had something tangible to offer her? Would she turn him down cold?

He remembered Mary's advise the night of the party. Annabelle was talking of a career in music and the theater. She was always in demand to sing or play at local events, weddings, and funerals. She had a scholarship for the Conservatory of Music in Minnesota anytime she wanted to attend.

Melissa suggested to Mary, "As soon as Annabelle passes her high school exams, you should consider sending her to the Conservatory of Music."

Joseph said, "Rod's about ready to leave. He's been going over plans for building a house and proving up a homestead. He asked for a year or two off to try and make it on his own. I'm gonna' miss him.

"In fact," Joe looked sideways at Mary, "I might consider joining him someday." He was feeling Mary out because he knew she disliked moving. It was only her strong will that had kept him in Vermillion these many years and made the store a success. Probably, if Mark hadn't left when he did, Joseph would have found a reason to go west.

It didn't take long for Joe to find out Mary's feelings.

"You really wouldn't move us, would you Joe? We all love it here and the store's beginning to pay off. Of course, it would be nice to visit Rod's place when he gets settled."

"The gold strike in the Black Hills is going to be the next boom town, Mark says. He wants us to come out there, if we can find a buyer for the store," Joe said.

"Now Joseph," Mary's voice was stern, "the Black Hills are too far away from everything. The children are in school and with a branch of the Conservatory opening up here soon, Annabelle can stay home. Dan is beginning to settle into law. I'm afraid it would split up the family if we moved. It's bad enough with Rod going off." She began to cry softly.

Joe tried to harden his heart, but he loved this kind, hard working partner of his. "Now, now, Mary. It's only for a year. We must move with the times. I'm amazed the lad hasn't wanted to move on before this, if he's anything like his Pa." Joe paused. "Wonder who the girl is?"

"Why do you ask that?" Mary stopped crying long enough to look up at him, knowing full well the only girl Rod had ever been interested in was Annabelle. How could Joe miss such an obvious devotion?

"Why else would he be looking at a cabin plan with two bedrooms?" Joe laughed. "And speaking of bedrooms, come along girl." He blew out the light. Putting his arm around her lovingly, Joe led her through the darkness to their bedroom.

The twins had decided to raid the cookie jar. They were listening outside the kitchen door and giggled knowingly. Their nosy dispositions bordered on the edge of criminal blackmail. They were the least popular members of the family in the community. Little Willie was the baby and spoiled by all.

Mary heard the lid to the cookie jar rattle. She knew what they were up to and laughed softly as she slipped into bed beside Joe. He took her in his arms and kissed her tenderly at first, then with more passion when she responded.

Until recently, their lovemaking had been frugal and somewhat frustrating. Both felt the hardship of more births would be too hard on Mary. With the new birth control device for Joseph, she had not gotten pregnant for the last three years. They were beginning to feel like honeymooners in their middle age. Only Rod noted their new satisfaction and connected it to the contraceptive device in the drug department.

In April, a wagon train gathered outside of town. Rod made arrangements to join it. Custer had sent the information on the abandoned homestead he'd mentioned to Rod and the price had been surprisingly low.

Custer had written: "Enclosed is the information you'll need to buy the place. The cabin has burned down and there is only the remains of an old Soddy, but the place has a small spring which feeds a big pond. The old barn will suffice until you get it repaired. Bring plenty of nails, tools and take a lesson in black smithery. An old forge is on the place . . . Good luck and I'll be stopping by to check on you. Elizabeth sends her regards."

Rod was both happy and sad to leave the Bennetts and his friends.

Instead of asking Annabelle directly to marry him, Rod s her the plans for the cabin, asked her advice and how she would feel about living on a ranch?

Annabelle was young. It did not occur to her that she would have to make an important choice between Rod and a career someday soon. "That would be fantastic Rod. I've always wanted to live on a ranch and have dozens of horses. Can I come visit you Rod?"

"I'll be back as soon as I prove up on the homestead and get a cabin built. Your dad said he might bring the whole family for a visit. If not, I'll come back and bring you myself." Both of them knew what he was saying and what she was answering indirectly.

Their bodies swayed together and Rod took her in his arms. At first their lips touched tentatively, and then clung. He pulled her closer. Annabelle's arms locked around his neck. She pressed her body against his in a passionate response.

Dan came rushing into the room. "Rod, the wagon master wants to start earlier than planned. He has news the spring snows are melting and that means the creeks are rising. You'd better get going." He stopped, flushed, and stammered, realizing he had interrupted a passionate embrace.

This was one time Dan had blown a special moment and was sorry. He knew how Rod felt about Annabelle and looked forward to having Rod as a permanent member of the family.

Rod released her but held her hand, squeezing it, reluctant to let go. His body felt hot where she had pressed against him. He forced himself to turn from her.

Mary and Joe heard the news and came in to wish him farewell. Mary cried as she hugged Rod. Joe had tears in his eyes. "I wish I was going with you, Son," Joseph said.

Dan walked with him to the wagon train. Willie and the twins trailed along side.

"Are you coming back, Rod?" "Uncle Mark left and he never came back," the twins said.

Little Willie began to cry and clung to Rod's knees. Rod picked him up and kissed him, handing him to the twins.

"You bet I'll be back just as soon as I get a cabin built and the sheep from Mackenzie enclosed; I'll send you a map. Next summer, either I'll come back or you can all come to see me. I'll have a horse for each of you and a lamb for Willie." He kissed the twins. They giggled. Willie continued to sob. "Take good care of

Nellie." Rod wasn't certain which of them Willie was crying for. He turned away quickly before he, too, began to cry.

Dan walked with him down to the cottonwood trees by the creek, their horses and Nellie trailing along behind.

"How I envy you Rod," Dan said. "I may just walk off someday and join you, so keep in touch. See you next year, anyway. You are coming back for Annabelle aren't you? Or is it Mom? If she and Dad weren't so crazy about one another, I'd think she was in love with you."

Rod smiled and hugged Dan. "Go visit Melissa often. She seems a bit sad since we've graduated. Tell her I didn't have time to say good-bye. And Dan, don't let Annabelle marry anyone until I return."

He looked up and there she stood. Her long black curls, and ruffled dress were flying in the wind, showing her lovely ankles above low cut shoes. He would never forget this picture of her.

"I'll wait Rod." Then tossing her head she said to Dan. "Besides, I'm a career woman. I'm not going to get married until I'm a big success." She winked at Rod and brushed back a tear.

"Why don't you just throw her across the saddle, ride off into the sunset and live happily ever after in a sod hut, like in her plays?" Dan teased.

Rod and Annabelle blushed, laughed and both lowered their eyes. What a clod he must have seemed, Rod often thought when he remembered their parting.

Move'em Out

Two Bears watched as Rod tossed and turned remembering his father, the Bennetts, Melissa, his mother and Annabelle, calling out to them in his feverish delirium. Sometime he fought with a buffalo or shivered from the cold. His shoulder burned with fire from the bullet wound. As he came back from the nightmares and the past, the faces of Sam, Brent and Rafe receded.

Often he heard a quiet voice which soothed him and a cold cloth was placed on his brow. A man's voice read poetry and Annabelle's letters. Later he was aware of someone bathing his body and coaxing him to eat broth, but he was too weak to open his eyes.

He slowly became conscious of the fact that he was alive, that the evil men in his mind were only dreams, but he could not raise himself above the lethargy. Each time he attempted, the burning shoulder made him conscious of his aching body. Rod lay quietly and tried to feed himself healing thoughts. Somewhere a chant was being sung, or was he dreaming again?

"Spirit of sickness, spirit of wounds, go with the night, spirit of fire, leave the body, heal the body, spirit of sickness leave this house." He smelled sulfur and strange herbs.

He visualized his mother reading to him and Annabelle playing the piano as the family gathered around singing his favorite songs. He pretended he and Annabelle were married and she was here with him, that it was her gentle hand which pushed him back down on the bed when nightmares surged through his body and screamed for action.

"Rod, Rod Anderson. Where are you? Come back. The animals need you. We all need you. Annabelle wants you to write to her. You must come back to us. Open your eyes."

For the first time he became conscious of wanting to wake up and tried to respond. "Mother, Mother," he whispered in a weak voice. Then he drifted back to the past again.

"Move'em out!" The call of the wagon master rang down the line of people, wagons, horses, and animals. It looked like an unmanageable group. Once they strung out across the trail the train was over a mile long and from a distance looked highly organized. Rod wondered it this creeping conglomerate would ever make it up the banks of the Missouri, much less west to the wild homestead land and the Black Hills on the west side of the Dakota Territory.

After the farewell party where several friends gave gifts, Rod had a sizeable pile of tools, a set of banty chickens, and assorted household necessities. He debated whether to take them or be slowed down by these new possessions. Everybody in the store had a piece of advice. "You'll be needing every shovel, grindstone and ax," an old farmer advised him, "even on the trail." His old classmates, Nancy and Josiah had married recently, "We're in the same boat. We want to homestead but have no wagon to carry our wedding gifts. Nancy won't leave 'em. Says she aims to have her spinning wheel and weaving tools."

"They're as important to a woman as an ax is to a man," she insisted.

"Tell you what I'll do," Joe said. "I'll give Rod a wagon and you two drive it for him. He can trail his horses and the milk cow Mary insists he take." Then he winked at Josiah and laughed, "Besides, he has to take that banty rooster Mrs. Brewster gave him so he can get up in the mornin'."

The others joined his teasing banter. "I can just see the pack horse carrying a cage of chickens when they start crowing. Probably have to chase him all the way to the Missouri," Rod acknowledged.

"You furnish the eggs and I'll weave you a blanket from your first wool," Nancy promised.

"It's a deal."

Joe was right. No one needed an alarm clock to get up. In fact, the darn rooster crowed off and on all night. Half the wagon trained wanted to have him for supper. He gave Rod an excuse to bunk out away from the wagon train. The stars twinkled and gleamed, the weather held crisp nights and sunny days. The quiet at night after the noise and dust of the wagon train during the day was relaxing. He often remembered his father and their traveling days with longing.

One night just south of a reservation three Sioux rode up near the circle of wagons. They dismounted and were creeping through the high grass when the rooster began to crow. Rod sat up and laughed as they raced back toward their horse and rode off into the night. After that, no one talked of eating Henry as he was called in remembrance of Henry Brewster.

He checked the map where Custer had marked parcels of land that were abandoned and the trail most often used by miners and daydreamed restlessly; until the wagon master asked him to do some scouting, The trail to the Missouri was deeply rutted but easy to follow without getting lost. Grass was already green and lush from melted snows. Farmers had put up signs that the land was taken and to keep animals on the trail. Fields of corn and winter wheat were beginning to sprout. Everything grew easily in the rich soil. Many farmers sold early spring onions, stored apples and potatoes to the people.

Until the Missouri breaks were reached, travel was reasonably safe. Across the Missouri the reservations had been divided again, in spite of past treaties, to leave a large amount of prairie land open for homesteading and travelers between the Missouri and the Black Hills. The rich fertile land on the West bank of the Missouri river was already claimed.

Rod usually rode with the wagon master or helped scout ahead. He was one of the many bachelors on the trip. Men led the way into the wilderness but never stayed long without women and families. Women gave birth, not only to children, but civilization. They wanted churches, schools, laws and community social life. Someday soon, Rod hoped, women like Melissa, Mary and Annabelle would settle the land. There was companionship and culture in a well organized community. The wide open spaces were beautiful but they often held hidden dangers.

Crossing the Missouri on rafts seemed to take endless days of hard work. Men cursed, women cried and animals roared, fought or moaned in fright. Hardships and interdependency brought people closer together.

The wagon train moved slowly without any unusual incidents. One woman died and cholera was suspected, but no one else became ill. Rod thought it was food that had set too long in a tin pan. Her husband dug her grave along side the trail and followed with his wagon in the dusty cloud behind the animals until evening.

Rod dropped back to keep an eye on him and helped fill the grave. By evening they were choking on dust. Rod was glad he had his own horses so he could ride off to the side. When they came to a creek he took off his boots and .44 colt, then jumped in, clothing and all. The wagon master frowned on anyone who got out of line, but they weren't in dangerous territory yet. The Sioux and other warring tribes were on the other side of the river breaks. The tribes on the east side had finally accepted reservation life; those that had survived.

After crossing the river, groups of people began separating into smaller groups going north, west or south. Many joined other wagon trains going northwest. The women hugged one another and promised to write or have someone write for them and the men shook hands.

Nancy and Josiah left the wagon with Rod at Mackenzie's. He loaned them a pack horse which they promised to return to Mac who would see that Rod got it in the near future.

Rod had arranged to buy his stock from Mackenzie via pony express which picked up mail and telegrams and delivered them to outlying stations.

He bragged, "I breed sheep and dogs to herd them, out in the middle of the territory between Pierre and Fort Bufort. Put my ranch on the west side of the Missouri river so's my customers don't have to haul them tother side. Yes siree, the Missouri, now there's a river. No crossing it excepting on a boat, raft or winter ice. That old Missouri is the second largest river ever discovered in this country," he said proudly. Mackenzie had promised him breeding animals and was as good as his word.

"I was thinking of raising horses and cows," Rod said, not wanting to dampen Mac's enthusiasm, he added, "maybe try a few sheep."

"Suit yourself, son. If'n you stay on the prairie, you'll come to sheep. But if it's horses and cows you want, I can fix you up. Have me a partner. Her pa drove a herd of Texas longhorns north and took over land right after the civil war, married his self a squaw and built up a sizable herd near the Missouri 'fore he died; but Snow Shoes knows more about ranchin' than anybody I've yet to meet. Just tell her what you want. Her ma was a Sioux and it shows. You don't mind buying from an Indian, do you?"

Rod smiled, "How could I, I'm one, too."

Mac laughed and slapped him on the back. "Knew you was different lad, but it don't show on the outside." He changed the subject.

"So far, most of our customers are soldiers and miners but as soon as I heard about the gold in them there hills, I begun to build up my flocks."

He and Rod had become good friends in Vermilion. He gave Rod so much information about sheep Rod decided to try his hand at more than he'd originally intended. With the coming of so many homesteaders and miners, Mac planned on making a fortune. I could use a little extra money myself, Rod thought.

With the help of Government maps from Custer showing the places available, Mackenzie had advised him on the best possible locations. He agreed the place north of the Badlands Custer had marked for Rod might have good water.

"You need a lot of watering holes and springs in dry years, if you're to raise livestock and even more to farm. Not enough rainfall in the summer.

Rod had written to the man who had originally homesteaded the property. He said he'd take a fifty dollar bill for the whole shebang and Rod could send it to him after he saw the land.

Mackenzie said, "There's plenty of tall buffalo grass, if not over grazed. Sheep thrive on it. Cows don't do well. Only along the creek beds can you hope to raise garden vegetables. Sometimes, during wet years, a wheat crop might grow. You can't predict when the rain will come."

Rod nodded. He felt fortunate to have such good advice on virgin country.

Mackenzie had permission from the government to train and hire reservation families. Some Indians were too proud to work for a white man, but others were happy to get off the reservations. The squaws worked harder than the braves, so Mac hired only couples. They carried their teepees and adapted readily to a shepherds way of life. When he could, Mackenzie arranged for Hopi's from the Southwest to stay at his ranch and help train shepherds.

"The Hopi have been raising sheep for hundreds of years in country drier than the prairies," he boasted as though it was his doing.

Rod laughed. He liked this large Scott who gave him advice like a father and didn't try to cheat him.

"I'll start out with five cows and fifty sheep." The horse and wagon team Joe had given him could be used for hauling and a bit of plowing and would produce foals in the spring. Mac trained dogs to help with the sheep. He gave Rod a choice of a dozen two year olds who were well trained. "A good dog is worth three men. They run, smell and hear, the shepherd mainly sees. Dogs are one of the reasons running sheep is more profitable than cows."

The Sioux woman was a sharp trader, but Mac was generous with his sheep. Rod figured it balanced out.

Rod asked Mac, "Can you train Nellie?"

"Too old," he commented. But Nellie soon learned to work with the sheep dogs even thought she preferred to be near Rod. With the help of the dogs and sheepherders, he headed west to his homestead area.

Rod found the stakes to the section for sale. It had several small creeks running through it. These made it rather hilly. He hoped, as a result of the rolling hills, there would be water, even in the driest weather. The air was filled with the aroma of Cedar trees growing along the sides of several small canyons. Warm sun filled the air with the clean smell of trickling water. He closed his eyes as he sat in the shade of a cottonwood trying to imagine what the place would be like in a year and in five years. Would

Avonelle Kelsey

Annabelle be singing and their children calling to one another as they splashed in the pond? He smiled to himself and rode on.

A couple of sheds and the abandoned Soddy would help with shelter until he could build a house.

One place had an ice cold spring that fed the creek and formed a small pond before it meandered off around the bend. Rod followed up the sloping ground to a point near the crown of a low hill and unloaded his gear. In his mind's eye he noted the location of the temporary Soddy, the cabin he would build for Annabelle, and where he would locate a dam, a barn, and a sheep fold.

After choosing his home site, Rod stood on the knoll, sighed and smiled, then raised his arms. An old Iroquois blessing rose from his lips. "Great Spirit of the Earth, Great Spirit of the Sky, on this land let men and animals dwell together in harmony."

The shepherds waiting on the other side of the creek laughed and applauded, giving enthusiastic shouts of joy following his chant. The old ways were still alive in their minds and blood.

Rod had contracted to keep the shepherds who led the flock to help him raise a barn, build fences, dig a new Soddy, and teach him the sheep trade. At least one shepherd family would remain to help him for a year. They could use the old Soddy and sheds just over the hill. Next spring, Mackenzie would send him another couple to help with lambing and shearing.

Cedar and cottonwood trees were not plentiful, but enough were available to use as supporting structures for sod bricks and a grass roof. Sod was free. To protect his tools and the sheep, they hollowed out a large room in the sloping bank above the creek and another cave opening around the bend from the other. One would be a sheep shelter and the other cave the Soddy where he would live for the winter or until he built the cabin and Annabelle came.

The following winter, Rod planned to dig a tunnel from inside the house to the back side of the sheep fold. In this way he could check on the animals without going outside and use the tunnel in between for storage.

On the animal side of the cave, he built a sod fence. It became both a sheep fold and corral until the barn was completed.

The other side of the hill would be his temporary dwelling. The shepherds helped him put up timber supports. Using gumbo bricks hewn out of the ground with axes; they sealed off the front, leaving room for a window, a door and a large fireplace. They mixed straw and dried prairie grass to strengthen the mud and to caulk between the layers of sod and timbers. With the large fireplace on the outside wall, the place would be snug in the winter and the foot-thick sod walls would keep it cool in the summer.

The sheepherder's wives and the dogs watched the stock, milked the cows, and made butter and cheese. By the end of the summer, they had fenced areas for corrals and built a barn out of sod. A small garden near the creek gave a few fresh vegetables. His new neighbors who had the section north-west of Rod's

Avonelle Kelsey

would share pasture and fencing in the future. In many areas there was fighting between the ranchers and sheep men. Since the prairie would not support many cows, that trouble was eliminated for Rod when his neighbors agreed to raise sheep as well.

Indian raiding parties were still a problem for many farmers and ranchers. Rod could talk with various tribes in sign language, and often befriended them. Sometimes they helped with chores or a barn raising in return for food. Rod shared what he could spare. There were buffalo and antelope when he had time to hunt.

Often a hunting party of braves and warriors camped by the creek. Renegade Indians hid out in the nearby badlands from soldiers who were trying to force them to stay on reservations. The farmers were more alert for desperadoes than wandering Native American bands.

As Custer had predicted, many people came to the spring below the house. It had been a watering hole and an old Native and animal trail. The spring water was sweet and cool. To keep the area clean, Rod and a wagon train that rested there for a few days built a toilet and some tables and light shelters to keep off the sun and rain. He put up a sign urging people to:

"Help yourselves to the spring water to drink and keep it clean for the next person. Wash clothing and bathe in the lower pond. Feed the stock in the pond below the springs and stake them out beyond it."

More and more people were heading for the gold strike in the Black Hills and needed food as well as water.

"Got any milk or cheese to spare," women with children often asked. Two of the cows produced more milk than Rod and the shepherds needed. If a family looked poor, he gave them the milk, but the milking and cheese making became such a chore he hired a shepherd's woman to come in each day. She soon earned her wages plus a nice profit for Rod. They also traded cheese and butter for eggs to a neighbor.

"Be durned if my wife ain't makin more money with them chickens than I do on the ranch," Clyde said looking puzzled.

"Seems to me that should tell you something." Rod laughed at his expression.

"What might that be?"

"Raise chickens."

"That don't seem quite manly."

"A chore is a chore," Rod said. "My milk cows are making as much as my sheep and I'm more than happy with the money."

"God moves in mysterious ways," Clyde said wrapping the butter and cheese in cloth and slipping them in the empty egg basket before riding away.

Rod grinned and shook his head. Some men had strange notions about men and women chores. "Reckon Father and I took care of ourselves on the trail for so long we forgot which is which."

He washed his face and hands in the creek and took the handkerchief from his neck, using it for a towel. On an impulse he slipped off his moccasins and slipped his feet in the cooling water. Before long it would be winter. If he didn't watch out, autumn in all her glory would slip away and he'd not even notice. He lay back in the damp grass and looked at clouds floating above. A flock of geese headed south. He could smell winter in the air as well as the brown and gold leaves from cottonwood trees. What were Annabelle, Dan, Melissa and the family doing this evening, he wondered.

A pony express rider passed south of Clyde's farm regularly. Sometimes he left a letter for Rod with Clyde. Communication would be easier when the train track was completed to the Black Hills. He wondered if buffalo would disappear here as they had every place the train ran. Rod dozed until Nellie licked his face. It was time to bring in the cows from the south pasture for milking.

Rod felt fortunate. The view from his small Soddy porch looked out over the cottonwood trees and pond. Trees held clusters of golden leaves until November. The Soddy window faced southwest so sunsets were a daily event. It was marvelous how the Earth constantly changed, yet remained the same. Sunsets often reminded him of his father and their evening talks around the campfire before he went to bed under the stars and his father went off for an evening of gambling. He wondered if somewhere the soul of his father still shared this rare beauty with him.

Winter came late. Mac had sent several loads of hay to be stored in the barn. He offered to share the profit with Rod should he sell the extra to nearby ranchers and farmers. They lined the walls with it and made it two stories high. The barn was warm and snug. Might be a good idea for a house, Rod decided.

The day before Christmas, Rod cut a small cedar tree, placing it by the scraped hide window. On it he hung a ribbon of Annabelle's he had found and kept in his pocket for two years, a picture-sketch from the twins, his mother's poem, a book marker from Melissa and the last letter from the Bennett family. Dan had slipped a bottle of whiskey into his saddle when he left. Rod decided he would spend Christmas Eve reading the letter and sipping a glass of the whiskey as he remembered home and the Bennetts. He fished out an old deck of cards belonging to his father, sat them beside the whiskey under the tree and laughed aloud. It was a strange sight, but comforting. Nellie nosed his hand and sat gazing at the tree as though it was special.

"You looking for a present, girl?" he asked scratching her head. "Let's go out and look at the stars. Then I'll cook you a steak. Guess this Christmas it's just you and me."

Outside a soft snow fell. Rod stood on the porch and searched for Venus, the Christmas Star his father had called it. Soft glistening snow flakes covered his beard and hair. He wondered if he should place his cedar outside and let Mother Nature decorate it.

Nellie whined and gave a small bark.

A snow-covered soldier came riding up the path. Rod's hand slid to his pistol. He stepped sideways so the light was not behind him and waited in the shadows.

The soldier kept both his hands high. "Howdy," he called, "and a Merry Christmas."

His voice had a cheerful note in it and Nellie, instead of growing, wiggled and gave a little yip of welcome.

"Mind if I get down? I'm supposed to be a scout for General Meade but this snow caught me off guard. It's a mite cold as well as purty."

"You're right there, soldier," Rod answered. "Nellie seems to think you're a friend. Step into the light and let me take a look at you."

The Sergeant stood for inspection in the doorway light rubbing his snowy arms. He held the reins to his horse which stood by the porch with bowed head, blowing cold from its nose.

"I'll take your horse to the barn and feed it. You and Nellie go inside. Under the tree's a bottle of whiskey. Looks like you could use a drink. Nellie and I could use some company."

It was the beginning of a life-long friendship.

Winter was short but cold with little snow until spring. The sheep could usually find buffalo grass to eat but the cows had to be fed with the hay Mac had thoughtfully supplied.

In March a series of deep warm snows began to fall. The homesteaders were hard pressed to feed their stock. Rivers flooded and the area turned the gumbo into an impassable, slick mess. The extra hay from Mac saved many animals.

Rod knew he would not be able to leave for Vermillion as planned.

Regretfully, he wrote to the Bennetts.

Dear Family, Annabelle, Friends & Melissa,

It is with regret that I will not be able to return this spring as planned. The animals gave birth late and I cannot leave the lambs. Mackenzie is sending me another shepherd family. Coyotes are everywhere. The rains have made many areas impossible to use until the creeks dry up. We should have plenty of grass later on in the summer.

I would like to invite one and all to visit me, if you don't mind sharing a Soddy. The railroad is being built in the direction of the Black Hills but it has not passed south of here as yet. I fear the rains will delay its progress.

My Soddy served me well during the winter. I've had a few leaks during the worst rains. It's strange to see the walls of one's house turning to muddy water.

During the winter I had a chance to read the books you gave me, Melissa, as well as repair harasses, mend my boots, make furniture and tan hides.

My home place has become know as Anderson Springs. So many pilgrims and wagon trains stop near the creek I could have sold off my entire flock by the end of last summer at a handsome profit, but I only kill from my herd when a wagon train is desperate for food and no antelope are available. I see Buffalo sometimes. They are such magnificent beasts I hate to kill them. An antelope now and again keeps Nellie and me in meat.

I sent a shepherd back to Mackenzie for more sheep before winter to replace those butchered or sold. I wish the twins and Willie were here to help feed the extra lambs and Dan to inject some humor into this rainy, slippery gumbo.

General Custer camped at the spring near the sod hut soon after I settled in. His soldiers stayed several days. "Scouting for renegade Indians,"he said.

As he sat on the porch and talked with me in the evening, the General insisted he was sympathetic with the Native Americans cause but must also do his duty. Some insists he's trying to making a name for himself. He's a man torn between his conscious and his duty, but I felt that so called 'duty' would win out.

It was winter when I heard the news of his massacre in Montana. For that alone he may become famous. I recalled him fondly and with sadness, as I remember the party the town gave me and dancing with his lovely wife, Elizabeth.

The few wagon trains to make it this far are plagued by mud, rain, cholera, flu, hunger and renegades after they cross the Missouri.

The wagon masters like to stop under the cottonwoods along the draw to rest and, hopefully, hunt buffalo for meat. Since so many people use my dam, I ask that each group repay me by helping construct a larger one farther away from the house.

Would you believe my milk and cheese business may be more profitable than sheep? The shepherd's wives want to raise chickens as well and promise to keep me well supplied. I barter milk and cheese with my neighbor, Clyde. He might not like the competition. There is a great deal of opportunity near the trails for anyone willing to work and risk a group of outlaws now and again. Maybe you should build a store near Anderson Springs, Joseph.

So far, only one homestead has been destroyed, but I rather think it may have been white men and Indians were blamed. Hungry Sioux and miners on their way to the gold fields in the Black Hills wander in to be fed. They often help with the work for the duration of storms or floods and then move on. The promises of riches in the Black Hills are more inviting than hard work on a homestead so it's not easy to get help, other than part-time Indian workers. A few have a tendency to get a full belly and money for whisky, then quit. Many, like the Shepherds, are very dependable. They would rather herd sheep than live on reservations.

I had two interesting visitors last winter. A soldier spent Christmas week snowed in with me and later an old Philosopher blew in on a sleety wind. I'll tell you about them when I see you. The house has yet to be built and there seems to be an endless list of chores which prevent its construction. The cows and both horses produced foals; it's a delight to see them racing about. The Arabian mare continues to give me a beautiful colt each spring.

My homestead is hard work but I enjoy it since it allows me to be outside a great deal of the time.

Avonelle Kelsey

Needless to say, I miss all of you very much.

A pilgrim awaits who is returning east and will see that this letter is delivered to you in Vermillion.

Yours, Rod Anderson.

By the end of the first winter, Rod had grown several inches to over six feet tall, as well as broader through the shoulders. He contracted with an Indian woman to make buckskin clothing from antelope hides he skinned and scraped. His beard grew long and curly. In the spring he trimmed it with shears. The reflection in the dam was one that he was not certain Annabelle would appreciate. His shaving mirror and razor were used very little. He decided he looked older and wiser with a beard.

Rod smiled again as he remembered the wise Plato.

There had been a late spring blizzard. Darkness on that stormy day came early. Rod finished his chores by lantern light and hurried inside out of the freezing storm. A warm wind from the Northwest seemed to collide with a Southwest snow storm. The winds struggled over the prairie like roaring giants bleeding a sticky, freezing sleet which clung to everything it touched. The large fireplace held a cedar log and a steaming kettle of stew. He hung his damp buckskin jacket over a chair to dry and flung himself down on the buffalo rug in front of the fireplace to remove his boots.

A horse whinnied. Throwing on the jacket, Rod rushed to the door with a lantern.

By the hitching post stood a horse nosing a man on the ground; the animal seemed to be talking to him. Both man and horse were encrusted with wet snow.

Rod spoke softly to the horse and scratched her ears. "I'll take care of him, pal. You go off to the barn with Nellie. I'll be down directly to give you some oats." The horse bobbed his head and stepped back so Rod could pick up the frozen man.

"Nellie. Take the horse to the barn and open the door." She had learned to push up on the wooden handle and let herself in and out. Rod grinned as he saw her circle the horse and it began to back toward the barn. He turned his attention to the bundle of blankets on the ground.

Rod filled a wash tub full of snow, letting it melt as he undressed the frozen bundle. Underneath the blankets and clothing was an olive skin. The man was not tall; his body was very thin, closed eyes slanted in a weather-beaten face. There was a sprinkling of gray in his hair. Chinese, Rod thought, about fifty years old. Maybe a run-a-way from the railroad work gang. His hands, feet and ears must be thawed slowly. He wondered how he'd be able to accomplish getting him into the tub and held upright while he packed snow on his frozen face and ears.

Suddenly, the large, liquid-brown eyes opened and looked directly into Rod's. For a moment Rod caught his breath. They were intelligent, knowing eyes and seemed to read his very soul.

Rod said, "I know it'll hurt, but I'm going to put you in a tub of cold water and hold wet snow to your nose and ears. You must thaw out slowly. Understand?"

The eloquent eyes blinked in the face still stiff from encrusted ice. Rod worked quickly. While the man sat silently watching him, he put cold packs on his face and ears. He must have some Hindu blood in him to have such eyes, Rod thought. One time on a river boat with his father many years ago he had met a Hindu snake charmer who had the same brown liquid eyes. The wise alert expression in them reminded Rod of Melissa.

I miss her as much as I do Annabelle, maybe even more, he realized. He yearned for good conversation about something besides the weather and sheep.

Melissa was only five years older than the young men, but she could read and speak French, Latin, quote Shakespeare, philosophers, Plato, and many great statesmen from the past. She knew more law than the lawyer under whom Dan apprenticed. With Rod she talked philosophy, mathematics and science. When any of the three were missing on long winter evenings, the others could often find him or her at Melissa's house. Rod knew she read far into the night.

Dan had a crush on her. Rod and she cared for one another as any two lonely people must when they can share questions and answers on any subject without embarrassment. Even Annabelle felt a deep affection and admiration for her.

"I repeat, I wish you'd become a teacher, Rod. The country needs men who think like you," Melissa said again before he left.

Rod had blushed and replied, "What have I to teach anyone?"

"What do you think a teacher is Rod?" He had learned from experience, her questions were a prelude to a deep insight. He did not answer because he wanted to hear what she would say.

"A teacher is not a person who teaches someone how to earn a living, set an example, or about the rules and regulations of church and society. When a teacher does this, the student becomes dependent upon the teacher. The student becomes fearful he won't live up to the ideals he has been taught. When fear enters into any relationship, it cripples the person who will always feel inferior to the teacher or person in charge."

She paused and the large intelligent eyes probed Rod's. When she was certain he was following her thoughts, she nodded, and continued.

"There is no freedom and creativity in conforming or following an example. If you tried to be like a hero, your teacher, or meet someone's expectations, wouldn't that twist and strain your life?" He nodded again.

"The function of a teacher is simply to help a student understand what he is and lead him to the gates of possibilities; to think with an open mind, probe, and use the mind and body as tools. The essence of being is neither the mind nor body. That can only be found in the quiet pool within each person."

When Rod left her home, he always found a great deal to think about. Often her words reminded him of the nights he and his father had lain under the stars and talked about the meaning of life from a Native American's point of view.

Rod thought of her words as he looked into Plato's eyes and pressed snow against his ears and nose. At least Plato was what the man murmured when Rod introduced himself.

He recovered quickly. Rod stretched his damp clothing over a chair to dry, gave him a blanket and a bowl of stew and went to tend the horse in the barn. The storm pelted him. By the time he returned to the Soddy, he too looked like a snowman. Plato smiled slowly as Rod shrugged out his coat and shook the snow from his hat.

The older man sat wrapped in a blanket by the fire for several days. Each night they talked about why people went west in spite of the hardships, the future of the Native Americans, and meaning of life.

"I believe we are here to experience truth, Rod." His accent was slight, his voice light and refined. "We can't do this by thinking. Our thoughts are based on past experiences which often bring bitterness and rejection of life along with it. A child lives from moment to moment, happily. That is, until some adult coerces it into conforming to society, or their beliefs. As a child learns to survive by doing what we expect, its happiness decreases proportionately. Conflict is only part of being human. It is when we deny and fight instead of investigating and arriving at better understanding and new plateaus of wisdom that problems arise."

As with Melissa, Rod listened thoughtfully.

"If you remain true to yourself, a quiet understanding can grow. Understanding never takes place when we let our mind run wild or try to conform, rather than trying new roads and thoughts."

They talked of the Native American's feeling of belonging to the Earth; whereas the white man felt the Earth belonged to him; of Melissa, his father and Grandfather. Plato claimed to have stayed at his Grandfather's saloon-church as a young boy. That would make him very old, Rod thought.

"You're very much like him."

"Tell me about Grandfather."

"The ideas of the church were too small for your grandfather." He smiled in remembrance. "A group of Indians came into the reservation church one day. As the young priest talked to them, a Native American girl stepped forward and said, "Why do we listen only to your ideas? Our people have been in this country since the stars were born. Surely we must have something worth while in our beliefs?"

"Show me." Your grandfather gave her his hand. She led him away. No one stopped them. After a month, a different man returned. He left his white collar and black coat on the church peg, put on a buckskin jacket and rode out of town. I met the two of them years later. He had built a saloon-church on a town near his wife's reservation. By then they had a son, John. Your grandfather always closed the saloon on Sunday and either spoke himself or made it available for funerals, weddings and discussions on that day. Often wise Native American women and men spoke of their own beliefs and smoked a peace pipe during the services."

Rod remembered enough of the story from his father to realize it was true.

Plato only stayed for two weeks, but he made a lasting impression on Rod. He promised to return again.

Letters & Poems

Dear Mary, Annabelle, Dan, Joe, the Twins, Willie, & Melissa:

There are many chores to do and often only two hands, so I hope you'll forgive the fact that I do not write individual letters at this time.

As I wrote earlier, I regret I cannot to return to Vermillion before snow flies. Roads and creeks were impassable last spring, grasshoppers and drought followed and now winter approaches.

My dear friend, Mackenzie has promised to come to my rescue with supplies for the animals which seem to be doing well in spite of the problems.

I had two colts, four calves, and forty baby lambs to care for in addition to the original fifty sheep, cows, the horses, and a stray mule I call Oscar, because he is so stubborn. (You probably know who (to whom) the name is referring.)

Avonelle Kelsey

Tell Willie Nellie is a great friend and helper. She may be a mother come spring and I'll save him a pup. Two shepherd families live near the other spring and help with the sheep. I intend to buy a couple of more dogs next year after returning to Vermillion. Also, Mackenzie has promised me Hopi couples who are supposed to be the most knowledgeable shepherds in the country; if I will run some experimental breeds for him. One of my neighbors has left and is selling me his section of land so I should have plenty of grazing pasture.

I hope to have a house built before I return next spring. The neighbors promised a 'house raising' when I'm ready.

So far, I have had very little trouble with Indians. In fact, they have been very helpful. Often small bands camp by the spring. One of my neighbors has not been as lucky. When a Sioux becomes angry, anything can happen. A few white men still persist in treating them as animals. They ask for some of the problems which arise as a result of this attitude.

My messenger awaits. Give my regards to Melissa and other friends who inquire. Remember that I look forward to hearing from each of you as often as possible. Needless to say, I miss my family very much and hope we can be together next summer, or sooner, if you see fit to pay me a visit.

Yours lovingly, Rod Anderson.
Anderson Springs, Dakota Territory.

The winter brought sporadic storms but snow drifts stayed on the ground and drifted aimlessly back and forth in the wind. Rod was glad the Soddy was underground. He decided to build the cabin just under the knoll on the southeast side to break the wind and, in the early spring, and plant rows of cottonwood on the north side as well.

One evening Rod ran into a herd of buffalo near the spring. A bull dug into the snow and snorted. Rod was able to side step his first charge. The bull and he circled one another. The restless herd behind the bull began to move.

As the herd ran past, Rod quickly moved in beside a female and raced along her side toward the grove of cottonwoods, threw his arms around a tree and swung around to the back side. The rest of the herd raced away but the bull continued to stamp around the tree until Nellie came barking and nipping at its heels. While Nellie distracted the buffalo, Rod slid across the frozen creek and hurried inside the milk house. The bull charged the small building, crashed through the wall and fell into the spring house pond, breaking a leg.

With regret, Rod shot the animal and then rode out to get the shepherds wives to help him skin the huge beast. He hung part of the meat in the spring house to let it freeze. The women made jerky out of the rest and brought him a large bag. The dried meat was handy when he went out riding during the day or didn't feel like cooking. The hide made him a warm mattress come winter.

Avonelle Kelsey

Sometimes stragglers, scouts or soldiers wandered in and stayed until a storm was over. They played cards, told tales, brought news from the outside world and often precious letters.

During long winter storms he found time to write a few poems.

Melissa and Mary always enjoyed them. Annabelle had even put a couple of them to music when he had been brave enough to show them to her.

Melissa: I'll pen a couple of poems for you as they often show how I feel at the moment. Perhaps an incident with a buffalo and Plato's visit made me take time to think about life . . .

Winters Dread

My icy whites a glittering prison,
A place of conflicts
When braving the great outdoors .
Inside, cozy crackling flames,
Tempting flannel sheets and hides
Cuddle me warm.

Crispy cold outside, sounds echo as
Snorting deer blow noisily
Crackle, rip, bang, bang . . .?
Scratching on the door—Poe's raven, "Evermore?"
Or is it just
Snow stacked limbs giving up their loads?

In the firelight,
Fairy sunbeams dance in rainbow swirls.
Silent Night and Christmas Candles
Echo memories eerily;
I wish I could be home for Christmas . . .
Smell air fragrant with pumpkin pies
And scent of loving bodies
Hugging me . . . tight . . .

A new year, a new beginning
For Nature, you and me.
I am renewed by the drip, drip of melting snow.
Welcome Sweet Springtime, I greet thee in song . . .
Forgetting winter's dread!

Avonelle Kelsey

Winter's Music

Loneliness brings sound like a drumbing band,
Bang, bang, bang, rat-a-tat-tat.
Bang, bang, bang, rat-a-tat-tat . . .
Rhythmic ripples, splashing raindrops,
Making concentric wavelets
Of over lapping circles.
Flowers bloom to the music of honey bees.

A Butterfly tastes disdainfully.
Reflecting colorful thoughts,

As crystal gazer I . . . Feel . . .
The intense silence of ages.

Sense isolated islands,
A pooled geoglactic period,
Mixed micro-fauna brooding, breeding . . .
Sleeping dragons stir, time ebbs and flows,
Into a titanic, gigantic, tidal wave . . .

Jungle drums keep time as raindrops thicken.
The hasty wave of man melts
 into future time of hazy doubts . . .
And noise . . .
Bang, bang, bang, rat-a-tat-tat.
Bang, bang, bang, rat-a-tat-tat . . .
R A T - a – tat t a . . . .

W H A T is t h a t . . .?

Dear Melissa and family,

I thought the first summer and winter on the homestead were hard work but the following spring and summer were one of ceaseless problems. The rain finally stopped so I could plant some late grain. Grasshoppers arrived in droves and anything which remained was stricken in the following drought. Dust blew from plowed or overgrazed fields.

Mackenzie rescued me by sending wagon loads of hay over the frozen ground in October. He said I could pay him back from the spring lambing and by raising some experimental breeds of sheep for him.

It is winter again and I can go to sleep at night without being too exhausted even to read. I finished reading all the books I have on hand, some a second time.

I can only apologize for not writing more often. I need more hands than I have, fewer grasshoppers and less dust and snow. It's been discouraging, but I refuse to give up. At least I have a friend like Mac to see me through and friends like you whom I know are wishing me well. When I see what little Native Americans have both on and off the reservations, I once again count myself as lucky.

An old man who called himself Plato, of all things, showed up nearly frozen in a storm last winter. He was wise and nearly old enough to be Plato. For the first time since you and I parted, I found someone to talk with about ideas and thoughts.

Avonelle Kelsey

The soldiers, miners, and stray pilgrims who wander by seldom talk about anything outside themselves, gold strikes, farming or weather.

Enough complaining. I trust all goes well with you. As soon as the lambing is under control, I'm on my way to Vermillion. Enclosed is a note for Annabelle. Give Willie and the twins a hug. Bet they've all growing up. I'm sorry to miss those years, but am certain they are doing well.

I would appreciate it if you'd round up some books for me to bring back. When I get lonely for someone to talk with, they help a heap.

You may not hear from me again before you see me.

Yours, Rod.

My Dear Annabelle:

It is hard to put into words how much I miss you and the family. I trust your career is going well and know your stage productions in Sioux Falls and surrounding cities are just the beginning of your success. Claudette sounds like a lovely, talented young woman. A friend with like passions is a treasured possession, I'm sure.

Melissa has always been such a treasure to me. When I talk, she hears what I say. I miss her as you would miss Claudette. Remind Melissa to get some books for me to read on the long winter nights, although I would much prefer your company.

The railroad will be passing within a few miles south of here, hopefully, within the year and will make other parts of the country easily accessible in a short time.

I could not make it back last summer as planned. I will be there this summer and hope we can spend a great deal of time together. Should you decide to pay a visit to the ranch, I would be delighted. However, I know your career is important to you and keeps you busy.

So Dan is a lawyer now? I suppose he still finds ways to tease and play pranks on others. Claudette sounds like a great companion for him and I hope they will be happy together. It will be a rare treat to hear him try a case one day.

I'm sorry the twins are still giving people problems. Let's hope they grow out of it. It's hard to believe Little Willie is old enough to go to school. Give him a hug for me. Tell him I'll be there soon.

The loneliness, especially in the winter is sometimes harder to bear than the hard work and endless problems . . .

My thoughts and love are with you daily.

Rod.

P.S. I sent Melissa a couple of poems. One may be something you'd like to set to music.

I don't mean to be presumptuous but am sending a few lines of poetry which I scribbled while thinking of you . . .

Avonelle Kelsey

Meditation on Love
Sitting in the garden, thinking of my love,
I see and feel:
The Music of Silence,
falling as rose petals,
on a buzzing pond of butterflies.
Our spirits dance together
above the water lilies.

Wrapping myself
In the soft isolation
Of your presence,
Smelling the perfume of acceptance
Fulfilling my contentedness,
Until my aloneness is no longer loneliness.
I Am Love!

Finally, hard work seemed to be paying off. The large barn, corrals, and sheep pens were finished. The timber had been cut and was being prepared for the two bedroom house which he hoped to build in the early spring before going for Annabelle.

She, Mary and Melissa often wrote and send their letters in one envelope. The letters might take a week or a month to arrive.

Rod saved each and read them over and over.

The Recovery

Rod's shoulder hurt. He moved restlessly, tossing the covers aside. His body ached from heat then shook with cold.

Again a calm voice would read from Melissa's books or Mary talked soothingly to him. Sometimes, he heard the old man, Plato, whom he had rescued from the storm, talking to him.

To Rod's surprise, the old man had seemed to heal himself. How had he done it, Rod often wondered? He tried to remember. Plato, he said was a name his father gave him as a child because he was always curious about what people and life were all about. He sat in the tub, meditating, and arose in a few hours, energetic and healed. Even the frostbite that had seemed so severe had left the flesh only pink.

Was he remembering or was someone reading Plato from a philosophy book? Rod's eyelids felt so heavy. He tried to open them to see if it was real or a dream. Again a cold cloth was placed across his forehead. He felt warm broth being put to his mouth, he swallowed. A sheet was pulled over him. He waited to see if it covered his face to find out if he was dead or alive.

Gradually the leering men and firing guns faded away. Rod's body mended. The stabbing pain released its hold and his mind could distinguish dreams from the sounds around him. He fell into a peaceful sleep.

For the first time his body temperature was not too hot or cold. A hand felt his forehead and again the voice said, "Come back, Rod. We need you." He felt Nellie's puppy nuzzle his hand and lick it with a large wet tongue. Rod smiled faintly and moved his fingers to scratch the puppy's ears.

Two Bears sighed with relief. Tears of gladness rolled down his cheeks. He looked around the sod hut which had been the first home he had lived in for many years and knew he would regret leaving this place. The door was open and the sun was shining. He stretched and walked outside to check on the animals.

When Rod opened his eyes and looked around he saw the hide had been removed from the window by his bed and the door stood open. A low fire was burning under a kettle which sent forth savory odors. Rod was hungry. He attempted to sit up, but it was too much effort.

For awhile he lay back enjoying the comfort of being safe again. His eyes traveled around the room. Through the window he could see Two Bears feeding a new born lamb. Tears of joy rolled down his cheeks. The quiet background sounds suggested order as he listened to the animals in a distance.

Outside the doorway, the puppy went dancing up and nuzzled a lamb. In a distance he could see cottonwood trees with new spring leaves bursting forth. His horse and a couple of cows were drinking from the creek. The ground was beginning to turn green. How long have I been ill, he wondered?

Suddenly Two Bears stiffened as he became aware that he was being watched. He looked questioning toward the open doorway.

Again Rod tried to sit up. The effort caused sweat to form on his brow and his shoulder throbbed. Two Bears put down the lamb and came into the room. He put pillows behind Rod's head and said, "Welcome back, Mr. Anderson."

Rod's voice was rusty from disuse. "Two Bears. How can I ever thank you? You saved my life and my ranch it appears."

Two Bears shrugged. "If you are feeling strong enough, I will leave." He was feeling uncomfortable. Many white men would not allow Indians in their home.

"No! Please don't go." It made Rod weak to talk.

"Are you hungry, Mr. Anderson?"

"Please, call me Rod." Two Bears nodded.

"Yes! I'm starved."

The stew was excellent. A large glass of milk and several biscuits later, Rod said, "Never has anything tasted so good."

He was grateful his right arm was free to move about. Each time he attempted to use his left arm a series of pains shot through the shoulder. He grimaced as he deliberately moved it, testing to see if any bones were broken. Except for the bandages, he was naked. This stranger has been carrying for me like a baby. How can I ever repay him, Rod wondered?

Two Bears stood in the doorway watching him. The puppy danced around his legs. Why is he hiding behind his Native blood so determinedly?

For that matter, why do I hide behind a white man's facade? Perhaps, like Father and me, he is not certain if he really belongs in either world.

"Children of the Cosmos," he heard Plato say, "Caught up in a transitional time warp."

Rod suddenly remembered many years ago, he had listened to an old Chinese man and his father talking by the camp fire under the stars until the wee hours of the morning. It could not possibly have been Plato, could it? Bits and pieces of the conversation came back to him now and again. He had shared the thoughts with Melissa. Now he looked at Two Bears.

"I was just remembering an old Chinese philosopher who wandered in here half-frozen last winter. He was a very wise man."

"I, too, met such a man. He gave me some advice, but I did not heed it." Two Bears did not say what the advice was.

"His name was Plato. I feel he would have preferred no name. One of his most profound statements about God, churches, fences and boundaries was, "Anything which divides and separates people cannot be good."

"Ah, yes. I remember," Two Bears said. "When I asked him his name he said, 'Names are a judgment. Words are for us to share information and feel safe with one another, not to limit people and things'."

The young man paused thoughtfully and continued, "Our Mother felt white man's words distract. Words should only be used in a limited way. It is the heart that speaks the truth to man through actions. Words deceive. Words cover deeds like a dark blanket."

Rod lay back with a sigh of contentment. He reached for the hand of his new found philosopher. "I am so tired. Please stay with me. I feel my spirit needs mending as well as my body." Tears flowed down his cheeks. Hands tenderly wipe his face as he fell asleep again.

The next time Rod woke, sun was streaming through the open door and windows. He was alone. What time was it? Where was he? He lay still and relived the events as he remembered them. How had he gotten from the hellish scene to his own house? He remembered Two Bears and the faces in the dream that comforted him. Was he really home and was Two Bears still here?

I must get up and take care of things. How am I going to complete the cabin and go after Annabelle before the spring thaw? Spring? The way the sun looked, it's already here.

It took all of his strength to put his legs over the edge of the bed. Finally, he used his right arm to pull himself to a standing position and lean against the wall. His left arm was in a sling. He exercised the fingers, slipped his hand out and moved the arm slowly up and down. It was not broken. He must exercise and eat to get his strength back.

Rod slipped on his buckskin pants and pulled a work shirt across his shoulders.

Old man Dolly came through each spring with a wagon of merchandise, taking orders and delivering clothing, pots, knives, sewing kits, and many other things homesteaders needed. Rod had outgrown everything he'd brought to the homestead. The buckskin clothing was great for winter but too warm for summer. It felt good to be dressed again, even if he was weak. He must get some new clothing.

Had Two Bears left? Native Americans drifted as clouds into ones life and drifted as causally out again. A shepherds staff leaned by the doorway. Rod took it in his hand and stepped outside into the sun. He stood for a few minutes with his eyes closed and let its warmth fall directly on his face. Then, he opened them to gratefully drink in the peaceful, orderly scene of his ranch.

The horses were in the corral, feeding on fresh hay and cows munched contentedly in the meadow beyond. On a ridge sat a sheep dog that looked like Nellie, gazing toward the direction the sheep must be. He took a few steps onto the porch and sat down gratefully on a bench.

By the spring-house where the milk cooled, a couple of ducks paddled. Chickens clucked and birds sang. It looked like a well run ranch instead of one that had been deserted for, how long? The angle of the sun indicated at least April or May. A month?

Two Bears came slowly up the path with two lambs in his arms, the puppy nipping at his moccasins. "You're very lucky and prosperous. Many of your animals have given birth to twins."

Rod smiled as the young man handed him one.

"I will get a bottle. The mothers can only take care of one."

Two Bears brought the milk. Rod stroked the lamb. It felt good to hold something in his arms and caress it. Nature has many forms of caring for those who will accept it, he thought.

"I should call you, Healer," Rod said, breaking the contented silence.

"I learned the art from Mother. She was a medicine woman with our tribe. A priest sent her east to learn white man's medicine as well. You lost much blood, and then the wound became infected. When I thought you were getting well, you had a setback and were too weak to have any resistance. It is through her teachings that you are here."

Rod nodded and sat listening in the sun. It was good to hear someone talk.

"My people called her Gentle Healer. Father called her many things." He paused, an expression of pain passed over his face. "He called me Fast Buck. His name was Martin Howe. May he rot in white man's hell when I find him," he said fiercely.

Then he changed moods again and said more quietly. "He was a cousin of General Meade."

Rod listened. He had learned people often need to talk, more than they needed advice.

"Mother called me Witty, short for Funny Soul. I am one of a twin. When we were small, my brother and I wrestled like bears. It was hard for her to tell us apart. She affectionately called us One Bear and Two Bears. As a young man, I used the name Witty Sky and acted like a white man. Never will I use the name Howe again. Now I am an Indian and I use the name Two Bears. White men enjoy giving us animalistic names."

He used sarcasm like a white cynic, Rod thought, nodded encouragingly and continued to listen.

"My brother often called me Sky Eyes. He said that when I became angry, my eyes take on the color of a stormy sky. You are a friend. I will let you choose whatever name you wish to call me.

"I would be honored to call you Witty Sky. Also, it might be safer for you to have a white man's name as troops often come by the spring looking for runaways from the Reservation."

"I do not seem to belong in either world. My brother and I chose to be Indian after we left our father's home. You have chosen to be a white man."

The young man was very observant. Not many men knew Rod was one-forth Native American.

"I understand part of it. It is as though I am two people," Rod responded thoughtfully. He released the lamb to Two Bears who fed it and set it on the grass. It ran joyfully around the yard and began to nibble a few blades of new growth. "My Native part is constantly observing nature and the way people act. The white side weighs words and responds to them. I did not trust my Nature when I went to sleep while those characters you were riding with were in the territory." His voice asked a question, but he did not wish to pry. "Please come and sit down. Tell me all that has happened."

"Let me help you inside. After you eat, I will try to answer your questions."

They sat at the table and talked.

"In the beginning my brother and I were looking for General Meade, not only to find our father and kill him, but in order to fulfill Mother's last request. She read in the papers just before she died that Custer had offended President Grant by condemning the War Department's Native American Policies and the frauds connected with it.

"Later Custer stopped by the Reservation where Father ran the distribution warehouse and store for the Government. Mother heard him disagree with Martin about the way he sold half the goods that were supplied for the reservations and only distributed the other half.

"Custer was kind to Mother and asked her many questions. Martin stayed in the room and glared at her. She knew he would beat her if she told the whole truth, but for her people she risked it, and eventually was killed for her words.

"The General told her the army had given him orders to shoot any Indians that were off the reservations, so they could not start a war. He had tried to plead the Indians claim to the land in Washington whenever possible, but so far, all they did was order him to search and kill. "As a Chief gives orders and warriors and braves obey, so must I," he told her.

"She believed he could be persuaded to help even more, if he could learn of the Indian's view of life. Martin would not let her talk with him during the rest of his stay on the reservation.

"After Custer left, he sought and killed many Indians, until they killed him. His face wore two sides." Bitterness filled the young man's voice.

"How did your parents meet?"

"Martin, an agent for the government, persuaded Mother to leave nurses training and go with him west to a new Reservation that was just opening up. He told her she could help more of her people there. She would be his interpreter. Besides a salary, she would have a house of her own to use for a clinic."

Rod nodded and commented, "The Iroquois Tribe of my ancestors was nearly wiped out by General Sheridan in the winter.

"Contrary to white man's opinion, many Indian women in the past were the healers and wise leaders of the communities. Men are hunters and warriors. A Medicine Man went with warriors. Women kept the communities going were in charge of religion and passing on the wisdom as well as traditions from generation to generation. When the religious leaders from Europe condemned the religion of the Native Americans, they outlawed the use of the true leaders in Council. An Iroquois woman is treated with respect by her family and tribe. Many white women are treated as slaves by their husbands and children.

"If a brave or warrior was mean to his woman and children, she could kill him or make him leave. The village belonged to the women. A Chief is in charge of hunting and war. A Medicine Man goes with the warriors and helps the Chief decide when and where to fight or hunt and takes care of the warriors until they return to the village.

Two Bears listened thoughtfully.

Rod chuckled, "Father said it was the white man who has made the Native American Chief so powerful. They make the treaties with the wrong sex."

Two Bears agreed, "Our women are more adaptable to white man's way of living. They understand farming and raise or gather most of the food. White men are fortunate to find a native who will marry them. Squaw is a bad name for one so helpful."

The puppy came in and raced to Two Bears, Witty Sky, and then sidled up to Rod, licking his hand.

Witty continued, "A Brave is closer to nature in many respects, a woman is more civilized, works harder and trains the children. That is why white men often find them to be good wives.

"Mother wanted to convince white men that women should be sought in council. She thought Martin was her opportunity to become a link between the two races." He paused and shook his head as though to wipe away bad memories.

"But once Martin had her away from other people, he forced her to become his squaw and kept her a prisoner. He let her heal people when they came to the store because it was good for business, but seldom let her out of his sight. When he went on a trip, he hired someone to watch her.

"Several times she ran away and was caught and beaten. Probably, the reason he didn't kill her and the reason she stayed, was because of my brother and me. In his own selfish, greedy way, Martin thought he loved us. Mother was intelligent, tall with thinner features than the local Native Americans. Many men admired her beauty as well as her skill in nursing and conversation. She tried to teach us all she knew so we would do what she was unable to, that is, help both sides appreciate the customs of one another. We had to learn both white man and Native American ways."

Rod nodded, remembering his own childhood.

"On Sunday she often took us to church. The wise, white father, Jesus, had many sayings Indians could accept, but often the preachers chose to quote from the part of the Bible that contained tales of cruelty and a separateness from nature. How could both be true, we asked?

"There are cruel Indians and cruel white men," she told us. "Perhaps the white man has lost something the Native American retained, when he built warm houses and wore so much clothing, even in the summer.

"Body and soul must be in touch with nature in order to communicate," Mother said to Father when he ordered her to put clothing on us and cut our hair.

"He brought her a white man's disease. When she was too weak to work for him, he threw her out to die and locked us in the house. We escaped and found Mother, but it was too late to save her. She made us promise to seek out the great white father with the long gold hair, General Custer. 'Perhaps if you tell him about me and the way the way Martin treats us here, he will try once again to help us', were her dying words. We did not tell her Custer was dead." He paused for a long time before continuing.

"We built a funeral rack for her and stayed by her side until Martin caught us. He put us under guard and made us stay in the fort and go to school. We escaped. We had a goal in mind; to elude Martin until we reached eighteen years of age. Then we would return to the Reservation and kill him.

"When we returned to kill our father, he was gone. The government had asked for Martin's resignation after so many starved to death.

"Our search for him took us west. We were told he had joined the army. We continued wandering and watching for him. Or, at least I have." For the first time Rod saw his face grow tender and he smiled.

Rod must have looked surprised.

"One day my brother and I heard giggling as we rode by a creek. We hid behind some bushes watching several Native American maidens swimming and playing in a creek. One Bear fell in love." Two Bears paused.

Rod noticed a slight flush when he talked about the maidens. So, One Bear was not the only one to fall in love.

Finally he continued, "Fawn Sue could not leave an ailing father. One Bear stayed on the reservation with her. They will join me when her father seeks the Happy Hunting Ground, or perhaps I will give up my 'will--o-wisp' life and join them. It has been very peaceful here," he said wistfully.

Rod said nothing but reached across the table and gripped the arm of his new friend in sympathy.

"You wondered how I happened to be with Sam and his crew. I camped in a forest with a group of Indians who were hunting for food. The Agent, like my . . . like Martin, had sold the food and supplies that should have been given to their tribe . . . they were starving. We slipped off the Reservation to hunt game. A group of Calvary hunted us down. When the warriors refused to turn back until they found game, they were shot. I escaped and beat the soldiers back to camp.

"I tried to warn the women and children who waited to skin the animals and prepare them to be taken back to the reservation. The soldiers came again and killed every man, woman and child. I escaped by putting on a uniform of a soldier I had killed in a thicket, stealing his horse and riding away. There was nothing I could do to help." He paused for a long time. The puppy licked his hand. Absentmindedly, he stroked its soft head.

"I promised One Bear, my brother, to continue my quest for Martin. We no longer acknowledge him as our father. The last time we heard about him he had headed for the Black Hills. He too, has long golden hair and blue eyes so he's not hard to follow. That has been my only goal, until you needed me.

"Thank you, Two Bears. How can I ever repay you?"

"I have received my payment. For the first time in many years, I have quit running and felt peace in my heart." Witty Sky, Two Bears, looked off into the distance.

Rod felt sorry for his new friend. They sat in silence. Finally, Rod reached out again and put his hand on the arm of Two Bears. "This ranch is on the route to the Black Hills. People come and go all year long. I get news here as fast as anyone this far out. Freight and wagon trains stop just south at the spring. There will be many more this summer and I could use your help. You are welcome to stay here as long as you like."

Two Bears looked at him as though trying to decide if it was pity or a true need.

"As a matter of fact, I need to leave soon and go back to pick up Annabelle, the girl I am to marry, from Vermillion. The cabin for her is not built and I should leave in a month. I would pay you if you could help me and stay with the stock until I returned. As they probably told you, the shepherds take care of the sheep and their wives milk the cows, make cheese and butter which we sell to wagon trains. Winter wheat and grass will take care of itself. But the dogs, lambs and horses need extra care. My arm is still not strong. After the neighbors build the cabin, I need to leave for a few weeks. I, too, have promises to keep."

Two Bears nodded slowly. "I will stay until you return."

While Rod's left arm healed, he rode the fences and stopped by the ranch of Lindsey Dodd who had offered the loan of his son and the sheep dog to Two Bears when Rod had been ill. They talked about his delay of plans. Rod asked if he could hire his son to build the house.

"I have all the material," Rod added, "but Witty Sky says I shouldn't use my arm for a couple more months."

"A house raisin' is what you need, Son," he said. "I'll give the word at church. Monday mornin' bright and early, we'll be puttin' up yer house."

True to his word, at the crack of dawn the neighbors with, their wives and children appeared with tools and food. The logs Rod had been gathering for two years were fitted together expertly. With so many experienced hands, it was like a big, well organized party. The women had a chance to visit and the kids to meet and play. By evening the cabin was raised and roofed.

Rod had used the cedar and cottonwood trees in the draws sparingly. Since fire wood was scarce for fire in the winter, he often used dried cow and buffalo chips for heating. He had saved the best of the cedar for finishing inside and used tall, young cottonwood trees for support.

Mackenzie had sent a wagon load of lumber, doors and windows. The wall crevices were caulked with gumbo and straw for binding and strength. Deep window wells would hold flower pots or cushions. The back of the cabin contained a large fireplace made from gumbo and straw bricks, fired at a low temperature for a week and then slowly increasing temperature as they hardened. River rocks were used where they could find them. They would import finishing stone for the fireplace later, Rod decided. There were windows on each wall with both inside and outside shutters in case they were needed for protection. He would bring back glass for the windows when he returned with Annabelle, he decided.

Rod stood inside the rough cabin, looking about doubtfully. It seemed large and empty compared to the cozy Soddy. Someday, it would contain hardwood floors, two more bedrooms upstairs and running water. Now, he was seeing it through Annabelle's eyes and felt sad, until he gazed out of the windows.

To the south was the creek with tall cottonwood trees blowing gracefully in the breeze, their silver undercoated leaves trembled and glittered in the sun as their wind-rippled shadows made the tall buffalo grass come alive. Birds flew in and out building nests. Ducks swam gracefully on the lower end where he had built up a small dam for swimming, lining it with clay so it would hold water. There were bullhead fish, in the dams and pond.

The back of the cabin had a smaller window and door. It was just a few steps to the sod hut which would be used for storage or where Witty Sky would live for the time being. He had planted a small orchard and intended to bring back a variety of fruit trees. In the corral were Annabelle's two year old and the work horses with several colts and calves.

Rod would sell some of these to travelers on their way to the Black Hills to finance new furniture, clothing and other items which Annabelle might need. The wool from the sheep and mutton were already bringing in money; the cheese and milk business were flourishing. He could sell all the animals he could raise, especially if he drove them to Deadwood City. Perhaps Dan would come back with him and they could drive any extra to market.

Rod smiled. He saw the homestead through the eyes of love. It was easy to forget the summer heat, lack of rain, and grasshoppers last spring. There had been some flooding earlier, Two Bears said, or Sky as Rod now called him.

Mr. O'Riley and his two strong sons agreed to finish the cabin floor, white wash the walls with lime, and give Sky and the shepherds a hand when needed. Rod's flock had nearly doubled in size again this spring. He wanted to keep most for breeding stock.

Rod had made wine from dandelions and buffalo berries the summer before. With gourd cups, the young carpenters, Rod and Sky toasted their workmanship and his trip. Only Two Bears knew he was intending to bring back a bride. The others suspected he had a woman in mind but kept silent.

Rod was anxious to get started. He would get new clothing on the way and shave his beard. His shoulder had not completely mended.

Two Bears suggested the trip would give his wound a chance to heal completely. The winter wheat crop was in. If they were lucky and the rain came once in a while, there would be wheat for feeding the stock in the winter. On the prairie, a crop was a fifty-fifty proposition. The climate and vegetation was not quite desert. Only in areas near the creek would a normal garden grow. Rod had brought seed from peddler, Dolly, and planted it. How well Sky and the shepherd wives would be able to keep it growing was yet to be seen.

Mackenzie, true to his word, sent the Hopi Indians with a strange new breed of sheep, a salve for the bite of sheepked, and an invitation to Rod to visit him on his way east.

Two Bears sensed his anxiety about Annabelle. "I know you're anxious to be going, Rod. Your shoulder needs time to heal. I will stay until you return . . . just pack up and go." He laughed at Rod's expression and eagerness.

"I'll leave at dawn." When the rooster crowed he jumped off his bunk, and was surprised to see his horse saddled just outside his door and a pack horse all ready to go. He gratefully took the jerky, bread and cheese Sky reached him, packed it in his saddle bags and threw a sleeping bundle on the back of the other horse.

They shook hands and looked into one another's eyes. Each felt comfort and trust with the other.

Rod also felt like a deserter, but he had promised to return to Vermilion for sure this summer and he was so lonesome for his family and friends.

"Thank you, my friend. I will return as swiftly as possible. There's a smell of rain in the air. I'll leave the horses at the nearest stable where the train track begins and pick them up on my way back, or at Mackenzie's." He looked fondly at Sky.

The two young men stood quietly gazing at puffy cumulus clouds rolling above the prairie. They contrasted beautifully with the deep clear blue sky overhead. A sudden gust of wind blew Rod's hat across the face of his hose which snorted indignantly. Sky rushed after it across the spring green grass and caught it just as it hit the pond where it slowed enough for him to wade in and grab it.

Rod held on to the reins and both laughed as water dripped on his shoulders.

"I hope you'll change your mind and remain after we return. There's so much to be done and the herds are increasing. If you don't stay, I'll have to hire extra help anyway. Maybe Mackenzie's has a couple more sheep dogs."

"I'll think on it."

Rod liked the young man and found both his wit and mind good company. The twinkle in his eye often reminded him of Dan.

Sky watched as Rod rode away. He waved when Rod paused on the cedar lined knoll and looked down on his spread, sighed and turned away.

Other than a bedroll, rain gear, rope, cheese, jerky, and bread, Rod had very little to pack. He had outgrown nearly all his clothing again this past winter. Like his father many years before him, he wore a holster on his hip when traveling and carried a rifle on the saddle. Before leaving, he'd bundled up the things he'd worn the first year and given them to Sky. "It might be safer if you wore these until I return."

Rod rode across his ranch, noting that the fence in which he kept his breeding experiment between a bull and a female buffalo would need to be strengthened and enlarged. There was a new calf in the corral. Sky was rounding up a couple more female buffalo to be bred next spring. At the rate the buffalo were being killed, they might become scarce. It was such a senseless waste. Native American used the hide for clothing, homes, bags, food, tools, storage, blankets, and numerous items. If they could have been left this one animal, along with antelope and the prairie dogs, they would not have to be fed by white men. Of course, a farmer thought the open land was wasted on wild animals and Indians thought wild animal and plants grew by themselves so why cut trees and plow. Their women gathered wild roots, bulbs and plants to supplement the meat the men hunted. They made clothing, blankets and homes with the hides, ran the villages and in many tribes, divorced husbands by stetting their bedrolls outside if they didn't behave. The simplicity of their way of life was foreign to white men.

The combination of an animal adapted to the prairie and a domesticated animal would make great beef stock because it could feed on the stiff buffalo grass more readily than a normal cow. Could Indians be taught to breed their own buffalo on their reservations? Sheep often ate the grass so short it would not grow back. He was careful not to over pasture.

Rod took a shot at a coyote slinking in the direction of the sheep herd. I'll have to track down the den when I return, he thought, but with a pack horse and Annabelle's two-year old trailing along behind, he kept moving.

His heart was full of both joy and anxiety. He carried a couple of letters from home and patted the jacket pocket. The rest he left in the niche in the wall of the old sod hut. They were worn thin from his many readings.

By the camp fire that night, he reread the letters which had passed from hand to hand until someone would ride the last mile or two and give them to the lonely homesteader. The pony express was going through just south of the ranch now and Wall had a postal station as well as a stage. The train spur on the way to the Black Hills would run near Anderson Springs. Within a year, there would be both mail and transportation a few miles from the ranch.

Annabelle and the family would be able to visit easily. Rod was pleased in that respect, but he did not like the idea of people riding trains to shoot animals for sport and letting the meat rot as they had done back east.

He felt a sense of freedom as he rode. A number of new homesteads dotted the land. Many were prospering and building houses in front of sod huts. The weather was warm. Storm clouds rose behind him, but overhead the stars were bright when he stopped at a tiny creek for the evening. By the firelight he re-read the last letter written in Mary's elegant style first. As usual, he sniffed each letter. Annabelle and Mary perfumed the first page. Each chose a different scent. Mary's was light lilac and Annabelle's was wild roses.

Avonelle Kelsey

By this time the fragrance was mainly in his imagination.

My Dear Friend & Son:

We miss you so very much. Dan is doing well with his law studies. It keeps him out of mischief part of the time. He's sweet on Claudette, the niece of Rev. Henry who has come to live with them. She's a very independent young woman, so he has his hands full. She lost her actor parents at sea and is a pretty good actress and musician herself. Annabelle and she have started a small acting troupe. It's like pulling hen's teeth to get either Annabelle or Dan to work in the store these days. But you know Annabelle. It gives her something to do until you return. We look for you daily and talk of you so often.

Mark is in Deadwood City. He's trying to get Joe to sell the store and move out there, but I have no intention of moving again. We moved so often before coming to Vermillion that I learned to hate it.

Melissa seems different these days. More restless. I think she misses you and Dan. She sends her love and says she hopes you are taking time to keep up with your studies.

She, Annabelle, and Claudette gave a terrific Christmas Musical for the school and are now working on a spring Cantata.

Joe says if you decide to give up homesteading, there is always a place for you in the store. It's so hard to get good help. All the able bodied men who were not killed off in the Civil War or off chasing Indians with the Cavalry, are headed for the gold strike. It seems to be larger and longer lasting than most. Mark has been there since he was discharged. *Says since Deadwood City and China Town burned, the shacks are being replaced with stone buildings, like a city. I think he still hopes to get news of Sylvia.*

He tells us the Black Hills are full of a large variety of minerals besides gold. I'm surprised you haven't felt the call. But then, greed isn't your nature. Thank goodness for that.

I miss you Rod. There is no one here I can really talk with as we did. Joe and your many friends send their regards. We look forward to your coming as we will not be able to make the trip again this summer. Mark is not returning and we are short handed.

Annabelle met a soldier who will carry our letters. He is on his way to the Hills.

May God be with you and send you safely home to us soon.

Lovingly, Mary

He folded her letter slowly and opened Annabelle's to read before falling asleep under the starry night. The brilliant stars above the prairie reminded him to the time he and his dad spent in Europe and an artist called Van Gogh. It was as though he painted the unseen pathway stars traveled that human eyes could not see. What else can't we see, he wondered as he gazed at the moon?

Was Annabelle looking at the same moon tonight? His body yearned to be near her.

Soon, soon, his heart beat rhymed with his longing . . .

Avonelle Kelsey

Dear Rod:

I'm still so mad at you for running away and having all the fun while Dan and I are stuck away in this old store. The only fun I had last year was when I could drag Dan away from his law books to go riding. Last week we saw a fox. Dan told me to shoot it. I drew my gun and looked over the sights. He was so beautiful. I could see your face if I killed it, so I let it go.

Dan called me a chicken and then we both laughed. We talked about you, your lectures on unnecessary killing and many other things. It's the first serious discussion I've ever had with Dan. Perhaps we're growing up a bit. He still pulls little pranks and teases, but he isn't as hard on me since Claudette came to town. She frowns on his tricks but we giggle behind his back. He's so crazy.

Later on Dan shot a pheasant. Claudette and I needed some feathers for costumes in our play and Mom made a great stew for dinner. Someday we may become famous playwrights and directors. Claudette is a great deal like you in many ways, an orphan, she writes poetry and stories as well as beautiful plays. Already, they want to hire her to play and sing in a saloon nearby, but straight-laced Rev. Henry, her guardian, is dead set against it.

We have our own small troupe. Melissa helps us and sometimes we set a stage up in the little High School she started. Wouldn't it be wonderful if she can get a University here in Vermillion as well? We're trying to help her raise money for it.

Dan will be a politician, I believe. He's protesting the capital of the Dakota Territory in Bismarck and believes that we should divide the large territory into two states. Melissa eggs him on. They attended the last legislative meeting together, each lobbying for their own cause. Two bad she's so much older than Dan. They'd make a great team. But he can't see anyone other than Claudette. You know how single-minded love is.

Dan and I have been giggling over Mr. Jacobs. His wife helps Mom out around the house and store part-time now.

Remember how his rooster always chased us when we went by his house and Dan tried to hang it? We all got into trouble for it. Anyway, old Jake got his paycheck and got drunk, as he did each month, and came home to beat his wife. Well, he began chasing her and she ran behind the heating stove. He was mad and grabbed the stove with both hands to shove it out of the way. The burns are so bad he can hardly use them to hold anything, much less a bottle.

Now she takes the broom to him when he gets uppity and makes him go to church with her every Sunday. I don't think he'll ever be able to beat her up again. She's in full control now and a different woman.

Claudette and I helped Melissa with the Christmas Pageant. We also plan a Musical which we hope to give at Easter. I have to teach the brats to dance and sing, but it will be fun. We're going to have such splendid costumes. Mrs. Walton is going to make them for us. You know what beautiful clothing she designs. If I ever get married, she will make my wedding dress.

Mom sure sighed and drooped around after you left. She misses you almost as much as I do. She says, "Rod's the only one who understands me." Dad certainly doesn't. Not that he doesn't love her. Sometimes they act more love-struck than Dan and Claudette. Imagine, at their age.

Don't tell Mom. Dad is learning to be a mule skinner. Uncle Matt wants him to move to the Black Hills and start a store there. He says there are fortunes to be made. Dan could practice law and there is a theater being built in town by a Professor Langrishe from the Denver Theater. Anyway, it would be closer to you and perhaps we could visit your place on the way. All of us think it would be exciting, except Mom. We're all working on her. She keeps saying, 'We'll see.' Meaning, no way.

A soldier who comes into the store says the Native Americans have been licked and they're breaking up the reservations, leaving room for a trail to the hills and making more room for homesteading and mining. Is that true? Are the Indians still dangerous? I forget that you're part Indian sometimes. If it is safe, please tell Mom. She'll listen to you.

I told the soldier that you're our brother. He might not be inclined to deliver it if he thought you were my bow. It's been awhile since we heard from you but the spring floods may have washed away the mail. Sometimes the Pony Express is more reliable than the stage coach or trains.

Well, I'd best quit writing before this gets so long the saddle bag won't hold it.

Dan says he envies you and we look forward to your return. I waited for you all last spring. Mom says homesteading is hard work and you'll come as soon as possible. I'll write again as soon as someone is going your way. How far are you from a Pony Express depot and the new railroad spur that is headed for the Black Hills?

Yours very truly, Annabelle Lee Bennett

P.S. Tell me more about my horse. I don't care much for sheep but the prairie sounds lovely when you describe it. Is the cabin completed as of this writing?
Are Plato and the soldier, Mike, still with you?
Give Nellie a hug and save me a puppy.

Rod lay for awhile, gazing at the stars. It was hard to get to sleep. He wanted to get up and ride again. Even yet nightmares often disturbed his dreams. A soft rain began to fall and he threw the rubberized rain tarp over his bedroll. Their last letters had been written in late March and here it was nearly June.

He had not written the family about his shoulder or Nellie's death, but just about having a small horse accident and that his shoulder was healing nicely.

Rod was not worried about Two Bears-Sky being able to take care of the ranch. He had proven to be very capable, but he was worried about his continuing to dress like an Indian. Soldiers might try to return him to the reservation, or worse. Rod had left his old clothing and suggested he wear it, but the youth was independent.

About two weeks earlier an evening storm had risen. Two Bears appeared saying, "Soldiers are coming."

"Sky, you go back to the Soddy. I'll take care of them."

There were four men, cold and wet even under their raincoats. Rod invited them into the newly built cabin. Sky had gone out the back door toward the sod hut where he slept, but Rod was certain he was on guard and listening.

Rod invited the small group inside. Soon the steam was pouring off their wet boots and pants as they sat by the fireplace. Rod made coffee, gave them bread and the rest of the meat left over from the antelope supper he and Two Bears had shared earlier. They wolfed it down, drank coffee and as was the custom, began to tell Rod the latest news.

"Denver is a growing boom town, but nothing like Deadwood City. Since Custer and his men discovered gold near French Creek in the Black Hills, the area is covered with people. It looks more like an ant hill. We were with the original group that discovered gold and have just been discharged from the army," one said.

"Yeah." The one with a slash on his cheek and a gray beard continued for him. "We're headed back to stake us a claim. We know where the real gold is. When I strike it rich, I'm gonna' build me a mansion right there and stay put. There are creeks running everywhere and small green valley's that would make rich farms. A warm wind can blow up all the way from Japan, they say. Right in the middle of winter, spring can come. Yep, that's the place for me." He stared into the fireplace in a dreamy-eyed way. Soon his head fell onto his chest as he went to sleep. The others laughed.

Rod could see they were all tired but he knew Two Bears was listening. "You rode with General Custer and General Meade's cousin. Did you ever hear of a Martin Howe? He was an Agent in the Northern Dakota Territory, I believe."

One man laughed. "Not since Custer got his. In his younger days Martin was some Injun hunter. Seemed to have a thirst for killin' toward the end. Even made the troops a bit uneasy. The General give Martin too much power. We went out with him one time on a rumor that some Injuns was runnin' away from the reservation. He give us orders to surround and kill every dang one of them."

"Women and children too?" Rod asked.

"Yer durn tootin'. Them squaws can be as mean as them bucks. They hide the guns and knives in their dresses. We had orders to shoot any that left the reservations. With them blankets on, we couldn't tell which was man or woman. Sure wish we had though. There was some real lookers, even dead, bloody and frozen the way they was."

Rod felt sick. He wished he had not asked. He could feel the hate and revulsion coming from Two Bears. A door out back closed softly. He knew that his friend had gone outside to seek solace for his grief.

"That there Martin is a heck of a lot meaner than Custer ever was. We was happy to get back to our own outfit. Ain't seen nor heered of him since. To bad he joined another troop before Custer got his'n."

Rod stood up. He'd heard enough.

"I'm leaving soon to go back east. You must have a long ride ahead of you. You can sleep the rest of the night in the barn and leave in the morning." Rod said stiffly. He wanted these men out of his house.

"That's mighty hospitable of you, but we got our tent set up down by the creek. The bedrolls are dry."

"Say, if you're headin' east, that there Missouri thinks it's an ocean. Better keep north. Rains been sneaking down from the Great Lakes area this spring. Might still be cross-able on the ferry 'round Pierre. Thanks fir your hospitality, Mr. Anderson. If you get to the Black Hills, we'd be obliged to return the favor.

"Come on Chester. Wake up. He's getting' too old for soldiering and such. Won't shoot an Injun unless they shoot first and has had nightmares ever since that raid. Chester thinks they're human."

"I happen to agree with him," Rod answered. He stepped closer to the bunk where he kept his gun. "My best friend is a Native American. I have Indian blood myself. Does that make me less human?"

They looked at him and backed toward the door. "Sorry about that remark, Mr. Anderson," Chester apologized for them all.

"Sometimes Jeff here has a big mouth. He was jest as sick about killin' them Injins as the rest of us. That's why we're all heddin' fer the gold mines and a better way of life than soldiering. Thanks again. We'll be off your place by morning, I reckon."

Rod was never certain what happened to the four. One day he came across a fresh grave and found four horses with army brands grazing near the little creek which ran across the north side of the ranch. The horses looked familiar but he and Sky never spoke of the soldiers.

Before Rod left he told Two Bears again, "If you don't start dressing like a white man, the soldiers are sure to take you in when I'm not around."

Rod tossed in his sleep with worry. Then he heard his father's voice speaking to him. "Enjoy today, my son. Don't be as the white man, always looking toward the future. The future's foundation is in the beauty of being in tune with nature, letting the past go and staying right here with nature." Then his father's face dissolved and Plato was beckoning to him . . . The rain had stopped.

In the morning the sun came out twinkling on buffalo grass and dancing in silver on cottonwood leaves. With a lighter heart and beautiful weather, Rod set out for the train. He sang, watched animals, played his harmonica and helped flood victims along the way to the train.

Because of flooding, it took longer than he had planned. The prairie was green. Spring sun flowers made patches of yellow

Avonelle Kelsey

and orange carpet. A few buffalo, elk, and antelope were still roaming the prairie. Pheasants were plentiful. Often at night he had a game bird or jack rabbit for supper and tucked some away for the next day. The horses ate the new spring grass.

Lonesome men and women were always glad to feed a fellow homesteader. They talked of weather, crops, Native Americans, massacres, weddings, cholera, wagon trains, pony express, the train and Chinese workers, gold strikes and the future.

Jessie James had been killed by a traitor. He was the Robin Hood of the west. It was almost as important to people to have a lovable hero who robbed the rich and helped the poor as Abraham Lincoln had been since he'd tried to help the slaves many years earlier.

The homesteaders worked liked slaves on their land. But it was their own. The weather was not always kind, but the land was free and they were not over taxed or harassed by land owners. What they earned, they kept; so hard work paid off.

Even though men sweated from dawn to dark, the prairie was harder on women. They raised gardens, canned, spun wool, made the family clothing, washed on washboards, while they bore children and took care of everyone, whether they felt up to it or not. Many of them had left good homes and big families that had servants. They seldom saw another female or even had help when they gave birth. Half of their children died before the age of five. Sometimes the loneliness and loss became too much. Often they died of childbirth or became old before the age of thirty. Many times the second wife was a Native American.

They, too, worked hard carrying for children, gathering, food but seemed sturdy and more able to handle the life of a pioneer.

Rod though about these things and wondered how Annabelle would like being such a person. Of course, he'd hire help, but . . .

I'm worrying about things that may never happen again. Soon I'll be home. That should be more than enough . . .

Avonelle Kelsey

Return to Vermillion

Rod's mind roamed over the past as he scanned the prairie. He thought of his Mother's Poem, The Sunflower Woman, when he watched the hard-working, bonneted women. He didn't want Annabelle to work like that. In fact, when he really thought about his house as home, it was not Annabelle but a faceless woman who roamed the rooms and greeted him at the door. He brushed away the thought.

Indian women were willing to take care of another man's children as their own. It also served another purpose. When they raided homesteaders, it often paid to have an Indian for a wife or an employee or two. These farms were usually left alone.

Even in their tribe, Indian women had lost a great deal of the respect they had commanded in the past. On reservations, they starved along with their children. As a homesteaders wife they usually had food for themselves and their children were safe.

There was no place for the warriors to go except to a humiliating reservation where they sat and dreamed of the past, happy hunting grounds, or revenge. Many tribes back east were nearly wiped out.

Just a couple of years earlier, the whole territory west of the Missouri had been set aside as one big Native American reservation. Since the discovery of gold in the Hills, the government was breaking up the area into the Pine Ridge and Rosebud Reservations on the south and the area just west of the Missouri on the east and to the north of the Cheyenne became a large reservation. In between was open to homesteading by people who were willing to risk the Native American outrage.

Some white women were more adaptable than others. Rod came upon one such 'Sunflower Woman'.

The rains had stopped but the run-off from the ravines and river brakes still poured into small creeks and added to the rising water of larger branches on the Missouri. One day Rod rode along a stream to find a crossing. He came upon a small house, a chicken coup, and a pig pen which were surrounded by water.

The Sunflower Woman stood in the doorway and surveyed the situation, then waved at Rod.

"Do you need some help getting to higher ground?" he called.

"No, thanks," she yelled back. I ain't got no man to build me another house so I'll settle wherever the good Lord sets her down, I reckon. The land won't be no worse than this land here." She was right.

He watched from the river bank as she knocked a hole in the roof with an ax, sat up a ladder of tables and chairs and hauled the piglet and chickens up to the attic. She put a cot springs on the peak and secured it. Then tied sacks of dried food and a few bundles of bedding and clothing, a spinning wheel, and anything she could haul up the ladder, to the ceiling. When finished, she sat down on the roof and began to read her Bible.

Rod and some of the neighbors who had come to help her, threw ropes to her to tie on to the corners. When the tiny house tipped as it pulled away from the chimney, they tied it to their saddle horns much as they would when roping a cow for branding and kept it upright. Slowly it moved down the river. By nightfall, the flood waters receded and the house came to rest in a grove of cottonwoods.

While the river was still up, they pulled it over to as near level as possible. The house settled down on the grass under a large cottonwood. It was a bit uneven, but she was happy and said, "Praise the Lord. Now we can have shade fir the meetins' in the summer. Some of you fellers build me a fire and we'll have us some supper."

By the time they built a fire, leveled the cabin, shoveled the mud out of the door and built a temporary fence for the pig which followed the woman around like a puppy, she had boiled up a chicken stew and dumplings. Other people came bringing odds and ends of food. After dark, they sang songs and talked of the future. No one bemoaned the loss of material things.

"We've decided it's time to build a school, and church fir you, Nola. You're always preachin' and singin' under a tree some place. Wilfred says you can have room here fir a house and a bit of a garden. Up on the ridge he'll give enough land for the buildin'. You can use it fir church on Sunday and we can get a teacher to use it during the week."

The Sunflower Woman beamed. "Praise the Lord," she shouted gazing up at the sky in such an appreciative way Rod caught himself looking up as well.

"Amen," the others shouted back.

The next day they build her a fireplace in the gaping opening in the end of the cabin where the other fireplace had been. By the next evening she had the floor packed down and smoothed, a woven rug spread across it, washed her curtains and dyed them orange with onion skins, took down the tables and chairs she had tied to the ceiling and made a home again.

Rod helped the men but watched out of the corner of his eye in amazement at this industrious woman. She moved in a sea of smiles. Food, clean floors, and beauty appeared as if by magic.

The next day was Sunday. By ten a.m. wagons, horses and walking people came over the ridge. They had Sunday school, singing of hymns and a prayer meeting. Nola took charge and everything flowed smoothly.

For noon 'dinner' they spread tablecloths on the ground and had a group picnic. Rod was reluctant to leave these good people and lingered the rest of the day listening as they exchanged news, recipes, plans and offers to help flood victims. Again, no one complained about his hardships.

Around four, he took his leave and found himself whistling and humming hymns as he rode along. It was a long, crisp evening. The stars reflected in the river. Further along a mist rose and the moon came out. Rod kept moving until he found a place to cross the swift moving water, and then sat enjoying the peace in his soul as well as the stars. The horses ate contentedly and their munching became a rhythmic sound in the night joining crickets, frogs, and night birds in song.

Rod rose as a blazing orange and red sunrise filled the eastern sky. He soon came upon a crew building the railroad track. He went along the line to the first town where he could catch a train going east; he felt sorry for the Chinese and indentured servants. Many of them were paying for their transportation from their homelands and had to work five to seven years for the person who paid for their ticket. Only on Sunday did they get a bit of rest. The rest of the week they worked from daylight until dark, receiving minimum food, clothing, no medical care and inadequate lodging. At least half died from exposure, overwork and malnutrition.

The Indians looked upon the Chinese as skin brothers, but most Chinese were deathly afraid of Indians. Their way of life seemed strange and primitive to the Orientals.

Rod had run across several signs posted by the army stating: *The Black Hills are off limits to anyone but the Native Americans due to The Treaty*; but everyone seemed to ignore them.

The railroad track would head for the Black Hills and continue north to Bismarck. Another track would connect with the one going to Cheyenne and Denver.

Beyond those areas, not a great deal was known about the land. On the west coast the Columbia River and California were explored inland and north to Canada.

Except for explorers, trappers and soldiers, few had ventured west beyond the Black Hills. Fremont had been sent out by the government and claimed that a large chain of mountains lay between the west coast and the Black Hills. The Mormons were said to have found a promised land and an inland sea. Few knew what it was really like or where an inland ocean could exist.

Around the camp fires, rugged mountain men and trappers told of a land where bear, rattlesnakes, furs, green valleys, and deep gorges were breathtakingly beautiful. The land seemed to go on forever. There was plenty for both white men and Indians. Oregon was proclaimed a paradise. Year after year the wagon train oxen and mules trudged along that tragic trail.

Often freed slaves worked on the railroad. Some were overseers. They were treated well. Many of them had been trained in the southern homes from which they had been freed and were better educated than white men. Few white men would work for blacks any more than they would for a woman.

Rod began to hear a great deal of speculative talk about the disappearance of young men from the reservations. It was said they danced in 'white shirts' and one brave had a vision saying the white man's bullets would not penetrate them. Others talked of Red Cloud and the treaty he had signed with the Government in 1866, stating that all land west of the Missouri belonged to Native Americans; a great Sioux Reservation. Red Cloud was now protesting the railroad to Montana as well as homesteading in the Dakotas.

Sitting Bull refused to sell or cede any Native American land to the government for any purpose. He also refused to take his large tribe to the reservation.

"As if a few Indians can farm all that land," one man said.

Rod tried to explain that the Native American's way of life was hunting and gathering. "They need more land than the farmer and the way in which they use it is self-renewing."

The man shrugged his shoulders and turned away. The homesteaders would fight and die before they gave up the stolen land. The homesteader's wives were frightened but they stood beside their husbands. Few of them had any other place to go where they could work and raise their children.

As more people settled west of the Missouri people complained, "The capital should be in the middle of the Dakota Territory when it becomes a state, and not at Yankton or Bismarck. The great Missouri River was the main transportation even though railroad travel was beginning to be competition for the river boats just as they had in the east.

Rod decided the problems were too big for him to sort out. As far as he could tell, the flood of white men from Europe had no end. The government had not enough force to stem the tides of people who hungered both in body and sprit for food, freedom, and the promise of riches if they were willing to work hard.

Many were ignorant people who wanted only to fill their stomachs and had a poor sense of right and wrong. Others worked hard and appreciated the land and the fact that the Native Americans were loosing a way of life. The white man felt the Indian's way of life took up more land than was necessary for them to live on, if they would just learn to farm and ranch, in other words live like white men, everything could work out.

Rod remembered the books and discussions with Melissa. The strong survive, vs. the Bibles, 'The meek shall inherit the Earth.' The weak could only fight back by banding together.

Abraham Lincoln had said, "Together we stand, divided we fall." Too late, Native Americans tried to stand together. By then, the weapons and number of white men were overwhelming.

Some form of order and compromise would have to be set up. Probably Indians would have been extinct by now if the North and South had not killed so many of their own people in the Civil War. Often the Native Americans had not chosen sides but been used by both groups. For a few years the war took some of the pressure off the tribes as each side tried to persuade them that theirs was the winning team. Some few Indians had adapted to white man's ways and appreciated them. The eastern Native Americans had been farmers and were more highly civilized. Many of them interbred and survived, but they lost a way of life.

Rod missed the debates with Dan and discussions with Melissa about world affairs, just as he missed the homey talks with Mary. But he loved the prairie and his ranch even more. It was home now. He had even killed for it; his only regret.

Finally, he came to Mackenzie's ranch where he could stable the horses and, after crossing the Missouri, get a train which would take him east to Sioux City and south to Vermillion.

Rod had been able to replenish his bank roll by selling wool and mutton as well as milk and cheese to travelers on their way west.

Before catching the train, he went to a barber shop getting a shave, haircut, and bath. The new clothing and boots felt stiff and rough. On the way back he would buy winter clothing for himself, Sky, and the shepherds.

Two of the passengers on the train were children, Nathan and Rebecca. The train crew had rescued them from Indians. Everyone else on their wagon train had been killed. The Native Americans had tied up the children and were about to put them on horses when the train crew arrived. They left the children and fled on their loaded horses.

The boy and girl were not harmed physically, but they were still frightened and grieving. They were going back to live with

an aunt in Vermillion. The conductor asked Rod if he would keep
an eye on them. At first the children were shy, but Rod soon
caught their attention by playing the harmonica. He made funny
sounds on it until they began to giggle.

"Could I try?" Rebecca asked quietly. Her large blue eyes, still
red from crying. By evening the children were smiling and he
took them to the dining car to eat. When they began to follow him
wherever he went, he felt like an old mother hen.

Melissa & Rod

The eastern half of the Dakota Territory was green and lush in contrast to the golden brown prairie on the west side of the Missouri. Rod told Nathan and Rebecca stories and pointed out landmarks. At night they snuggled down beside him to sleep. He smoothed their soft cheeks and curly hair and wondered what his children and Annabelle's would be like. Word had been telegraphed ahead to Vermillion for the children's aunt to meet them at the station.

The round, cheerful woman waited with open arms for the boy and girl. Nathan and Rebecca were reluctant to leave him.

Rod said, "I promise to come see you tomorrow and bring you a present." With that they kissed and hugged him, and reluctantly let their aunt take them home.

Rod went to a barber shop near the Bennett store. For twenty-five cents he could have a shave, haircut and bath. He changed into his new flannel shirt and clean clothing after his luxurious bath before sitting in the chair for a shave. Rod had gone to school with the barber about four years earlier. They shook hands. It was the same boy he had fought when he attended school just before his father had been killed.

"How's the homesteading business these days, Rod?"

"Couldn't be better. Got me a spread that goes as far as I can see. Which is the next ridge," Rod said and laughed. "I mainly raise sheep and sell them as fast as I can raise them."

"Is that a fact?" Sheepherders were without prestige.

"The prairies not much good for cattle, but sheep do fine on the buffalo grass. I keep a few milk cows and a couple to breed and butcher when I get tired of antelope, buffalo, and mutton."

"Didn't expect to see you back here since the Bennett's moved to the Black Hills. Thought you were sweet on Annabelle. Guess you forgot about her by now though. You've been gone a long time."

Rod turned white and flinched.

"Oh, sorry, did I nick you? I'm finished anyway." He took the towel from around Rod's neck.

"No, it's all right. I didn't know they had gone. Guess I didn't get their letters. When did they move?"

"Well, let me see. It was kinda sudden like. Guess it was around Easter sometime. A drummer come through and made Mr. Bennett an offer on the store. Heard Mrs. Bennett was real upset, but Joseph, Dan and Annabelle decided to go along and take a load of supplies to Mark. Also, some politician came through and offered Dan a job at his new law office in Deadwood and he accepted. Reckon Mrs. Bennett was outvoted." He either didn't notice Rod's upset expression or took pleasure in it.

"Half the people in town went to see them off. They had so many wagons they were purty near a train in themselves. Mrs. Bennett wouldn't leave without her new stove and Annabelle had to have her piano. Then Injuns could have a good time with that 'un," he said laughing and winking.

Rod gave him a cold stare. The barber knew he had gone too far and began to procrastinate.

"They'll be all right. That was one of the biggest wagon trains to leave here yet. Mr. Bennett and Dan can sure handle trouble if it comes. For that matter, I'd hate to tangle with Annabelle. She's a handful, that girl is, why I remember once . . ." his voice trailed off when Rod thrust the money and towel on the chair and stalked out the door.

So he was too late. He passed through Vermillion without seeing it. Different people spoke to him. He nodded a brief greeting and kept on walking.

"And he used to be such a friendly lad when he worked in the store," one woman said. "Guess fightin' them Injuns changes a body."

He was stopped by Melissa outside the old Bennett Store. She guessed from his unhappy expression he had just heard the news about their leaving and had not received the letters from the Bennetts.

"Well, I do declare, if it's not Rod, Rod Anderson." She hugged Rod and released him quickly, conscious of the stares of school children and parents.

"Miss Melissa!" Rod picked her up, swung her in a circle, kissing her impulsively.

She blushed and laughed, "Come on home with me. We'll have coffee and supper. I'm dying for some good talk and to hear about your homestead."

"Well, I'd like to ma'am. I just want to step in and find out about the store and where the Bennetts went first."

"Oh, I can tell you. But go ahead to the store. Mary left you a letter with the owner, in case the one she wrote got lost or you came back before you received it. When you're through, come on to my house. You can leave your bedroll there."

Rod was beginning to recover from the shock. "Fine. Thanks Melissa. I'd appreciate that. Be there directly." He tipped his hat in respect even though she was only a few years older than he.

Melissa smiled in anticipation. Over the years when she tutored Rod and Dan, Rod often stayed and helped her with odd jobs around the house and school. The boys had both been 'love struck' when she first came to teach. As Dan and Rod grew older, they became friends as well as students.

"It's a pleasure to have someone who thirsts for knowledge instead of having to cram it down reluctant throats," she had told

Mary. She missed Rod. Now the Bennett family had gone and she felt bereft. A tear slid down her cheek as she lowered her head and hurried home.

Many students counted the days until school let out, or came to flirt, or to have something to do socially during the long winter months. She managed to get some learning into them and they had a lot of fun with spelling bees, Christmas Programs, socials, and learning games. Melissa had a way of teaching with a flair for the dramatic. Often the student didn't realize he or she was learning. She was not above turning a student over her knee when she taught grade school. But in High School, she turned an unruly student over to the Truant Officer or the parents. Usually parents were even stricter at home. When the children complained, the parents would often give them another punishment saying, "You don't get a lick-a-miss."

She knew many thought of her as an old maid, but she often grinned to herself. If anyone could have seen her before her soldier-lover rode off with Custer's Army, they would have been shocked and fired her on the spot. The two were to have been married when he returned at the end of the year.

The week before he left, she called off school saying she was sick. They would have spent every minute making love, but many of the children's parents sent hot dishes, advice, and gifts, or their children came by to ask when school would start again. Finally, she put a "Do Not Disturb" sign on the door and locked it. When Mary came by concerned, she said, "Mary. I'm not sick.

I'm just worn out. Please don't tell anyone. I need a few days alone."

"I envy you," Mary said. "Wish I could join you." She kissed Melissa's cheek and never mentioned to anyone the army jacket lying on the sofa.

What a glorious week it had been. The miracle of it all was that she never got pregnant. Now, she wished she had. She would not be so lonely and would have someone of her own, even though disgraced. She could have moved and pretended to be a widow. Six months after he left, Melissa received a letter from her lover with a note from his commanding officer saying he had been killed in a skirmish with Native Americans. A letter addressed to her had been found in his pocket.

Men tried to date her, but few of them were as well educated as she would have liked them to be, or they were just plain boring.

Melissa often sighed as she looked in the mirror at the 'teacher act' she put on with her glasses, bun at the neck, and high collars. She was young. The Superintendent and town fathers often mentioned her age, but her disguise, sincere interest in educating children and good reputation, fooled them, she thought. Now she was twenty-five and still looked eighteen. She acted so mature and sensible at school meetings and town council sessions, they had even discussed letting her set on the board. The High School had been built much earlier than planned because of her nagging and fund raising. A University was almost certain to begin breaking ground soon as the result of her pleas to the Members of the House in Yankton.

Only Dan, Annabelle, and Rod, saw her at home with her hair down and the clear-glass glasses off.

Rod had been a rare and sensitive child. The two hit it off from the beginning. She often wished his father, John, had been more persistent in his courtship. If he had not been shot . . . it was something to daydream about when she was alone at night and the face of her soldier began to dim.

After Rod left Vermillion, Dan finally became a serious law student. They burned a lot of midnight oil together. When her lover died, only Dan knew of it and comforted her in her grief. That night Dan stayed over. After that, she let him spend one night each week in her bed. It kept them both out of trouble. She insisted he use the new birth control condoms, made him agree that when either of them became attached to someone else, that would be the end of their affair, then swore him to secrecy.

When Dan fell in love with Claudette, they stopped sleeping together but Melissa still missed his healthy, passionate, young body.

As she rushed around cooking supper, she remembered one evening when she and Rod had been reading and discussing poetry. He asked her if she would ever marry.

"But of course, when I find someone like you who is about five years older," she teased. They both laughed and he blushed.

When he left that evening he had an arm load of books. At the door he turned and said, "Miss Melissa, if I wasn't going to marry Annabelle, I'd marry you." She checked her impulse to laugh, stood on her tiptoes and kissed him. He laid the books down when he tasted the salt of tears on her lips and took her in his arms, soothing her as though she was a child.

Another time he had asked, "Miss Melissa, is it possible to love more than one woman at a time?"

Her answer led to a long philosophical discussion. She often discussed the nature of human beings when she had a group with whom she could talk frankly, or students who would not take word home to parents who might threaten to have her fired if she taught heathen ways and even mentioned sex.

Now that Rod, Dan, Claudette, Mary, and Annabelle were gone, she was lonelier than ever. That is, until Rev. Henry started calling on her.

Rev. Henry had first come to see her about Claudette, or so he said. Now, he often slipped in the back door and stole an hour to have tea and talk with her. When he left he would hold her hand for a long time. At first she thought he was just a loving man. Then he began to look at her adoringly and talk about his nagging wife and spoiled kids.

"I have no peace at home," he told her. "In church I always have to act happy and pious."

Only with Melissa could he make a joke or be impulsive. Often he picked bouquets of wild flowers and left them on her doorstep. She was trying to get up the courage to tell him to stay away. If it had not been in the middle of the spring semester, she would have gone to Deadwood with the Bennetts.

Melissa had been saving as much as possible of her small wages to pay her way on a wagon train when summer came. Now that Rod was back, she would beg him to help her get out of town. This had been the last week of school before summer vacation. Surely they needed teachers in Deadwood City. If not, perhaps she could open up a hat shop, nurse, or something.

There might even be some extra men around. Many of the eligible ones her age had been killed in the Civil War or Native American wars; others had gone off to homestead or strike it rich in the gold fields.

Melissa preferred living alone to accepting just anyone, but she wanted children and a man with whom she could be a partner, even though she could not love him as she had her soldier lover.

If she could get away, she would not sign her contract here again. Rod would surely head for the Black Hills to find Annabelle. She made her plans as she cooked their supper and waited for Rod.

The store hasn't changed much, Rod decided, but different faces behind the counter made him want to turn away. If he pretended, he could see Mary measuring cloth, Joe helping a woman shovel sugar or beans from a barrel. He asked for the owner.

Simon Shultz came forward and extended his hand.

"Mr. Anderson. I've heard a good deal about you. You looking for a job? We could use you. This is gonna' be the biggest store in town," he gloated.

"Thank you, no. I have a job. I rather liked the store the way it was. Did the Bennetts leave a message for me?"

"Oh, yes. I'm certain they did. It's in the office. I'll get it for you." Mr. Schultz soon returned with an envelope.

"Thank you and good luck." Rod thrust the letter in his pocket and hurried out.

Melissa's small cottage was just a few blocks from the store. She let Rod in. He took the letter from his pocket and waved it, smiling. She stood on her toes to kiss his cheek and began to turn away.

"Not so fast," Rod said taking her in his arms. "That's twice you've kissed me. I owe you one."

Melissa giggled as he kissed her lightly on the lips, paused and kissed her again. "Well," she said when he released her. "Your kiss tells me you've grown up since I saw you last."

Rod grinned and replied, "Yours tells me I've been missing something special. Want to try for seconds?"

"Now, Rod. Quit teasing and go read your letter. Supper's nearly ready. Go into the parlor so you can read it alone. I'll finish supper."

"Thanks, Melissa." Her parlor was more like a man's den. Rod had been there often. He loved the smell of her books, the shiny wooden desk, and leather couch. He closed his eyes remembering Dan, Annabelle and Melissa and their evenings of good talks. Someday, I want a room just like this one, he thought as he sat on the couch to read the letter from Mary.

Dearest Rod,

If you arrive here before our letters reach you, I am so sorry that you had the long trip to find us gone. Mark is now living in Deadwood City. He purchased land and built a store and asked Joe to bring supplies to him.

Dan has been offered a law practice there and Annabelle insists on going out to check on the new theater with Claudette. The great Langrishe is to be there this summer and she's eighteen.

Needless to say, I objected, but rather than split up the family, I finally consented to a trial move of one year.

Joe had a good offer for the store here. It seemed he has become an excellent mule skinner and has been practicing for such a trip. He brought nearly all the wagons in town and we'll leave as soon as possible before the rivers begin to flood. I wanted to wait until you returned, but they all say we will be much closer to you and will see you sooner as you are not far from the Black Hills.

The Missouri will flood soon and the mules and oxen only go about ten miles a day, I understand.

Yesterday Annabelle insisted on taking me out for a shooting lesson. I think I am supposed to shoot myself rather than be taken by hostile

Avonelle Kelsey

Indians. She doesn't know that as a girl, I was quite athletic. Father taught us to ride and shoot. In those days, the east had not been tamed either, but I enjoyed our afternoon together. We so seldom have time alone. You were the main topic of conversation. Her feelings for you run very deep.

We'll send notes along the way, hoping a letter gets through before you leave for Vermillion. Dan and Mark will ride out to see you as soon as we get settled. If the Indians are not on the warpath, Annabelle wants to come along. Send mail to us at Deadwood City and come there as soon as possible.

All send their love. Mary

Rod brushed the tears from his eyes. They had been gone for nearly two months and must be settled by now. He would go home as quickly as possible. If they met trouble, they could all be dead. But that was nonsense. Someone would have heard by now if they had run into trouble.

He rushed into the kitchen. "Melissa, did they reach Deadwood safely, or does anyone know?"

"Of course they did, dear. Come over and sit down at the table. While you eat, I'll read Dan's letter to you." She took his arm and patted his hand.

"Sit here. I've even poured us a glass of wine. Dan left it with me and said we were to share it, should you came back and miss them. That family really cares about you, Rod. I missed you, too.

Somehow, after both you and Dan left, there was an empty spot in my teaching. No one around here stretches my mind or imagination. When I learn something new, there's no one to talk with about it, except Rev. Henry." She broke off and stared into space.

Rod looked at her inquiringly. "I'm still here, Miss Melissa." They looked at one another and laughed. She had been putting food from a large iron skillet onto his plate. Impulsively she leaned over and kissed his cheek. He felt the nearness of her body and smelled its womanly fragrance with appreciation; resisting a strong impulse to put his arms around her.

"Oh Rod. It's so good to have you back."

They sat in her cozy kitchen. The gay tablecloth and linen napkins gave the meal a party air. The sun was setting outside the window and painted the interior of the room a warm orange. Her face and body picked up its color. The auburn braids wrapped around her head were thick and heavy. One had come lose and softened the stark effect she tried to assume as a teacher.

Rod sensed something was on her mind so he waited, watching her closely. If Annabelle hadn't been wrapped so tightly in his heart, this woman would have been there. He wanted to take her in his arms to comfort her, but was not certain this was the time.

In silence, she finished serving the food and took her place opposite Rod. They raised the wine glasses in a toast. "Here's to you, Rod. I hope you have a good trip to Deadwood and find

Annabelle waiting for you with open arms." They touched glasses and drank.

"Here's to you Melissa and the University you propose. May it pass the legislature this year and be named after you."

"Ah, but it has passed. You could come back Rod, go to school and teach here."

"Thank you, Melissa, but at the moment, I have other plans for my life."

They looked into one another's eyes. She knew he was wondering what he would do if Annabelle refused him. He must be very discouraged and disappointed. To bring him back from his brooding, she began to chat about the Bennetts.

"Honestly, Rod. You should have seen Annabelle. She worked so hard getting ready for the trip that we thought she had a fever. Once she set her mind to go, Mary never had a chance. She lives for that family, and you Rod. After you left, we talked often. Both Mary and I were lonely for you. Dan fell in love with Claudette. Between his law practice and her, he seldom came by." She blushed and laughed self-consciously.

"That's right. You haven't met Claudette. She's a lovely young woman; Rev. Henry's niece who came to live with them, after her parents went down at sea. Her parents were successful actors and she was on stage with them. Fortunately, she had the chicken pox and couldn't go with them when they went to Paris. They left her with an aunt. After their death, she became too much for the aunt to handle so she shipped Claudette off to poor Henry."

Rod noticed her tone and high coloring when she talked about the minister. There was something here she wasn't telling him.

"Claudette's tall, beautiful, reddish-blonde, freckled nose, funny, and very independent. So very talented. She and Annabelle make quite a team." Melissa's eyes sparkled as she sipped wine and talked, hardly touching her food.

"Claudette wrote a story about Joseph and Mary in the olive grove and Mary telling him she was pregnant. The church fathers raised their eyebrows a bit, but the play was such a success they couldn't say too much about it."

Rod noticed she had finished her second glass of wine and her eyes were bright. Usually, she only sipped one glass with him and Dan on special occasions. Melissa had changed. Rod could sense a restlessness within her he'd never felt before. He watched her closely as she talked.

"Claudette and Mrs. Henry fought from the time she came and nearly drove Henry out of his mind. She became twenty-one this year and he had to turn her inheritance over to her. That really upset his wife. She hates Claudette. In fact, I'm not sure she likes anybody. Her kids run all over town, except when they're in school. He's such a fine intelligent man," Melissa sighed and stopped talking, looking into space again.

"What is it Melissa, what's bothering you?"

"Oh, I'm sorry Rod. Nothing." She stood up and began to clear the table. Rod stood too, turned her around and looking into her eyes, saw the tears she was trying to hold back. He pulled her in his arms, patting her shoulders. She leaned against him letting the tears flow.

When they slowed, he held her at arms length, "All right, out with it. "You're always helping others. Now, will you let me help you, if I can?"

"Oh, Rod. I have to get away from here. I must. Will you take me to Deadwood with you? I'm certain I could get a job there. I must get away or . . ."

"Or what? What has you so upset?"

There was a light knock at the open doorway and a man's voice said, "Melissa, are you home? In stepped Rev. Henry. He eyed Rod who still had his hands on Melissa's arms. They stepped apart. She blushed. It was one of the few times Rod had ever seen Melissa at a loss for words.

"Rev. Henry, I believe. I'm Rod Anderson. I just returned to town and Miss Melissa is filling me in on the news." Rod seldom went to church but he remembered the minister from the programs Annabelle and Mary dragged him and Dan to on holidays. The minister was a good speaker. He hadn't preached hell and damnation like so many. Rev. Henry seemed gentle and kind. His congregation found him a comfort during deaths and weddings. He was more liberal than many preachers of the day. They shook hands.

Rod wondered at the tension in the air. From the way Melissa stammered and the hurried leave Rev. Henry took, Rod turned to her asking, "Is that the problem?"

"Yes. No, partly. In Vermillion, I'm simply an old maid school teacher. If I look at a man, I could get fired."

Rod looked at her with raised eyebrows. She had removed her glasses; her long braids had fallen down her back. Short wispy curls framed the upper part of her face. Her gingham, blue dress with short sleeves and low neck lined with lace and ruffles, gave the impression of a young girl trying to look mature. Rod had to laugh. Melissa began to giggle from the wine and at the look in Rod's eyes.

"It's true. I get so lonely. Especially in the summertime. Rev. Henry began to stop in last fall and talk about his children. Now he finds excuses to stop by nearly every day. I'm beginning to feel like Hester in *The Scarlet Letter*." She sighed and giggled again.

"Oh, nothing's happened, yet. I know I should stop him from coming, but I have no one else I can talk with about art, science, school and travel. To a certain extent, he's taken your place and Dan's in my life. That's why I must get away. I'm sure I could find work and not be a burden to you, Rod."

"You could never be a burden to me, Melissa. If you left with me, your reputation would be ruined. There's a wagon train going to the Black Hills this week, I understand. How soon could you be ready to go?"

"Anytime. I own this house, but with so many people moving in, I could leave it with Josh, Rev. Henry, to sell or rent for me. The books and furniture can be shipped later. In the meantime, I'm sure they could be stored in the shed out back. My school teaching clothes, I'd enjoy leaving behind. I'd walk out that door this minute, if I got a chance to leave."

"Wait a second. You can't leave before you do the dishes, my good woman," he said and the tension left her face.

"Thank you Rod," she threw her arms around him and kissed him on the lips. Each felt the longing and need in the others body. They clung together for a long moment and withdrew silently.

"We'd better light a lamp and get these dishes done so I can pack," she said laughing a bit nervously. "I never read Dan's letter to you, did I? I'll give it to you and you can read it in bed. Since I'm leaving, you can use the extra bedroom. No point in getting a hotel room. They expect me to sign a new contract. When I don't, my reputation will be ruined anyway."

Rod watched her as she poured hot water over the dishes from a kettle on the stove. If Annabelle hadn't loomed so large in his life, who knows what would have developed between himself and this wonderful woman. Some man would be lucky to have her for a wife. Rev. Henry must not be allowed to spoil things for her. He would see that she got to the Black Hills, if he had to take her himself, he decided. He owed her a great deal more than that.

Rod dried the dishes and felt as though he had never been away. He told her about his homestead, the children on the train and that he was sorry she wouldn't be there to teach them one day.

She caught him up on all the town gossip and the family.

Rod smothered a yawn.

"I know you've had a long day. We can talk in the morning, although I'm so excited, I think I'll read awhile." She lit another lamp. "You take this one and I'll get Dan's letter for you."

He sat on the bed and removed his boots. The newness had not yet worn off and it was a relief to free his feet. He longed for his moccasins.

Melissa returned with the letter, leaned over and kissed his cheek. "I'm so happy you came Rod. Goodnight and thanks so much."

He watched her walk from the room and close the door softly. The night was still warm from the heat of the day. He opened the windows and undressed, then lay back against starched pillows to read Dan's letter by the kerosene lamp at the bedside.

My Dear Melissa,

And I do mean dear. Often on the long trip, I thought of you and how much more you'd get out of it than most people. You're like Rod. Where most of us let our glance float across the world, you see it as an onion. Each thing has layer upon layer of unexplored mystery and beauty. Perhaps we see things on one level collectively, what we expect to see, and you two look at things and people, not only seeing the shape and color but action, feelings, and many other possibilities. You seem to have time, whereas I am always too busy. Enough philosophizing.

The oxen teams plod along and the mules slow us down because they can't keep up a steady pace and are so stubborn; ten miles a day if an axle doesn't break or a wheel comes off. At that we are lucky.

(A week later)

If we had waited a week longer, we would have had to camp by the Missouri for a month. The Missouri breaks were hell but so many wagon trains have gone through that the trails are practically highways with deep ruts or streams when it rains. All along are remains of massacred wagon trains, pieces of furniture, cans, graves, like bits and pieces of hundreds of lives.

It's better now than any time in the past. Many people have built along the trails. Most of the Native Americans are on reservations or off raising hell up north with Red Cloud, or Sitting Bull. We saw one sizable group, but soldiers came. When they rode up the Indians high-tailed it. Annabelle said she'd write to you about it or maybe Claudette will do a play about the incident and the moccasins.

"Just renegades who managed to escape from the reservations," the soldiers said. "They only prey on small parties or stragglers, like wolves."

Claudette and Annabelle keep the party lively. Every evening we have a sing-a-long, dancing or something. You may hear some wedding bells as soon as I get my law practice going. Maybe by then Annabelle and Claudette will have acting out of their systems and Rod and I can have a double wedding. If the train is running, you'll have to come and wipe Mom's tears.

Speaking of Rod, have you heard or seen him yet? Mom's worried. As soon as we get settled, I'm heading out to find him myself. We sent letters by pony express and soldiers. The flooding rivers may have held up some of them. I hope he hears from us and beats us to Deadwood. Our caravan passes about twenty five miles south of the place he has homesteaded. Dad needs every hand he can get on the wagon train or I'd stop off on the way.

Even the twins, Mom, and Annabelle take turns on wagons to spell us now and again. The women work as hard as the men on the trail.

I'm writing this on my way and will mail it as soon as we hit town. The pony express has been hard hit by renegades. They mainly want the horses and scatter the mail to the winds.

Deadwood City.

So much happened on the rest of the trip that I will try to summarize a bit of it for you. Claudette was bitten by a rattlesnake. Thanks to Annabelle's quick action, she's all right.

We arrived in Deadwood Gulch and as Mom says, "It's a hell hole. Building and mining noise, muddy roads, ruts and animals as well as the stench from the fires and mine tailings. It's horrible, yet exciting in some perverted, Poesque sort of way.

Sometimes I envy Rod and his simple life on the homestead. I'm sure it's hard work, but setting up a new law office isn't easy in this crazy town. It's swinging twenty-four hours a day. Even our store is open until midnight and again at five a.m.

Uncle Mark has finally settled down. Remember the daughter of the Doctor who became a woman Doctor? She lived on the other side of Vermillion. Maybe you didn't know her. He was sweet on her and there was talk around the house about them getting married when he came back from the army.

Then, she took off with her relatives in a wagon train to meet him near Denver and Indians killed everyone on the train. Something seemed to go out of him. Now he's as settled as Dad. Oh, he still gambles and drinks a bit now and then, but whenever I'm with him, I get such a lonely feeling.

The railroad finally surveyed the Black Hills. Harney Peak, the highest point is near here. I'd like to climb it someday. The Black Hills are fantastic. They have more minerals than the whole country, I think. Cortez should have come here.

It's difficult to get down into the gulch except by footpaths and ropes, but they're finally cutting a road down the mountainside by using lots of dynamite.

It was a major feat getting Mother's cook stove and Annabelle's piano down the mountainside. When the miners heard about it and the pretty girls, hundreds of them turned out to help. Claudette carried her violin and guitar down by herself, but Mom and Annabelle danced around and shouted like line foremen. It was a real show.

The great Langrishe is building the theater again. The girls are like two giddy birds that've eaten fermented apples. I know Annabelle loves Rod but if he comes for her while she has this acting job, it may be a hard choice for her to make. After the troupe goes back to Denver, she may be more ready to settle down. I have the same problem with Claudette, but at least I live in town.

Both girls are filling in at the theater. Annabelle is an understudy for the leading lady. You know Annabelle. We have to keep a twenty-four hour watch on her to make sure she doesn't trip her.

It's my job to pick the girls up after the show and walk them safely home. I get to see all the performances free. It's a sad state when decent women can't walk down the street in daylight without men trying to take advantage of them. There are a great number of houses of prostitution. I think Mom's planning a secret campaign to wipe them out when she gets time.

The judge from the territory is here now. He wants me to help him campaign and says that I should plan on running for office someday. His daughter is just in from a finishing school in the east. She's a bit haughty, but seems to like me. Annabelle says she's making eyes at me, but Claudette is more than enough woman for me. Thanks to you, and Melissa, the political life is enticing.

This is really the west. Nearly everyone wears a six shooter on his hip or carries a rifle. Claims get jumped often. Half the time I'm out in the mud trying to locate stakes. I'm becoming a real detective. Uncle Mark is grubstaking several miners and making a killing.

Calamity Jane has a hospital, believe it or not. Since wild Bill Hickok was killed here, they say she's become a drunk because she was so in love with him. She looks like a pile of rags and more like a man than a woman. Mom, Annabelle, and Claudette help out in the place they call a hospital. Calamity Jane was in charge until she started drinking so much. It's choice comedy to see Mom and Calamity together. Melissa, this place needs you. We all do.

Annabelle slips out in overalls, a fake mustache and hat at night. One evening I knew she was going to sneak out when she was suppose to be in her room. I hired a man to pretend to be drunk and pick a fight with her; thought she'd run, but suddenly she lowered her head and butted him in the stomach. He went down with a moan and thud. She took to her heels. It cost me an extra buck to cool him down.

It's time to pick up the girls. There is so much more to tell, but I'm sure Mom and Annabelle will write you about the trip and Deadwood, so I'll save something for them.

I miss you, Daniel

PS. If Rod comes, have him bring you out, if you haven't signed your contract. This place could use some education.

Rod blew out the lamp and lay in the dark thinking about Dan's letter. Am I being unrealistic when I think Annabelle might settle in the country, he asked himself? Apparently, there was no reason to hurry back with the hope of marrying her. He decided to write to her, declaring his love openly and then go home to wait for her reply. After he and Sky got caught up on the work in the fall, he would go to Deadwood. Maybe October or November before the snow came and after the summer crops were in. Perhaps Two Bears could be persuaded to stay through the winter.

Tears slid down Rod's cheeks and soaked his pillow. His hopes had been so high. To have the whole family gone was a real blow. Thank goodness Melissa was here.

Rod fell into a restless sleep. His old nightmares came back again. The gunfight in the snow, a man's heads coming apart and the bits of flesh covering him, burning into his skin. He cried out in his sleep.

"Rod, Rod. Wake up." Melissa was shaking him by the shoulders. His mouth felt dry and he was trembling.

"What is it Rod? What are you dreaming about?"

He felt dazed. Rod's childhood nightmares about his mother had finally ceased, until he had shot the three men. Then they came again, as well as the shoot out, anytime he became upset. Sometimes, he wished he had let the men have the horses. They were not worth a human life. He knew that those men would have killed others and probable had done so in the past. Could he have lived with himself, he often wondered, if he hadn't tried to regain the animals? Sam had fired first, but still something deep within Rod was not satisfied with his response. He shuddered.

Melissa sat down on his bed and put her arms around him. Like a child, she rocked him back and forth patting his back and talking softly to him. "It's all right, darling. Everything is fine, Rod. It was just a bad dream. I'm here, Rod. There, there. Relax, Dear."

They sat with their arms about one another, his head on her breast.

Gradually the tenseness drained from his body. Her light summer gown and the odor of her body began to penetrate his senses. She felt warm and soft in his arms. Slowly, his hands tightened on her back and his lips kissed the curve of her breast. All the wonder and mystery of womanhood filled his body and mind.

Melissa tensed for a moment, and then let her body soften in his arms. She stroked his hair as his lips continued up her neck to her ear.

"Stay with me tonight, Melissa. Please. I need you so."

She hesitated for a moment, and then slipped under the covers with him. She continued to stroke his hair as he held her close. Melissa had just finished brushing her long luxurious braids. Her hair fell across his body. He buried his face in its silken folds.

She felt her own flesh respond to the call of Rod's. His body was strong, clean smelling, and eager.

Rod remembered at night when he was a boy how he had snuggled against his father's arm while they read his mother's poetry. When it was very cold and they could not afford a hotel, they would curl up together by the camp fire; how Mary would come to Dan's room when he had a nightmare after his father was killed. When she heard him calling out, she would sometimes take him in her arms soothing him in much the same way as Melissa. He had held no one in his arms since, or been held, except to kiss Annabelle good-bye.

Just the touching of this woman set his flesh yearning and full of desire. He trembled with the force of it.

"Don't think about the dream, Rod. Think about our pleasant evening by the fire. Would you like another glass of wine?"

"No, no, just hold me." He thought of Melissa sitting at the table laughing with him. The way the sun had turned her face glowingly warm and her hair flaming orange, her kiss. Suddenly, his body felt as hot as the sunset and he yearned to dive into her body, become one with this beckoning desire.

Her body was soft and yielding. Slowly, his free hand began to caress her back. Their lips met. She did not pull back. It was the first time he had ever made love to a woman outside of his dreams. His dreams had never been this great, he thought.

As Rod slipped the straps down over her shoulders, she wiggled out of her gown and felt his lean hard body against hers.

Pressing her body against his, she whispered, "Is this the first time?"

He nodded as he slid his hand down her body and slipped his hand along her thigh. She opened her legs and rolled over, sitting above him. With her hands she squeezed him gently and guided him into her. He moaned with the sweetness of it all.

She knew he would come too soon, but it had been so long. She wanted to let him use her. In a little while, his youth would again ready his body. She would take what she needed then.

Rod had never dreamed anything could be so demanding or so fulfilling. They slept, rested awhile and made love again. She taught him how to help a woman enjoy love making.

They talked of his nightmares, the shooting and she of her fears of the lonely years ahead. Then, it was morning. The night had been a memorable experience and neither had expectations of the other in the light of day.

Melissa prepared a pitcher of water, towel, and washcloth for him and took it to his room. They bathed one another's bodies lovingly. He brushed her long hair and braided it, Native American fashion, down her back. She made him sit down in front of her mirror while she brushed his. He watched her glowing, naked body behind his, turned with shining eyes and began to kiss her breast.

"Not again," she whispered softly. He picked her up; her legs went around his body, even as she protested.

"I can't get enough of you, Melissa," he said, kissing her. "How could you have withheld such a wonderful experience from me all these years? Did you know how exciting making love was when we were learning about law and philosophy?"

"Oh, yes. I was in love once, Rod. Just as you and Annabelle are. You think this is thrilling. We're just in heat. Wait until you make love with someone you care about with all your heart. It will be even better."

He had entered her as he held her, standing up. Now he paused and looked into her eyes. "Do you really believe anything could be more wonderful than this night has been Melissa? Surely you know I have always loved you in a different way perhaps, but more satisfactorily than Annabelle." He searched her eyes, but she waited, her hands rubbing his back.

"I know you love Annabelle, Rod, and that's OK," she whispered softly.

"Yes, I still love her, but I asked you once if a man could love two women. Your answer was that the human heart is much larger than most people's minds. Tonight, today, I know I love you both and I hope you won't be offended by my saying so."

She gave him a mysterious smile, "You have yet to have an act or thought that has offended me, Rod. This least of all."

Then, her eyes took on an intimate, passionate expression of urgency as she placed her finger to his lips. "One more time Rod," she whispered leaning back in his arms, eyes closed.

He laughed softly, moving slowly, rhythmically, as she'd taught him the night before until she began to moan softly. Then he moved swiftly and they climaxed together. He had learned a great deal in one exciting night. They clung together for a long time before dressing.

"Promise me one thing, Rod."

"What, my lovely teacher?"

"After you and I part, neither of us will ever let anyone know we had this wonderful time together, that it will not come between you and Annabelle in any way, other than enhance your sexuality? Promise, Rod."

He hesitated, looking so young and handsome. What a beautiful man, she thought. Sex with him was almost as wonderful as it had been with her soldier.

"You must promise, Rod, or I will never forgive myself. You will always be someone special to me, but I want to marry a man my own age or older. Someone whom I shall never have to worry about being younger than me. Promise me you'll find Annabelle as soon as you can and marry her. You must never let me stand in the way."

"Melissa, I promise. Don't get upset." He sensed she was about to cry.

"Thank you, Rod. Now will you talk to the wagonmaster for me, or must I give you my soul as well as my body, sir?" She asked lightly.

"If your soul is half as delightful as your body, I'll be more than happy to take it off your hands, madam." He bowed courtly, put on his cowboy hat and kissed her tenderly before he dressed and slipped out the back door. There were enough gossips in town to tear Melissa's reputation apart, if they saw a man coming out her door in the wee hours of the morning.

As Rod walked toward the stable he thought he saw Rev. Henry's black coat in a distance and smiled ruefully.

Near the creek, he paused by the old swimming hole where he and Dan had spent every moment they could steal on hot summer evenings. Sometimes Mary would make Joe hire someone to run the store and the whole family would come here for a picnic.

He stripped off his clothes and dived in for a refreshing swim. All his worries about Annabelle seemed to have vanished. He watched the sunlight turn the silver-backed leaves of the cottonwoods to a golden flicker as he lay on his back in the water. A possum and a parade of ducks floated lazily by. Somewhere a rooster crowed. He realized it was time to be on his way.

Rod found the wagonmaster by the campfire having a cup of coffee. Rod introduced himself.

"Say, young feller, bet I knowed yer Dad. Weren't he the gambler what was shot a few years back? 'Twas a sad day fir the ladies. They still talk about him. Met one in Deadwood last trip that was sweet on him. She says they would have married if he hadn't been shot."

Rod flinched.

"Sorry Son, didn't mean to bring up bad memories. He was always a straight shooter, that one."

Rod looked at the aged, rugged man. The morning sun fell on his battered hat, leaving his face in the shade. The woolen shirt was worn and frayed and would be hot during the mid-day sun. A bit of underwear showed at the neckline. The worn boots reached his knees and looked as though he never removed them, even to sleep. It would be an interesting trip to ride with such a man. His life as a wagonmaster must have been more adventuresome than that of Captain Cook. Melissa would probably enjoy a great many of his stories, if he knew her. She had sheaves of notebooks with hundreds of stories about the pioneers. Rod hoped she would put them into a book someday.

"What can I do fir you, son?"

Rod explained about Melissa.

"There be a Mormon woman that's travelin' light. The teacher could spell her, if'n she'd take a turn driving. Goin' to Deadwood to see her son before headin' to Salt Lake to join her people. The teacher might have her hands full, but reckon she can handle her if she can handle a room full of kids. Can she be ready in two days? As soon as the train from the south comes through, we'll be headin' out."

Rod met Mize Bingham, as well as several business men and would be homesteaders. They asked him dozens of questions about homesteading. It was several hours before he could get away.

Melissa was pacing the floor when he returned. Boxes and bags were strewn around. "Tell me quick, Rod. Will they take me?"

"Yes, they will, but I'm not sure you can pay the price," he said with a twinkle in his eye.

"My kingdom for a ride. Tell me." She danced around him tugging at his shirt. "Don't tease me. I can't wait."

He laughed, scooped her up in his arms and twirled around the room with her. "You leave in two days. Now give me my reward. She gave him an enthusiastic kiss. I'll do you one better if you come into the bedroom," she whispered.

After lunch, Rod went to the Post Office. Mail now ran regularly to Denver and the east coast. At Christmas each year he heard from the Sunflower Woman, Mrs. Johnson, with whom his father had left their old farm. The last two years the small check for rent and a larger one had been sent to the bank along with a letter saying that this was part of the stock receipts which his father had left with them.

"We're getting older and Mr. Johnson is doing poorly so we wanted you to have the money now. Your homestead might need some stock. Come see us soon, if ye can."

Rod knew he should go east and see them. He had considered taking Annabelle there for a honeymoon, or when the train track was completed past his place in a year or two maybe they'd just hop on the train and go. Both of the Johnson's had been 'ailen' she had said in the last letter.

But, there was another letter from a lawyer saying the Johnson's had died within a few months of one another. They had willed their place to Rod, along with a sizeable amount of money. He could send the money to a bank in Vermillion, if Rod couldn't get back at this time.

"A letter of credit is enclosed. The town has grown out to your old place and it is going to be worth money someday. It is still rented. I will wait until I hear from you for further instruction."

Avonelle Kelsey

The telegraph office was near the Post Office. Rod sent a telegram saying: "Send the money to the Bank of the Dakota's in Vermillion. Rent both places and hold on to everything. I'll be back within a year."

With the letter of credit in his pocket he went to the bank and opened an account, then went shopping using some of the money he had been saving for Annabelle to furnish the house.

He bought two harmonicas and a toy for each of the children. For Melissa, he bought a big box of candy and then going to the stable, purchased a beautiful riding horse and saddle. He couldn't resist and rode out into the country visiting places he, Dan, and Annabelle had frequented.

When he returned to town, Rod rode up to the children's door playing his harmonica. They must have been waiting for him. The door burst open and they ran shouting down the steps to greet him. He had to give each of them a ride around the block.

Their aunt waited on the doorstep laughing. She seemed a happy, jolly soul. As they danced around the room to their own music, she looked on with dignity for awhile. Then, picking up her skirts, she waltzed around with them.

Finally, Aunt Thelma plopped onto a chair, out of breath. "I can't take it anymore. I'm all out of wind. Nathan, Rebecca, go outside and practice your music for awhile. I want to talk to this young man. Then we'll have some nice cold milk and a bit of cake."

They protested but obeyed.

"Now young man. Tell me all you know about what happened to their parents."

Rod told her what little he knew. Then he said, "If anything ever happens and you, or the children need anything, will you promise to write or telegraph me?"

She assured him she would.

"The railroad will be finished within twenty miles of my place soon. Perhaps you could all come for a visit next summer, if I send the tickets?"

"That would be lovely. I'd always admired to take a trip west young man. You just gave me something to look forward to. Now let's have that cake and milk."

The children clung to him and cried when he left. He promised them Aunt Thelma would bring them to see him next years. "I'll have a horse for you to ride and you can help herd sheep." He didn't mention Two Bears. Any Native American talk would be too close to their sad hearts at this time. He wondered how they would react if he told them his Grandmother was an Indian?

Rod rented another horse and went to see Melissa. As he came up to her door, a red faced Rev. Henry came out, slamming it behind him. He stumbled down the street without seeing Rod. After waiting for a few minutes, Rod knocked.

"Who is it?" came a muffled voice. When she finally answered, he could see she had been crying and took her in his arms. It was his turn to comfort her. He sat down in the rocker and held her until she dried her tears. Giving Melissa his handkerchief he said, "Now blow your nose and tell Poppa all about it." She giggled at the thought and began her tale of the day.

"Oh, first I caught hell from the Superintendent of Schools for handing in my resignation. Then Henry, found out and tried to blackmail me into staying. He said he knew you spent the night here and he would tell everyone if I left. He needed me and if I wanted to leave, he would take me away."

"I became angry and told him if he said anything to anybody about either of us, I'd say he forced himself on me."

Then he tried to kiss me. I slapped him and shoved him out the door. I'm crying because what we said is not what either of us really felt."

She sniffed, wiped her eyes again and continued. "He's really a kind man, but so lonely. I feel sorry for him, but each of us must be responsible for solving the problems which result from our own mistakes. Anyway, I'm certain he won't try anything. Let's forget about it. Tell me, what have you've been doing?"

"I have a couple of surprises for you."

"I feel better already. What else could I need more than a trip out of this town?"

"Come and see." Rod led her outside and lifted her onto the sleek black mare, "It's yours."

"Is it for me? Really?"

"If you wish to trade for an English saddle you can, but it's a long way from here to Deadwood."

"Oh, no. This is perfect. Annabelle and I rode often after you left. I have a couple of split skirts. Let me put one on and let's go for a ride."

When he lifted her down, she hugged and kissed him. "I don't care if everyone in town sees us," she said. "This is the nicest gift anyone has ever given me Rod, and the most thoughtful. Thank you, dear man.

"Be back in a flash," Melissa called over her shoulder as she raced in to change into a riding outfit.

Rod smiled. It was fun to be able to give people he loved gifts they could use. It was hard to believe he had a great deal of money. When he went to see Annabelle in Deadwood, he would get her the fanciest saddle money could buy.

They rode down to the wagon train and Rod introduced Melissa to Mize. Bingham. Then they raced along the creek to the swimming hole. By this time it was getting dark.

They sat by the creek throwing stones in the water and talking. Rod brought out the box of candy and some jerky. It made a strange picnic. Eventually, they went for a moonlight swim, made love under the stars, and slowly rode home again.

"If you were still here, this wouldn't be such a bad place after all, Rod," Melissa said softly.

"I suspect neither of us would enjoy being here without the other, or our friends." Rod answered.

On the door was a note telling Melissa the town was having a farewell dance for her in the barn in the center of town the following night.

When Rod went to take the horses back to the stable, she whispered, "The back door will be unlocked."

The next day the bank received the telegram transferring the money to Rod's account. Rod again went shopping, this time for the house. He ordered glass for the windows, plumbing fixtures, a large copper bathtub, and a kitchen sink. The man showed him a stove like Mary had purchased and he ordered one as well. Then he went to a music store and ordered a piano. In the corner stood a harp. When Rod strummed it, he could feel the vibrations all the way to his soul. It was one of the few material things he really coveted for himself. Reluctantly, he ran his fingers across the strings and left. After an hour, he returned and added the harp to the equipment.

"You be the only person 'cepting Miss Claudette, Rev. Henry's gal that ever took notice to the harp. Yes siree, that there gal and Annabelle could make music from a rain pipe. Miss Claudette was goin' ter buy hit but they took off sudden like for Deadwood City, so she jest come in here one day, played hit fir me all afternoon and left. Shore miss that young lady. I shorley do."

The cabin would be full. I'll have to finish the second story as soon as possible, he thought. I'll wait until I go to Deadwood. There may be better lumber there and it's much closer. Annabelle can help me decide on things she might like. If she doesn't come, I won't need the extra room. He hurriedly put the thought aside. Next he purchased dozens of books and a desk. He had them ship everything to the end of the railroad line. He would leave after seeing Melissa off and be there when it arrived to off-load it into wagons.

Knowing that clothing was scarce on the prairie, Rod brought clothing for winter for himself and Sky. Extra gloves, boots, underwear, socks, caps, overalls, rain gear and extra warm, sheep-lined jackets, blankets, bed rolls and utensils. They would be used eventually by hired hands, or a cold traveler. Maybe Mr. Dolly should open up a branch store near his ranch.

He picked up a mail order catalogue. In it was displayed a steam engine car. Rod was fascinated and longed to see one.

He stopped to talk with several people and was less hurried than on his first day in town. After another shave, he brought a dress suit, shirt, tie and slippers. Melissa would be surprised to see him. As he paid the man, he noticed a green silk dress on the model in the women's department. A fur coat was draped across the shoulders. It was one of the loveliest dresses Rod had ever seen. "I'll take three coats and dress, too," he said to the surprised store owner.

When he returned to the house, Melissa was in the bedroom getting dressed. "Can I watch," he asked outside the door.

He took the dress out of the box. Holding it up he waltzed into the room saying, "How do I look, my dear."

"Oh, Rod. It's so beautiful. Who's if for?"

"Do you see any other women around? Now take off the one you have on and let's see if it fits."

"I'll wear it even if I have to leave it unbuttoned."

He slipped the dress over her head and buttoned it up the back. She twirled before him in a swirl of green silk. Tiny pale orange rosebuds nestled in lace around the low cut neckline. She stared at herself in the mirror with shining happy eyes. Then she noticed Rod's new suit.

"Well, aren't we both beautiful? We'll give the whole town something to talk about tonight, Rod." She threw her arms around him and kissed him.

He held her tightly. "I'm looking forward to the hours after the ball," he whispered kissing her ear and throat. She caught her breath.

"Oh, me too. But you'd better slow down, we'll be the last ones there as it is."

He picked up the coat she had worn for so many years and wrapped it around her shoulders, silently vowing she would have the new one for her trip. If she wore the fur coat tonight, people would know he gave it to her and jealous tongues would lash out at her. "Your carriage awaits, milady."

"You rented a buggy. Aren't you spending too much money Rod?" Melissa asked concerned.

On the way to the dance he told her about the inheritance. "I paid your fare so you can use your money to get settled when you arrive in Deadwood. I would like to give you some more, if you need it."

She protested. "Absolutely not."

"You've done so much for me over the years, Melissa. The things you taught me and given me to think about can never be bought."

"Thanks Rod, but I cannot in good conscious take any more from you. Oh, Rod. I'm so happy."

"Guess what, Melissa? I am too."

The barn was already crowded. The fiddler struck up a square dance. When Melissa and Rod appeared, people stood and applauded. The students were awed by the sight of the teacher in a lovely dress with a handsome man. Very few people had ever seen her without her glasses and in other than high necked dresses. Some hardly knew her.

Men who had seldom given her a second glance clamored to dance with her. She and Annabelle had taught Rod and Dan to dance for one of Annabelle's musicals several years earlier. None of the men danced as well as Rod, Dan or the ones who had been in one of Annabelle's shows.

Rod danced with any lady who looked lonely and watched with a happy smile as the men lined up to do a folk dance or waltz with Melissa.

Nearly everyone had bought food and a lantern. The lights were hung all around the barn giving it a bright festive air. At ten o'clock, they took a break, eating a late supper. There was apple pie, fired chicken, pork, beef, deer, pheasant, salads, and berries. The poor as well as the rich ate and danced. Later, the whole group of people sang and danced in a circle. Folk dances were done by Swedes, Germans, and groups from several counties.

Some of the more talented students put on a little skit. One of them wore her hair coiled, glasses down on her nose and pretended to be Melissa scolding a six foot four kid, then turning him across her knee when he didn't obey. He kept falling off her lap.

Both Melissa and Rod would remember these days as a couple of the happiest in their lives.

The next morning at daybreak, he helped Melissa take her bags to the wagon train. They kissed a fond farewell and promised to see one another in Deadwood in the fall. She would let the Bennetts know where she was staying. Rod slipped a hundred dollars into her saddle bags before he rode back to town to the train station.

On his way to the train, he stopped and paid a boy to catch up with Melissa on the wagon train and give her the gaily boxed coat.

Tears fell from her cheeks as she held it to her face. She felt Mize. Bingham's disapproving eyes, but Melissa didn't care. It was a lovely red velvet on the inside and fur on the outside. The feel of it would always remind her of Rod and the past week. She folded it carefully in its box, hiding it away until she reached Deadwood.

"The twins and Annabelle will be green with envy. But it will be my secret." Ouch! Rod thought. He'd have to find something for the twins and Mary. Christmas presents, by mail order.

Avonelle Kelsey

Home Again

Rod's return trip on the train was hot and dusty. He rested and caught up on his sleep. In his dreams there seemed to be confusion between the faces of Annabelle and Melissa.

Rod thought of the first time he saw Annabelle. She had been playing the piano and whistling along with the music. Long black curls hung to her waist and a big pink bow was perched on top. Perhaps because her name was the same as his sister, Annabelle Lee, and in the poem his mother had been listening to him recite just before she died, had helped him fall in love with her.

Did he love her like a sister? Had he transferred the love he felt for his family to Annabelle? Did it matter? He loved her.

How was his feeling for Annabelle different than his feelings for Melissa, he wondered? Melissa left him with a feeling of peace, thoughtfulness, and satisfaction. Whereas, thoughts of Annabelle were often filled with drama, excitement, and anxiety.

Would it always be like that, even after they were married?
Somehow, the thought of Annabelle making him wait, or turning
him down, did not upset him as much as it had before.

The nights spent with Melissa would always be special. They
had left him with a feeling of self-confidence and maturity which
he had never known before. An intelligent beautiful woman had
found him exciting. Women who had passed him by with hardly
a glance before, found excuses to stop and chat with him, or smile
invitingly before lowering their eyes.

Annabelle would find him greatly changed, he supposed. For
the first time he could smile when remembering his father and
other women. His father had tried to explain sexual attraction to
Rod once, but sensing the young boy's resentment at the idea of
anyone taking his Mother's place, he gave up.

"I'm sorry Father," he said silently and went back to sleep to
dream of Poe. I wonder what his Annabelle was like.

"She was a child and I was a child,
In that kingdom by the sea,
But we loved with a love,
That was more than love,
I and my Annabelle Lee . . ."Poe

Annabelle smiled to herself as she remembered Rod's voice
saying these words to her. The tall buffalo grass on the prairie
was nearly up to her waist. Her kingdom was a bit different. A
gentle spring wind blew through the tall stiff buffalo grass as it

rolled across the flat land, giving it the appearance of enormous waves under a setting sun. They had been on the wagon trail a week. Long enough for her to learn that these inviting waves often hid danger in many forms.

This was the way Annabelle liked to live, on the edge. In their own way, both she and Dan kept life around them stirred up. They were as restless as the wind on this sea of grass. She had never really had a chance to drink deeply of adventure. Her parents, Rod, or Dan had always been there to protect her. Annabelle was determined to taste life before she settled down on a ranch with Rod.

The early morning dew twinkled like diamonds in the sunlight as the grass moved. Rod would love it. She remembered the time they had been out riding just after a rain. The world sparkled so beautifully; she jumped off the horse and tired to pick a raindrop to wear. Finally, in frustration, she stuck her head in a bush and came out triumphant but dripping wet. She felt like a grand lady standing in a diamond crown with Rod her royal knight, until Dan rode up and said she looked like a drowned rat.

It always amazed her how one man could make a woman feel like a queen and in the same moment another could turn her into a tramp. She got even with Dan later by scaring the deer he was about to shoot.

Annabelle looked at the grass. Sometimes Indians hid in it. Last evening about a dozen warriors sat above them, silhouetted on a small butte. The wagons circled and put the animals inside the enclosure. They had sung, as usual, to keep up their spirits while the men sat watch with guns ready.

Now, Annabelle scanned the horizon. She wondered if they were still out there, watching her. What would it be like to live as a Native American? She decided she wouldn't like it. White men said the Warriors treated their women as slaves. Rod said it wasn't true, there was always lots of work to do and the women did it willingly, just as the men hunted and protected the village.

Annabelle was determined to be an actress and marry Rod both. She would persuade him to move to town. Dad and Mark would give him a job. She must write to him and let him know her decision. We could go and visit his old sheep once in awhile and ride the horses. That would be fun, but a stinking sheep ranch was no place for Annabelle Lee.

There were lots of other young men around but they teased, were clumsy and didn't seem to know what a girl needed or wanted. She preferred older men. They were polite and never teased or fell over their feet. Rod would look at her and wait quietly for her to say what she thought and felt. Then help her get it.

"Try not to hurt Rod, Annabelle," her Mother said the day they had gone out for her shooting lesson. "He's a very special man. There aren't many of his kind around."

"What is there about Rod that's different, Mom? Is it because he's part Native American?"

"Since he left us, I've wondered, too. Some men have a special charm for women. His father had it and he cultivated it when he became a gambler, I'm sure. Perhaps it's his way of really being with a person when he talks with someone. He looks upon women as interesting people," Mary said thoughtfully.

Annabelle nodded. "Do you notice many men keep glancing at a woman's legs or breasts and never look into her eyes? Almost a furtive look, afraid if you knew their secret thoughts you'd run away? Others act as though they know too much about me."

"Many men mainly want sex and a slave. They aren't really willing to accept the rest of a woman as being a worthwhile companion to cultivate," Mary said.

Annabelle grinned, "Sometimes they follow me about like a dog in heat. I'd like to bash them over the head and throw them in an icy stream to cool off."

The two women laughed and lay back on the grass in the cool afternoon shadows.

Mary frowned, trying to find the right words. "Men and women are different in many ways, but they usually want the same things in the end. You're more like a man in your attitude, Annabelle. You take what you want. I was a bit like you when I was younger; determined to be a career woman. Then I met Joseph," she said dreamily. "Things I thought were important seemed frivolous compared to our love."

"You and Dad have never told us how you actually met. You both just laugh and say, 'in Boston', but I bet there's more to it than that."

Mary turned over on her side and plucked a wild flower that painted a yellow spot on the velvet moss beside the creek, then lay back and smiled.

"I had opened my 'Hat Gallery', I called it. One summer day it was terribly sultry. Business was slow, so I closed the shop, took my buggy and went for a long lunch hour to read and have a picnic at a secret place where I could swim in the nude. I hate the heavy woolen bathing suits women are supposed to wear when bathing," Mary said scornfully and both of them giggled at her daring.

"I had never before seen anyone around my swimming hole. Bushes lined the creek on both sides and there was a bend on the north end. I could see anyone who came from the south in time to head for the shelter of the bushes."

"Get on with it Mom," Annabelle said mischievously.

"Under a large drooping willow tree, I undressed and hung my clothing over a limb. I had just waded in to my waist when a man's voice said, "Come on in, the water's fine.""

Normally, I would have screamed and run, but you know what a kind, deep, mellow voice your father has. I stopped dead still, then dropped straight down in the water like a shot, went all the way under and picked up a rock.

When I peeked out with just my eyes showing, he said. "I'm Joseph Bennett. Welcome to the best swimming hole in the country."

"I'm . . . I'm Mary Calhoun." Surprise and resentment at a stranger using my private swimming hole must have given me courage. Keeping my eye on him I slowly began to edge toward the bank.

"Mary and Joseph," he said slowly. "Tell me Mary, are you pregnant?" It was a bit off color. An old school joke that has been over done so often I hardly thought of it as anything except stupid. But, you know the way Joe has with words, everything he says can be funny when he uses that certain tone. Perhaps it's because he says so little we wait for him to say anything." She shrugged as though she had given up trying to solve the mysterious affect Joe's words had on her.

"For some reason, we both began to laugh. When we gained control, he suggested that we both stay on our sides of the creek, finish our swim and then share my picnic lunch.

"I never went back to the shop that afternoon. We talked and talked; we fell in love. Mother came looking for me that evening. She knew my favorite spot.

Joseph shook her hand and put his arm around my shoulder. "I would like to declare my intentions to you, Mrs. Calhoon. I intend to marry your daughter, today, tomorrow, or in ten years. Just as soon as she'll set a date."

"It took me all summer to set a date, but my heart had said yes the first moment he spoke to me. I was twenty-two, my business was going well and I had plenty of suitors. Joseph was patient. He insisted that I could make hats in his store or could keep my own shop. I had really wanted to be a painter but Mother taught me to make hats and we needed the money after Father died. Father was one of the first people to be killed over Civil war issues," she said sadly.

Annabelle didn't want to loose the gaiety of the afternoon. "Have you ever regretted marrying father and having a passel of kids? You said you had been invited by a large New York Store to come back and design hats for them. Wouldn't that have been more exciting?"

"Each time I get pregnant, I regret it, until Joseph takes me in his arms and I look into the face of the new born baby. When a mother's eyes lock with that of her child's for the first time, it's like looking all the way into a shiny new soul and knowing she alone has the responsibility to keep it shining. It's more important than hats."

"Why is it, Mom that I dream of being with Rod so much my body aches; yet, with my mind, I know we're so very different and each want a different kind of life? I feel torn in two at times," Annabelle turned her beautiful blue eyes toward her mother.

Mary saw a lovely young girl turning into a woman. It was like watching the opening of a rosebud. Her hair was jet black, waving in the breeze around flawless white skin. For the first time, she saw signs of maturity in her expression. She reached over and pushed back a lock of hair that had fallen over Annabelle's eyes and stroked her cheek. For a moment she wanted to protect her from the pain the world had in store for her. With Annabelle's temperament, there would be plenty.

"Sexual intercourse is an almost overwhelming desire for most men. They see it as necessary and their right. A woman sees it as a way of being close. After the first time or two, she enjoys it as much or more than a man, but it's not the most important aspect in a relationship. For a man, sex can stand alone. The couple need have little else in common, if he is ego bound. But for a woman, the act is only a small fraction of the relationship. It presents her with life, children, health problems, and a necessity to make a home. She has almost no alternatives once she becomes a Mother. Men still have choices about the kind of work they do, where they live and with whom."

"Men often marry to have sex handy, you're saying, Mom?"

"Often that's the case. Women use men to get wealth, provide a home and further their own ambitions, so they have their ways, too." Mary suspected Annabelle knew too much about this angle already.

"Passion comes in many guises, Annabelle. A true love is rare. Jumping into a relationship without exploring and satisfying your own talents, often leads to regrets. Unfortunately, when a woman follows up on her desires, she's called ugly names, if she chooses a path not directed by social customs such as marriage."

Mary paused, searching for right words. "A man and children take over a woman's life soon enough. It can overwhelm a woman and she may become bitter, a viper in a marriage, when she feels she has been cheated. Do what you must do, but don't rush into a marriage without first deliberately deciding to take the consequence of your choice."

For the first time Annabelle seemed to be listening to her. "That's why parents keep such a close eye on their daughters. We want you to have time to stretch your wings. Both a man and woman need this time. It was good that Rod went away for awhile and each of you have time to mature into individual possibilities. Sometimes this separation time helps two people know their minds, to learn things about themselves and their own needs for the first time. Please don't try to maneuver Rod to suit your needs, Annabelle. Promise me?" Annabelle nodded silently.

The sun was setting. Long blue shadows danced over the bodies of the two women stretched out on a blanket. For the first time in many years, they felt the closeness that had not been there since Annabelle was a child. The water smelled damp and dew began to form on the warm grass. A bird swooped down to bath, shaking the water from its feathers. A cowbell rang and peep frogs began their evening chant as the two women lay silently contemplating life. Darkness descended. Mary knew Joe would be worried about them, but this might be the last time she and

Annabelle would ever have to themselves, so she did not break the spell.

Finally, Annabelle sat up. Quietly they gathered up the picnic scraps, folded the blankets and stood in the cool of the evening. Annabelle put her arms around Mary for the first time in years and hugged her. Both women had tears in their eyes as they walked slowly back to town and their lives. They had come to the river as mother and child and returned as friends.

Annabelle would tell Rod about it some day, she thought. Only he would understand. I'm becoming a woman. It did not occur to her that Rod was also becoming a man.

"Annabelle, Annabelle. I caught you day dreaming again," Claudette called. "Come down off the wagon and let's have a race along the wagon train while we're in this flat stretch. I brought Whirlwind." She rode up beside the oxen with Annabelle's horse in tow.

Annabelle laughed. Claudette was the first person who really understood her and such a wonderful friend. Becky, her grade school pal, had been a good friend but they were so very different. After she'd married at sixteen, Annabelle had relied on Rod, Melissa and Dan for companionship. She kept busy partly out of loneliness.

"I'll have to find a driver."

The twins came rushing up." Can we drive now, Annabelle? Can we?" Dad said we could sometime on a straight stretch."

"Well, all right. I'll tell Mom."

After scanning the ridge for Indians, Annabelle turned the reins of the oxen team over to the girls. "If you see anything yell, and I'll come right back." The thought of anything exciting happening to a slow plodding oxen team seemed pretty far fetched. A whole army of Native Americans wouldn't push them to more than a fast walk.

"Mom, I'm going for a ride," She called as they rode up beside Mary. "The twins are driving for a spell."

Mary nodded, looked back and smiled. She and Annabelle took turns letting the men walk and rest their backs on straight stretches. She watched the two young women racing toward the head of the wagon train which stretched out for over a mile. Her arms had ached all night at the beginning of the trip but now she actually enjoyed each change of scenery. She knew they had been unusually lucky because the weather had held back the rain. It had been nippy and one snow storm held them up for a few days, but they had missed the spring rains and floods.

She looked to the north and wondered what Rod was doing on his ranch. I still miss him as though he was my own flesh and blood. Is it true that some people are old souls, she wondered? If so, Melissa and Rod must have them. Wonder if he got our letters or went to Vermillion? Could he be in Deadwood waiting for us? I feel uneasy about him, as though he's calling to me . . . . If she had known he was lying on his bed fighting for his life, Mary would have taken the fastest horse and headed for his ranch.

Up ahead Claudette and Annabelle raced along side the wagons until they came to a small creek. The day was hot and the trail dusty. "Let's take a quick swim until our wagon catches up," said Annabelle when they came to a deep pool. They pulled the horses to a stop and let them drink.

"Looks as though they're stopping to let the stock drink any way. It'll take an hour for them to finish."

They'd made better time today because the prairie was much flatter than the Missouri Breaks. To the north loomed the peaks of the Badlands. Often in the heat of the day when a creek was spotted, the children and women took off their boots and waded into the water, split riding skirts, dresses, overalls and all. As their clothing dried in the hot sun, it kept them cool.

"Mr. Clampet, Annabelle and I are going to swim right over there. You can see us from the wagons. Tell the wagonmaster, if he asks," Claudette called to an old scout.

There was one rule that was strictly enforced. No one left the lineup without checking with him. No one went ahead or drooped behind at any time. When some one had to go to the toilet, three or four men with guns surrounded the area. Usually, the trains stopped for short time every couple of hours. While the animals grazed, toilets were made on one side for the men and the other side for women. A toilet break was one time the long dresses came in handy. Few women wore underwear other than slips. They could stand up and retain their modesty to a certain

Avonelle Kelsey

extent. Umbrellas and blankets were often held by women for privacy.

The whole trip was leisurely because of the slowness of the animals and their need to graze and rest. Wagons were loaded heavily with food, cloth, tools, and various supplies for the new store; mining and farming equipment were the heaviest items. The twelve wagons the Bennett's had brought, plus Mary's buggy and horses for the children as well as extra cows, pigs and chickens in cages on smaller wagons, was a caravan in itself.

After two days on the trail and wrestling long skirts, many women took a pair of their husbands or sons overalls to wear. Modesty was secondary to their lives on the trail.

The wagons would all come back for another load when the train reached its destination. "If we had waited another year," Mary reminded them, "we could have ridden the train and saved all the trouble."

Actually, except for the mud when it rained and crossing the creeks, it hadn't been as bad as she expected. The girls played music in the evenings. Often the entire wagon train or evening camp echoed with singing. Mary wondered if the Native Americans watching were being entertained or waiting for a chance to kill them all.

One morning, Claudette and Annabelle woke up to find two pair of beautiful moccasins by their wagon. When warriors were spotted on the ridge above, the girls shivered and giggled.

Joe ordered them to ride on the opposite side of the wagon train. "They might decide to kidnap you."

A rule of the wagon master was that each person must always carry a gun or knife, whether man, woman, or child. The young children were not allowed to unsheathe their knives unless attacked by Indians or a wild animal. They were allowed supervised practice time throwing them and target practicing with guns from the age of seven on up. Little Willie could hardly wait until he turned seven to get a knife and to practice shooting.

Several other women who were not driving teams waded in the creek on both sides of the wagons as their teams drank.

The wagonmaster passed the word down the line, "We'll stay here tonight. Any clothing, washing, and bathing, should be done today. We're approaching the badlands area and there be little clear water until we get to Cottonwood creek. Men, take your guns and stand guard while the women wash clothing."

Sluice mining muddied many creeks near the hills, they had been told.

"We'd better go help the twins," Annabelle said, giving Claudette a splash and racing out of the creek. She squeezed out her long curls, retied them with a scarf to keep off some of the dust and bent over to pull on her boots.

Claudette screamed. She had taken off her light jacket, thrown it on the ground and a rattler had crawled under it. It bit her on the hand as she picked it up.

"Help me, help me, Annabelle. I'll die, I'll die," she moaned over and over. Annabelle grabbed her gun from the saddle and shot the snake. Then she slapped Claudette to calm her down. Several people came running up.

"A snake bit her. Get Dad." Annabelle pulled her knife from her pants pocket while Claudette sobbed; holding her hand out from her as though it was attached to the snake.

Annabelle led her away from the writhing, rattling body. Claudette continued to cry and look away as Annabelle cut two slashes across the wound and sucked the blood. She spit the blood and poison out onto the ground. Other members of the wagon train put their arms around Claudette, gave advice, tied a tourniquet around the wrist, and held her still. Dan came rushing up. "Give her to me," he shouted. The men reached her to him and he rode back to Mary's wagon.

Several women, as well as Mary, were both nurse and doctor to their families and neighbors. They gathered around giving advice and offering tea and herb polices.

Annabelle stood watching Dan ride away with Claudette.

"Annabelle, wash you mouth out well. If you have a decayed tooth or cut in your mouth the poison will get you same as her." Mr. Sully warned.

"Come back to the wagon train with me. I have some good strong tea fir ye," a kindly Quaker woman said. "Ye acted real fast, young lady." She could see Annabelle was shaken and put her arm around her.

"Whirlwind, our horses," said Annabelle as she picked up Claudette's jacket. She felt sick. It was one of the few unselfish acts of her life and she might die for it.

"Milt," take these here horses to the Bennett wagons. Tell Mary, Annabelle is with me."

Annabelle knew people thought she was stuck up and aloof, except when she got fired up about something. After acting so quickly and perhaps saving Claudette's life, people treated her more kindly.

Avonelle Kelsey

Claudette

There was no music around the camp fire the evening Claudette was bitten by the rattler. Annabelle was often considered to be a bit on the snobbish side but Claudette was loved by children and adults alike. She both teased and took teasing good-naturedly, often picking up children to swing in the air, teach them songs and dancing or giving someone a helping hand.

The delegated camp midwife-doctor arrived to press a freshly killed chicken's breast to Claudette's hand. Dan held her on his lap while the poison was drawn out into the fresh meat. The midwife bandaged the swollen hand, gave her several cups of nasty tasting tea and told her to rest. Claudette was running a fever by evening. One of the wagons was partially emptied so Claudette could lie down in it.

Dan sat by her side, holding her hand. Her nightmares seemed worse than the fever. During the night he lay down beside her and held her tenderly in his arms.

Mary reached in and felt Claudette's cheeks. Claudette's fever seemed to have lowered. All they could do was wait for the body to reject the rest of the poison. She pulled the canvas across the end of the wagon so the early morning sun would not shine in and went to bed. Her children were growing up. She hoped it did not mean moving away as well.

Claudette had come to Vermillion shortly after Rod had gone west. After her parent's boat sank, she was very lonely. Her whole life had been wrapped up in show business. She was mature for her age and could act the part of an adult. The 'old maid' aunt with whom she had been left was a 'Bible thumpin' Baptist'. She and the headstrong girl fought over every act Claudette committed.

Finally, the unhappy girl ran away to join Vaudeville. The authorities picked her up and she consented to go to her Uncle Rev. Henry's rather than stay with her aunt. Claudette would not receive her inheritance until she was twenty-one. The last thing she wanted to do was be stuck in the hick town of Vermillion, she told him. "If you will just give me part of the money to live on, I'll leave."

Henry's wife resented Claudette's beauty, talent, and funny ways. The children loved Claudette and willingly helped with work as she danced, sang, and joked with them. Rev. Henry would have enjoyed the girl, if his wife hadn't met him at the door every time he came home to complain.

"You're suppose to be a preacher but I don't see you doin' anything about her ungodly ways. You mark my word. That girl's gonna' get in trouble. She don't deserve the money. We could use it fir clothes on our back and food on the table."

"Now, Margaret. It's the money my sister set aside for Claudette. The girl's just full of life. She doesn't hurt anyone and does her share of the work when you leave her alone. When she's twenty-one the money is hers, so don't go coveting it."

Claudette was confident she could earn her living by acting. The money would give her a chance to start her own theater troupe. Aunt Margaret, Henry's wife, had been a beautiful woman when she seduced him, but now, her unhappy face and jealous anger made her seem ugly. She gazed at the world with an accusing eye. After Claudette arrived the eye settled on her as the cause of all her problems.

The other reason besides money that Claudette stayed in Vermillion was the Bennett family. She and Annabelle complimented one another in acting, producing, song writing, singing, and dancing.

Claudette was good at costumes, writing scripts, scenery, and as a comic.

Annabelle had a talent for talking men and women into helping with sets, selling tickets, training dancers, and singing as well as publicity. Both girls were musical and could play any instrument that was placed in their hands. They were together every minute possible. Claudette was the closest friend Annabelle ever had and vice versa.

Mary took Claudette under her wing, giving her tea and sympathy when she complained that she couldn't stay under Mrs. Henry's roof another minute. She knew a girl like Claudette was special and sensitive. It would be easy for someone to take advantage of her aloneness and her eagerness for life.

Claudette and Dan were attracted to one another from the beginning. At first, he flirted with her lightly as an attractive friend of Annabelle's, but when Claudette chose to turn on her charm, few men could resist. Dan resisted very little.

He talked with Melissa about it, as he did nearly everything, and she approved of his interest in the young lady. As they had agreed earlier, there were to be no string, other than mutual respect and silence, about their intimate relationship. She kissed him goodbye and reminded him that they would no longer be sharing her bed. "I'll miss you, Melissa. Are we still friends?"

"Always, Dan. Remember, it's our secret."

Melissa and Claudette became friends when the girls helped her produce a high school play for a fund raiser.

Mark's invitation to the Bennett family to move to Deadwood and his mention of the fact that Langrishe was going to build a theater in Deadwood, made Claudette and Annabelle determined to go there, one way or another.

Rev. Henry refused to let Claudette go, saying he would not turn over her inheritance, if she went to Deadwood. She promptly quit helping around the house. Mrs. Henry complained more than ever.

Dan asked Claudette to marry him so she could go to Deadwood with the family. Mary said she would approve, provided they waited for one year. "Dan has his law practice to launch and you, Claudette, should have some time on the stage." They agreed to wait if Claudette was allowed to go to Deadwood.

Mary talked with Rev. Henry, promising that Claudette could stay with them. He finally agreed to let her go, in order to keep the peace at home.

On the trip west, the two girls made the trip one of the merriest wagon trains that ever crossed the prairie. The weather was a balmy spring with very little rain, except for one late spring blizzard, which melted off in a day or two. One child was playing in some abandoned wagon parts along the trail and a rusty piece of iron punctured his foot. He died of tetanus.

Claudette was a favorite among the people with her funny remarks and clown routine. At night she sang ballads or folk songs and played the guitar.

She and Dan had not had slept together until the night he stayed with her when she was snake bitten. After Claudette's fever broke, she turned to Dan in the night. The temptation of two, young, yearning bodies was too great. It was both a comfort to her and a thrilling experience. Being close to someone outweighed Claudette's desire to act.

Dan stayed by Claudette's side as much as possible during the rest of the trip, even though she recovered quickly. She couldn't play the guitar for a few weeks but seemed no worse for the experience, other than the fact that she jumped every time she saw a stick, and often had nightmares.

When they came in sight of Bear Butte, Annabelle said, "Let's slip away and go see Rod. Wouldn't that be fun? Bet Mom would go with us."

"You and Dan talk so much about Rod. I'm already in love with him. If I wasn't so in love with Dan, I'd make a play for him myself when he comes."

The girls laughed at her statement.

Deadwood Gulch

"Come mornin' we be leaving Fort Meade and movin' up the canyon to Deadwood Gulch," the wagon master said. A loud cheer went up. But it was a long haul up to the rim of the canyon.

The family looked down into the gold mining town with various reactions. Deadwood most nearly resembled an ant hill. Buildings were in all stages of construction. Stone masons had been imported and the large, red sandstone cliffs were being used to construct numerous hotels, stores and permanent homes. There were rows of canvas stretched over wooden frames between half-finished, large red-stoned buildings. On the hillsides black burned areas of trees stood like guardians of evil. People were everywhere. The noise level was high, even on the hillside. There was shouting, cursing, singing, music, saloons going full blast, mining, sluice boxes, shooting, banging, and building. Noise, mud, dust, and excitement hung in the air.

People were leaving as well as coming. A few had struck it rich, some were ill, others discouraged or just plain lonely for their families. Women were few in the 'hellhole' as Mary called it.

Even with all the extra men who turned out to ogle the girls and see the piano being lowered over the edge, it took two days to unload the goods and take it on to the empty store building Uncle Mark had waiting for the merchandise.

Oxen and mules were left on the rim and would return after a few days' rest with a smaller load going east as far as the train track. There they would pickup another load of supplies and return. They would do this until the railroad arrived. Even milk cows, pigs and chickens were lowered over the edge. Men tried to buy and even steal the supplies as they moved down the hill and along the way to the store.

Joe could have sold all the merchandise before they crossed the valley. But Mark was waiting for everything to furnish the store.

Mark was happy to see the family. "I hope you won't mind living above the store for a few months, Mary. When I heard you were coming I bought a lot and drew up plans for a house. It's being built on a hillside; that's the only place left that there isn't mining these days."

"I'm only here for a year, Mark," Mary said. "Thanks all the same." She didn't see the wink Joe gave Mark over her shoulder.

While Dan, Mark, Joe and the twins helped unload supplies, Annabelle and Claudette rode ahead into town amid applause, whistles and admiring remarks.

"Can you tell us where we can find the theater," Annabelle asked a man who stopped to admire the young women.

"Ye are standin' by it, miss."

"But this building only has two walls and a canvas roof."

"Yep. Mr. Langrishe only stays here for the summer. He'll be puttin' the rest up next year."

Claudette laughed and shook her head. "At least it's a theater, Annabelle. Let's go inside."

The stage was large and attractively draped and the backdrop scene was lovely. Mr. Langrishe was directing the leading lady, Bella, a handsome, middle aged man named Sheldon and other members of the cast.

During a break, the girls introduced themselves. Langrishe auditioned them on the spot. "You're hired. We only bring the basic troupe with us from our central theater in Denver. When we travel I hire local talent. You're the first ones who've shown up and we need you."

The girls were elated. They rushed back to tell Mary who needed help more than actresses. She dampened their enthusiasm. "Your Dad and I will meet him in good time and talk with him."

Avonelle Kelsey

Mary went with them to the theater after seeing Mr. Langrishe and his troupe at church. "You can try it for a few days," she said reluctantly.

Annabelle and Claudette kissed and hugged her, then waltzed around the room. Dan came in with the twins to see what all the shouting was about.

"We want to go on the stage, too," Bettie pouted.

"Yeah," Nettie continued, "and we can sing just as well as you, Annabelle." She ignored the twins, but if Annabelle had seen their glance as Mary did, she would have realized they intended to cause trouble.

Later Mary took them aside and laid down the law. "You girls are on probation as it is. One more trick and you get separate rooms and schools."

"I wish Rod could be here to see me perform," Annabelle said as she dressed for a bit part one evening. She was also the understudy for the leading lady. "Somehow, he makes every thing I do seem worthwhile. He says it's the trying, even if we don't do it perfect at first that is important. I always look ahead to the goal. He's happy just living," Annabelle chatted on.

Claudette teased her, "You're a very lucky girl. If I didn't have Dan, I'd envy you. I know I tease you about a sod hut and a dozen brats hanging onto you, and getting old before your time, but your parents have something very worthwhile in their relationship. I only hope we're as lucky."

Annabelle looked at her in astonishment.

Even though Claudette loved Dan, she had been a bit relieved when Mary requested they wait a year. But now, she was beginning to long for a home and family. In the past she'd often put down marriage.

Annabelle looked up surprised. "Do you feel all right, Claudette?"

"Well, I do feel a bit down, in spite of this opportunity. Maybe it's something I ate. It's about that time of the month, I guess."

Claudette did comic skits or played the guitar and sang between acts. She was to understudy any woman who could not show up for her part, except the leading lady.

"I've decided to write to Rod and tell him I won't marry him for a couple of years, until I've had my chance at stardom. Unless he'll move to town, of course. I wonder if he got our letters before he went to Vermillion." Annabelle said. "Wouldn't it be terrible if he went one way and we went another?"

Claudette nodded and smiled. "Wouldn't it be wonderful if you, Rod, Dan and I could have a double wedding?"

"That would be great, but what would happen to our careers if we became pregnant? As much as I love Rod, I'm not willing to take a chance. Are you, Claudette?"

"It's so hard to decide. I do love Dan, but he'll be living in town, so I don't have to choose like you, if Rod decides to stay with his ranching."

Avonelle Kelsey

"Well, I don't have to decide now. I've always been able to get him to do what I want; all I need to do is get him here." Then she laughed and said, "We do have choices. Half the men in this 'hell-hole' are in love with us." They giggled.

"That's not too flattering considering the fact that there's no competition," Claudette reminded her. "What if your Mom hears you talking like that, Annabelle? She'll think you learned it from me. Bet you've been talking to Calamity Jane again. Didn't Mary say to say away from her hospital?"

"I slipped out last night disguised as a boy. Calamity dresses like a man all the time and she's had all sorts of adventures."

"Right off hand, I'd say not all of her adventures have been happy ones," Claudette observed.

"What do you mean?"

"Well, look at her. She's not much over twenty and she looks older than your Mom. I hear she drinks like a fish. Have you seen that card-playing Marshal and his cronies she hangs around with?"

"Annabelle, Annabelle, get down here and help with the store. What are you girls doing up there?"

"Coming Mom," Annabelle answered. She opened the door suddenly. The twins fell through at her feet. "How dare you eavesdrop? I'm going to tell Mom. You're up for a good spanking this time."

"You let us go or we'll tell Mom what we heard."

"Yeah, and you'll be in big trouble. You won't get to be in any show." "She's tired of doing your share of the work, too. Besides, play acting is the work of the devil. I heard Rev. Rout tell Mom in the store."

Bettie ducked as Annabelle swung at her. Nettie let out a screech. Both girls went racing down the stairs almost knocking Mary backward.

"What in the world's going on here?" she asked.

"Oh Mom, you wouldn't, would you?" Wailed Annabelle.

"Wouldn't what?"

"Wouldn't make us quit acting just when everything is going so well. Mr. Langrishe says he might take me to Denver for the winter shows." She covered her mouth with her hand. He hadn't said for certain and it was suppose to be a secret from Claudette, unless Mr. Langrishe asked her, too.

"Winter show in Denver? I wouldn't hear of it. Besides, you've just begun here."

"When did he ask you?" Claudette wanted to know. "He didn't ask me."

"It was suppose to be a secret until he talked with Mom and Dad," she stammered tearfully.

"We'll talk about it later. The store is knee deep in customers. Even the twins have to help, so let's get busy."

Claudette followed slowly. This was the first time she had felt resentful toward Annabelle or been in direct competition with her. She knew a great deal more about show business than

Annabelle and was nearly as pretty. Maybe he would ask her later. As soon as she could, she slipped away to the theater where the main cast rehearsed.

"Mr. Langrishe. Are you going to take me to Denver for the winter shows, too?"

"I only need one person and since Annabelle looks so much like my leading lady, I've asked her. We'll be back next summer, perhaps next time you can go too, if you aren't married."

"Mr. Langrishe, I'm not getting married for a long time. You must take me. I've worked so hard. I can do wardrobe, makeup, write, and clean, anything, please."

Mr. Langrishe sighed. It seemed nearly everyday some pretty girl begged for a job. He had learned to answer firmly.

"No, Claudette. You are extremely talented, but I have more than enough staff in Denver. However, I've been thinking of establishing a permanent theater here. With your background and a little training from me this season and next summer, you could become my assistant. I'd be willing to have you in charge of putting on some winter skits from whatever talent you can come up with, or just do singing and monologues. If we don't get the theater winterized, Jake at the Waggoner has promised to let us use his saloon stage when the weather becomes too cold."

Claudette wondered if he was just being nice.

"Come to dinner with me this evening and we'll talk about it."

"Thank you, Mr. Langrishe." She left slowly. True, it wasn't Denver, but in the long run, perhaps this was better. Her own theater. Claudette ran joyfully back to the store.

Annabelle could not believe the change in her. As soon as they had a moment, Claudette and Annabelle got their heads together in one of their important conferences that were so familiar.

Mary was happy to see they were getting along again. She must talk to Joe tonight about Annabelle. What would Rod think? Where was he? She really needed to talk with him. Annabelle was young. Some actor could easily turn her head. I've done everything in my power to keep her safe for Rod, she told herself. He's going to have to take over now. I'll send for him.

"Mark, I need help," Mary said when he came into the store and they had a moment between customers.

He was surprised, Mary seldom asked a favor and Mark was more than happy to be of service.

Joseph and he were the only two left of their family. Mary was probably the only person who knew Mark was still carrying a deep wound at the loss of Sylvia.

"What can I do for you, Mary?"

She told him of her fears about Annabelle and asked if he and Dan could go for Rod.

"Let me think about it. Perhaps Dan and I could take a quick trip to the ranch next week, if you haven't heard from Rod by that time. Would that be soon enough?"

"Thank you, Mark," Mary stood on her toes and kissed his cheek. He blushed and hugged her awkwardly.

Claudette was having dinner with Mr. Langrishe when Dan walked in the dining room. She saw him look at them across the dining-room saloon. There wasn't much choice of a place to eat in Deadwood. The partially built Bodega was the best restaurant available. Women did not normally go into the saloons, 'nice women', that is. The troupe had a choice of two places to eat, the Franklin Hotel or the Bodega. The Franklin was unfinished but would be the grandest structure in town. It was to be made out of cut pink stone. Many of the other buildings like the Waggoner Hotel were also being erected from a local red rock cut from the nearby cliffs. When all these buildings were completed it would be a city. At first workers were hard to come by but as more and more miners became discouraged or needed to work to supplement their partners in their mining claims, the buildings were going up swiftly. Many stone masons from Europe had promised to work for their passage, room and board.

Claudette waved at Dan when their eyes met across the room but he turned on his heel and left. It wouldn't hurt him to be jealous of her for a change. She wondered if their making love had made a difference in his attitude toward her. Something was changing Dan. Perhaps he'll be all right when he finds out I'm going to stay in town, she thought, and continued making plans with Mr. Langrishe.

After dinner, Claudette found Dan in his office. It was small but adequate until the one in the Franklin was completed. Dan had plenty of clients. The store was busy and noisy, so he had made a bedroom for himself in the 'lean to' behind the law office.

Claudette rushed in to tell him the news. He was sitting with his muddy boots upon his desk. Dust and mud were on everything. It was impossible to keep floors and shoes clean in Deadwood Gulch. When the mud dried up, dust floated every where.

The story was told that once when it rained the mud became so thick a team of horses and a wagon sank right out of sight.

"Dan, guess what?"

"You're eloping with Langrishe?"

"Oh, Dan." She came around the desk, pushed his feet to the floor and sat on his lap. She took his face in her hands and kissed him. There was nothing subtle about Claudette. He laughed and kissed her back, becoming more passionate as he pressed her body against his.

Then he picked her up and carried her into the back room. With all the layers of skirts and petticoats, spontaneity was hard to accomplish but Claudette and Dan managed.

When they lay back exhausted, Dan asked, "What was your news?"

She ran her finger across his chest as she pulled back in order to look into his eyes and see the response to her news. "Mr. Langrishe has offered to let me start a winter theater right here in

Deadwood. Isn't that wonderful?" She kissed him again. Later on she whispered, "We could be married right away."

He pulled away and sat up. "Claudette, we promised Mom, remember? One year. Speaking of Mom, isn't it time you went home? They'll be looking for you."

"Don't you love me Dan? Is it the politician's daughter who makes eyes at you that causes you to seem so distant sometimes?" Her eyes flashed.

Dan laughed and took her in his arms again. "I do love you, Claudette. I have a hard time waiting until next year. Every time I see you I want to do what I did tonight. You want a career and so do I. The only way I can resist you, is to stay away from you. Mom has asked Mark to go and bring Rod back before Annabelle leaves. I'm going with him. You'll like Rod, Claudette."

"The great Rod. I've heard so much about him he's bound to be a disappointment. I see a big, innocent, clumsy buck in my mind."

"Don't you ever talk that way about Rod," Dan said angrily. "He's like a brother to me and the most intelligent, decent person I've ever met. If Native American blood makes him what he is, we all need some of it."

"I'm sorry Dan. I'm sure I'll love him."

He smiled his quick beautiful smile, so like Annabelle's, and kissed her lightly. "You don't need to go quite that far, young lady."

Claudette walked thoughtfully to the Bennett's store. She needed some time to think. It was past time for her monthly. If she was pregnant, they'd have to get married. But Claudette was independent; she didn't want him to be forced into marrying her. She realized suddenly how much she wanted a home and family.

Did she sense a withdrawal in Dan's attitude? It was as though he loved her, but something was standing between them. Was it because she let him make love to her before they were married? Was he really such a prude underneath? She hadn't been seeing him very much, except when he walked the girls home after a show.

Was the other woman a real threat? She raced around town in a fancy buggy and beautiful clothing. One Sunday Dan had even gone to church with her and her father. Claudette had let Dan know how she felt and it had not happened again.

She tossed these thoughts aside and went in to talk with the Bennetts about her new career. At least she had something to look forward to and think about when Annabelle left. Perhaps someday Annabelle would even ask her for a job. Somehow, her good news felt a bit empty. She watched Annabelle in the lamp light and suddenly felt old. Claudette excused herself and went to bed where she cried herself to sleep. The next morning she had an upset stomach. Annabelle thought she was just jealous.

The family received a letter from Rod telling about his return to Vermillion and that he would come to Deadwood after the fall harvest. Melissa was on her way to Deadwood.

Everyone was delighted except Annabelle. She wouldn't be here when he came.

"Dan, will you take me out to see Rod?"

"You've waited this long. A couple of months will go fast."

"I have a secret; I'm going to Denver for the winter theater."

"I'd like to but I'm off for a two week swing through the territory on a campaign tour next week."

"Does Claudette know?"

"I'll tell her tonight."

Claudette found Mary's copy of Melissa's poems and added music and a chorus to the words of one.

Roses for My Love

Mysterious Stranger,
He . . .
Who with these lovely roses,
Buys my life and love.
So thrilled am I,
Equating these fresh beauties
With the one I dream
Will come for me and life renew.
I won't look beyond this day,
Let myself know that on the morrow
Our love will wither on the stem,
Like blossoms cut off from nourishment.
Your love withdraws,
Only the seed remains for me to tend, and
Like a Honeybee,
You're off to other blooms,
Sowing, sowing, never hoeing,
or staying 'round to harvest.
For a while I feel so sorry for myself.
But nature knows that I will love
That straying seed.
Care, share, and in my bondage,
Detest, accept, adore,
your bud carelessly planted and
The memory of the roses
From a thoughtless Honeybee,
One moonlight night.

Avonelle Kelsey

One Bear, Two Bears & Fawn

In spite of his disappointment at finding the Bennetts gone and Annabelle a bit dubious about their relationship, Rod didn't feel unhappy.

On the way home he hired another Hopi shepherd couple, picked up more breeding stock and two more sheep dogs from his old friend near Pierre. Mackenzie promised to send another shepherd along the following spring and yet another breed of sheep that had a special kind of wool, if Rod could find another section of land to rent or buy.

At the last train depot Rod bought a wagon and team to freight his purchases to the homestead. Two miners on their way to Deadwood agreed to drive it for him, provided they could carry their gear as well.

Spring flowers had brightened the prairie on his way to Vermillion. Due to a late spring rain, sunflowers bloomed for miles along the wagon road. He smiled as he remembered Melissa and her happiness when she joined the wagon train to Deadwood.

What a strange four days, he thought. First the children on the train, Nathan and Rebecca, his sudden inheritance of money and land in New Salem, and then Melissa. The sexual experience alone was a terrific adventure. If Annabelle put off marriage for a couple of years, would he be willing to wait?

'Know thyself,' had been a favorite saying of his fathers and Rod had agreed. Now he was not as certain he knew himself. A few short months ago I killed three men. Now I've had an affair with a woman other than my bride-to-be.

He laughed aloud and said to his horse, "Father should have added, 'control thyself'. I must admit, I can hardly wait to repeat the experience."

The horse pricked up his ears and blew through his nose as he shook his mane.

Again Rod laughed, "Oh you agree, do you? You just keep to the middle of the road when we pass the O'Leary's pasture where that little mare hangs out." Rod whistled and gave the horse a nudge. They raced across the miles toward the setting sun and home.

It felt wonderful to be home again. Two Bears had run things smoothly, it appeared. A new calf and colt were out to pasture. Rod was surprised to see another Two Bears come out of the barn while he talked to Sky. Then he remembered, they were identical twins.

"My brother and Fawn came to join me. They stayed on to help until you returned. I hope you don't mind?"

"Of course not." Rod held out his hand and went to meet Sky's brother. "I presume you're One Bear." They shook hands. "Now, how can I tell you apart?"

"If you look closely, I am slightly heavier than One Bear and he is a bit taller." They stood side by side. "We share our thoughts, so it really doesn't matter much, does it?"

"Probably not to you. I brought a couple dozen handkerchiefs; how about Sky wearing the blue and you the red until I adjust?"

"Oaky-doky," One Bear grinned, good naturedly. "And I'll be Witty cause I'm funnier." Rod learned later it was a favorite expression of his.

"Fawn has food ready if you would like to eat before unloading. It would seem you took up white man's collecting habits and purchased the whole town."

Rod laughed and looked at the wagon. "By Jove, I think you're right. I did get a bit carried away. I hope one of you can play an instrument so they don't go to waste.

A lovely young Native American woman walked gracefully out on the Soddy porch. Then turned shyly and retreated into the house when she saw Rod.

"So you are Fawn," Rod said as he entered the sod hut where Sky led him as they talked. "I am very happy to have you here."

She lowered her eyes and clasped her hands in front of her. Then she raised her large round eyes to his and said, "Welcome, thank you."

"That's about all the English she knows at this point," Two Bears said, "but she is a quick learner."

Rod used both sign language and a combination of Native American dialects saying. "The words you speak are good words. My home is your home and I hope you dwell long in my house."

Fawn gave him a surprised, merry smile and began to chat with him while the two young men looked on in astonishment.

"Hey, Fawn, this man's hungry," Sky said, "you can talk later. Feed him."

After Rod had eaten of the rabbit stew and roots, he apologized for not leaving orders for them to kill an animal should they ran short of supplies.

"We learned to garden as white men do. Your garden is doing well. We kill the jackrabbits because they are eating it. Save the sheep for wool."

"What I said to Fawn was meant for all of you. I hope you will give up your quest and stay here on the ranch. Your help would be appreciated. If you get tired of the sod hut, we can build you a cabin. You can have some of the land to do with as you wish."

They looked at one another. It was as though they were speaking without words. They turned to him as one and held out their hands. He laughed and took one hand of each. It was a happy homecoming for Rod. No one mentioned the fact that he had returned alone.

The mail had been delivered the day after Rod left. There had been a storm and the wagon carrying the letters from the Bennetts had been washed down stream. The mail bag had been leather and caught on a bush. By the time the water receded, it was found stuck in a tree. The next wagon train found the bag, and eventually the letters the Bennetts had written about their moving had reached the homestead. Some of the letters were a bit moldy. Rod knew what was in most of them so he laid them aside to read in the evening.

"You must wonder why we are wearing your old clothing and have cut our hair." Sky asked.

"I was hoping you would for your own protection. What happened?"

"Last week Mr. Pulaski rode over and told me the army was on the way, looking for stray Indians and that I should hide. One Bear and I have often posed as white men because of our light skin and light brown eyes. We didn't want to leave your place alone. We put on your old clothing and cut one another's hair.

We hid Fawn out in the sod house, made a willow screen over the outside wall and hung beans on it to dry. When the soldiers came, they thought I was you. I told them I had hired a half-breed to help me but he was out herding sheep. They said as long as I gave him a place to live and a job, he could live off the reservation.

"You now have three hands for the price of one. We don't want Fawn and Newly to live on a reservation. If there was any chance we could win, we would fight. As it is, we have decided to educate Newly and send him to Washington to represent Native Americans. On the reservation there's starvation, disease and mistreatment. We will work here for nothing but our food and a place to stay."

Rod held up his hand for silence. He laughed and said, "It seems I am a family man. I take it, Newly is a baby? You're all more than welcome and you're hired." They smiled happily and nodded.

"I came into some inheritance when I was gone and I can pay you wages. You are more than welcome to use the sod house and food. Now, where's Newly?"

Rod watched Fawn as she moved gracefully across the room to a curtain in the back. She brought forth the baby and presented it to Rod. He looked into its brown face and large brown eyes. "Hi there, son. How about a smile? The baby blew a bubble and burped." Every one laughed."

"He just ate," said Sky.

"How old is he?"

"He was born two weeks ago."

"Shouldn't you be in bed?" Rod looked at Fawn concerned?

"Native American women do not give birth like white women. Often they have babies in the field and go on working," One Bear told him proudly.

Rod held the baby against his shoulder and patted it. The baby's skin was soft against his neck. He moved his new growth of whiskers away from its face.

Giving the baby back to her, he said, "You rest anyway." She nodded.

"Why Newly for a name?"

We will let him choose his own name according to his experience, in the old way. When the time comes, he will be given a sign and a name. For his sake and Fawns, we will live as white men on the outside, but inside, we will be Indians. Perhaps as you say, we are the link between the past and the future. Newly can decide how the future will be for his generation. On the outside, we are Witty and Sky, although Two Bear's is really funnier," their teeth flashed white against tan skin. They were relieved to have Rod home again and things settled so easily.

The three ate and went outside to unload the furniture from the wagon into the new cabin. The big, high-backed copper bath tub was unloaded first.

"Looks like a hog trough," Sky commented.

The cabin, which had looked large and spacious without anything in it but Rod's bed, began to take on the look of a storage shed. When they unloaded the harp, Rod sat a moment and tried to play it. Fawn came into the room. She carried Newly on her back. Reaching out, she plucked a string. Then jumped back shyly. She and Rod played around with it for a bit. "Wait until the piano comes," Rod said. "You'll enjoy that, too." He caught Sky's questioning glance.

"I did not see Annabelle, Sky. They had moved to the Black Hills. I didn't receive the mail in time. Now, I'll have to go there but I'll' wait until fall."

Sky nodded. The others said nothing. Native Americans have a way of being silent when something personal is discussed. Rod was grateful he didn't have to explain. Sky must have told them he planned on getting married.

They finished unloading. Fawn moved swiftly around the rooms, re-arranged things until it began to look like a home. She was delighted with the material he had picked up for curtains, the needles, thread and colorful blankets.

Witty, Sky, and Rod watched her face as she fingered the materials. "She probably won't rest until she makes up every bit of it into something," Sky said, affectionately. Rod glanced at him.

If I can love two women, why can't two men love one, he asked himself? During the coming years he would see both of them hug and kiss her impulsively. The baby seemed to be our child, not Witty's child. The three lived happily in the sod hut with never a word of jealously.

That night, Rod sat in a rocker he had purchased. He placed a kerosene lamp on a carved mahogany table. Rubbing his hand over the polished finish, he rocked for a moment looking around the room with satisfaction at the deep red wood of all the furniture. A dining room table would follow soon with a dozen chairs to match. The mahogany bookcase held a new set of encyclopedias as well as several books Melissa had given him. The copper bath tub glistened warmly in the corner. It would be a pleasure to take his Saturday night baths in it. He let his imagination carry him away and thought about Annabelle using it, but somehow it was Melissa's image that stood by the tub. Perhaps it was because he had never seen Annabelle naked.

I'll get the bathtub, the kitchen sink, and pump installed before I leave for Deadwood Gulch, he thought with pride and satisfaction. Pulling off his boots and socks, he rubbed his bare toes over the wool rug covering the wooden floor.

In the lamp light, he read the mail. The musty letters were from the Bennetts telling him about their intended move. The latest letters came from the west. Annabelle and Mary had written separately.

Dear Rod,

Melissa has arrived and says you helped her get passage to Deadwood. Also, that you came for Annabelle and were very disappointed.

I am extremely worried about Annabelle. In order to avoid further disappointment, I felt I should tell you that Annabelle has been invited to go to Denver with the Langrishe troupe for the fall theater. There has even been some hint of Paris next winter, but since Annabelle doesn't confide in me very often, I cannot be certain just how far her plans extend. She is eighteen now and will have her own way. Anyhow, she promised to come back for Thanksgiving. I hope you can be here then.

I would love to see you sooner, but I would not want you to come with the anticipation of marriage this fall. Perhaps a years' engagement would work out, but I leave this up to you and Annabelle. Things are moving too fast, not only in the careers of Annabelle and Dan, but this whole area. I do not like it here.

We have a comfortable enough home in the rooms over the store and Joe is having a house built for me on the side of the hill, hoping to keep me happy. I miss my home and friends in Vermillion and most of all, you. Thank goodness Melissa has come.

I though Claudette and Dan would get married next spring, but now he is seeing the daughter of Mr. Taylor, a politician who hopes to become governor. Dan insists it's just because she helps with the campaigning, but it upsets Claudette. Dan is to help him with his Territorial Governor campaign this fall. I fear it will interfere with his practice, Claudette, and take him away from us a great deal of the time.

Claudette is developing into a lovely young woman. Mr. Langrishe has decided to let her head his winter theater here, such as it is, and perhaps next year, have the summer one enclosed so it can be used all year round. She is at liberty to develop it in any way that she sees fit. When it gets cold, the Waggoner Hotel will have a stage in its large dining room. They have offered to let her use it for plays, if she will sing and play a couple of nights a week for them. The saloons here are hotels and dining rooms, but in my mind, they still are not very good places *for young ladies to be. I wish Annabelle would stay another year and help her.*

All send their love. Come anytime. You are always welcome whether Annabelle is here or not. If we don't hear from you soon, Dan and Mark are coming to find you.

Take care, Lovingly Mary.

PS Melissa and Joe just came in. They send greetings.

Annabelle's letter was short and to the point.

Dear Rod.

I'm so sorry we missed you in Vermillion. Our trip was long and not too unpleasant until Claudette got bitten by a rattler. She seems to have changed since then. It may be because Mr. Langrishe has invited me to Denver and she has to remain behind, or because Dan is seeing another woman.

Anyway, Rod. I'm going to Denver for the fall theater season. I hope you will be as happy about it as I am.

I must have a few years to work on my career. If you wish to come to Denver with me, I would love to have you, but I just can't spend my life on a sheep ranch. Please understand. No one else does except Dan.

You'll always be like a brother and good friend to me. I think of you often with fondness and love.

Annabelle

Avonelle Kelsey

Rod smiled through the tears. Dear Annabelle. She was never one to beat around the bush. Deep down, he had expected something like this ever since he found out she was no longer in Vermillion. He wondered if he had known about this when he and Melissa had been together, if something more might have developed in their relationship.

I would like to see Annabelle once more, he thought, and let her turn me down in person.

Dear Mary and Family,

I'll be there as soon as the crops are in for the winter and hope to spend a couple of weeks with you and the family. Before Thanksgiving or at the very latest, the end of November.

Unexpectedly, I am a family man. The young Native American, Two Bears-Sky, who saved me, has an identical twin brother with a wife and baby. They are here with me and will look after things when I come to see you. Faun, Sky's wife, does the cooking and house work, which frees up a lot of our time. The babe, Newly, is a delightful gift to all.

With the railroad just about finished, we may be able to visit back and forth often after next winter. The Indians are concentrating more on the army and the reservation problems than on we small homesteaders.

Next summer, you may be able to pay me a visit as it will be only a day by train. I am amazed at the progress the track has made, but I suppose it is partly due to the lack of opposition by the Indians.

It would seem that the whole family has had a busy summer and I am looking forward to hearing about it in detail.

Melissa was very helpful when I went to Vermilion. She made my disappointment in not finding you there, a bit easier. I was late in arriving due to an accident which she may have told you about.

Annabelle wrote saying she needed a few years to work on her career. I was disappointed; but I would not want to stand in her way and wish her every success.

Tell Dan not to leave until I get there and not to get into too much trouble.

Lovingly to all, Rod

It was a golden autumn. The crops had been slow due to the late rainy season, but they had escaped some of the heavy summer heat. There would be plenty of winter feed. Rod purchased a neighboring homestead after the man died of cholera and his wife decided to move back east, so there was plenty of grass to cut.

The rest of the furniture arrived. While others saw to the crops, Rod installed a sink with a pump above it in the kitchen. The new stove had a large reservoir and kept hot water on the side and back. Faun was reluctant to use it and cooked outside or in the sod hut. He finally convinced her to use the oven to bake bread and that the heat was easier to control. He also taught her how to bake a cake and decorate it when his twenty-second birthday rolled around. She was delighted. Though she rarely used the top of the stove at first, she used the oven often.

Onto the side of the house behind the stove, Rod added a bathroom and piped water that would drain from it and the kitchen stove reservoir into the tub and all water would flow into the orchard. Then, added a porch all around the cabin.

He divided the large room and made one area into a bedroom. The cabin roof and foundations were built with the idea of being able to add another story. The front would have white pillars and a deck upstairs just like he'd seen from the steamboat years ago. He would let his future bride help him plan this part of the house. Above the stove would be drying racks for vegetables such as beans and peas. The fireplace was at one end of the cabin and the kitchen stove at the other. This gave a more consistent heat in the winter time. One wall of the bedroom had large panels which would fold back and could receive the view and heat from the fireplace in the coldest months of the year.

Rod wanted a family. Perhaps Melissa or having Newly, Fawn, Witty, and Sky around made him miss more keenly, the pleasure of having an intimate relationship of his own. He would give Annabelle some time to see if she wished to remain an actress, but he was doubtful that she would ever change her mind about the ranch. Acting was too much a part of her. He would put his thoughts of her away and look for another bride, he decided.

He would ask Melissa to marry him but knew her too well to deceive himself. She would never be content just to live on a ranch. Perhaps Mary could help him find a bride.

In spite of himself, Rod began to let his thoughts stray more and more to Melissa. He knew she believed he was too young for her.

Sky and Witty tended the harvest. Rod and Fawn turned the cabin into a home. She sewed quietly while Newly slept in a cradle the men fashioned or played around their feet. As they worked, he taught her English. They often took time to practice the piano and harp. Sometimes Rod and she would stop for a cup of chicory coffee when she'd baked cookies or make a cake. He would show her a new dish to cook or she would introduce him to a new herb or root. She treated each thing as a delightful adventure.

One day Rod showed her how to make frosting using an egg beater. Fawn became so excited. She couldn't believe that an egg could turn from a liquid into a cloud. The first evening, she served egg whites on everything. She was almost in tears when they flattened out and became runny.

Fawn and Newly added humor and relaxation after a hard days' work. Rod was amazed how much was accomplished with a few extra hands and a cheerful woman. The Shepard's and their wives and families often gathered on Sunday afternoons near the pond. Sometimes he played the harmonica and one neighbor played a fiddle. They might dance, sing, talk, or just rest in the shade. Often the women came early and heated water in an iron kettle and washed clothing and bedding. More and more neighbors showed up and they talked of building a school and church.

Rod began to feel crowded but he eventually agreed to give an acre of land for a building quite a way down the stream. "I think we can use it for a school during the week and church on Sunday should a parson settle here."

"By dang we don't need a parson with you around Rod," Dolly said. When Rod tried to protest the others backed him up.

"If you'd sell me a plot for a store, I might just make a tradin' post with a house attached. Met me a widow woman who has a couple of kids. She said if'n we had a school hereabouts she might just marry up with me."

"I'll tell you what, Dolly, if you folks will build the building I'll furnish the land and material."

"Who'll we get to teach way out here?"

"Well, Sky and Witty here have had a good education. If they'd take the job and each of us gave a day a month to help out, we could have a couple of months of school in the fall and in the spring for the first year or two. I think the shepherds kids would like to attend and even some of the adults might like to learn to read and write."

People began to clear their throats. Before they could protest, Rod continued, "If all ages and colors are not welcome, I won't lift a finger to help or give any land. Anyone who is against this policy can take their children into Wall."

People nodded and began to make plans. "We can have a house raisin' for a school church and one for Dolly if you can get the timber here before the snow flies," Clyde said.

Rod said, "We'd best draw up some plans. Mackenzie's ranch is practically a town. He has a saw mill and a sizeable amount of lumber on hand. As soon as you men get the plans drawn up and lay out the foundations, we'll send the wagon teams to the railroad tracks just south of here and before we know it, you'll be pounding nails in your new school."

By October a post office was opened in Wall, a few miles from Rod's place. That, and the addition of the railroad nearby, gave Rod a feeling of being more connected to the world.

He was only two or three days on horseback to the Black Hills. Rod could hardly wait to be off, and yet, what would it be like to see the family without Annabelle? Would Melissa consider his proposal? She had said she longed for a child of her own. She had a teaching job in Deadwood already. Perhaps she, like Annabelle, would not want to live on a sheep ranch.

True, he had horses, cattle and buffa-cows, as he called his buffalo-cow combinations, but he was basically a sheep man. The dogs and shepherds took care of the sheep and Rod did most of his work from a horse, chasing down strays, rounding up a few horses and cattle, or riding fence lines. It seemed there was always a fence that needed repairing or a stray animal to be rounded up.

One day in September, Rod helped Fawn take the laundry down by the creek where they built two fires under kettles. She would boil the clothes in the kettles and raise them in a tub, then hang them on the line or spread the white ones on the grass for the sun to bleach and dry. A chemical reaction between the grass and the sun made the linens sparkling white. On wash day summer evenings, Sky and Witty would come in from the work and the group would have a picnic by the creek, then help her carry the clothes to the house. It made Wednesday's a special day for all of them and varied the activities.

After helping Fawn with Newly and the wash kettles, Rod saddled his horse and went to check the buffalo and cows. It was nearly time to bring them closer to the house in case snow fell early. They would need their grazing supplemented for the winter.

Suddenly, he heard Faun screaming and several shots.

"Let's go boy," he said to his horse and nudged him into a run. He pulled his gun, which he always wore when riding the range, and raced toward the creek. Soldiers were holding Faun and shooting at Witty.

The body of One Bear fell on the bank of the creek. When Rod came racing down the slope, the soldier holding Faun pushed her in front of him and began shooting at Rod. Rod jumped off the horse and darted behind a cottonwood tree. The two soldiers backed toward the creek using Fawn as a shield. The body of another lay near Witty.

One Bear had taken a bullet in the shoulder.

As they passed him, he rolled over and shot one. Faun reached up and clawed the eyes of the man dragging her. He let lose of her, shoving her into the creek before realizing he had lost his cover. Rod shot him. He fell face down into the water.

Rod fired three rapid shots into the air. This was a signal for help. It would bring in Sky. He would help One Bear if anyone could.

Rod and Faun rushed to him and found he had been shot twice. One grazed the side of the skull. The other wound in the shoulder was spurting blood from both the back and front. The bullet in the shoulder had gone on through. He was breathing. They tried to stop the bleeding.

"Is Fawn all right?" he whispered.

"She's fine. Aren't you Fawn?" Rod assured him. She bent over and kissed him. He sighed and lay back. Sky came riding up, jumped off the horse and began to work over the wound.

"Hold it," a commanding voice said, as Rod stood up. Rod's hand hovered by his gun belt for a moment before he slowly raised his hands and turned around. A Captain and a dozen soldiers were pointing guns at them. Sergeant Mike O'Leary who had come by in a snow storm last year rode up beside the Captain.

"It's Rod, Captain. This is Rod Anderson, the homesteader I told you about. He saved my life last year. If he shot these renegades, no doubt they were asking for it."

Rod was thankful to see him. "Hello, O'Leary. Good to see you. You too, Captain. As you can see, we had some trouble here."

The captain slowly lowered his gun and gave the orders for the others to dismount.

"It looks as though you've done a good deal of our work for us by killing some low down, desertion' possums," he said as he looked at the dead men. "Can we be of service to you?" He nodded toward Sky and Witty.

"Maybe you could bury those three," Rod said pointing to the bodies of the renegade soldiers.

"It would be our pleasure. What happened anyway?"

Rod shook his head and said, "Could we get Witty up to the house first. Then we can talk over a cup of coffee."

"Sure. I'll get the troop organized and be up shortly."

Rod said, "Let's take him up to the house Sky." Then he looked at Fawn. Her dress had been ripped from the shoulder to the waist. Tears rolled down her cheeks. She was holding her dress up with one hand while she bent over One Bear, talking to him in crooning sounds. Sky went to her and talked to her in gentle soothing tones. Putting his arms around her he held her for a moment. Then he smoothed the torn dress back over her shoulders, tying it with another scrap. Newly slept through it all in his cradle nearby.

"Sergeant O'Leary," Rod called. "Could a couple of your men help us?"

"Why yes, Mr. Anderson. We shore could. How can we help?"

"If you had a stretcher we could carry Witty, it might be easier on him. Also, someone could bring the cradle and help pick up the laundry, before it gets trampled on."

"I'll see to it, Sir."

"Thanks. Join us for coffee at the house when you get time."

The medic pack-horse was brought over and a stretcher unrolled. Fawn gathered Newly in her arms. Rod put his arm around her and led them home. She seemed to be in a daze. Two soldiers carried Witty up to the sod hut. Rod had O'Leary put the cradle down near Witty.

When the soldiers left, he took Newly from Fawn's arms and placed him in the cradle. She stood gazing at Sky who was still trying to get the bleeding to stop. Rod went to the kettle on the fireplace, dipped up a pan of water, wet a wash cloth and brought it to her, placing it on the table. Gently, he washed the bruise on her cheek, pushing her hair from her face. She must have fought back, he thought.

"Tell me, Fawn. Just what happened?" Rod hoped if she talked about it, it might relieve her of some of the tension. For a long time she did not answer.

Avonelle Kelsey

Still staring into space, she finally whispered, "I had finished the laundry and it was drying. I decided to go for a swim, like always. I had just finished putting my dress back on. One Bear had returned to the house and I knew he would be down soon. I wanted to get lunch started." She paused. "I must get lunch."

"No, Fawn. You don't need to cook now." Rod looked past her to see Sky watching them. "What happened after you swam?"

"They must have been hiding in the bushes. They slipped up behind me and grabbed me. I kicked and screamed. One of them hit me and I fell down. Then Witty came running from the house and they all began to shoot. He fell down. They killed him." She looked wildly around.

"No, Fawn. They did not kill Witty. See. His eyes are open. He's looking at you."

She turned to the bed and ran swiftly toward it, sobbing.

When Rod left, the three were smiling and holding one another. Just as he went out the door, Newly began to fret. He picked him up and said, "I'll take him for awhile." There was another cradle in Rod's house, plus diapers and bottles. From the smell, he would say that a diaper job was the first order of the day.

Rod stepped out of the Soddy onto the back porch, and into his house. After he freshened up Newly and given him some tidbits to eat, he went out onto the front porch and surveyed the scene. The baby was across his shoulder. Somewhere in a distance he heard the clang of pick and shovel. That would make six men buried on his ranch and all shot by him. He did not include the four Sky might possibly have buried. Rod felt a tremor run through his body. I hope to God this is the last time I'm forced to kill.

The captain came up with a couple of soldiers. They carried the laundry; all folded neatly, the stew kettle, and coffee pot. "Thought you might need these."

"Thanks. Come on in and put the clothing on the table."

The soldiers were surprised to see such nice furnishings way out on the prairie. They looked about in appreciation.

"That will be all fellows," the captain said.

Rod put Newly in the cradle and busied himself with making a pot of coffee. He put the stew on the back of the stove to heat. Out of the corner of his eye, he saw the captain looking at Newly. He tentatively put out a finger, which Newly promptly grabbed and began to chew. He laughed and blew a bubble when the captain pulled it away.

Rod put a stack of plates on the table and some silverware. He had purchased silver for twelve after he received his inheritance. It was a relief to have enough for everyone to be able to eat for a change. By this time the captain and Newly were sitting in the rocker. There was a damp spot on his uniform, but he didn't seem to mind.

O'Leary came in and joined them.

Fawn came in silently and looked at Newly and then Rod. "How's Witty?"

Avonelle Kelsey

She smiled shyly. "Be well, Rod." She said in English. Rod walked over and took Newly, handing him to Fawn.

"I think it's time Newly had his dinner, Captain." She saw the damp spot on the uniform and put her hand to her mouth to hide her smile. The men laughed.

Fawn had used the material Rod brought back to make herself several dresses. She did such a beautiful job, Rod ordered more material from the catalog so she could make shirts and pants for the rest of them. Her designs were unique. They combined the Native American fringed and laced designed with the dress of the white woman. The skirts were about a foot off the ground and sometimes flared like pants between the legs.

Fawn was tall and rounded. Neither fat nor skinny. Her walk was stately. She had apparently bathed and changed. Rod was proud of her as he and the men watched her walk across the long room and out the back door. She turned and asked, "Do you make me to supper Mr. Rod?"

"No, thank you. We have the stew and your bread. That will be enough for the evening. You take care of your patient."

She nodded.

"Her English is getting better." Rod said.

"She's a lovely young woman," the captain said. "She's lucky you were there. Whose squaw is she?"

"She's married to Sky, my hired man."

"Hope he appreciates her."

"They do," he answered and did not pursue their puzzled looks. "Who were those buzzards, anyway?"

"Well, there were eight of them originally. A versatile bunch of bastards. Sometimes they dressed as Native Americans all painted up, other times like today, they wore uniforms. We caught up with them once and got three of them. They were headed for the Badlands and we were trying to cut them off. They must have swung back north, or maybe decided to head for the Black Hills, when they ran into your place."

"You said there were five. We only saw three."

"Your man must have shot another one. We found him in the bushes. The fifth one, we haven't located yet, but the scouts are out after him. One of the scouts is a Sioux. After what they tried to do to your woman, my guess is he won't be brought back alive. Be on the lookout for him just in case he didn't hightail it. He's a big son-of-a-bitch."

Rod looked worried.

"Rod, "Mike said, "I told the captain about your offer of a job when my time was up. If you still have one for me, I'll be staying on. I can wait for the scouts and send them on to Fort Meade, Captain."

"You bet I can use you." Rod said happily. For a moment the thoughts of the death disappeared."

"Starting right now. The dogs, a shepherd and a neighbor who works part-time when I need him, are with the sheep, I suppose. In the excitement, I almost forgot about them."

"Just point the way and I'll start to work."

"You can have supper and some coffee first. Then I'll go with you. I just remembered, we left our horses down by the creek."

"Not to worry, Mr. Anderson," Mike said. "We put the tack in the barn and the horses are in the corral. The men brushed them down and gave them a handful of oats."

"Thanks," Rod said. It would be good to have this man working for him. "I missed you after you left. No one to cheat me at cards. Sky's too honest." He reached out and shook Mike's hand. The handshake told each what the other was feeling.

Capt. Spaulding stood up, knocking the ashes from his pipe into the fireplace. With a sigh, he reached for his hat and extended his hand.

Capt. Spaulding's grip was strong. "In spite of the shooting, I've enjoyed being here. My own little tike was not much older than Newly when I left last year. It's been a bit like being home. I'll write to my wife tonight about Newly and your homestead. Let me know how the buffalo experiment turns out. Might be interested in a breeding ranch myself. We're heading for the new Fort Meade being built east of Deadwood. The army, as you know, gave up trying to keep people out of the hills. We're now ordered to police the area until it can get its own law and order established."

"What about the treaty with the Native Americans?"

"God knows, we tried to keep people out, and we might have succeeded if gold hadn't been discovered. It's become an impossible task, unless we want to shoot our own people for years to come. I can sympathize, but like Custer, orders are orders. There's no stemming the tide of people's greed and lust, as you saw today. Reckon you know about that."

Rod nodded sadly.

"If you get to the Black Hills, look us up. To get to Deadwood Gulch you have to pass right by the fort. You too, O'Leary. I'm gonna' miss you. If you change your mind about the army, come see me."

Capt. Spaulding shook hands with O'Leary. Then slapped him on the shoulder, saluted and marched down the steps toward the waiting soldiers and his horse.

Rod and Mike followed him outside. "Tell the young woman, I'm sorry about today and that they weren't real soldiers. We didn't give them a headstone. Thought you'd just as soon not remember. Don't forget, there's still one of them loose. Keep a sharp lookout."

Rod could tell the Captain was reluctant to go back to a cold dark tent.

As he nodded his eyes scanned each bush and the horizon. The soldiers rode away. Rod stepped back into the shadows out of the lamp light.

Mike and Rod stood in the shadows of the porch, listening. There was a bird call like an owl near the barn. Rod gave an answering night bird call.

Soon Sky joined them on the porch. "Clem and I put the sheep in the fold. He'll sleep in the barn tonight and stay over a couple more days if you need him," he said quietly. "I heard what the captain said. Witty said he thought there were five. I scouted around and it looks as though the fifth one is headed for the Black Hills. The scouts trail followed his purty close. I doubt he'll escape. Just to be safe, after we milk the cows, I'll check things out again and keep watch tonight."

"Come inside, both of you."

"Sky, this is Mike O'Leary. He's a retired soldier looking to become a farmer. Reckon he can milk a cow or two for starters, eh, O'Leary?" The two men eyed each other for a moment, and then shook hands.

"Well, let me tell you, Son," he teased Rod. "Reckon I be milking' cows 'fore you was out of diapers. Just hand me a pail and point me to the back side of a cow."

"You go have some supper Sky and check on Witty and Fawn. Stay with them until I return. Get some rest for awhile. O'Leary, Clem and me will take the first two watches. I won't be able to sleep anyway. You tell Fawn to keep the door bolted on the inside and put the shutters across the windows. Not to let anyone in but us."

Summer evenings were still long. They had all been up since daybreak. The evening sky was beginning to light up the prairie with a bright moon. Rod thought of the lifeless forms buried on his land. O'Leary saw him shake is head as though to clear away the ghosts.

"Well, dog gum it, Rod Anderson. You promised me a bucket for milk. Am I supposed to put it in my pocket?" Rod knew Mike was trying to cheer him up. He smiled as he loaded his gun, putting extra shells in his pocket. O'Leary picked up his rifle. "I already put my gear in the hay mow."

"You can bunk in here," Rod offered.

"Seems to me a man can't be three places at once. The boy and I can take watches in the barn. You and Sky can take turns up here and the Soddy. The animals will give us some warning. The captain didn't want to worry you, but one of them men you shot was a brother to the one that got away."

Rod nodded, anxious to be outside. "The milk buckets are in the spring house. Who ever does the milking strains it and leaves the buckets clean. Drink all you can hold," Rod said as Mike headed for the spring house. It was always amazing to Rod when things got done without his ordering it, or doing it himself.

A scratching began at the door. Then a low whine that would turn into a howl if Rod didn't respond. It was Nellie's pup. She came in each evening to watch Newly if he was around and then go to sleep by the fireplace. The other dogs would stay near the sheep fold at night. Rod had let her become a house-hound. Now, he decided, Slurpy would be trained to guard Fawn and Newly from this day forward.

He closed the shutters on each of the windows and latched them inside. You guard the door, Slurpy," he said firmly.

In the Native American fashion, Rod had let him name himself. He loved to greet people with a lick of his tongue that left a wet slick of saliva. An embarrassed guest never knew what to do until Rod handed him a towel to wash his hand or face. Slurpy was still a bit clumsy and lovable but was growing fast. In a year, she would look like Nellie. She had already taken a place in Rod's heart.

Slurpy stood by the door as he turned the lamp low. Rod knew she was feeling abandoned. Before he slipped through the back doorway, he bent over and scratched the silky ears. "We'll be back soon. Go lie down and guard the house."

Slurpy rolled over on her back, trying to act cute. Rod laughed, scratched the white belly and slipped out closing the door, quietly. At the barn he called up to Clem.

"Come on in, Mr. Anderson. Them cows was getting' impatient to be milked, so I obliged them. Had myself about a quart to drink. Reckoned Mr. O'Leary is too late to milk. He can spell me come morning."

"I'm sorry Clem. You know what happened today?"

"Yep. Sky told me how you saved his whole family from a band of ruffians."

"That's only partly true. But that's no excuse for not feeding you. Slurpy is guarding the house and Sky is in the Sod. Let them know it's you that's coming. There's a kettle of stew on the stove.

The back door is unlocked. A fifth man escaped. You and O'Leary can keep watch down here and Sky and I will take turns up at the house. In the meantime, I'm going to take a little walk around."

Rod knew Sky was as good or better scout than he. O'Leary probably was too, but he needed to touch the animals and see where the trail was leading with his own eyes. There would be little sleep for him tonight anyway.

The signals that Sky and Rod used were bird calls, two in a row with the bird that sings that time of night or day. If there was more than one bird like an owl and a whip-per-will, they might answer with the other call.

Rod left O'Leary in the barn and took Clem to eat. Keeping to the shadows, he slipped up to the window, whistled and Sky soon stood beside him. Rod slipped inside to check on the patient. Newly sat on Fawn's lap cooing to his father. Witty's arm was tied across his chest and his head bandaged. He managed to smile at Rod. For a moment, Fawn's face looked startled, and then she tried to smile. "Thank you for to save our lives," she said starting to rise.

"It was Sky who gave me back my life. I'm glad to do the same for his family." It was beautiful to watch a family giving healing comfort to one another. Rod took a deep breath. The pain he felt about killing was lessened by the sight.

"We'll take turns being on guard tonight. I'll be up for hours anyway. O'Leary and Clem are in the barn. Clem's eating in the house. After this is over, I'll send him home. Try to get Sky to rest, Fawn. The scouts are on the trail. One is a Sioux. I doubt that anyone can get past him. It looks as though he's headed for the Black Hills. I'm going out to take another look. Clem will leave Slurpy on guard in the house. One man can't get past all of us, so rest easy."

He picked up Newly and tossed him in the air to hear his cheery, trusting giggle. Then gave Fawn's shoulder a squeeze.

"Rod," she said determinedly, "if Fawn be much trouble, she leave. Go away."

"No," both Rod and Sky said together. It broke the tension in the air. They smiled at one another, then, laughed as Newly seemed to catch the joke and join in.

No one got very much sleep that night except Newly. The next day the Sioux scout rode in and reported to Mike. The last of the outlaw gang had met his death, but not before he had killed another scout. O'Leary thanked him. The scout ate, slept in the barn that night and left early the next morning to catch up with Captain Spaulding and give him the news.

Rod checked often on One Bear. He was running a fever and talked in delirium; sometimes he shouted and Fawn or Sky comforted him. "Like you last spring Rod. His body is fighting and rebuilding itself. He will be better soon."

Fawn and Sky took turns sponging his body to bring down the fever. They spooned herb tea into his mouth often. From his medicine bag, Sky applied ground leaves and roots to the wound.

"I have plenty of help for the time being, Rod assured Sky when he worried about the chores. Clem will stay on a few more days if I need him and O'Leary is here permanently. If the shepherds need help, one of us can spell them from time to time. When Witty gets better, I'll head for the Black Hills. In the meantime, taking care of him is the most important thing you and Fawn can do." Rod knew that keeping her mind on Witty would help Fawn forget some of her own traumatic experience.

He called Slurpy and Mike. "Slurpy and I are going to show you the place and what goes on around here. I just brought the Clutter Homestead so you came at the right time. If you find yourself a wife someday, and have a mind to, there're a reasonably good house and barn there."

O'Leary got off his horse and presented the back of his hand to Slurpy. She gave it one of her watery licks and then presented her ears to be scratched. He laughed as he obliged her. "She's a winner, Mr. Anderson. Where did you get her?"

"For God's sake, call me Rod. I thought we had that out last winter."

"Well, if you call me Mike like you did last winter."

"Now that that's settled, Mike, I'll tell you about Slurpy as I show you the place."

For my eleventh birthday, my parents gave me a collie which I named Nellie. Nearly every year, she presented me with a batch of pups. There was no problem finding homes for them. By the time I homesteaded, she was getting old. In her last litter she had one pup, Slurpy.

"You remember Nellie from your visit last Christmas? She was killed by horse thieves last spring." Then he told Mike about the horse thieves, Two Bears caring for him and the coming of Fawn and Witty."

As they rode the range, clouds moved in. By noon a fine snow began to fall. They rounded up the cattle and moved them into a pasture near the house. Both Rod's barn and the Clutter barn were filled with hay. They found Clem and told him to help the shepherds lead the sheep home early. He whistled and a sheep dog began to round up the stragglers, heading them back to the fold.

"You can go home, if you want, Clem. It looks as though we may be snowed in for a couple of days. Everyone has been working hard and needs a rest anyway. Stop by the house and I'll give you your pay. The new dogs seem to be working well."

"Shore is." They all laughed as Slurpy joined them. The dog was fast but due to the puppy stage was a bit clumsy on her feet. One of the rams turned and pretended to chase her but she stood her ground.

"He's got the makings of a good sheep dog, if'n you don't spoil him around the house," Mike said laughing as he watched Slurpy roll in front of a sheep to turn it around. "I'll be dogged if he don't have a sense of humor."

Rod grinned. "He's a she. I've decided we need a dog to guard the house. You should see her try to herd buffalo."

They put the horses in the barn for the time being. Rod was glad they had made the barn roomy. There were four stalls for cows and six for horses. The new sheep fold was around the bend north east of the house. One end of the barn served as a bunkhouse.

"Slurpy, bring the milk cows home." With a happy yip she went racing off. By the time they finished with the horses, the cows came trotting into the barn.

"Hey, slow down a bit, girl," Rod said bending over to reward her by scratching behind her ears. She wagged her tail and closed her eyes, snuggling up to Rod's knees, laying her muzzle across them.

"It looks as though we're stuck with the milking again this evening, Mike. I told the shepherd's wife who makes the cheese we'd take care of the milk until the storm's over.

"Our family seems to be expanding. I may keep another cow for milking this winter. I'm teaching Fawn to make cheese and butter. She's fascinated with the churn. So many things seem like a miracle to her. When she sees the butter begin to form, she stops and peers at it, then laughs and churns faster and faster."

Rod went up to the house and gave Clem his wages. "May be Hattie could come over for a couple of days and give Fawn a hand after the storm, Clem."

"Sure, Mr. Rod. You wouldn't be trying your hand at match making would you?"

Rod laughed. "You caught me Clem. But seriously, with four or five men to cook for, Newly and now Witty being sick, Fawn has more than enough to do. We could really use her."

"I'll put in a good word for Mike and bring her along, soon as the snow lets up. Reckon the Hopi and sheep dogs will take care of the sheep on the Clutter place, but I'll ride past and double check things on the way home."

"Thanks Clem. Give my regards to your folks."

The storm lasted three days. It was an early freak storm and the snow melted off by the end of the week. Witty's fever lowered and he sat up. Sky was able to get back to work.

Hattie came the day after the storm ended. She was a large strong woman, nearing middle age, with a good sense of humor. She stayed several days, caught up on the mending, taught Fawn to make pies, cheese, made a couple of shirts, spun wool on the spinning wheel, set up a quilting frame and insisted the men help tie a quilt in the evenings, cleaned the house, and chatted with Fawn. They exchanged recipes, gossip, sang and made the place so interesting the men hated to go to bed at night.

Hattie was a widow and had two children. Mike was pushing forty, and to Rod's knowledge, had never been married. He received a small pension from the army and probably had very little money even though he'd worked hard all his life. When he was around, Hattie had more color in her cheeks. She let her hair fall a bit softer around her face. Fawn made her a dress. She looked like a different person than when Rod had first met her. When she left, they all felt sad. The house seemed quiet.

"Cheer up, everyone. I've asked Hattie to come back and help out a couple of days each week." Fawn clapped her hands; Sky and Witty smiled their approval and Newly laughed.

"Course, Mike wouldn't care if she didn't come back, would you Mike?" Rod teased.

His Irish eyes twinkled under his red bushy brows. "Well, it's a long time until next Wednesday, Rod. Seems Hattie and me are goin' to Wall to do a bit of shopping, if the snow melts by Saturday. Might even have us a fancy dinner out and come home by the light of the moon. That was what you wanted, wasn't it?"

Rod laughed. "You didn't need any help after all. Check on the mail while you're there and I'll bet Fawn has a list of things she needs. Next spring Dolly might have his trading post going."

"You wouldn't be expecting a letter from Annabelle, now would you Rod?" It was Rod's turn blush, although it hardly showed beneath his tan.

"If everything's under control, I'll be heading out about Sunday for Deadwood Gulch. May stay until after Thanksgiving. If anything goes wrong, you can send for me.

Avonelle Kelsey

A Ghost from The Past

The week before Annabelle left Deadwood for Denver, she was working in the store while Mary took an afternoon off to help at Calamity's hospital. A mining accident had claimed the lives of two men, broken bones and crushed legs and feet of five others. Uncle Mark and she had a break between customers and were chatting about her proposed trip to Denver. Mark was a handsome, romantic figure. Annabelle always felt flattered when he took time out to talk with her.

"Where's Dad?" she asked.

"He went to help the mule skinners bring supplies down the hill. Sure glad the road will be open before winter."

An old miner opened the door, peered around it and then stepped inside. His whiskers were scraggly, boots muddy, and clothing ragged. He smelled like a skunk.

"Pewee. You take this one Uncle Mark."

Mark grinned and went to wait on the old 'geezer'.

"Say partner, name's Bill Wade, Polecat Bill they calls me now. Went to town 'tether night. When I come home, had me a visitor waiting fir me. I run fir hit but t'was too late. He got me. Yes siree. Wouldn't come ter town again but another two legged skunk stole all my gear."

He probably doesn't smell too good at any time, Annabelle thought. She was trying to measure out several yards of calico for a miner who had followed Polecat Bill in, holding his nose. Another couple stepped inside, sniffed the air and left.

"Uncle Mark, could you take your friend into the back room? We can't stand it in here."

They both laughed and Bill good-naturedly followed Mark into the storeroom.

"What are you going to do with all this material?" She asked the miner as she measured out yards and yards of material.

"Gonna' cover the holes in me cabin fore winter." She smiled in amusement at the thought of the miner in his polka dot cabin.

Two little boys came rushing out of the storeroom holding their noses. "Willie, Markie, you can't play in here," Annabelle called. "Keep out of the candy jars." They headed for the door. "It's raining outside. Where are you going?"

"To the barn, it stinks in here."

Annabelle laughed and wished she could go with them. She put away her shears. Mark would probably furnish the miner a new 'Pilgrims Outfit'. He often did so and in return, had an interest in several small mines which were beginning to pay off. Also, Annabelle suspected he had a reputation as a 'soft touch'. She would miss all this. Not the work, but her family and Rod. Wonder what he's doing today? Sighing, she turned to the door to greet the next customer.

A woman was standing just inside the door. Annabelle had seen her in town once in a while and knew she was little Markie's mother. Someone said that she lived in an old shanty up the draw with a trapper-miner.

The miner had come to the store earlier in the summer and traded furs to her Dad for credit and supplies. "I want some calico fir my woman." He seemed to be bragging, but this woman didn't look very pretty, more like sick. Or, maybe she was pretty but her eyes were so sad and she was thin even under her raincoat. Her eyes seemed to be filled with deep hurt.

Annabelle smiled and asked, "May I help you?"

"A little sugar and flour please. I believe Sam Spencer has some credit coming on some furs. Will you please charge it to him?"

"Sure," Annabelle said looking in the ledger. She did wish Mark and her Dad wrote more neatly, like Mom and Rod.

Usually people took a paper sack and helped themselves, setting the food on the scales. The woman was so hesitant that Annabelle scooped a pound of sugar and about five pounds of flour for her, asking, "Is this about right?"

"Yes, thank you." The woman hesitated.

Avonelle Kelsey

"Is there something else?"

"Have you seen a little boy, Markie, here today?"

"Oh, yes, he and Willie were here about ten minutes ago. It's my guess they went to the livery stable to feed Willie's pony candy."

"I'll look for him there, thank you," she said and walked toward the door. There she paused, turned and said, "If Markie comes back, will you tell him to come right home, please?"

"Sure will," said Annabelle. As the lady turned and left she heard a gasp behind her and turned to see a white-faced, tight-lipped Mark staring after the woman who had just walked out.

The door opened and a group of ladies from the saloon came in. They smiled widely at Mark. "Hello, Mark," they chorused.

Mark rushed past them without speaking. They turned and looked after him in surprise.

"What in tarnation was that all about," asked Joseph as he came in the back door and saw everyone looking after Mark.

"Thank goodness you've come," said Annabelle. "This place is a madhouse. We need another clerk. Mom went to help at the hospital, Willie is running wild, a stinking miner is in the back room and now Mark just ran out on me," she complained. The twins are hiding out at the church to get out of work."

"I'm certain a little work won't hurt you, Annabelle. Be glad you can give your mother a few hours off to help needy souls. Now let's get busy and see if we can help these good people." His vibrant voice and smile welcomed the women who still waited just inside the doorway.

Mark had frozen in his tracks when he heard the voice of a woman from the past say, "Tell Markie to come home, please."

How often he had dreamed of going home to her, even yet, after all these years, the sound of her voice made his heart pound furiously in his body. It couldn't be her. She was dead, killed when her wagon train had been massacred. He had been a soldier. They were to be married on his first furlough.

He would have to see her just to make sure, or he would never be at peace again. Mark rushed out into the rain. Oh, yes, the livery stable, Annabelle had said. If she had a little boy, that must mean she was married. As he stood outside the door, the woman brushed by him with her head down, half dragging the reluctant boy.

"I'm coming, Mom," he said. "Just don't go so fast."

"You're soaked to the skin, Markie," he heard her say. Then the rain closed in around them.

It can't be, but it is. No one has a voice like Sylvia's. I must not lose her again, he thought desperately. But, perhaps she's not mine to lose anymore. The thought stabbed his heart.

She had been his for one beautiful day and night so many years ago. How could she be here? Had the Native Americans captured her? Had she waited for him to rescue her and he never came? I must know if she's well and happy. He was soaked and chilled when he finally spotted them again going up a gulch.

Just last week he had ridden down past miners claims and shacks. A woman was standing on the porch of one, shaking a cloth. For some strange reason he had thought of Sylvia and felt very close to her. Was this where she and the boy were going? Surely his Sylvia could not be married to that louse, Trapper Sam. Mark had been in Deadwood for over two years and knew everyone who had been there any length of time. He tried to return to Vermillion after the army but there had been too many reminders of Sylvia. He had felt strangely at peace here in Deadwood. Perhaps his body sensed she was nearby, even though his mind had not known.

As they climbed up the steps to the porch, they were met by an angry Sam. "It's about time you got here. Where'd you find the little rascal this time? If he was my son, I'd skin him alive."

Mother and son went past him without a word. He slammed the door. Mark crept close to the cabin and pressed his face to the window. Night had come early with the rain. Droplets fell off the roof and ran down the back of his neck, but he hardly felt them.

Inside an oil lamp burned on the table. The fireplace was burning low. "Send that kid out to get some wood. I've worked hard in this rain all day and come home to a cold, empty house with nothing to eat. How about you two earning your keep for a change?" The trapper shouted.

Markie stole a glance at his mother and started for the door. "Wait, Markie, come back and change your clothes first and put on a coat. Your cold isn't better yet."

Mark was spellbound. Suddenly the woman turned and walked directly toward the window with her head down. Tears were streaming down her face as she leaned against it, not a foot from Mark's face. She opened her eyes and looked directly into Marks. Then she sank slowly to the floor.

"Markie, bolt the damn door," Sam shouted. "If that no good Limpin' Wolf is back again tryin' to steal your Maw, I'm gonna' kill him dead." Markie bolted the door and ran to his mother's side.

"Git me that bottle of whiskey off the table and help me give her a snort. That'll bring her 'round quick enough."

"Mom, Mom," Markie wailed, "Wake up."

Sam poured whiskey into her slightly parted lips. For once he was ashamed of the way he had acted and muttered, "Sorry Sylvia, didn't mean to yell at you like that. Come on, wake up." He picked up her frail body and laid her on the bed.

She coughed, moaned and opened her eyes. Then she sat up and stared at the window. Sam took a shot of whiskey himself.

"What's wrong, Mom? Did you see Limpin' Wolf?"

"Reckon she saw that redskin," said Sam. As Sylvia flinched, he said in a more gentle voice. "You just lay still. I'm goin' out and catch me an injun." He grabbed his gun and started for the door.

"No," Sylvia cried. "I didn't see anything. Just didn't feel too well today. Guess the rain and mud got to me. You don't need that gun."

"I'll just look around while Markie gets the wood."

Mark could see that things were under control so he ducked around the side of the house and headed for home.

Sylvia had known Mark was in town so she seldom went there. Often she watched him in a distance when he drove a wagon or rode a horse in her part of town. Most of the houses and shacks were built against a hillside. The valley was narrow with a small creek which raged over its banks in the spring. As new stores, saloons. and hotels were built along it's beds, the land was filled in with loads of dirt and deep basements were constructed from the cut sandstone rock on the hillside. Main Street was two long rows of buildings, reaching from one bend in the river to the other; filling the small valley which ended in a cliff, with only a small outlet for the creek. Long stairs were built up the hillside where house hung in rows, one street above the other. To the south a road had been blasted into the hillside. Sylvia thought each time she sat on the porch the town had grown louder and larger. It was like a live thing. Big, rough, and at another time, might have repelled her, but it was such a relief to be away from the Indian village. Sylvia knew the Native Americans were battling a lost cause against the white man and she didn't want Markie raised to be killed as a warrior, perhaps even by a soldier's hand, or his father.

She had composed a letter for Markie to take to Mary Bennett in case anything should happen to her. He was not to let Sam see it. She had been going to mail it to Vermillion but when Sylvia found out Mark was in town and that Mary was coming, she decided to wait a bit longer to reveal her presence. From her porch she watched the town grow and often caught glimpses of the people she loved. This was reward enough.

Sylvia listened intently for a shot. She should not have gone to the store, but Sam would be angry if he returned and found Markie gone again. She had not seen anyone who might recognize her in the store, so had ventured in to inquire about him. There weren't many small boys his age in town except Willie. Her throat felt irritated. Sylvia coughed. She pulled a cloth from the pocket of her dress. The white turned to scarlet as it had been doing often recently. She tried not to think about what it implied. Soon, she must face up to her last ordeal.

Sylvia had promised Sam Spencer that if he would help her get Markie away from Limping Wolf, she would live with him for as long as treated Markie well and sent him to school.

He often reminded her; he had done so at great expense and risked his life for them. She would not marry him. She had pretended all these years that Mark was her husband and often escaped from the harsh reality of her existence into this day dream.

Living with Sam had been a hard bargain to keep, but anything was better than being a hated, white slave in the teepee of an old woman and her only son, Limping Wolf. Sylvia had lived in dread of the return of the warriors from battle. If he was killed, her life would pay for his death. Only Limping Wolf treated her with some kindness and stood between Sylvia and death. The other thing that kept the old woman from beating her was the fact that Sylvia was a doctor like her father. She learned from the medicine man and woman how to distil herbs and roots to ease pain. He was envious of her but also traded healing secrets with her. She combined these to ease the old woman's pain.

Limping Wolf had adopted Markie and was good to him. She again wondered if she had done the right thing in going with Sam.

Since coming to Deadwood, she had heard that nearly all the Indians were all on reservations. Perhaps in a couple of more years they would have been freed anyway, if she had lived. Many times she saw things in Deadwood that were as cruel as anything done by the Sioux. The Native Americans at least practiced what they believed. If the treaties had been kept and the people in charge of the reservations had been picked for wisdom instead of greed, it might have saved many lives on both sides.

Sam had ignored her sickness and said when he struck it rich in Deadwood, he would take them south to a warm climate where she could get well and Markie could get the best education. So far, Sam had not struck it rich. In fact, the only money left was the credit the on the furs which he had traded to Joseph Bennett.

Sam didn't know about Mark or that she even knew the Bennetts. He must not know.

Trapping was Sam's great love. Sylvia knew if he didn't find gold before long, he would want to go back to trapping. She also knew her health would not stand another bitter-cold winter.

The three years after she had been captured had gone by in a hopeless dream state. When the wagon train was attacked, Sylvia tried to hide as her Aunt, Uncle, and friends were being killed and scalped. She sat trembling under an overturned wagon, mute, waiting for death. Limping Wolf found her when he bent over to fire the canvas, grabbed her by her long gold braids and pulled her out. Almost worse than the dreaded blow of the tomahawk, was his cry of delight at seeing a beautiful young woman. Until Markie was born, she never spoke.

That she was pregnant didn't seem to bother him. He had used her body and took her to his Mother's teepee. She was beaten when she did not understand what was being said. One day she simply walked over a cliff. Limping Wolf carried her to the Medicine Man's hut. His wife, Healing Hands took care of her when the labor pains began. She almost died. After his birth she looked into the baby's eyes and spoke, "Mark. You came back to me."

With Markie's birth, she began to take an interest in her environment. She lay with him in her arms and for the first time tears streamed down her face. The Medicine Woman gave her herbs and tended her body. Finally, the blood ceased to flow and she slowly recuperated.

Avonelle Kelsey

Limpin' Wolf let her stay with the Medicine Woman until Mark could sit up. Then he came for her. The Medicine Woman talked with him in an angry tone for a long while, warning him that the girl had been seen by white men, and if she were to die, it might be reported. He must see that she and the child were treated better. No more beatings.

This time, he told his old mother that if she touched Sylvia again, he would put her out in the cold. She still berated Sylvia and ordered her about. Four fingers from her left hand were gone. Each time she lost a son in battle she cut one off. She looked at Sylvia with hate in her eyes.

"One for each of my sons who have been killed by the paleface," she told Sylvia often.

The Medicine Woman and Sylvia became good friends. It was she who made Sylvia's life tolerable all those years. Medicine had been Sylvia's great love all of her life. She was interested in the cures and herbs the woman used and learned a great deal from her. Gradually, she gained the respect of the Native Americans as she helped when they were ill and did her share of the work.

Her skills were recognized by Curing Wind, the Medicine Woman. "My father was a doctor, a white medicine man and I went to his school and became a medicine woman," she told the old woman.

After that she insisted that Sylvia have better food and time to spend with Markie as well as help her. They learned a great deal from one another. As Sylvia gained strength and confidence, she began to plan her escape.

Sylvia's father had been a country Doctor. When her mother died, Sylvia was nine. Her childhood ended. After her death she spent each summer in her father's buggy making house calls with him, or in his office acting as his assistant during operations. She cleaned, cooked, and did whatever she could do to ease the tiredness in his face and shoulders. She had gone away to college, determined to become a Doctor and practice with him, in spite of the prejudice against a woman in medical school.

Sylvia had been going to medical school back east when she received a letter saying her father had suffered a stroke and needed her. After his stroke, he had recuperated for a time and decided to train her himself. She became his assistant and sometimes he hers.

Sylvia met Mark for the first time when she helped deliver the twins. Mary was older than she but they had become good friends.

Many young men besides Mark were in love with the Doctor's daughter. He was shy. She waited for a long time for him to ask for a date, but hesitated flirting with him because she did not feel free to leave her father for a home of her own.

After her capture she knew Mark must think she was dead. He had not come for her. She also knew that any woman who had been captured by the Native Americans was treated as a whore and unclean by white men. Mark would stand by her, but she did not want pity.

She found the dress she had been captured in, washed and hid it. If she and Markie could escape, she would take it along and pretend they had wandered away from a wagon train. She would start a new life for them in Denver, perhaps. She watched and waited but Markie was never let out of sight. When she went for food gathering or roots and herbs, he was kept behind.

Sam Spencer came ever winter to trade with the Native Americans. She approached him with food and said under her breath, "Please help me escape. I am a white woman." When he approached Limpin' Wolf and wanted to trade furs for his woman, they nearly came to blows.

The next winter, Limpin' Wolf said he would trade her but not Markie, his son. She told both of them she would not leave with out Markie. They drank and talked for hours. Sylvia decided Sam was too drunk to know what he was doing and finally returned to the teepee to bed.

The old woman was sleeping soundly.

She heard a scraping sound outside the teepee. Sam was outside whispering to her. "Come quick. Bring the kid." She picked up Markie and crept outside.

Sylvia never knew how Sam had convinced Limping Wolf to give Markie up. When Sylvia acted restless, Sam often said he had seen Limping Wolf's tracks near the trapping cabin where he took them for the winter.

Sam's trapper shack was cold and lonely but Sylvia cleaned it up, washed the dirty blankets and sunned the buffalo robes. When spring came, she and Markie picked berries and swam in the creek. Her soul and body began to heal.

To her surprise, Sam was bashful in bed. That first day, she had heated water and made him take a bath, washed his clothing and trimmed his beard.

He had been a lonely trapper for nearly all of his forty years. Except when he had too much whiskey, he treated them with a gruff sort of kindness.

The second winter, Sam trapped a bear. He thought it was dead when it swung around and broke his ribs. Sylvia heard his signal for help. She rushed to his rescue, picked up his gun and shot the bear. Using the hide like a travois behind his horse, she dragged Sam back to the cabin. Sylvia had learned a great deal as a Squaw and Doctor's daughter.

She took care of Sam, but he was never quite as strong after that. It was while bedfast that he told her about the gold strike in Deadwood.

"If we go as soon as the weather breaks, we can be one of the first ones there." When he was well, they bundled up all of the furs and headed for Deadwood.

Several of the pelts had been traded for his 'Pilgrim's Outfit,' as the miners called the pans, picks, axes, etc. needed to get them started in the mining business. He had sold the pack mules and kept the horse. The last of the pelts had been sold to Joe Bennett and no gold was forth coming. Sylvia had been planning on seeking out the doctor and hoped to practice with him when the accident happened. .

She had been helping Sam at the claim. The air was crisp. Ice nearly covered the creek. The ground was hard to dig, but it had felt good to be outdoors for awhile.

The day was sunny and Markie had been playing nearby. Suddenly she looked up to see that he had crawled out onto the ice. It was not strong enough to hold both of their weights. She thrust him to the shore as her body plunged through the ice. Sam pulled her out. By they time they returned to the cabin, her clothing was frozen to her back. She developed a bad cold, which turned into pneumonia. Her chest pains and cough never let up completely. Then she had begun to cough up blood. Sylvia had hoped the warm summer months would cure her. She sat on the porch in the sun as often as possible. Sam would not face up to her illness and accused her of being lazy, not living up to her bargain.

The Bennetts moved to town that spring. She began to lay her plans. When Markie went to play with Willie, she worried at first and then realized that it would be better if he had friends when she was no longer able to take care of him.

Sylvia thought of all this as she lay in bed. With a sigh, she forced herself from the bed, made herself a cup of peppermint tea and began to cook supper. Perhaps it was best that Mark found out. There was no cure for tuberculosis. The dry air in Deadwood could have helped but dust flew everywhere. The rain and dampness made her chest feel as though it was on fire.

If she did not feel better by tomorrow, she would send Markie for Mary. Sylvia would have her ask Mark to leave them alone and let her die in peace. She had made a promise to Sam and must keep her end of the bargain. However, if she died, she wanted Mary to take Markie. She gave a sigh of relief and managed to smile as Sam and Markie came in again, soaked to the skin. Evidently, they had not seen Mark.

Sylvia was ashamed for Mark to see her in this condition. Even though she had no hope for a better future, her heart betrayed her and she felt the song of loves renewal within herself. She was not alone with the responsibility of her beloved son. For him it was not too late.

Mark stumbled and slipped in the mud as he went down the gulch. What could he do? It was too late. Why hadn't he looked longer for her? His head throbbed and he began to sneeze.

The last time Mark had seen Sylvia was five years ago. He had signed up with Custer's Army that morning and was on his way back to pack his gear. He would be leaving at daybreak.

Sylvia had been visiting with Mary and was just leaving the store. She almost bumped into him thinking of Mary's words.

"He's in love with you, Sylvia. Don't you think you should let him know how you feel before he leaves? He has no idea that you return his love. I think he's joining up because he can't stand to be around town and see the other men flirt with you."

"I haven't wanted to get involved because Father needs me so badly, Mary. You know that. But perhaps you're right. I'll speak with him."

Sometimes Mark had felt Sylvia was interested in him and at other times he thought she liked Sidney Potter, the son of the local banker. No woman would turn down a catch like him, he thought.

He was hoping that being out of town would ease his longing for her. "Hello Sylvia. You going to the barn dance tonight?"

"Well, if the right person asks me, I might," she teased with a twinkle in her eye.

"Guess I'd better not ask you then, I'd hate to be turned down," he began to turn aside.

"Mark," she said, taking hold of his arm, "I was only teasing. There's no one I'd rather go with than you, if you're asking me? In fact, I feel like a ride in the country and a picnic, it's such a lovely day. If you could get away, I was going to invite you along."

"You bet. How soon can you be ready?" His eyes were aglow and for the first time she looked directly into them. He saw what he had always dreamed of seeing there but never dared hope for. She stood on her tiptoes and kissed his cheek.

"The sooner the better," she whispered and raced home to make a picnic lunch.

His heart sang until he remembered that tomorrow he would be in the army for two years. How could he stay away for two whole years? What had seemed like an adventure an hour earlier, now seemed like a life sentence to hard labor. Would she wait for him, if he could get up the nerve to ask? Maybe he had misunderstood the look in her eye.

He rushed into the store to tell Mary and get cleaned up. Hurriedly he packed his bedroll and gear. Then he borrowed Mary's surrey. She smiled and shook her head as she watched the transformation love had made in this tall rugged brother-in-law. His blue eyes and reddish brown hair were touched by sunlight. He was taller than Joe, over six feet. Muscles rippled under his shirt from loading and unloading supplies for the store in which he and Joseph were partners. They would miss him, but he was nearly twenty-five and had felt life passing him by, she supposed.

Mary sighed. They would all miss him. Rod and Dan would have to take his place. If Sylvia's dad had not been so ill and needed her to run his practice, Mary was certain she would have been married to Mark by now.

Within the hour, Mark had loaded enough food from the store for a dozen people, hitched up Mary's high-stepping horse to her sporty buggy and went trotting up to the Doctor's home.

Sylvia had changed into a soft pink blouse with ruffles and tied a ribbon in her blonde hair. Usually she wore a uniform jacket of her father's or a severely tailored blouse with her hair in a bun. Today it hung down her back and she looked more like sixteen than twenty-three years of age.

Mark put his hands around her waist and lifted her into the buggy. He let his hands rest there and they became lost in the moment until Mrs. Jordan came by and spoke to them. She smiled and walked on when she realized the lovers were alone in the world.

They went swiftly down the street and out into the country lane that led from town and along the creek.

"Am I dreaming?" He asked.

"No Mark. Because of Father's illness, I've tried to avoid showing you how I felt. He's dying, but so many people need him that he can't quite give up his practice. I try to ease his load and take care of him. It would not be fair to you to make you wait. I thought we had plenty of time. Now Mary tells me you're leaving. I won't play games with you any longer, Mark. I love you, but I know that if you return my love and touch me, I'll turn to jelly." Sylvia had seen too much pain and sorrow to be bashful.

Mark turned the horse to the side of the road and into a grove of cottonwood trees. The leaves had just burst forth throwing a cool blue shadow underneath.

"Can I touch you now?"

"Please do," she whispered breathlessly as they reached for one another. The horse munched his way slowly toward the creek. Finally, they realized the buggy was setting at a precarious angle and they were about to go for an unscheduled swim.

"Do you think this is a good place for a picnic?" He murmured, kissing her again before she could answer. The surrey shuddered. Laughing, Mark picked up the reins and with a flick of the wrist, encouraged the horse to move to a level spot.

Mark carried the blanket and picnic basket behind a clump of wiliows, tied the horse loosely so he could graze, and returned in a happy daze to Sylvia.

She had spread the blanket on the soft velvety grass by the creek. He stood looking at her as she threw a pebble into the sparkling, gurgling water. Feeling his presence, she turned, reaching for him with a welcoming smile.

They forgot to eat. In the course of the afternoon, they made love, swam and made love again. The moon came out.

"Just once before I go, I would like to spend the night with you," he whispered. She nodded, with her lips against his bare chest. Neither of them could face the fact that in a few hours, they would be parting, perhaps forever, if a stray Indian arrow or bullet should find Mark in the next couple of years. So, they clung to one another, wrapping themselves in the blanket as the spring night became cooler. The horse waited patiently.

They tried to pretend the night would never end. In the wee hours of the dawn, they drove slowly back to town. "Will you wait for me Sylvia?"

"I'll wait for as long as it takes for you. Promise to come back home to me, Mark."

"If I get posted to a town or fort, could you leave your father long enough to meet me and get married?"

"I'll have my wedding dress ready. Mary can be my bridesmaid."

"Write to me every day?"

"Does Custer's army have an address?" They both laughed breathlessly. He was going to be late his first day in the army.

A ray of sunlight lit her hair as it flowed around her face in the breeze.

"I love you Sylvia and always will, never forget that." He hugged her fiercely and turned away.

She called after him, "I love you too, Mark. Come home to me soon."

Those had been her last words to him. Now, as he went up the steps to the back door he shouted, "A son. I have a son." Sam had yelled, "If he was my kid . . ."

Mark stumble into the kitchen. "Mary, Mary, I've found them. I've found Sylvia."

He was soaking wet and shivering but his eyes held a light that Mary had not seen for many years.

"Who's Sylvia?" Annabelle asked. She was a bit put out. The Drama Troupe had decided to leave in the morning and she wanted the attention of the family for herself this evening.

"Never you mind," Joseph said. "Mary, you see to Mark. I'll send Dan to his room for some dry clothing."

"Come with me Mark." He realized they thought he was delirious. Mary felt his burning forehead and led him into the bedroom. He began to shiver with cold. She slipped his wet shirt from his shoulders and left the room while Joseph finished undressing him and pushed him back on the bed, covering him with a warm feather tick and blankets.

Mary returned with a bowl of soup and a cup of strong hot tea. "Now, you sit up, eat this hot soup and drink the tea. Then we'll talk." He began to shake and realized that she was right. There was no way he could help Sylvia if he became ill.

Quickly, he did as she instructed drinking the soup from the bowl. Joseph came in with dry clothing and helped him slip into a warm flannel shirt.

For a moment he closed his eyes leaning back against the pillows. Mary thought he was going to sleep.

When Mark opened his eyes, the glow was still there. "She's alive, Mary," he said excitedly. "I saw her. She's Markie's mother and I, I think I may be his father."

Tears slid down Mary's cheeks. She had loved Sylvia as a sister. Could it be true? She felt the commanding pressure of his shaking hand on her arm and knew he must not get excited.

"Mary, was Sylvia pregnant when she died, disappeared? Did you know?"

Mary nodded. "If you'll lie back and relax, Mark, I'll tell you about it.

"Sylvia's father died shortly after you left. Apparently Custer was traveling in Sioux country. She received your letters when you were close enough to a town to mail them, but you did not have an address other than the fort near Denver. Both of us were pregnant. We didn't know if you were dead or alive half of the time. Her aunt and uncle were going to the Denver area where their son lived to open up a sawmill. Sylvia decided to go with them and have the baby quietly in the country, saying she was your wife. She did not want Markie to be called a bastard. When you returned, or she could meet you to be married, she would do so. She didn't want you to know she was pregnant until she met you again."

"Oh, Mary, what hell she must have gone through." His teeth chattered as the tears he had contained for so many years ran down his cheeks.

Mary was worried. Her eyes met Joseph's questioning look as he stood in the doorway, keeping the children outside and waiting to see if he could help. She felt Mark's burning flesh and nodded. Joseph turned and quietly told Dan to go for the doctor. "If he isn't in his office or at home, leave a note for him to come as soon as possible." Dan nodded silently.

Mark tossed restlessly and muttered at times, then again, he would talk clearly.

"Mary, will you go see her for me first thing tomorrow morning? Tell her; tell her, I'm sorry. Tell her I love her and make certain Sam is treating her right. She's sick Mary. So thin and she was crying, Mary." He sat up and tried to get out of bed.

"He yelled at her. He must not yell at my wife and son. Tell him. Tell him." Joseph came over and helped her get him back into bed.

"We'll take care of Sylvia," Joseph said in his deep reassuring voice. "You must rest so you can get well and help her yourself, Mark. Do you understand?" Mark relaxed and lay back. Mary squeezed Joseph's arm gratefully.

The doctor came and said Mark had pneumonia. He recommended steaming, sulfur plaster packs on the chest, and at least a week of bed rest. "Feed him fish liver oil and lots of good strong tea and soup. Mary, bathe him with cool water to keep the temperature down. Put a bit of soda in the water, but above all, he must rest."

By this time Mark was tossing restlessly, alternating between shaking from cold and burning up with fever.

Joseph and Mary took turns setting up with him.

Annabelle left in tears the next morning. She loved Uncle Mark and volunteered to stay.

Mary told her to go ahead. There was very little she could do. "He seems to be resting this morning and Claudette can stay with him while I rest. Melissa can come by after school and grade papers by his bedside, so there's plenty of help.

Melissa and Mark had begun to see one another. There had been a real affection developing between them. It was the first time Mark had taken an interest in any woman since Sylvia had died.

Mary was happy to hear that Sylvia was alive and anxious to see her old friend, but she sighed when she thought of the problems and heartache they would all be going through.

After the stage left with Annabelle and the Langrishe Troop, Mary took off her large white apron, called Willie, and went to see Sylvia. Only Joseph knew where she was headed. He volunteered to go with her, but she knew Sam Spencer from the store.

"I think it's best if I go as an old friend, not as an intruder who has come to rescue Sylvia," she said.

Mary put her hand on Willie's shoulder. They smiled as he drew himself up proudly when she continued. "Willie will protect me."

The rain had finally stopped but the damp air always made Sylvia's coughing spells worse. She spit up blood often during the night.

Sam cursed as he got his own breakfast in the morning. The sun shown through the window and fell on her face and chest. She closed her eyes and dozed. Markie sat by her and looked at his school books. Sam had told him to stay home with his Maw.

Markie liked his new teacher, Miss Melissa, and being with Willie, but he would not have left his mother alone anyway. As he pretend to look at his book, tears fell from his eyes. Markie was certain she was going to die. She was a doctor, why couldn't she make herself better, he wondered? He had promised her that when he grew up, he would study his Grandfather's books and go to school to become a doctor. Also, that if she should die someday, he would go to see Willie's Mother and take a letter that he had hidden under his mattress.

"You will not be alone, if I die," she had told him the last time she had been sick like this. "Do not let Sam keep you with him. Promise?" It was an easy promise to make, but he wasn't certain after he took the letter to Mrs. Bennett where he would go. Maybe back to Vermillion, wherever that was. His Mother had said that his grandfather had a home there but she wasn't certain what had happened to it. She would ask Mary, Mrs. Bennett someday.

"But promise, you won't tell Willie or the Bennetts until I talk to them, that I knew them?" He nodded and felt comforted that his Mother had a friend.

Little Willie was proud to show his mother the way to Markie's house. He chatted and Mary learned about her dear friend. "Did you know he can talk Injun talk?"

"Native American, dear."

"Most of the time she makes him speak English like us, but he's teaching me when we're alone. He says Limping Wolf was his father for a long time but his real father was a soldier that rode with Custer and maybe died with him. His mom's sick and don't say much, but she sure makes good cookies."
"Doesn't Willie."

"She does too. Almost better than your'n." Mary gave up and smiled. Very few people in Deadwood spoke the King's English. Most of them weren't English, for that matter.

So dear Sylvia had survived, she thought. How had it affected her? What terrible things she must have lived through. She looked at the tumble-down shack with the sun shining on it and shivered. The sun was warm but winter was in the air.

Mark still had Sylvia's last letter that caught up with him. It was yellow, tattered and worn. He kept it between the pages of the little testament Mary had given him when he left for the army.

Dearest Mark,

My father has died. I am going to Denver on a wagon train with Uncle Denny and Aunt Sally. It will be closer to the Fort from where you wrote last. I'll leave my where-a-bouts at the fort. If I can find a job at the hospital in Denver, I'll wait for you there.

When you get leave, come to me and we will be married.

All my love, always, Your Sylvia.

A report had come in to the Fort near Denver, asking for a cavalry guard to meet the wagon trains coming from the east. In his delirium the words kept going over and over in Mark's mind and intermingling with the scene of the massacre.

A wagon train from the eastern part of Southern Dakota Territory, the Vermilion area, had been massacred by an Indian rebellion from the new reservations. Mark had just returned with a group of soldiers for supplies. The letter from Sylvia was waiting for him. He sent a telegram to Vermilion to Mary and Joe. "Yes. Sylvia was on the way and probably on the missing train."

He asked permission to ride out to the site, saying that Vermillion was his hometown. The last wagon train had already buried the bodies in a common grave. From letters, books and papers they made up a list of passengers. These were placed in a trunk and sent to the Fort.

By the time Mark reached the site, the trail was cold. He road in large circles around the area for a week but could find no trace that could identify the direction the murderous band had taken and there were no survivors. His group was ordered to put down an uprising at a nearby reservation.

Now, in his feverish nightmares he imagined he could hear the screams of Sylvia as the warriors drug her away. By mid-morning his fever broke and he fell into a deep asleep.

As Mary and Willie walked up the gulch, sun glittered on the scattered, dark green pine trees. The red cliffs made a lovely backdrop. Many trees had been cut for wood and buildings.

It's almost winter, Mary thought, and Rod still isn't here. The house had seemed quiet an hour after Annabelle left. Her family was leaving, one by one. Dan would be next. He was too interested in politics to stay in Deadwood for long. What would happen to Claudette if Dan turned to Miss Taylor? Had she been wrong in asking them to wait a year to be married? Mary sighed. Troubles seemed to come in bundles.

Just outside the door of the shack, Mary paused. "Willie, don't say anything to anyone about them having lived with Indians. Ignorant people can be very mean about anyone who has lived with them."

"I know, Mom. I won't. Markie already told me to keep it a secret."

Mary knocked. Markie opened the door quietly and said, "Hi Willie, hello Mrs. Bennett. Mom's sick." Mary could see Sylvia across the room and walked inside past Markie.

The boys looked on in amazement. Sylvia turned her head weakly and the two women looked at one another. Then, Mary put her arms around her old friend and they were both weeping.

"Let's go outside Markie and catch leaves. Mom will take care of her. She's a good nurse."

When they drew apart, Sylvia wiped her eyes. Mary saw the spots of blood on her handkerchief and gown. She knew what they meant. Sylvia nodded silently.

Mary was trembling inside but tried to put on a smile. "It's so good to see you Sylvia. But before we talk, I'll make us some coffee."

"There's tea on the shelf above the stove. It seems to help for awhile. An old Indian recipe," she said with a wan smile.

Mary called the boys and had them haul some pails of water and wood for the stove. An iron kettle hung over the fireplace. Mary dipped up a pan full of hot water and found a towel and cloth. She took it to Sylvia's bedside and helped her bathe and change into a clean gown. Then she brushed her long blonde hair, tying it back with a bit of cloth.

Sylvia sipped the tea as she leaned against the pillows. Mary sat in the only chair. The sun had warmed the cabin.

"I'm sorry you didn't come to me Sylvia, but I'm here now. I'm going to send for the doctor." She could see Sylvia about to protest and held up her hand. "Sam Spencer does not intimidate me. I know you're a doctor, but I want a second opinion."

The question that hung between them needed to be answered so Mary plunged in. "Mark would have come himself but he caught a chill and is running a fever." She saw the alarm in Sylvia's eyes.

"No, he's going to be all right but the doctor insists he stay in bed for a few days. Then he'll come to you. He sent me to tell you. Do you feel strong enough to talk, Sylvia?"

Mary had toasted a slice of bread over the fire, found some jelly to put on top and set it by Sylvia. Her skin was like parchment and even though she was not thirty years old, there were streaks of gray in her hair. Round red spots glowed on each cheek as though a fever burned inside her. A feeling of dread gripped Mary. "Oh, God, don't let us lose her again so soon," she prayed silently. Sylvia had always been so vibrant, full of enthusiasm, teasing, and charming. She had her father's gift for healing everyone but herself, Mary suspected.

As if she read Mary's thoughts, Sylvia said, "I know I look a mess. The rain and seeing Mark so suddenly were too much for me, I guess."

"You look lovely," Mary lied. To give Sylvia a bit more time, she chatted on about how Sidney Porter had run away with the French Maid, Melissa was here teaching school, Rod was grown up and ranching not too far from here. Annabelle had just left to become an actress in Denver; Dan was a lawyer here in Deadwood and going into politics with a man who was running for Governor. Mary knew she sounded glib, but Sylvia had enough problems without hearing Mary's.

Sylvia nibbled on her toast and sipped the strong tea. A bit of color came back to her face.

Mary decided to get to the core of the problem. "Mark never married, Sylvia. After your death, or we believed you had been killed in the wagon train massacre, he lost a spark that I have not seen again until last night. After the army, he never returned home. He had been in the same corps that discovered the first gold in the Black Hills. When the territory was opened up to miners, he came here." Sylvia listened to her words, hungrily.

"Rod took his place in the store when he left for the army and continued to help out until he brought an old homestead and has become a sheepherder. He won't live in cities and Annabelle doesn't want to live in the country. They seem very much in love but at least they are wise enough to give each other time.

"Mark seems to have found a home here in Deadwood. I preferred to stay in Vermillion but with Joe, Mark, Dan and Annabelle wanting to move here, I had little choice.

"When we found a buyer for the store and Joseph joined their nagging, I finally gave in. The store here is making good money. Joseph is having a house built so they can enlarge it. We hope to move in soon and would like for you to come and stay with us until you feel better.

"Perhaps with the help of you, Melissa, and Claudette, we could make this 'hellhole' into a town after all."

Both of them laughed at Mary's daring language.

"Mary, it's been years since I've had anyone to talk with, so bear with me if you will. I . . . am going to die." She saw the tears roll down Mary's cheeks and reached for her hand. "Mary. I'm tired. If it wasn't for Markie's sake, I would have done so long ago. I know you don't need another burden, but perhaps he can receive some of the love from Mark that I missed.

"I promised Sam if he would help me escape from Limping Wolf and be good to Markie, I would live with him. He promised to help educate him. I will keep my end of the bargain as long as he keeps his. However, if I die, I want you to take Markie and raise him, with Marks help, of course. Will you do that? Please?"

Sylvia's voice rose and her chest heaved as she began to cough. The cloth was covered with blood when she lay back, exhausted.

Mary patted her shoulder and said, "You know I will Sylvia. We'd love to have both of you, but rest assured, Markie will be well taken care of. Why don't you just concentrate on getting well? Even Sam would want that."

She bathed Sylvia's face again and brought clean cloths from a shelf, tossing the bloody ones into the fire.

Finally, Sylvia was able to talk again. "Thank you Mary. You've always been a good friend. Mary, please don't let Mark grieve too long. Help him find another woman, like Melissa or someone. Tell him Markie needs a mother and that is the way I want it to be."

They talked, cried, and talked some more.

Sylvia was finally able to tell Mary about some of the terror she had felt when the painted warriors swooped down upon the wagon train. How they had shot her uncle, who was driving; the team ran away and the wagon overturned on her. She could not get free of it before Limping Wolf found her.

She waited for death but worse was the lustful eyes of his painted face. He had thrown her across a horse and tied her to the saddle horn. After they finished scalping and looting, they set off at a dead run. Every few miles a group would split off. Part of the time she was unconscious. She was bleeding and certain she would lose the baby, but they finally reached a secluded Village in the hills. An old Medicine Woman's wife befriended her. Limping Wolf protected her sometimes from his malicious mother who hated white people for killing her other sons. She had not spoken and lived in a daze until Markie was born.

"I'm grateful to Sam. He says he went to a great deal of expense and danger to rescue us. I know that Limping Wolf wanted to keep Markie and may still kidnap him if he gets a chance.

I suspect that I'm becoming a handicap to Sam, now that my consumption is worse and that he may go back to trapping. I had thought if I got well I could help at the hospital Calamity Jane has started, but I know I'm fooling myself. Mary continued holding her hand while she talked.

"I don't want Markie to see me die. Will you take him before that time, Mary? Just give me a couple of days with him. There's so much I need to say to him."

The boys had been playing under the house. When Markie heard his mother say she was going to die. He sat up and went pale. Willie tried to get him to come outside, but he shook off his hand and continued to listen. Willie felt they shouldn't be there, but he didn't know what to do. Then, he too became fascinated by Sylvia's story of Indian life. Tears ran down both their faces. When his mother asked Mary to take him, he buried his head in his arms and sobbed quietly. The voices went on relentlessly.

"Is my Aunt Hannah still alive?" I was going to try to contact her to take Markie until I found out Mark was in town, and then your whole family arrived."

"Your aunt is living in your old house, Sylvia. I'm certain she would welcome you with open arms. Your estate went to her.

"Sylvia, I have heard that sometimes the warm dry climate in New Mexico area can cure people with lung problems. When Mark is well, let him take you there and try at least." At her protest, Mary continued. "You owe him a chance to try to help you, Sylvia."

"I won't break my word to Sam," she said faintly turning away as tears slid down her cheeks.

Mary could see she was exhausted. "You rest now. I'll send help back and come again. Mark will be here as soon as he's well enough. He sends his love. Mary rose. At the door she turned and asked, "By the way, Sylvia, just what do you owe Sam? How did he help you escape?"

"Usually, when a trader, trapper or priest came, they penned me up. Some one was with me at all times. They took Markie away when I went outside camp so I wouldn't leave. Sam came often to trade for furs. Eventually, they let me see him. I deliberately flirted with him and when I served him food whispered, "I'll do anything to get away, please help me." He laughed and for a moment I thought he was going to give me away. Later he walked past me and said, "All right but you're mine.

"Only if my son goes and you promise to be good to him and help educate him."

"No."

"Yes."

"You drive a hard bargain."

The old woman came and pulled me away from him. I knew the tribe had been talking about moving as the white soldiers were getting closer. They were going to join a larger group and wage war against the whites. Custer's name was mentioned and the warriors bragged about taking his blond scalp. One grabbed me by the hair and said, "Like Custer's." He put his knife to my forehead. Limping Wolf knocked the knife from his hand and sent me to the teepee.

The next afternoon, Sam and Limping Wolf settled down by a tree and began to drink and talk. They argued for a long time and when I approached, Limping Wolf waved me away.

About dark Sam scratched on the teepee and called, "Let's go."

If we did not make good our escape, I knew I would be beaten and possibly killed, but I shook with excitement.

We were south of here on the edge of the hills. There was talk of our tribe going north to join other tribes and using the western side of the Black Hills to avoid the army. I think they were joining up with the group that killed Custer.

"I bundled up Markie. Before I left I took Limping Wolf's knife and stood over him trying to get up enough nerve to kill him. As I looked at his scarred face, I remembered all the times he had saved me from the others. Sometimes, when I hear Sam say he has been lurking around the cabin, I wish I had stayed. Markie and he loved each other." Sylvia paused.

"With the knife I slit the back side of the tent because I knew the old woman would try to stop me if I went past her. I would gladly have killed her." She paused again as if to gain strength.

"As you can see, Mary, I turned savage myself. I'm not the girl Mark once loved. Tell him that and to let me die in peace."

Then, she seemed to remember the story. "Sam was outside and grabbed my arm. He had already loaded the skins on the horses telling the Native Americans he wanted to leave by day break.

He had traded more whiskey to other warriors for pack horses, saying he had more skins to pick up along the way. He helped me on one horse and took the sleeping Markie in his arms. Quietly he led the horses through the woods in back of the village.

"He took us to his cabin where we stayed for nearly two years. After a bear attacked him, he brought his furs to Deadwood and decided he would find gold. He is good to us unless he drinks. Then Markie and I hide out until he's sober. His temper is violent when he's drinking but he has never hurt Markie."

She lay back exhausted. Mary straightened the covers around her shoulders. "I am having Dr. Adams come up and see you." She went to the door and called the boys.

"Is, is my mom going to die?" Markie asked. Mary took the child in her arms. "We'll do everything in our power to make her well, Markie, but sometimes we just have to trust in the Good Lord. Whatever happens, we'll take care of both of you. That's a promise. You stay with her and keep the fire going. See if you can get her to eat something and keep the water hot. She sets a great store by that tea."

"Yes, Mam. I've taken care of her lots of times. Thank you Mrs. Bennett. I'm glad you're her friend."

"I'll send Willie back with the doctor to show him the way." She looked at Sylvia and turned away quickly, kissing Markie again. He was old and wise for his age, like Rod had been, Mary thought.

Mary sighed as she hurried down the mountainside toward town. Both Mark and Sylvia sick. She was anxious to get Sylvia out of there and decided to send a note to the doctor with Willie. Mary would tell him to insist that Sam let Sylvia come stay with the Bennetts until she was well. Perhaps Sylvia could have a few days of peace before she died.

Mark was waiting for her. His fever had broken. He was dressed and sitting by the fire. "Did you see her, Mary? Was it really Sylvia? I didn't dream it, did I?"

Avonelle Kelsey

Mary smiled at him, "Just calm down. Yes, it's really Sylvia, or partly Sylvia."

"For God's sake, what do you mean?"

"Sit down, Mark," Mary said firmly. "We must talk." When she used that tone of voice, people obeyed. Joseph had left the door to the store open and came quietly in to listen.

She sat by him and took his hand, "Sylvia is very sick, Mark

"No. No. Not again. I can't loose her again. I won't." He stood, wild-eyed, trying to pull free.

Mary held on to his hand firmly and he sat down again, burying his head in his hands. "She has consumption and is dying." Putting her arms around him she held him tightly and patted his back. Sylvia had been her best friend.

"I've sent Willie for the doctor and I want to bring them here, but you must be strong Mark. She needs you now more than ever. She needs all of us. Let's not let her down again."

Joseph came across the room with two glasses of brandy. "Drink this Mark, and you too, Mary." She took it and sipped, feeling the reassurance of Joseph's hand as he patted her shoulder. He went back to the doorway so they could continue their talk.

Mark drank his brandy. Mary set their glasses on the bedside table. "Isn't there any cure?"

"The only one I've heard is moving south to a warm dry climate, provided the patient gets there in the early stages. Sylvia is in the last stages, Mark. I don't mean to seem cruel, but she wanted me to tell you not to grieve. She says she can't break her promise to Sam."

Mary told him about Sam's rescue and the story pretty much as Sylvia had told her.

"I'm going up there."

"Don't go off until you're stronger, Mark. We'll take care of her. Joseph and Doctor Adams can help me bring her here."

Mary looked at Joe and he answered, "The twins are helping Claudette. Dan is here, too. If need be, we can lock the door for a couple of hours." Joe put his arm around Mary, "You look tired, woman. Did you eat?"

"Mark, you and Mary sit down at the table and have some soup. You and Mark aren't going up there alone," Joseph said. "If I know Sam, he won't be giving in easy. Man like him will get his dander up."

Mary sighed. It was a relief to have Joseph take charge.

"So that's how the scoundrel got her to live with him," Mark mused. "Limping Wolf was killed in Montana. More likely, they would have let her go with Sam willingly to get rid of her at that time. That's probably why they let Markie go, too. The reservation Indians that fled had been told that if they gave up all white hostages and returned; there would be no vengeance taken. Sam probably knew that."

Then he paused and his eyes lit up. "Mary, is Markie my son?"

"Yes."

"I'm going up there and get them."

"Yes. Mark's your son. But he's going to need a Father. A live one. Think of him first. Even before Sylvia. She's been a Squaw and you know what people will say."

Mark's face was livid with anger. He would have struck anyone but Mary. "I never thought I'd live to hear you, of all people, say something like that Mary. If you were a man, I'd have your hide for it." He stood up but his voice ended weakly. He leaned against the back of a chair to steady himself, his anger spent.

"I want you to face that fact, as you will have to live with it when you rush to her rescue. She won't leave Sam and break her promise, even though it's killing her. She's locked out everyone but Markie. You and I are a part of a very hurtful past," Mary pleaded for understanding,

"You're weak now. If you'll rest a couple more days, we'll look after Sylvia. If not, Dan, Joseph and I are going with you."

Little Willie came rushing in. "Mom, Dad, Sam Spencer came back and tried to run the doctor off. Doctor Adams told him Markie's Mother is dying and that she has to go to a hospital. I'm supposed to get the Marshall and have someone come with a wagon to move her."

"That does it. I'm going up there." Mark went to the closet and put on Dan's jacket.

Joseph took over. "Willie, you go get the Marshall. I'll get the buckboard and bring it around back. Mary, you get some bedding ready. If you insist on going Mark, you can lie down in the back. You're in no condition to go anyplace. Knowing Mary, she'll bring her back here instead of the hospital. It would be a sight lot easier if both of you let the Marshall and I handle things?" It was a question as well as a statement. Both Mary and Mark were very determined people. He felt very little hope they'd sit and wait.

"With Sam up there raging around, Sylvia will need a woman. I'm going," Mary insisted putting on her coat.

"Me too," said Mark. "I'll meet you there," he mumbled and left as soon as Mary and Joe went to get ready for their assigned duties. It would take too long for them to get ready. He'd waited years too long already. At the stable he had a boy saddle his horse. Mark stopped by his room at the hotel for a gun. He felt weak by the time he climbed on his horse and began the climb to the cabin.

Doctor Adams was coming down the hill in his buggy. Sam was on the front porch waving his gun at him. "Don't send anybody up here to get her either, Doc. You hear. She ain't goin nowhere."

Mark rode his horse around to the back of the cabin, drew his gun and opened the back door. Markie was cowered beside the bed on which Sylvia lay. She opened her eyes wide at the sight of Mark and tried to sit up. He crossed to the door behind Sam, closed it quickly and placed a chair against a rung under the knob, securing it solidly. Sam was locked on the porch with a twelve foot drop on an incline. He slipped his gun back into the holster and went quickly to Markie and Sylvia, putting his arms around both of them.

"Please Mark; everything will be all right if everyone goes away. He'll calm down. Take Markie with you. He won't come after the boy. I'm dying anyway, Mark. It's too late for me, but not for Markie and you. Please go," she pleaded.

"I'll never leave you again, Sylvia." Mark watched as Sylvia had a coughing spell and the blood gushed forth on the cloth she held. She had a fever. Her fair skin looked like porcelain with two round spots on her cheeks. She was so thin he could see each bone. Her big eyes glowed brilliantly in the sunken hollows under her brow. Blonde hair curled round her face. If it wasn't for those eyes and that mysterious something about her that always held him like a magnet, he would not have known it was his beloved. He soothed her hair and held her, rocking back and forth making a crooning sound. She laid her head on his shoulders and closed her eyes with a little sigh.

Markie watched in amazement. He had a Father. Little Willie's uncle whom they had both often tried to emulate.

Out on the porch, Sam gave up pounding, kicking and cussing. He finally hung over the edge of the porch and dropped to the ground.

The back door burst open and Sam came in waving his gun.

"So this is what you do all day when I'm out workin' hard." He brought his rifle to bear on Mark.

"No, Sam, No," Sylvia protested and tried to get between them.

"Hold it, Sam," said Joseph's commanding voice from the doorway.

"Like hell I will," answered the angry, bull-bellowing voice. "I'll kill both of 'em and no one will blame me one bit." He cocked the gun and squeezed the trigger as Mark pulled Sylvia aside and they both rolled onto the floor. The bullet went through Mark's sleeve and tore a hole in the pillow. Feathers flew. Before Sam could fire again, Joseph hit his arm with his pistol, knocking the gun out of his hand. He cursed and screamed, holding it and repeating over and over, "You broke my arm."

"Shut up or you won't be able to yell again," Mark said leveling his pistol at Sam.

"Please don't kill him, Mark," Sylvia pleaded.

"Why shouldn't I? I heard about the promise you made him. Now Sam, tell Sylvia about that big rescue. Tell her Limping Wolf paid you to take her away because the Cavalry was coming. You probably told him they would hang him for keeping prisoners. Isn't that true? Isn't it? Tell her or do you want a hole in the other arm?" Sylvia sat on the floor holding her chest.

"Yeah, Yeah. I guess so, but I give up a good tradin' business, too."

"The fur trading business with the local Indians was all over anyway because they were being kept on reservations. You knew that. Tell her how you've kept her as a slave in isolation so she wouldn't know Limping Wolf was dead."

"All right, maybe so, but I treated them good."

"In this shack? There are holes in the walls that wouldn't keep a rat out, much less winter snows. Have you heard enough Sylvia?"

She nodded weakly and said, "Yes, Mark, quite enough."

The Marshall, Doctor, and several miners had gathered in the doorway by this time.

"I'll take over from here, Mr. Bennett," the Marshall said. "We have a couple of other claims against this jaybird, and with the kidnapping charges, we can send you up for quite a spell, Sam."

Sam began to grovel and beg, saying he had none-the-less helped then get away when the Indians would have killed and buried them both.

Joseph nodded to the Marshall.

"If you're out of town by sundown and never come close to any of these good people again, I'll let you go. The jail's mighty crowded with the likes of you and we're going to have to hang a few of the worst to thin it out. Take your choice."

"What about my arm?" he whined.

The Doctor said, "Joseph, maybe you'd best take the lady and Mark out to the wagon. Both of 'em are on their last leg. Mary's having a tizzy. Some of you fellers help him," he motioned to the miners to come in. "I'll take a look at this here skunks arm before he rides."

By sunset, Mark and Sylvia were tucked in bed in Dan's warm snug bedroom. Sylvia's hair was brushed and a bright pink ribbon to match a flannel gown was tied around her clean shiny hair. Doc Adams had advised bed rest for both. The preacher was coming to marry them after supper.

This had been a long day for all of them. It seems like a week since Annabelle left, instead of a day, Mary thought.

The Doctor took Mary aside. "If she should gain some strength back, Mark might take her to the desert, but I doubt that she could make the trip. She could go anytime, she's so weak. Ain't been eating right. You and your brother shouldn't get your hopes too high." He shook his head sadly and left.

Sylvia leaned back against the pillows. She was in a hazy comfortable state from the medicine the Doctor had given her. It was like a dream. Mark sat by her on the bed holding her hand and she was warm. Her chest didn't hurt.

Melissa came to the door, looked in at them and turned to the kitchen. Tears fell from her eyes. She had fallen in love with Mark.

Mary put her arm around her and gave her a hug. "She's dying Melissa. Maybe he can finally bury her in his mind."

She nodded and mumbled goodnight as she hurried out the door.

Melissa looked at the stars. Tears ran down her cheeks. She pressed her hand against her stomach. She had missed all her monthly periods since Rod put her on the wagon train at Vermillion. Her dresses were getting tighter. She had hoped that Mark would return her affections and understand enough to marry her anyway.

Before long she would have to marry someone or go away and pretend for the child's sake that she was married.

Rod would marry her but she cared too much to come between him and Annabelle. She sighed and with bowed head made her way back to her little cabin behind the schoolhouse.

Markie and Willie were excited about staying in the same house. Joseph closed the store for the evening. The family changed clothing for the wedding and gathered around the kitchen table for supper, waiting to hear the story and for the preacher to come.

The twins had been taking turns all day doing their usual eavesdropping and knew most of the story, but they loved secrets and smiled knowingly as Mary and Joe told Dan and Claudette the story, or as much of it as they felt they needed to know.

"Mark and Sylvia were engaged to be married. Before they could do so, he was sent to Denver with the Cavalry. Sylvia was on her way to meet him and be married, when Indians captured her. Everyone thought she had been killed along with the rest of the people on the wagon train.

Sam Spencer rescued her and Markie a couple of years ago. In return for this, he exacted a promise from her that she would live with him. What Sylvia didn't know was that the Indians were releasing all of their prisoners. They were being sent to a reservation so she need not have made the promise to Sam to stay with him if he would help her escape. Sylvia and Mark will be married tonight because she is very ill and will probably die within the week." Mary's voice faltered and Joseph squeezed her hand. He took over for her.

"The date they were married is no ones business. She will be buried as Mrs. Mark Bennett. Only a few people know anything about Sylvia. They will forget soon and I advise you to forget, too," Joseph said looking directly at the twins, then at Willie, Dan, and Claudette. They all nodded.

"Does that mean Markie can stay with me, in the same room?" The boys looked eagerly at Mary and Joe.

"Yes it does, Willie. Why don't you show Markie where he'll sleep tonight. We'll call you when the preacher comes."

Markie went to the doorway and looked at his mother and Mark. He was feeling both elation at having a father like Mark and sadness at his mother's illness. He just couldn't believe that she might die.

Her eyes opened and she looked at him with a quiet smile. "Come here Markie. I want you to meet your father."

"My real honest-to-goodness father?"

"Yes. Your real, honest-to-goodness, wonderful father," she said weakly.

Markie extended his hand to Mark, but Mark took him into his arms and held him for a long time.

Sylvia looked at them and said, "Now I can die happy."

Both of them turned and looked at her in protest. Markie said, "No, you can't die now, can she Father?" He rushed to her, throwing his arms around her, sobbing.

"You're not going to get rid of me that easily," she said stroking his hair. "Everybody dies, Markie. I can not get well. Your father will take good care of you. Your grandfather was a good doctor. You have healing hands. I hope you'll follow in his footsteps. Dr. Adams says he'll help you. Promise me you won't cry for me very often and try to become a good doctor?"

"I promise, Mom. I'll be the best Doctor in the whole world for you, if you don't die."

"I won't go very far away. Just remember I love you with all my heart. My spirit will always be with you. You have been the best son any mother could have," She ran her fingers through his hair and held him close to her.

Mary came to the door. "The minister is here."

The whole family filed into the bedroom.

Reverend Rout performed the short ceremony and left quickly.

As they said goodnight, each member shook Marks hand and kissed Sylvia on the cheek.

She smiled faintly. Her hand clung to Markie's for a moment and she said weakly, "I love you Markie. Goodnight." He paused at the door and looked back; her large luminous eyes followed him. He tried to smile bravely, but his lips trembled as he turned away to hide his tears. Mary waited outside and took him in her arms. Joe picked him up and together they took him upstairs to share Willie's bunk beds. Like she had the others and Rod, over the years, she sat with him in the rocking chair until he fell asleep.

Sylvia sighed and closed her eyes. Mark looked at his frail bride and took her hand in his large brown one, pressing it to his mouth. It felt cold to his touch. "Sylvia, Sylvia, are you all right?"

Her eyes fluttered open. She smiled faintly. "Dear, dear Mark. You've been through so much and now we must part again."

"No, No, Sylvia. I can't let you go again. I can't live through it again."

"You will and you must. You have a son who needs a father. Give me this one last gift, Mark. Take good care of him, love him for me," she whispered. Her eyes closed, again.

"Hold me, I feel so cold," she murmured. He slipped off his clothing and slid under the covers, taking her in his arms.

She leaned against his chest with a deep sigh.

After awhile she whispered, "Talk to me Mark. Tell me all about your life since I saw you last."

He talked until his voice became hoarse, hoping to tie her to this life. Along toward morning, she had a weak coughing spell, and then fell across his chest.

At dawn, Mary knocked lightly and opened the door. Mark held Sylvia in his arms, but her eyes were vacant. Sylvia was no longer alive. Joe led Mark from the room.

Melissa came in every evening to help with Markie and Mark. It was a couple of weeks before Mark recovered. His son's needs were the only reason he could see for going on. As the days passed. Sylvia's return seemed more like a dream to all of them, except for little Markie.

Sylvia was buried in the Deadwood cemetery. A single rose carved in the stone marked her grave.

Fate Twisted Lovers

It was November before Rod left for Deadwood.

"As the crow flies, it can't be more than fifty miles to Deadwood Gulch," Mike said.

He and Rod had climbed to the top of the highest knoll to watch the sun set over the top of Bear Butte. He drew a map in the dirt. The Black Hills are just about five miles beyond the Butte. If you continue straight west and follow the dirtiest stream in the country, old Whitewood Creek, it'll take you plumb into the heart of the hills. Lots of pilgrims coming and going so won't be any problem finding Deadwood.

"Even the soldiers stay away from the Butte. It's the Native Americans sacred mountain. You never see anyone and you never return, is the impossible tale. But I'd keep south along Rapid Creek. The railroad is aiming at a small city by it. So far it's just called the town of Rapid. Then, swing north past Ft. Meade.

The Captain should be there. Give him my regards. The Cavalry post will be a large one. If you have any horses to sell, that's a good place to take 'em. You can stay over night there and follow the old wagon trail up the gulch to town."

Mike had decided to set up a blacksmith shop at the edge of the property near the road and spring. He would help take care of Rod's animals and work for him when he wasn't busy. After he had saved enough money, he would buy up some land with Rod and become partners.

Old Dolly had parked his tinker's wagon across the road from Mike one day, unhitched his team and decided to quit traveling. His battered hat and faded clothing make him look like a tramp. Rod watched as he limped around the bend, past the spring house and came toward the house. He walked with an outstretched hand and went to meet him.

"Good to see you again, Mr. Dolly. Anything I can do for you?"

For the first time Dolly removed his hat. He's still a young man, Rod thought surprised. It must be his battered clothing and limping that made me think he was an old man.

"As a matter of fact, there is. I figure with Mike and his Blacksmith shop down by the road and a store beside it, we'd be might handy to you and the ranchers hereabouts. We'd have the makings of a small town. Could you spare a wee bit of land for a trading post?"

"Well, Mr. Dolly, you and Mike are welcome to stay as long as you like. But, I'm not hankering to have Anderson Springs turned into a city. You keep the place clean down there; you can have a spot, if you like. I don't want to sell my land, but I'm more than happy to share it. "

"As a matter of fact, some of us have been thinking of building a school/church where the creek leaves my property and were wondering if you'd want to build a permanent place by it. I'd let them lease the land for a dollar a year for the school and church. If the adjacent land comes up for sale, Mike and I are thinking on buying it. You might like to come in on the deal.

"I'd like you for neighbors. You understand?"

"Your words good enough fir me, Mr. Anderson. I'll make it worth your while. I just set here fir a spell and when they build the church/school, I'll build me a regular store."

Mr. Dolly had planted flowers, roped off an area south of Rod's dam and rocked it in, made a swimming hole for people to wash and bathe, as well as a little park under the cottonwoods. He always wore flowers in his hat and played the fiddle for wagon trains that passed on the trail going west. Word got around. People lingered and rested before heading for the Black Hills.

Rod often sat on his porch or opened the window to hear the music. Sometimes he picked up his harmonica and joined in. Fawn, Sky, Witty, and Newly wandered out on the porch. They took turns dancing with the baby while he giggled and blew bubbles.

Even Slurpy joined in the fun.

A widow and two boys stopped at the spring with a broken axle. They didn't seem in any hurry to leave. Rod often noticed her and Dolly working together. Until her arrival, Dolly had been content with his wagon trading post. Before Rod left, he asked if he could build a cabin large enough for a store and house, the other side of the property where Rod had already ordered the material for the church and school. Rod suspected there would be wedding bells when it was finished.

"Get your horse and we'll go take a look at it. We'll draw some plans up on paper in case one of us develops a bad memory. I'm happy to lease you an acre and some grazing rights for a couple of horses until you can afford some land."

Rod believed in a handshake and the word of people, but his father had warned him, "Get money or land down on paper. People tend to forget in favor of themselves. You'll save yourself from turning a friend into an enemy."

"That's fine by me. I reckon I'll frame it."

It was November; the first snow had fallen and melted.

Witty had completely recovered. They urged Rod to leave for the Black Hills and bring back a bride.

The evening before a few neighbors, the shepherds and their wives and Fawn, Witty, Sky, Newly, Mike and Hannah, who had married in September, came to see him off. Dolly and his new family showed up with a fiddle up as well. Faun, Rod and Mike accompanied him when they weren't dancing. Faun had learned several songs and to read notes. She played the piano, the harp and even strummed a bit on Mike's guitar. In teaching her, Rod had picked up a few tunes as well. Some of the others used kettles for drums and after Rod had told Sky about Dan's saw and drums, he made up a set. Everyone had a good time and talked of a Christmas dance.

"The Schoolhouse materials have been delivered. If you get the foundations in before the ground freezes, maybe we can have a house raising before Christmas."

Rod didn't know they had planned to have the school built by the time Rod returned as a surprise.

It was late when the party wound down. Dolly and family had come in his old store wagon and Mike and Hannah stayed in the bunkhouse. Early in the morning, Hannah cooked a big breakfast. The women packed him a large basket of food. He was taking a pack horse and Annabelle's horse with Christmas gifts for the family. They waved at him when he stopped on the ridge and looked back at his friends and ranch.

Rod smiled as he remembered his first lonely year. There must be a dozen people living on my land, he thought. A new bride wouldn't be lonely.

The creek made a rainbow-shaped curve feeding water to the roots of the huge cottonwoods on its edge; the new orchard still held a few golden leaves. His barn and haystacks were bulging with hay. In the corral roamed several horses. A dozen cows were in the barn lot and would be put out to pasture during the day unless a blizzard was blowing up. South of the house a small village had sprung up in tents in spite of his wanting to keep a quiet site around his house. On the far horizon nearly two hundred sheep were being led out of the folds.

The cabin looked cozy. Smoke rose lazily from the chimney. It was a peaceful scene. Rod smiled and rode down the other side. He was already missing it, he thought, or was he reluctant to face the Bennetts without Annabelle?

In spite of all the people he seemed to have collected on his ranch, Rod wanted someone close to him, a family. In his mind he tried to accept the fact that his future bride would not be Annabelle.

I intend to propose to Melissa, and if she won't have me, ask Mary to help me find a bride, he thought as he turned in the direction of the Black Hills. Mike had warned him, "Deadwood is no place to be lookin' fir a bride. There be fifty men fir every woman."

Rod liked women but knew that he would not want just any woman. He loved Mary, Melissa, and Annabelle in different ways but he was certain there was room in his heart for another. There would be regrets that his life mate would not be Annabelle or Melissa. Rod felt lucky to have shared his life with each of them.

Badlands: Prairie dogs had made holes and mounds across the prairie. Carefully he threaded his horse through these treacherous acres. A few buffalo wallows and the white flagging tails of antelope told him large animals were nearby.

At a little cluster of buildings called Wall he stopped for lunch. He was at the mouth of a gaping hole called the Badlands.

"Yep. That's where the bad ones go," an old timer said. "Whether it is Injuns or Outlaws. Pears ter me that more go inter that place than ever comes out."

One large wall of orange rock loomed up by the side of the town. Nature had weathered soft stone and clay of many colors as far as the eye could see. It looked like a fairyland and went on for miles. Small valley's with green grass in the bottom, now sprinkled with spots of snow, made it look even more unreal. Many formations resembled castle walls and turrets. They ran down both sides of the valley walls. Like looking into a huge cavern without a ceiling, he thought.

The old timer, an arthritic retired miner said, "That's what we call our place here, Wall. Can't mistake where we're to be found, eh? Gonna' build me an eating place here, watch the outlaws and sun come and go over the purtiest part of the world I ever seed."

Rod laughed and agreed. The sun was high in the sky. The black-green of the Hills loomed ahead, but they were not as close as they looked.

He was not following the windy wagon trail where most of the game had been killed for food. He saw Native Americans in a distance as he passed just north of the Pine Ridge Reservation. If he could get within a day's riding distance of the Butte by night he could cut northwest toward the fort and gap leading to Deadwood Gulch. He rode leisurely on into the night before placing his bed roll on a tarp and horse blanket and fell asleep. Annabelle's Destiny, as she had named it in a letter, was green broke. By taking turns riding his own Satin and her Destiny, he could help gentle him and make better time. The land was quiet under the rippling grass.

In a distance a shot rang out. Rod sat quietly on the top of a crest, watching. Down in the valley a group of men rode toward the hills.

Buzzards circled in the air overhead.

Rod rode cautiously. They had killed a buffalo, cut out the best parts, and left the rest to spoil. Suddenly he stiffened. Looking up, he found himself surrounded by Native Americans. His hand was near his gun.

Then, he raised his left hand and made the peace sign, palm outward. In Sioux he said, "Greetings Brothers." One stepped forth and raised his hand.

"We come to take our brother, the buffalo so the waste of his flesh does not poison the soil."

"That is good," replied Rod. "May the strength and warmth of the cow go with you."

Rod rode on; glad the flesh of the buffalo, as well as the bones and hide would continue to be of use after all.

The autumn weather continued. Trees gleamed golden yellow with sunshine in the draws where tiny creeks ran chuckling toward the Missouri. Cedars, sculptured in wiry twists and turns, smelled crisp and fresh. The trip was a vacation. He enjoyed each turn in the road and often paused at the top of a small ridge to study the lay of the land and listen to the sounds around him. When spotting homesteads he knew where there was a home, there was water and people as thirsting for company as he was for a drink. By the next evening he came to the creek which led into the hills. It turned from crystal clear to milky and then red to black with soil and chemicals. The water was poison. There was no life in the creek or near the edges. He decided to spend another night out of doors and visit the fort the next day.

That night he lay with his back against a log and kept a small fire going. The wind had come up. The stars were crisp and clear, but the temperature was below freezing. He pulled his buffalo robe off the pack horse covering his body and head. The next morning, ice was beginning to form along the edge of the creek.

I'll be glad to get to the Fort tonight if this freezing weather keeps up, he thought. Just hope it doesn't snow before I make the climb up the gulch.

The sun soon warmed up the day as the Indian summer continued. Rod played his harmonica. The closer he came to the hills, the more his mind began to dwell on the reunion with the Bennetts. He looked forward to seeing Melissa and meeting Claudette. By now, she seemed a part of the family to Rod. He had often wondered about the woman who had played his harp before he purchased it.

Being alone was always been a healing and planning process for Rod. Annabelle would not be a part of his life unless he moved to the city. I must face it. I must care more for my ranch than I do for Annabelle, or I would gladly give it up to be with her. He wondered what would have happened if he had never gone off to homestead. Would we have been married now?

Shaking himself out of his reverie, he began to study the interesting formation that loomed before him, Bear Butte, the sacred mountain. How long would the homesteaders leave it alone? At the foot was a small lake which reflected trees and sky. A wagon train sat by it. At least two cabins sent forth smoke on the far shore.

It took most of the morning to ride past it and go north along the hills to the trail which pointed the way to the newly built Fort Meade.

The soldiers who had been with Mike asked about him. He spent the night at the Captain Spaulding's house.

"In the spring my wife and family will join me," he told Rod happily. "Sometimes it's been tempting to take a squaw just to have a touch of female companionship, but now I'm glad I didn't." Rod nodded in understanding.

The next morning Captain Spaulding rode part of the way up the canyon with Rod and wished him well, telling him to stop again on his way home.

Deadwood City: Rod looked down into the gulch at the busy
town of Deadwood. The new road was muddy and rough. He
smiled to himself as he remembered the description of
Annabelle's piano and Mary's stove being lowered over the cliffs.
Noise echoed from the orange-rose canyon walls. Blasting, drills,
construction, shouting men, and saloons, gave a noisy welcome.
After the quiet of the woods, it took a bit of getting used to. He
rode down the dusty, long main street and could understand
why Mary referred to it as a 'hell hole.' Many of the building
from local, rose-colored rock were surprisingly large and elegant.
Next to them would be a miner's shack. Most of the new houses
were being built high against the hillsides. It was certainly
cleaner and quieter where they perched. Many had at least a
hundred steps leading to them.

Rod stopped at a barbershop to have a bath, shave, and
haircut. He put on a new shirt, pants, boots and a sheepskin
jacket. After looking in the mirror at his beat up hat, he went into
a store and brought a new one. A few of the men wore guns on
their hips but he decided to leave his in the saddle bag for the
time being.

Rod walked into the large Bennett store. The twins spotted
him first and ran to him, throwing their arms around his waist,
screaming in delight. They were fifteen and looked so grown up
he hardly recognized them, except they still talked and acted as
one. "Rods here," "Rods here," they shouted.

"Wait until Annabelle sees you." "She'll be sorry she took off for Denver," they giggled, each clinging to an arm as they led him toward the back of the store. Joseph came forward and hugged him so hard it took his breath away. Mary rushed in from the back with two little boys at her heels. He lifted her off the floor swinging her high in the air. Both shed tears of joy.

"Now that you're here, she'll never stop talking," Joe said.

"He hears me," Mary said tartly.

"Is this young man, little Willie?" he teased.

"Don't you know me, Rod?" Willie asked anxiously. Rod picked him up and tossed him into the air like he had when Willie was two.

"And who is this young man?" he asked.

"This is Uncle Mark's son, my cousin, Markie?"

Rod glanced questioningly at Mary, then reached out and shook hands.

"Hello. I'm very proud to meet a cousin of Willie's. I'm Rod."

"Willie, Markie, run and tell Dan that Rod's here." When they hesitated she laughed and said, "He won't go away."

Mary continued to hold his hand as though she wasn't certain. "I promise Rod will still be here when you get back. We're going to keep him a long time." She took both of his hands and looked at him. Joe watched in amusement. Rod always brought out the best in Mary. She glowed and chatted, seeming more comfortable with him than with her own children.

"Let me look at you. Why, you're as tall as Mark. Maybe taller and so handsome, isn't he Joe?"

Rod grinned and Joseph laughed. They looked at one another understandingly over her head.

"Let's all go into the kitchen and have some tea. I bet Rod's hungry aren't you?"

A beautiful young girl came out of the door as they entered the kitchen.

"Oh, Claudette, this is Rod. He's come at last."

She looked in surprise at this handsome young man. "Well, I can see why Annabelle is in love with you." Rod blushed slightly and she apologized.

"I'm sorry. As Dan can tell you, I'm not one to mince words."

"And I can see why Dan is in love with you," Rod replied. It was her turn to blush.

"I, I think that is past tense. Was, would be a more fitting word." Tears began to flow and she ran from the room.

"Oh, dear," Mary said. "I thought when all of you grew up, things would be so simple. Let's have our tea. After she has a good cry, I'll talk to her. We're getting ready to move into the new house in time for the wedding . . ." Mary stopped and put her hand over her mouth.

"Who's getting married?" Rod asked as the answer dawned on him.

"Sit down Rod. I'm sorry to be the bearer of bad news. It's Annabelle. We received a letter from her last week. You may as well read it, while I pour the tea." Rod turned white under his tan and gripped the edge of the table. He felt like joining Claudette. The words of the letter swam before his eyes.

Dear Mom, Dad, and Family,

I don't know how to say this, I'm so excited. The troupe from Paris, France I wrote you about has asked Sheldon and me to join them for the spring theater season.

You met Sheldon last summer. He was the male lead at the Langrishe Theater. We are going to be married and leave from New Orleans on a boat at the end of November. I insisted that I must come home to be married and say good-by to my dear family before we depart.

Don't stew, Mom. I've always dreamed of Paris. It will only be for a year. When I return, I'll be famous. You'll be proud of me and of Sheldon, too, of course.

I know you always wanted me to marry Rod. I thought I would someday, but I would never forgive myself if I didn't take this opportunity.

Only married couples can travel with the troupe overseas. Sheldon and I have a great deal in common and we work well together in the theater. I do not love him as I do Rod but I hope our love of acting will help us build the kind of wonderful life in the theater I've always dreamed of having.

We will be leaving for Deadwood next Saturday via train and then stage, and will be there in about five days. If all goes as planned, we may lay over two days in Cheyenne for a special performance.

Mom, I can't write to Rod. He's such a dear person. I'll always love him like a sister and perhaps more, but I just can't spend my life on a ranch and he wouldn't be happy in the city. We both must face that. He's been such a part of the family for so long. When he isn't with us, something is missing. I tell my self it's time I grew up and made mature decisions about my life.

This is something I must do. Please have Claudette help with the wedding. I won't have much time there, only three days.

Your loving daughter, Annabelle Lee.

Rod gazed at the letter. Mary sat down beside him and put her arm around him, remembering the night she found him outside her door many years ago.

Finally, he stood up. "I need to be alone, Mary. I'll be back," he headed for the door.

The twins had dropped back when Mary blurted out the truth. They followed him outside and watched the direction he took.

Rod climbed the side of the mountain until he reached a cemetery. He sat down by a freshly dug grave with a broken lily carved on the headstone. The sun was warm on his face as he looked out over the town. The cool Earth seemed to draw some of the misery from his heart. After an hour he got up and brushed the tears from his eyes. He and Claudette. Two of a kind.

Rod told himself that he had not expected to see Annabelle, yet the shock of facing up to the reality of never marrying her, finally hit home. He squared his shoulders and decided he was here with the family he loved and he would enjoy them. Yes, and even go to Annabelle's wedding. At least he could love her as a sister; it was not a total loss. The thought comforted him and a spring came back to his step as he started back down the hill.

"Hail, fellow traveler," sang out a voice from below. Dan had found him. They threw their arms around one another and pounded backs, laughing. Then, they stood back and admired one another. Dan's sturdy figure had filled out. He had grown several inches, his blonde hair gleamed in the sun and the dark blue eyes sparkled. Except for the eyes, he and Annabelle would not have passed as brother and sister. But then, every member of the family seemed to have different colored hair, except for the twins who had Mary's auburn hair. Joseph's was blonde like Dan's.

"God, how I've missed you, Rod. I hope I'm not intruding?"

"No, no, I'm at peace with it now. I was just coming down to see you. So, you're a lawyer?" Rod changed the subject as they walked down the old trail from the Deadwood Cemetery. "Melissa told me what a good lawyer you've become."

Dan laughed. "I have to be since there aren't many. Strangely enough, I'm getting a kick out of it. Maybe because the law's more personal out here. Melissa says it's because I can get by with more of my tricks."

Rod grinned and clapped him on the shoulder. "I'll bet you do. How is Melissa?"

"Great. She told us how you helped her escape Vermilion. Seems many people run away to Deadwood for various reasons. Like Uncle Mark." Dan quickly gave him a run down on Markie and Sylvia.

Rod nodded in sympathy. "I met Markie and Claudette, briefly. Whoever said true love never runs smoothly, knew what he was talking about," Rod said looking closely at Dan. He saw the emotion that flashed in Dan's eyes before he looked uneasily away.

"Is she the one you wrote about?" Rod knew how hard it was to talk with anyone about feelings, yet how helpful a sympathetic ear was in clarifying his own.

"Yes, no. I don't know. In some ways, I'm mad about her, but I'm like Annabelle, Rod. I'm ambitious. I have a chance to get into politics and this very influential man has a very attractive daughter. Claudette gets jealous when we work together. If I marry an actress or someone who has even sung in a saloon, my career won't get off the ground.

"If I give up my career for Claudette, I would probably end up resenting her, as Annabelle would you. Or, as you might if you moved from city to city following Annabelle's stage career. I'd get bored staying in one place the rest of my life. So, as you can see, we're both damned if we do and damned if we don't. I guess what I'm saying, now that I hear myself trying to explain my actions to you, is that I'm going to choose a political career."

"What will you tell Claudette?"

"I think she already knows and understands. She's upset, but so am I. She has said she'd give up her career for a home and family, but in this case, her past would always be dangled in our future."

"It would seem to me that after a few years, if you gradually built up your practice and went into politics, her past would not be so damaging and perhaps forgotten. After all, so far it has only amounted to a bit of acting and a few months of singing, hasn't it?"

"Perhaps. But right now I have an unusual opportunity to get into office on the tails of a successful politician. It may never be this easy again. I want to take this next year and give it all I have. Marriage to Claudette cannot enter the picture. If she wants to wait in the background and see if I should lose, there might be a chance for us, to put it bluntly. If I win as a territorial representative and he becomes governor, I'm on my way, providing we gain statehood as seems likely. To ask Claudette to hang around in this event would be unfair. In any case, single women do not stay that way long in Deadwood. There are too many men waiting to step into my shoes. I only hope you can understand, Rod. I know I sound like a cad." He broke off and looked at Rod anxiously.

"It's a hard decision to make. Only time will tell if it's the right one. Each of us is different so no one can make decisions for us," Rod said, patting Dan's shoulder in sympathy.

"From what I've heard and seen of Claudette, I can understand why you hesitate breaking off with her."

Dan nodded soberly. "Say, we'd better be getting back to Mom. She has a late lunch ready for you and a million questions." They both laughed and quickened their pace toward the store.

Dan changed the subject. "The store's really making money these days, so Mom doesn't have to work in it unless she wants to. Dad and Mark have built her a house out of the local orange rock. It's ready to move into.

"In the spring they're going to build a larger addition to the hardware store. Soon the whole length of Main Street will look like a city. This area has a future, Rod. If you should decide to move back, there's plenty of room and money for a person like you."

When they arrived at the house, the family was gathered around the table. Melissa hugged Rod and looked closely at him. She longed to comfort him as he had comforted her in the past. Mark came in, shook hands with him and sat down beside Melissa. They made a handsome couple. Rod felt a jealous pang and smiled at himself.

He looked around the table at his friends and family and felt fortunate. Mary was showing some streaks of gray in her auburn hair, but retained a freshness of spirit. Melissa must be about twenty-eight. In Deadwood she had taken off her glasses, let her hair fall loosely in a clip at her neck. Her dress was simple but not overly modest. She had gained some weight. It became her. All together lovely, he thought as their eyes met. They smiled at one another in a mysterious comradeship.

Mark looked up and caught this exchange. He, too, felt a stab of jealously as he turned to look at Melissa with new eyes.

Melissa noticed his glance and blushed. This was the first time Mark had really seemed to see her since Sylvia died.

Mary observed the 'by play' with a glad heart.

Dan sat down between Mark and Mary leaving the empty chair by Claudette for Rod. The two avoided one another's eyes and said very little as the family chatted and ate.

Dan soon excused himself saying, "I'll be back in a couple of hours to show you the town, Rod, if everyone will excuse me for now."

He took his handsome cowboy hat from the peg by the door, giving an exaggerated bow with a stage smile as they stopped chatting and looked at him. His eyes flickered over the family and rested on Claudette as though asking forgiveness. She nodded curtly and looked away. The smile left Dan's face and for a moment, the pain of his decision flared across his features. His face became pale and taut beneath the tan. Turning quickly, he retreated outside.

After an awkward pause, Mary turned to Rod. "All right. Don't keep us in suspense any longer. Tell us about the past few years and your ranch."

He looked at their dear faces and felt their sympathy, love and support. The heart-sickness faded away. Like his father, and grandfather before him, he could spin a yarn, adding color, smells and personality. Even Willie and Markie sat spellbound without wiggling.

He told them of Two Bears, One Bear and Fawn, of Nellie, the shoot-out, Mike, Old Plato, the animals from the sheep to the buffalo experiments he was conducting, Fawn's attack, the purchase of the farms next to him, down to the cabin, the shining copper bathtub and ending with the harp. He turned to Claudette when he heard her sigh.

"Oh, Rod," she breathed, "Your place sounds wonderful. I'm so glad you got my harp. May I come out next summer and play it?" She had leaned forward, fascinated, her lips parted in anticipation. The sadness was gone from her eyes. The warm quality that came over her face when she was happy, transforming it to one of exciting anticipation, took Rod's breath away for a moment.

He could feel her femininity surrounding him and pulling him toward her. When she reached over and patted his arm, he wanted to pick her up and swing her around the room. She made him feel the place he had just told about was the most enchanted place in the world. The family watched the two with various degrees of satisfaction, except for the twins, who felt that now Annabelle was out of the way, Rod would become their special property. They'd find a way to get even with Claudette for getting Rod's admiration.

After the snakebite, Claudette had put the countryside out of her mind. Now Rod had made her remember its special wild beauty and see it in a new way. She recalled the morning dew sparkling on waving buffalo grass, antelopes, and prairie dogs.

"Can we come too?" Asked Willie.

"He promised us," said the twins.

They laughed with Rod as he said, "Of course. Why do you think I brought the extra horses?"

"Oh," said Claudette, "I'm sorry to leave you with the dishes, Mary, but I'm late for rehearsal. Thank you for the story, Rod. I'd love to hear more about your ranch. Will you excuse me, please?" She smiled happily as she left the room. Mary and Joe looked at one another and he shook his head quietly. No matchmaking, she was being told. Mary only smiled.

"Since Dan isn't back yet, Claudette," Mary called, "perhaps Rod could walk you to the Waggoner." Joe shook his head and smiled looking at Melissa and Mark. They both laughed knowingly.

"What are you laughing about?" "Yes, tell us." The twins didn't want to miss anything.

Rod smiled and rose. "I'd be more than happy to walk with Claudette. Then I'll come back and help you with the dishes,

Mary. I miss our old talks." He bent over and kissed Mary's cheek. She smiled appreciatively.

"Melissa. Will you save me a couple of hours Saturday? I'm anxious to get caught up on everything that's happened to you since I saw you last. Whatever it is, it has agreed with you."

She blushed and nodded. Again Mark turned and looked at her closely as though surprised she was there.

Claudette appeared in the hallway wearing a deep-blue velvet cloak, a fur collar and muff to keep her hands warm. Rod reached for her guitar as she picked it up in the hallway. Their hands touched. They looked searchingly into one another's eyes for a long moment before going out.

"Can we come along too?" asked Markie as they started out the door. "Willie says you can talk Sioux."

"When I return, we have big pow wow." He said in Sioux. Markie and Willie cheered.

"You boys haven't done your chores yet. Rod can talk to you all week. Let him get settled in," Mary said.

Mark nodded, "I'd best unload that wagon. See you tomorrow?" He tipped his hat to Melissa. For once he didn't seem to be taking her for granted.

"Of course, Mark," she said a bit surprised.

Both Rod and Mary notice her coloring as she rose and began clearing the table.

Avonelle Kelsey

There's more going on there than I realized, Rod thought, as he opened the door for Claudette, gave the boys a Native American farewell and closed the door behind them.

Rod took her arm as they crossed the street. "Where is this grand theater I've heard so much about?"

"In the wintertime it isn't so much. Mr. Langrishe didn't get the roof put on, so we rehearse and use the Waggoner for shows during the cold months. Dan promised to help get a roof on, but hasn't made it yet. If I sing for Mr. Timmons, the owner of the Waggoner two nights a week, he lets us use the stage for performances on Saturday nights. On Saturday afternoons he closes down the bar and housewives can come to the matinees.

"I write the scripts, direct, and sometimes act in the plays. It keeps me busy, but I'm gradually getting a trained troupe and staff." She sighed a bit tiredly.

Rod glanced down at her. "Aren't you taking on quite a bit for one person?"

"No. Of course not. I love the theater," she said defensively. "Oh, you're right. Annabelle always said you could see right into people's minds. I am a bit tired, but I'm learning a great deal about myself." Her voice was deep and surprisingly clear. When she paused, Rod had a feeling that she had sung her words and he wanted to hear more. There was something comfortable and familiar about her. He waited for her to continue.

"There's no question about it. I prefer to write and let others act. I guess I had enough applause when I acted as a child, before my parents died." She paused. Rod squeezed her arm in sympathy. Claudette had an impulse to throw herself against his strong shoulders and bawl her eyes out. She shook her head slightly to clear away the feeling.

"I think I was stage struck and wanted to act to hang on to a bit of my parents. Suddenly it's clear to me that I want to go off by myself and write and write. I have a play in mind, as well as a story. In fact, I'm considering doing just that."

"It seems to me the world has more actors and actresses than it does good writers. You may be making a better choice for yourself in the long run."

Her cheeks had taken on a warm pink and her eyes lit up. She became a person of passion. "For the first, time I seem to know what I want and where I'm going."

"What else do you want besides being a writer?"

"I want a home. A husband. I never really had a home, except with the Bennetts these past few months. Mary and Joe have something special between them, like my parents, but they also have friends and a family. Something I've never stayed in one place long enough to have. Maybe I not only fell in love with Dan but with the family." She faltered and became quiet.

"My God, Claudette. Thanks. I think you've defined what happened to me, too."

They stopped on the street. He laughed and said, "That's why I'm not as upset about Annabelle as I should be. It was a shock to lose her, but when I sat at the table with the family, I felt comforted. I too, love the whole darn bunch. Thank you, Claudette." He laughed merrily and swung her around in a circle. She laughed with him as he set her on her feet.

Neither of them saw Dan standing across the street. He brushed a tear aside and turned away, stumbling over a wooden step on the sidewalk.

"Would you like to come inside?"

"Sure. I haven't seen many stages other than the ones Annabelle had Dan and me build in Vermillion."

She looked at him. "Oh, Rod. Annabelle is such a fool to trade the stage for you." She stood on her tiptoes and brushed his cheek with her lips.

"Oh, Claudette. Dan is such a fool to trade you for a political career," He mimicked laughing. Her laughter joined his. He pulled her to him and kissed her lips. They looked at one another surprised.

The door opened and Mr. Timmons appeared.

"I was just looking for you, Claudette. Everyone is waiting." He looked at Rod.

She introduced them and the men shook hands.

"I'll go along Claudette and talk to you later."

"Thanks for walking with me. I'll be singing tonight until eleven, if you want to catch my act. Someone usually comes and walks me home."

"I'd like that. Thanks. Be seeing you." He tipped his hat and departed.

Rod returned to the store and went to find Mary. She and Melissa had finished the dishes and were chatting away like magpies about the wedding. They were looking at Annabelle's dress which was stretched out over a chair. When they saw Rod, Mary picked it up to take to the other room.

"Mary," Rod said taking her by the shoulders, "I will stay, only if you don't let my being here make a difference. I am through feeling sorry for myself. That is a lovely dress. I'm glad for her sake that you're accepting Annabelle's decision as an adult. Now, what can I do to help?"

Mary gave Rod a hug. "Oh, Rod. Thank you. Mark and Joe are so busy in the store. Dan's in and out, but of no use to me. I could really use you tomorrow. I'm leaving all the old furniture here for Mark. He and Joe can come up here for lunch. We'll make it into apartments when the new store's finished, unless Mark gets married and needs it." She looked pointedly at Melissa.

"Don't look at me," she said coloring. "I know nothing of his plans."

Rod looked closely at Melissa. There was something very different about her. See seemed so mature. There was a bloom about her as well as the fact that her waist line had thickened. Perhaps it was her gown. It hung loosely around her body and was charming but . . .

She interrupted his thoughts. "Well, I'd better be getting back. Loads of papers to grade," she said as thought trying to get out from under his keen scrutiny.

"If you'll excuse me again, Mary. I'll walk back with Melissa."

They strolled along in silent companionship.

Melissa told him about her trip and the diary she kept which she wanted to share with Rod sometime. She did not mention the part she kept in her own special shorthand about the morning sickness that had developed on the way out, or the fact that she had signed the teaching contract as Mrs. instead of Miss. The students and parents stilled called her Miss Melissa because Willie called her that the first day.

They passed the Waggoner and Rod asked, "What about Claudette and Dan? Is there any hope for them? They so obviously love each other."

"You and Annabelle obviously love each other, but are you together?" She turned and took his arm, "Rod, she may have talked herself into being in love with that actor, but if I know Annabelle, she's in love with the idea of Paris. You could make her change her mind." She paused and looked earnestly into his eyes.

"Melissa. I've made peace with Annabelle's way of life and mine. Neither of us could accept the way the other chooses to live without loosing a valuable part of himself. Anyway we tried it, one of us would be the looser, much like Claudette and Dan I suspect."

Melissa listened to his quiet voice. "I believe you have Rod."

"What about you, Melissa?" He stopped and turned to her. Taking out his handkerchief, wiped the tears from her cheeks.

"Are you sorry you came to Deadwood? What is it Melissa? Is it Mark? Are you in love with him?"

"Yes, Yes, I did fall in love with Mark and I thought he was beginning to return my affection when Sylvia came back. I'm sorry Rod. I've turned into a sniveling sop these past few months. I declare, I've shed more tears this past year than I have since I was a kid.

"The schools just over this way. Would you believe that we have three classrooms and three teachers. One of us must live here to keep the fire going in the winter and since I live alone, I was elected. That way they don't have to hire a janitor and I'm always on time."

She was making a valiant effort to change the subject. Melissa would work things out in her own good time. Rod didn't press the matter.

Her classroom was rich in materials on the walls and bookshelves. It even smelled like her classroom, Rod thought. The lamplight fell gracefully upon her hair and her eyes lit up with their old fire as she spoke about education and the high school they were planning. In her own way, she was as ambitious about it as Annabelle was about the stage, Dan his politics, Claudette writing, and Rod ranching. She laughed when he told her what he was thinking and they fell into a long philosophical discussion.

"I wonder what the world would be like if society didn't have so many rules?"

"If there weren't rules, would we enjoy life as much? Even the Native Americans make up seemingly unnecessary rites to keep the game of life more exciting when they could have been free with abundant food and shelter, Father often said. Trouble and War are more exciting than peace. It keeps people from worrying about the meaning of life." She listened thoughtfully.

Rod added, "Somehow, we always want excitement from the normal but yet search out the familiar. You've said often enough that in education, most people want to learn formulas and conclusions instead of attempting new ideas and embracing failure. It's the need to feel secure, but only on the edge. A good trapper has to learn that each animal has its own pattern and territory. If he has only one set way of trapping, he may only catch skunks. The beautiful and wily fox will never come near the trap."

Melissa nodded and took up the conversation where he left off. "If education has value it's to learn to think and relate intelligently and wisely to any situation that may arise. The first thing parents want to know about school is can Johnny say his multiplication table or Suzy her ABC'S. If so, they sigh happily and the teacher's off the hook. They tend to think the problem of education is taken care of, just like religion is a safe harbor for their soul . . . People want simple recipes for living a tremendous adventure called life, then want to be rewarded in the end with heaven and of course their enemies punished in hell." She said with a rueful smile.

Rod watched her in puzzled silence.

"We've talked about how heaven as described from most pulpits would be a bore, but sometimes I'd like to have a rest from problems for a few days," Melissa broke off and looked away.

"When are you going to tell me what's bothering you Melissa? Are you uncomfortable because of the nights we spent together in Vermillion, or are you pining for Rev. Henry after all?"

"No, Rod. Those nights with you were some of the most memorable ones of my life. I'll never forget them. I'm not pining for Rev. Henry. It's . . . I have a few decisions to make. When I make them, I'll discuss them with you. Be patient with me please, Rod." She laid her hand on his arm.

"You're not sick?"

"No, my health is normal."

"Remember, I'm always here for you Melissa. Since Annabelle's going to be married, I'm looking for a wife. Anytime you want to become a rancher's wife, let me know."

"Why, Rod, are you proposing?"

"I'm available, Melissa."

"Thank you, Rod darling. You've made me feel better. Now, go home and let me grade papers," she said firmly.

She walked him to the door and kissed him on the cheek. "It's so good to see you again." He hugged her, but she pulled away. "Goodnight dear."

She closed the door firmly and leaned against it. It would be so easy to take advantage of Rod's kindness, tell him about their child she carried and let him take the responsibility. He deserved better. Rod must have a chance to win Annabelle back.

Melissa had come to Deadwood with high hopes. She fell in love with Mark and he was beginning to return her affections. First the bout with flu she thought she was having was actually morning sickness.

Then, Sylvia returned from the past. Melissa hoped to disguise her pregnancy until after Christmas. Bulky winter clothing made it easier. She knew Mary suspected but when she broached the subject, Melissa said, "I'd rather not talk about it just yet," and turned away.

This day has flown by on wings, Rod thought. He hadn't even visited with Mary. As usual, when he and Melissa began to talk, the time went by unbelievably swift.

The town was busy during the day. Rod was amazed to find it even busier at night. Saloons and restaurants were going full blast. Every place had several lamps and torches burning outside. The buggies and people all carried lanterns. None of the stores were closing. At the Bennetts apartment, Mary had left a note for him:

Rod--We eat at strange hours here. There's a pot of soup on the back of the stove. I'll be back soon. Help yourself. Mary.

He penciled: Gone to hotel, I'll catch Claudette's show and walk her home. See you in the morning.--Rod

Rod decided to freshen up. Mary had asked him to stay with them. The store apartment would be empty when they moved into their new house tomorrow. He had told her he'd wait until then and sleep at the hotel this first night. Rod returned to the Waggoner to have dinner and listen to Claudette sing.

She sat on a stool on the stage in an elfin costume with garlands of flowers draped around her waist and shoulders. They trailed to the floor. Her voice was low and mellow as she sang several quick, catchy tunes, but the miners requested ballads. The last one she sang was new. It was sad and lonely as her eyes searched the crowd. Rod suspected she was looking for Dan. Her gaze lit up when she spotted Rod. It annoyed him when the applause after each song turned into noisy hoots and whistles.

She changed her costume in her dressing room and came out to join him. They had a long leisurely stroll back to the store. It was nearly midnight and the family had gone to bed. At the door he hesitated a moment, then bent and kissed her goodnight.

She quickly opened the door and went inside. Rod walked back to the hotel with a quickened heartbeat and a thoughtful manner.

Avonelle Kelsey

Annabelle & Sheldon

Annabelle and Sheldon were on their way to Deadwood. About five miles out of town, the stagecoach broke an axle. The carriage sat at a slant.

It was midday so the sun was out. The ride had been composed of long cold nights, hot days and rough roads. Sheldon was in a disgruntled mood.

Annabelle was impatient but full of anticipation about seeing her family again and hardly seemed to notice his sulky face. The shows in both Denver and Cheyenne had been a success. She had been applauded with enthusiasm by the audience.

"Oh, damn," she said and slid out to stretch and look at the damage.

"We're going to unhitch the horses and one of us ride ahead to Deadwood for help. You can either walk or stay here," the driver informed them. "It's about five miles and may take awhile to get another axle and put it on."

"I paid to ride and I'm staying put," Sheldon said.

"Oh, come on, let's start walking," Annabelle said. "I can't stand to sit around all afternoon."

The other passengers decided to walk also. Sheldon grumbled but came along rather than remain in the country by himself and the shotgun riding cowboy who would stay to guard the luggage.

Suddenly, over the hill came two men and three horses. They gave loud war-whoops and swept down upon the group.

"It's Dan and Rod," screamed Annabelle dancing in delight. They rode up on a cloud of dust, jumped off and hugged her, each swinging her in the air.

Dan said, "We were worried when the stage didn't show up on time. Rod and I decided to ride out and rescue my fair sister from the Injuns, if need be.

"I'm so glad you did. We broke an axle."

Sheldon came forward, red-faced and angry. "Did you only bring one extra horse?"

"Oh, Dan, you remember Sheldon?" Dan pumped his hand and squeezed until he flinched. "Welcome to the family." He said with a mischievous twinkle in his eye. What a handsome wimp, he thought, as he released Sheldon's hand.

Rod shook hands and came away with an uneasy feeling about the man. He tried to tell himself it was jealousy. Annabelle had run to the large black horse."? Did you bring my horse? Rod, is this Destiny?" The stallion snorted and stomped as she scratched his ears and made crooning noises to him.

"Annabelle, don't you get on that thing," Sheldon said alarmed.

"Don't be silly, Sheldon. I cut my teeth on horses. Besides, the sooner we get back to town, the sooner you'll get rescued, unless you want to ride behind me?"

He looked pale and stepped backward almost falling over a clump of sagebrush.

Rod held Destiny and talked to him a bit, then helped Annabelle into the saddle. She pulled up her long skirts which showed high button shoes and a trim, stockinged leg. They rode off at a gallop.

"See you in town, Sheldon," she called over her shoulder. "I'll beat you both," she grinned back at Dan and Rod as they raced down the trail.

This is exciting and such fun, she thought. Just like old times, they were all thinking. But would I be willing to go back to the old ways full time, Annabelle wondered? She had rushed off to hide the excitement she felt on seeing Rod. He had changed from a boy to a man. Her blood was on fire. When she felt herself under control, she slowed down and the men followed suit. They began to laugh and talk about the old days back in Vermillion. On a hill outside of town they looked down into Deadwood Gulch. Annabelle said, "I'd swear it's grown in the two months since I left."

"We figure it's growing at the rate of a hundred or more people a month," Dan said proudly. "The train spur is almost to Rapid City now. Should be here next year or two at the latest. The men are hoping the first train is loaded with women.

"A train might make Sheldon happy," Annabelle said. Everyone became silent.

"Are you sure you want to marry that guy, Annabelle?" Dan asked.

"Sheldon's all right. He's just a city boy and not used to roughing it. On stage, we're a real team. I do intend to go to Paris." she said defiantly. As usual, Annabelle had made up her mind and nothing would stop her. Dan shook his head and Rod remained silent. Annabelle stole a look at his face but could not read his expression.

"Only married couples can go. Langrishe insists that it causes too much trouble when there are extra men and women to take care of. Besides, we have everything in common. That is the most important thing. More important than love." Her cheeks colored. She dared not look at Rod.

"From your letters, you've made the same choice, haven't you Dan, or are you willing to admit it?"

"Don't get nosy so soon, Annabelle. I'm sure Claudette will tell you all about it."

"That is the new house," Dan said pausing at the bottom of cemetery hill for her to admire the tall, three story structure perched against the cliff. The top two stories had windows across the front but the back was built into the hillside. The top floor faced the road above. There were porches and stairways to each level.

"Rod and Mom hung the curtains yesterday. She ordered the new furniture from back east. Looks pretty good. Only your piano was moved from the store apartment. We'll have the outside painted next summer."

"It's so tall," Annabelle looked at the house with three balconies across the front and around the side.

"An upside down house, Dad calls it. The top floor, where we enter from the street at the back, is the living room and kitchen. The bedrooms are downstairs on the second floor. The first floor in back is mostly storage and a spare room. Both an inside and outside stairway go down to the lower level. We even have a yard at the bottom," he said proudly. Not many homes in Deadwood had room for a yard because of the steep hillsides. "On the top of the mountain is the cemetery."

Rod glanced up at it and then at Annabelle as he remembered going there for solace the day of his arrival. He was excited and happy to see Annabelle but the hurt he had expected to feel was not as painful.

The family came pouring out of the house, calling and laughing as Annabelle jumped off the horse and went rushing to her mother. Claudette stood on the porch.

She looked at Dan who waved at her and said, "Just leave my horse here, Rod. I have to go to the office in a few minutes. Then her glance fell on Rod. He met her eyes, grinned easily and winked at her. She gave him a wide grateful smile and wrinkled her nose. Dan glanced at Rod but said nothing.

"Can we ride the horses back to the stable with you Rod, huh, can we," Willie and Markie danced about him. He looked at Mary. She nodded.

"Will you tell Joe and the twins that Annabelle's home, Rod?"

Annabelle turned and gazed after him for a moment as he put the two boys on his horse and rode Destiny himself. She caught her breath and turned to meet Mary's look of concern.

When Rod, Joe and the twins returned from the store, Melissa had joined the group. They were all listening to Annabelle tell about the theater and Denver at the supper table.

Finally she stopped to catch her breath and asked, "Claudette. How is your theater going?" I keep talking on and on and haven't asked about anyone here."

The happy chatter was interrupted by an angry voice. Everyone had forgotten about Sheldon. "Annabelle, Annabelle, where the hell are you?" His face was red and his manner belligerent.

Shocked silence fell upon the room as they looked at the angry man who barged into the room. Joseph was livid with anger. He stood up and said tautly, "Young man, we do not talk to the womenfolk in this house in that manner." Dan and Rod both rose to their feet.

Annabelle rushed to him. "Oh, I'm sorry Sheldon. I was so excited about getting home. I forgot about you. Time has gone so quickly. Do apologize to everyone and come in. You'll feel better after you've had something to eat and a bath," she chatted on hoping to restore his good humor.

"No, thank you," he said stiffly. "I'm going to the hotel," turned and stomped out.

Annabelle sat down, tense and white-faced with anger and embarrassment. Finally, she stammered. "I'm sorry. He's used to all the comforts. It's been a long hard couple of days. He'll be fine tomorrow."

"I had the stage send back a buggy," Rod said quietly, "So they got here sooner than they would have. Should I help him find a hotel?"

"No, let him simmer down. He was here last summer so he'll probably stay at the Franklin again." Annabelle wasn't too worried about Sheldon. He needed her for the act as much as she needed him. If only he hadn't embarrassed her in front of the family and friends; she shrugged.

"I think Annabelle must be very tired," Mary said. "Why don't you let Claudette take you down to her room before she goes to work? You can get caught up on girl talk. Tomorrow, everything will work out."

"Mom, you're a jewel. I am tired." She hugged each member of her family until she came to Rod. Then she laughed and hugged him, too. The tension lightened as everyone left to go about his or her own business.

The young women went out with their arms about one another's waist and their heads together, talking. Mary smiled. It reminded her of Vermilion.

"I can hardly wait for you to try on your wedding dress," Claudette said.

Mary watched them for a moment, shaking her head sadly.

Joe put his arm around her, "Now Mother. It will all work out, you said so yourself. He's probably a fine young man, but all the same, I'm going to have a talk with him before the wedding." Rod and Melissa watched with envy at the love that flowed between them. The twins slipped silently out of the room and followed Claudette and Annabelle.

"I have to help Mark," Joe said. "Rod, how about coming along and giving us a hand?" He really wanted to get Rod's advice about some land and cattle he was thinking of buying.

Dan went to his office and sat with his head in his hands. He did love Claudette, but he couldn't give up his career and just settle for being a small town lawyer the rest of his life.

Rod knocked on his door. "It's me, Rod. Can I come in or is two a crowd?"

"You may as well join the mourner. What do you think of that animal Annabelle's marrying? She doesn't take things lying down. You may win by default yet, old buddy, if you play your cards right."

"I have no intention of 'playing my cards right'. Annabelle and I both know we could never live the same kind of life and be happy. I for one intend to be content, if not happy. I want a home, wife, and children. When I find a good woman who will have me, I will love her and be happy. You and Claudette could work things out if each of you were willing to give a little, settle for a bit less than everything."

"I don't see you and Annabelle settling for less."

"Perhaps in her own way, she is. If you can't have everything, second best may not be too bad. Nothing will stop her from going to Paris, or wishing all her life that she had. My traveling urge left me when I rode with my father all those years.

"Now, I want a home, which I have, except I want to share it with a family of my own. I love Annabelle, but I find that I can love other women, perhaps with more satisfaction, if less passion. If I was riding herd on sheep and she sat home dreaming of Paris, how long would the fire last?" Rod became a bit self-conscious. "I'm preaching, sorry."

"No, I'm interested in what you're saying. God knows I need some new thoughts about the two women," Dan said and Mark nodded."

"From what I understand, Miss Taylor is intelligent, a social asset, and not altogether unattractive. Were it not for Claudette, you might find loving her very easy. If you told most people that you loved them both, they wouldn't find that acceptable." Dan listened thoughtfully.

Avonelle Kelsey

"Melissa and I were talking about the game of life. If there weren't rules to break, would it be a bore? There are other societies were the rule allows for more than one husband or wife."

 Dan nodded and looked a little less miserable. "I feel like a criminal around Claudette. Since you've come, she seems to have accepted it better and I feel jealous."

"I try to picture the kind of life I really want, leave guilt behind, and go for it. Hopefully, it won't be too weird for a conservative society. Sometimes it helps me to go off by myself for awhile. Usually, time makes the decision for me. Not making a decision is really a decision."

There was silence as Dan thought about what Rod was saying.

"Anyone home?" Mark called. "I saw your light on and wanted to invite you to a drink and listen to our Songbird. Claudette has a new ballad and promised to sing it for me. Eat your heart out old buddy," he said as Dan stood up.

"Come on Rod, let's tie one on. Have our own bachelor party. Let the mighty Sheldon buy his own drinks." They laughed and headed for the Waggoner.

"I notice you and Claudette seem to be hitting it off pretty well, Rod," Mark teased.

"Watch out or I may challenge you to a duel," Dan said as they walked along.

"At the risk of breaking up a good fight into thirds," Mark said. "I must congratulate both of you on your taste."

Their spirits rose with a couple of drinks.

Then the stage lights went on. A boyish figure in buckskins came onto the stage. She sat on a stool with her guitar. The room became quiet as she sang:

Lies

The other night it snowed and rained,
I thought the sky had cried,
But then the sun came out and said,
My thoughts to me had lied.
The rain the snow is like the dew
And like my love for you.
The changes that we dread today,
Will polish love anew.
The fog rolls out across the land,
In search of lovers true.
The words of love he said last year,
Today do not ring true.
Now winter winds and moonless nights,
Have let the stars shine through.
The fog the rain hid sparkling dew,
And a love that will be true.

The applause and whistles were deafening. When the miners liked something, they let the world know it.

A drunk jumped upon the stage and shouted, "She really does love me," lunging at Claudette. Before the bouncer across the room could get to her, the stage was alive with bodies. Dan, Rod, and Mark tried to push through. Claudette was being crushed against the side wall.

Rod stood on the table and jumped up, catching the balcony rail. He pulled himself along until he was above Claudette's head. Extending a foot to Claudette he shouted. She looked up and grabbed his boot, hanging on until he could pull himself up and over the rail of the balcony and she could get a grip on the bottom rung. She let lose of his foot and hung onto the rail while he swung himself over and pulled her up beside him. Her clothing was torn and she seemed to be in a state of shock.

Rod shook her gently until she looked at him. "Rod?"

"Come on. Let's get out of here."

"My guitar," she said, "and my beautiful song."

"It was beautiful, like you. I'll get you another guitar. Where's your dressing room?" She pointed down the hallway. They raced to it, closing the door on the bedlam.

In her dressing room, she began to shake. He took her in his arms and talked soothingly until she was calm.

"Your song is lovely. You took the words to the dream I told you about and put them together in a very special way. I'd like to hear it again.

"You were going to let me read some of the stories you're writing. Melissa says you should take them to the newspaper editor. He's printing some of her things and he would probably publish yours."

Her face began to get some color back and he could feel the tremors of her body subside.

Suddenly, the door burst open. In rushed Dan and Mark. "What's going on? We've been getting our brains beat out trying to rescue you and here you are chatting with Rod."

"Oh, Dan, are you hurt?" Claudette rushed to him. "Come, sit down and let me look at your poor head."

"What about me?" Mark asked mournfully.

"You too," she said as they laughed. She bent over their wounds like an old mother hen with baby chicks. Rod watched her, thinking how lucky Dan was to have this woman in love with him. He glanced at Mark who was watching her also. They looked at one another and Rod nodded.

"Dan, if you'll see Claudette home, the hero and I will wander off to our lonely bachelor pad."

They stepped outside and Mark said, "You know something, I don't think they'll miss us. We'd better go up to the house and tell Mary that she and Dan are all right, in case they hear about the fight. Let her know Claudette's in good hands, or she'll be sending out a searching party."

"You just want an excuse to see Melissa again," Rod said, searchingly. If there was something between Mark and Melissa, Rod didn't want to come between them.

"If Sylvia hadn't returned, I might have considered asking Melissa to marry me. She's such a lovely, intelligent woman, but now, I just can't get up any enthusiasm for life. Except for Markie.

I just go through the motions. How do you handle it so well about Annabelle, Rod? Or, were we all mistaken? Do you really love her?"

They went up the steps to the house and paused on the porch by an open window. The lights were low but unknown to them, everyone was awake.

The twins were delighted. One went from the stairway door near Annabelle and Claudette while the other slipped to the listen in on the men on the porch.

How often in the past week had he been asked about love, Rod wondered? It seemed to be the biggest issue at the moment. Perhaps they all sensed they were at the point in life where both careers and companions chosen were important crossroads. The action each person decided to take would direct the events of his or her future.

He wondered if there was an answer, other than just living and working out the knots as they appeared. We're all trying to make lifetime decisions with no experience to fall back on. None of us want to consult parents who might be able to give us good advice. Education had failed to teach the most important issue in life, human relationships. Religion mixed simple human values with so many myths and threats people couldn't sort out that which was truly valuable in everyday living. Rod shook his head.

Someone should write a book about decision making and love, he thought, as he wondered how to answer Mark. Not everyone was ready for his open viewpoint about men and women. 'Course most of his knowledge about men and women had come from Melissa and his father. There seemed to be a bit of his grandfather's preaching in him as well.

"I've been exposed to many kinds of love, Mark. When Mother died, Father nearly joined her. Eventually, he was able to love again. The human heart has room for many people, many forms of loving. Not just one. One form of love may be the burning flame that scorches our hearts and to which we rush blindly like a moth to a flame.

"True love may be the wisdom found in the ashes after the flame has died out a few times. Or, it may be an attitude of sharing and a willingness to forget one's self and ones own wishes in order to be intimate. A sharing of the deepest emotions of two human beings. Or, perhaps three or four people sharing a loving relationship, if our society allowed us to think in those terms," Rod said thinking of Fawn, Witty and Sky.

"Our culture has a great deal to do with our attitudes. Native Americans often have more than one wife because they believe each man and woman has a right to family, food, and shelter. Sometimes, there may be a lack of women and a woman can just as well have two husbands." He told Mark about Fawn and the identical twins.

"They have, in a very natural sense, adjusted to their environment. With houses and possessions, white people have moved away from nature and set ups rules and customs that may have fit their society yesterday more than it does today. If you love more than one person of the opposite sex at a time, it is unlawful, you're fickle, something's wrong with you. But the rule does not account for the strong sexual drives that make the race survive.

"Being a son of a father who was half Indian, I had the advantage of his attitude toward woman. He loved Mother dearly and I'm certain was faithful to her. It took him a long time to seek another woman after she died. When he did, I felt he betrayed Mother. He tried to explain the healing qualities of physical intimacy, but I refused to listen. Now I know it was not a betrayal but a healthy attitude toward life."

"You're a wise young man, Rod," Mark said, "but how does a person close out the past?"

"I feel we should cherish the good memories and try to build new ones every day. If life is a learning process, each new love will be a different flavor and a new adventure into its depths." He paused and smiled at himself.

"Grandfather, the Priest is talking again, Mark, but at the moment, I could love and appreciate any of the wonderful young women that live in this household." They stood talking on the porch, not realizing they had an audience.

Annabelle and Melissa had been downstairs talking and waiting for Claudette. They heard the men approach and stepped out onto the porch below to call up to them, then stopped to listen. Mary and Joe were waiting up for Claudette and talking of last minute wedding plans. The new fireplace was smoking. They had opened the window onto the porch to let out the smoke.

The twins had their ears glued to doors in the hallway and by the porch. They didn't want to miss hearing anything

Secret information was spilling out of everyone.

The women and Joe had become silent when the men walked up on the steps, expecting them to come in. In the silent night, Rod's voice carried distinctly inside the house.

There were many reactions to his words. Mary and Joe listened amused. They knew he was making a pitch for Melissa to Mark.

Annabelle felt a bit put out that Rod could take their love so lightly.

Melissa was proud of him as she listened to his thoughtful words. The twins giggled in triumph as though they had heard a dirty secret.

"You make a great deal of sense, Rod. I'll give it some thought. I had given up having a home like Mary's and Joe's after Sylvia passed away the first time, but now with Markie, I'll always have a part of her. Do you think Melissa would have me?"

Rod chuckled. "What the devil have you to lose? A cold empty bed and lonely days and nights, always living on the edge of your sister's life, not having a complete one of your own. Try to imagine a home with Melissa and Markie to come back to after a hard day's work. Just the thought of it makes me want to beat you to the schoolhouse to propose."

They laughed. "Say, we'd better get off the porch. We'll wake everyone. Apparently they're asleep after all."

Mary went swiftly to the door. She heard the twins bolt down the stairs to the bedrooms on the lower floor. She decided to wait and talk to them later. Mustn't let Mark to know they'd all been eavesdropping.

"I thought I heard someone," Mary said. "We're still up waiting for Claudette and talking. Come on in."

Melissa walked into the room. She was staying overnight to help with last minute wedding plans.

Mark looked at her with an open heart for the first time and caught his breath. He eyes met his. Her hair was down and there was a warm glow in her beautiful eyes; he felt puzzled at the unexplainable sense of mysteriousness that emanated from her being. Rod's words echoed and kept seeing mind pictures. He let his breath out sharply.

"What is it Mark?" Mary asked.

"Oh! Rod and I just stopped to tell you not to expect Claudette for awhile. There was a bit of a ruckus at the club. She's all right," he reassured her. "Dan's with her and I think they need some time together. I didn't want you to be worried and send out a posse."

Joe stepped out on the porch with Rod. He and Mark were now staying in the living quarters at the store the family had just vacated.

"Mary, would you mind if I talked with Melissa, alone?"

"Of course not. Isn't Rod with you?"

"Yes," he opened the door and said, "Rod, I'm going to stay for awhile. Why don't you go back to the store? I'll be along."

Joe said, "See you in the morning' Rod," and gave his arm a squeeze. Tears were in his eyes. This was the man he wished Annabelle was marrying in the morning.

Mary took his arm when Joe came inside and said, "Let's go to bed Joseph. Goodnight, Mark and Melissa." When he looked inquiringly in their direction, she gave his arm a meaningful squeeze and he followed her like a lamb.

Annabelle, on the porch below, had put on her cloak and waited, hoping to get Rod's attention. As he went down the steps, she whispered, "Rod. Rod."

The twins heard and dashed to their door by the stairway. They opened it a crack and listened.

"Wait a minute." She went swiftly up the outside steps and joined him on the street. "Walk with me for a minute. I can't sleep." She gave a shudder.

"You're cold," he said taking her small hands in his to warm them. When they came to a gas light, he turned her around and looked into her face. Rod knew this was a fragile evening for her and that she needed his strength. "What is it Annabelle?" He dropped her hands because the blood in his veins had begun to race madly when he touched her.

"I want to ask a favor of you, Rod. You can turn me down and probably will. I feel like a shameless hussy. I deserve it, but . . ."

He cupped her face in both his hands and looked into her eyes. Pure desire blazed in their blue depths. It both repulsed and attracted him. She saw his reaction and lowered her eyelids.

"Where does Sheldon fit into all this?"

"Please, can we go to your room and talk?"

Never had Rod felt such an uncontrollable desire for a woman. He asked himself if he should take this enchanting siren back to her home and ride out, or relax and enjoy it. If Annabelle had been anyone other than Mary's daughter, he would not have hesitated. Melissa had taught him to enjoy intimacy in a healthy way and not to feel guilt.

They walked swiftly down town and hurried up to the apartment above the store. Rod lit a lamp, added a log to the fire and turned to Annabelle with a questioning look.

The answer was in her eyes. Gently he untied the hood of her cloak, slipping it slowly from her shoulders, letting it slide to the floor. Rod felt a hypnotic, magnetic force settle over them . Where can I get the strength to turn away, he asked himself? Perhaps if Sheldon was a man that he admired, he could do it for his sake. What reason have I to turn away from a moment I have dreamed about all my life, he wondered?

Rod looked at Annabelle. She was wearing a light robe and gown.

He followed as she walked slowly into the bedroom, closed the door, locked it behind her and slid the robe from her shoulders. When she had played this part on the stage, the lights had gone out. Each night when she went home to bed, she completed the scene. Sheldon was never in the last scene.

"Rod, please treat me as a woman and accept what I am saying. I will marry Sheldon tomorrow and go away with him. In our own way, I feel we have enough in common to build a good life together. We're both spoiled and selfish and will do nearly anything to further our careers. However, I will never love anyone as I love you. I have given up all of my dreams of you except one." She hesitated and took a deep breath, "You are the one I want to make love to me for the first time. Will you grant me this one last request, Rod? No one but us will ever know."

He looked at her searchingly.

"Do I have to beg, Rod?" Tears streamed down her cheeks. This was an Annabelle he didn't know existed. Humbleness was not one of her stronger characteristics. His heart beat wildly. This part of his dream could come true. So often in the cold, lonely sod hut, he had lived through this night and anticipated it. Now he felt like an actor on a stage as he smiled and walked toward her.

Slowly he took off his suit jacket. She reached up and helped him unbutton his vest and shirt, watching every movement with glistening eyes and swollen red lips. Finally, he stood naked before her, a tanned, muscular, handsome man. With one finger she reached out and touched his chest.

"Are you certain about this?" He asked softly looking into her eyes as he reached for her.

"Yes, oh, yes," she whispered.

He slipped the straps of her gown over her shoulders and guided it down over her hips. Her body trembled as his hands touched her naked skin. For a moment their eyes devoured one another. Slowly they came together. In spite of his urgent desire for her, he wanted her first time to be the memorable sharing experience it had been for him. He carried her to the bed and kissed her tenderly but with passion.

"Since this is your first time, I want it to be a memorable one. Tell me if I hurt you, and I'll stop."

Annabelle had never dreamed her body could scream out for another person as hers was doing. My desire for the stage is a wilted flower besides this, she thought as she begged him to enter her. It was as though the world exploded in a flash of heat, pain, and light. They laughed and cried together.

With loving hands and lips they explored one another's bodies. Somewhere a rooster crowed. Hastily they made love again, rose, and rushed through the dawn to the Bennett house. One last time he held her and she clung to him.

"Thank you Annabelle for sharing this precious night with me," he whispered.

"Oh, Rod," she sobbed. "Thank you for understanding."

A door closed downstairs as she hurried inside.

When Mark asked if he could talk with Melissa alone, Mary smiled knowing and said, "Goodnight, see you in the morning," pulling Joe with her into the bedroom.

Melissa sat on the sofa. Mark stood looking at her searchingly. In this woman he saw all the wonderful qualities that he had seen in Sylvia and perhaps even more depth. Her large eyes never faltered as she looked into his open face. She let her love for him radiate from her whole being. Melissa was wise enough to know that the fate of her love and life with Mark was being weighted.

She waited, letting herself become vulnerable. At this moment she gambled her heart. Finally, he sat down beside her and took her hands. They looked at one another. He searched her face for encouragement. She blushed finally and asked softly, "What is it, Mark?"

"Melissa, I know I'm supposed to bring you flowers and do a lot of things before I ask you this. You know that I'll always love Sylvia in a very special way, but I need to get on with my life. Do something to give it meaning. Heal myself. Rod suggested that I visualize my future and put into it possibilities that would enrich my life.

"I want a home and loving companion for Markie and myself, more than anything in the world. The only woman I can see in the picture is you. I realize you have a career and I would never try to stand in your way, but do you suppose you could make room for us in your life?" She looked at him as she searched for an answer. When she told him, would he reject her? She held on to the moment she'd believed would never come.

"You may not love us now, but we would try hard to please you," Mark continued.

Melissa reached out and touched his lips as if to sush him. He kissed her fingers, then her hand. She felt warm and the scent of her filled his nostrils. Suddenly, his heart was beating wildly. He pulled her to him and kissed her passionately. When he realized she was responding, he was so surprised that he stopped and looked at her. Then, he laughed joyfully.

Melissa did not know why he was laughing. She had never heard him sound so free and happy, so she joined him. Their laughter rang throughout the house.

Mary realized she had not heard Mark laugh like that for many years. She sighed as she turned in Joe's arms and went to sleep.

Secrets & the Twins

The twins had given up waiting for Rod and Annabelle to return. They crept back upstairs to listen in on Mark and Melissa. They couldn't understand why everything was so silent and tried to peek around the corner of the door.

"Then it's settled. You will marry me?" He said and began to kiss her again.

When Mark and Melissa stopped to catch their breath, she remembered that she had a confession to make. He reached for her again, but she pushed against his chest with a sigh.

"Is something wrong?"

"No . . . yes."

Marks face turned white and grim. "Your aren't going to die?"

"No, dear Mark. It's nothing like that." She leaned over and kissed him until she felt him relax. Then, she sat back, brushed her hair from her face and looked into his eyes. "I have something that needs to be said. If, after you hear it, you still want to marry me, I can't think of anything more wonderful than to be your wife and Markie's mother."

Mark held her hands as though to give her courage and keep her from running away.

"About three years ago, I fell in love with a soldier. We loved much the same as you and Sylvia must have loved. Our time was short. We had one long lovely week together. He was to be discharged from service in the spring and we would be married when school let out. Jarel never returned. He was killed. I dared not let anyone except Mary, Dan, and Rod know the grief that I bore, or I would have lost my job. I longed to be pregnant and have his child, but no such luck.

"Last summer, Rod came back looking for Annabelle and the family. I invited him to stay at my house. During the night he had a terrible nightmare about a gunfight where he was forced to kill three men. I heard his shouting and ran into his room. In my attempts to wake and comfort him, I realized how starved both of us were for the intimate touch of a loving person. We made love. It was something both of us needed. He helped me get a wagon train to Deadwood and went back home. There were no commitments other than the strengthening of our friendship. I made him promise not to let out need for bodily comfort let me stand in the way of his love for Annabelle and to keep it our secret. Under the circumstances, I am going to break our promise." She sighed and pulled her hands out of his; stood up as though to gain courage and leaned against the fireplace with her head down.

Mark went to her turned her around to face him. "Tell me."

"Rod does not know it, but I am expecting his child. I love children and I want it. It may be my only chance to have one." Melissa glanced away. Tears ran down her cheeks.

Mark stared at her as though trying to absorb it all and she continued, "I came to Deadwood and met you I fell in love with you . . . you seemed to enjoy my company. When I realized I was pregnant, I decided to tell you and hoped I would not lose you, if you would accept the child . . . . Then Sylvia came back. Knowing you would never love me, I wanted the child more than ever." She faltered . . . he reached out, took her hands and squeezed them gently. It gave her courage to go on.

"You're the only one that knows who the father is. I signed my school contract as Mrs. saying I was recently a soldier's widow. During Christmas vacation, I plan to be called back east to the bedside of a sick relative and return with the child, if the school board will accept us back. If not, I will stay in the east. In the event anything should happen to me, will you see that Rod gets the child?"

The room was silent. The Grandfather's clock ticked and struck the hour of midnight solemnly. Melissa stood with bowed head; tears fell on their clasped hands. Mark let out a sigh of relief. "Are you through, Melissa?" She nodded silently.

He reached over and took her face in his strong hands. Tenderly, he kissed the tears away. She looked at him unbelievingly. Melissa, can't you see that Rod would welcome you both? He would never turn his back on you. Do you have the right to deprive him of his child?"

"No! Rod is young. He must have his chance to fall in love and marry someone his own age. I care too much for him to force myself on him. Perhaps, I'm selfish and want that opportunity, too."

Melissa's tone softened. She turned to the fireplace and stood gazing into the glowing embers as if they might hold the answers to her feeling of desolation.

Suddenly, she felt strong arms around her. Mark pulled her to him. He stroked her hair tipping her head back.

"My lovely, wonderful woman. Don't you see? If you can accept my love child, I can yours. Especially a son of Rods. I love you, want you and need you. The community and school need you. Now, will you marry me?"

She looked searchingly into his eyes. The answer she wanted to see was there. "Yes, by Jove, I will marry you Mark Bennett."

"Tomorrow, after Annabelle gets married?"

"Yes, tomorrow, today," she murmured as their lips met.

They finally parted so he could go back to the apartment and get ready for the big day. Melissa lay down on the couch and went to sleep.

When Mary entered the parlor in the morning, she found Melissa on the couch and the twins asleep on the stairs. She shook the girls roughly and sent them to their room. "We'll deal with you after this day is over. Enjoy it. It will be your last one together."

"No." "No. you can't part us."

Joe stood above them. "This time you've gone too far."

Mary hoped what they'd heard had not been more than a proposal. She looked at Joe and shook her head.

"Don't spoil Annabelle's last day or I'll skin you alive. Go get cleaned up and help your Mother. Tomorrow we're going to put a stop to your trouble and spying."

Mark had returned home to the apartment above the store that he was sharing with Rod and hung his coat on the peg. A woman's cloak lay on the floor. It looked like Annabelle's. He shook his head in amusement. What does Rod have that women find so special, he wondered? Then he smiled at himself as he answered the question, I think he's special, too.

Mark remembered Rod's dad. As a young man he had envied the handsome gambler and his way with women. He hoped Rod would not die over one as both his father and grandfather before him had done. At the rate he's going, he may. Would Sheldon have the guts to challenge Rod?

He lay fully dressed on his bed and thought of Melissa. In a few hours he would get up and get ready for his own wedding. That is, if Annabelle still wanted to marry the actor after tonight.

Melissa . . . she would have a mind of her own . . . But so had Sylvia . . . She would have liked Melissa . . . have to tell Markie. For the first time in years, Mark fell asleep with a smile on his lips.

Mary went into the bedroom where Joe was dressing and they talked about the twins. "I'm going down and talk to them. I want you to help me decide what to do about their problem. Someday they'll hear something that will really hurt someone." She had not told Joe about Melissa and thought the soldier was probably the father of her child. They had not talked about her condition; she knew Melissa would confide in her when she was ready.

They marched downstairs to the twin's room. Had Melissa told Mark about her pregnancy and the father? Had the twins heard? She bit her lip. Had she somehow neglected these two because they always had each other and their own little world?

They had been born within a year of her loss of another child. Dan and Annabelle had been too young to be of any help and Joe had needed her in the store when she felt well enough to help. They seemed to have their own world, which had few scruples as far as she could tell. They spied on people, blackmailed, tattled, went to church often and professed to be pious. Sometimes she felt they were spawned in a different heaven than the other children.

What were you doing on the stairway listening to Mark and Melissa?" She demanded.

"Nothing." "Nothing."

"All right, out with it." She knew that a great deal of emotional actions and conversations must have been carried out during the night. If she knew what they knew, she might stop tragedy. Mary went over to the bed and took each one firmly by the arm and squeezed.

Mary seldom fell back on physical violence, but these two deserved to be dealt with firmly. Joe stood in the doorway. He had never seen Mary so angry. "These two have been up all night listening to people and I want to know what they heard."

He, too, was worried about the twins. "Either tell your mother everything or I'll get my belt." They looked at one another and then defiantly at Mary and Joe.

"If we tell, you won't punish us?"

"You will tell and you will be punished." Joseph's face was one of fury. Neither of them had ever seen him look like this. They trembled and held hands . . . He pulled their hands apart, shook each one and stood each at the end of the bed. "Now talk."

"Annabelle and Claudette were out nearly all night."

"And what else?" They looked too smug.

"Melissa and Mark are going to get married and . . ."

"And . . ."

Melissa is going to have a baby and we know who the father is."

"All of it girls."

They wanted to keep back a small part, but Joe was unfastening his belt. They began to sob.

"It's Rod's."

"Oh, my God," exclaimed Mary.

Joe looked shocked and the girls gave a triumphant look. He saw it. The worst punishment the twins could have was separation for any length of time.

"As of today. You girls sleep in separate rooms. For the next week, you will go to your room after supper and not come out. If at any time you sneak or set foot in on another's room, I will add another week to your punishment. If you don't do as I say, you will each be sent to a different school in different parts of the country."

They began to sob. "No Dad. Please don't. We won't ever spy again. Please." Mary felt herself soften for a moment, and then remembered what she had heard and her face hardened.

Joe stood over them threateningly, "I've known you should be parted for a long time. Together, you're a thorn in the eye of God. So help me if you ever breathe a word about anything that went on in this house last night, I will beat the living daylights out of you and ship each of you to different schools in different parts of the country. You will never be together again. Do you understand me?" They nodded miserably.

"Now Nettie, pack your clothing. When Annabelle leaves today, you put your things in her room. If you slip back in here just once, you're off. Understand? Betty, you go start breakfast."

Mary went to her room and began to cry. Joe sat on the bed and took her in his arms. "Oh, Joseph, how did such a thing happen?"

"There, there, Mary," he said stroking her back and kissing her hair. "Sometimes two lonely people seek comfort in one another without thinking of the consequence. We know them both to be good. When Annabelle leaves, you can talk with Melissa, and I'll have a word with Rod, if necessary. It seems she has been open with Mark about it and they have made a decision. We're obliged to abide by it, but she should know that the twins overheard their talk."

"I worry so about the girls. What's wrong with them Joe? Do they feel left out? They're very artistic. I let them make all the flowers and decorate the house for the wedding. They did a beautiful job. Have we been too easy on them or left them together too much?"

"Don't know, Mary. People just seem to be born the way they are for the most part and nothing much can change them. Look at Rod. He's more like you than any of the others, except Willie. Those two have more goodness in their little finger than all the rest of them have together in their whole bodies.

"Come on, Mary. It sounds as though someone's getting married today, anyway. Best thing that could happen to Mark and Melissa. Isn't this what you've wanted? Be happy for them. If they've accepted it, who are we to complain?"

She nodded, smiled through the tears, and wiped her eyes with the end of her long white apron. He gave her a kiss and pulled her to her feet. What would happen when Rod found out? Just when Mark had been recovering.

"How about a cup of coffee before I check out the store. I have a feeling people are going to sleep in today."

They had just finished breakfast when Sheldon knocked, loudly. A subdued Nettie answered the door.

He barged on past her into the hallway. "Betty, Nettie, whom ever you are, where's Annabelle?"

"She's still in her room. Mom and Dad are in the kitchen." The formal dining room was decorated for the reception. Usually the family liked to gather around the table in the kitchen where the delicious smell of food and Mary's warm presence filled the room before their busy day started and again at night." Nettie felt slighted. Other than Annabelle, only she and Bettie had liked Sheldon.

He walked past her into the kitchen waving a telegram. "Langrishe is waiting for us in St. Louis. He wants Annabelle and me to be there as soon as possible. Let's get this wedding over with so we can catch the two o'clock stage. I'd better wake Annabelle." He turned toward the stairway.

"I'll call her." Mary said. "You have a cup of coffee with Nettie. Joe, you'd best wake Mark and Rod, if they aren't up when you go to the store. Tell them there may be a change in plans." She looked at him meaningfully and headed for the stairway, then turned back.

"You'd best knock on Reverend Rout's door as you go by and tell him to try to be here by noon."

Joseph grabbed his coat and gloves, glad to be away from Sheldon who stood looking a bit helpless with his telegram in hand. Nettie put a cup of coffee and a plate of bacon and eggs in front of him. He reluctantly sat down to eat.

Annabelle came slowly up the stairway. Again he made a remark slighting the importance of the wedding. "Let me see the telegram, Sheldon." She read it and looked him in the eye.

"I resent your attitude, Sheldon. Ever since we've been here, you've sulked like a school boy. This makes twice you've come shouting into my home. If you wish to call off the wedding, now is the time to say so. Mr. Langrishe made it clear; it was both of us or neither. It might take me a bit longer to get to Paris without you, but I will do it. Can you?"

Sheldon looked startled, trying to decide whether to turn on the anger or charm. He tried the latter. "Oh, come now, Annabelle, darling. I was just tired. We'll not rush. I didn't mean to upset you." He put his arms around her. "Come on now, love, give me a smile and a big kiss.

Joe pretended to shovel a light snow off the porch before leaving. He put his head in the door to see if he was needed.

Annabelle looked over his shoulder and winked at him. "Sheldon, I think Dad is waiting for an apology also."

"Oh, Mr. Bennett, I do apologize for my rudeness last night. We've been under a stressful time schedule. It's my only excuse. I do want to marry this brilliant daughter of yours." Sheldon extend his hand and exuded charm. Annabelle had seen him do a similar scene in a play.

Joe hesitated, looked at Annabelle and quickly shook hands. "I need to get down and make sure Jim has the store open. Do you intend to get married this morning and make the stage this afternoon, Annabelle?"

She hesitated. Sheldon squirmed. "I'd hate to keep the great Langrishe waiting, Dad. Let's try for noon, if the minister can make it. Tell Mark and Rod."

For a moment her voice softened and her eyes misted. She turned away. Joseph hesitated in the doorway; she ran to him and hugged him. "Dad, in case things get too hectic later, I just wanted to say that sometimes I've been a problem but I do love and appreciate your not standing in my way." They hugged each other for a long moment.

"If you ever need me Annabelle, I'm here for you, and Sheldon, treat her well." There was a warning note in his quiet strong voice that he didn't try to veil.

Mary stood watching with a slight smile on her lips. Sheldon turned to her, still oozing charm. "Mrs. Bennett, I apologize to you as well. In the excitement I forgot my manners. I'm sorry we won't be able to stay longer." He smiled boyishly.

Joseph nodded and left.

Melissa, Claudette, and the twins gathered in the kitchen. Annabelle sent Sheldon back to the hotel to get ready.

"Are you certain you want to get married like this Annabelle? This isn't play acting, you know. It won't be over in a couple of hours. Marriage is a lifetime contract." Mary said.

"Oh, Mom, please don't lecture me now. You can't possibly know how much thought I've given it." Her voice was hard and her eyes brilliant.

There was a pause and Melissa said, "Annabelle, Mark and I decided to get married last night. Would you mind if we got married after you?"

"Well, that was quick." Then realizing she had made a blunder, ran to Melissa giving her a hug, and said, "I'd love sharing my wedding with you and Mark. Claudette, why don't you and Dan tie the knot too and we'll make it a threesome. I would hate to miss your wedding."

"Dan and I talked it over last night. We won't be getting married." There was a sympathetic silence as they all looked at her. "Please don't let me spoil you happiness."

Mary leaned over Claudette's shoulder and hugged her. Looking around the table she said, "Hadn't we better help both these brides get ready?

Claudette managed a smile, "What are you going to wear Melissa?" They all began to chatter at once.

Suddenly, Melissa said, "Did anyone tell Mark, Rod and Dan about the change in time?"

The women laughed. Willie and Markie had wandered into the bright warm kitchen. "You boys eat as fast as you can. We need you to take a message to the store. "

The boys ate and giggled as they made chocolate mustaches, taking their time. They were dressed in warm clothing and sent out find all the men.

Melissa decided the dress she had planned on wearing for Annabelle's wedding would do for her own. The twins got out a needle and thread and made her a veil for her hat, cleaned up the kitchen and became very industrious. They often glanced at one another and made faces or shrugged. Mary frowned and shook her head at them when she caught their communication. Behind her back they grinned. They had not told her about all the secret activities of the night.

By eleven forty-five, only Sheldon and the Minister were there. Had Mark changed his mind, Melissa wondered? She felt the baby kick and her hand went to her stomach. Mary caught her glance and realized she forgot to tell Melissa about the twins. The girls looked at one another, knowingly. What should I do, Mary worried? She was about to call Melissa to her room when the men arrived.

Rod had rented a sleigh and came racing up the hill with Markie and Willie who stood up waving at people on the street as though riding in a parade. The men, including Sheldon, rode their horses into the stable across the road from the house.

There was a great deal of laughing and stomping outside. They all looked handsome and smelled of shaving soap and new clothing. Mary rushed Joseph to their room to get dressed, and then took the boys into their room to supervise their attire. People rushed about getting in one another's way and several talking at once.

Sheldon sat alone on the sofa, watching in disapproval at the joking, laughing and good-natured mix ups of the last minute wedding plans of Melissa and Mark.

Melissa wanted Rod to read the poem his mother had written about the Secrets of Loving for the wedding.

She asked Claudette to sing a love song she'd written and Nettie and Bettie to play the piano.

Avonelle Kelsey

Secrets of Loving

The secret of loving is seeing,
Your loved one as a beautiful star,
Whose light is shining to guide you,
And loves you just as you are. (The chorus repeated)

Blending, now weaving and threading
A blanket of life worth sharing,
The woof intersecting the warp,
Each touching the other so lightly,
While letting the colors meander,
Patterns fall into place.

Bright satin ribbons, made up of friends,
And families darting about.
A bit of dark shadows, sometimes made of sorrows,
Weave the beauty of starlight nights,
Composing a comfort, tied with soft laughter,
Lots of fun as you experience your lives.

Looking into eyes, sharing your souls,
Discovering intimate delight,
Speaking often with love and mirth.
In your life you'll fell reflected,
Quilts for warming up the nights.

Claudette sang the song in her lovely mellow voice. Everyone pretended not to see the tears that rolled down her cheeks or hear the catch in Rod's throat as he stumbled over some of the passages. He and Claudette sat side by side when the ceremony began. Rod took her hand. She squeezed his in sympathy as

Sheldon kissed the bride, not letting herself look in Dan's direction.

The glow that was missing during the ceremony for Annabelle and Sheldon filled the room when Mark and Melissa took their vows. In spite of what Mary had learned that morning, she shed tears of happiness for her friend, and brother-in-law. Joe patted her hand in understanding.

After the ceremony, they went into the new dining room. The twins had decorated it beautifully and set the new crystal on the table. Mary let Joe serve a bit of wine.

Mark toasted and said he had never seen two lovelier brides at any wedding.

Joe said, said, "I've never seen so many beautiful women in one place."

Rod added, "It also means that everyone gets twice as many kisses."

No one paid any attention to Sheldon as he cleared his throat, nervously, and said. "Hear, hear."

"I have an announcement." When they all turned to Dan, he continued, "Mr. Taylor wants me to leave today and meet him in the Eastern part of the territory to begin campaigning. Perhaps by next year at this time, I will be a Territorial Representative and he the Governor. That is, if we gain statehood. I may become the youngest Representative in the country. Melissa, I'm counting on your support in this area."

Dan didn't say he'd added a couple of years to his age or that his career depended on his marriage to the daughter. They drank a toast to Dan. The men shook hands with him and the women kissed his cheek. Rod stepped back beside Claudette as Dan continued, "I still have to pack, and so if you will excuse me, I'll ride back with the Reverend and see you at the stage. He kissed Mary, the twins and Melissa, and very gravely shook hands with Willie and Markie before giving them a hug.

Dan and Rod shook hands. He brushed Claudette's cheek lightly with a kiss and rushed out the door.

Rod put his arm sympathetically around Claudette's shoulders. A fact Annabelle didn't miss, or Claudette's brave little smile as she looked at Rod with affection.

Outside, fat snowflakes floated lazily onto the ground. It was decided Rod and Claudette would take Mark and Melissa to the store in the sleigh to see if they would like to live there until they built their own house in the spring. Then, rush back and take Annabelle and Sheldon to the stage.

"Is this a plot by Mary to give Annabelle and Dan a chance to be jealous of us and perhaps change their minds?" She whispered to Rod.

"You're a brave young lady, Claudette. If you can take it, I can."

The punch made them giggle. Annabelle felt a stab of jealousy.

"Throw the bouquets Melissa, Annabelle," the twins called. It was not often that one threw a bouquet up stairs. She threw hers rather grudgingly in the direction of the twins who caught it together, giggling. They looked at Rod. Someday . . .

Melissa deliberately threw hers between Rod and Claudette who automatically reached out and caught it together. Everyone laughed, except Annabelle who turned, rushed to her room and burst into tears.

Earlier, Rod had given Willie a package to put on Annabelle's bed. She threw herself across it and brushed aside the tears, angrily, to see what lay beneath her. Inside was a long, lovely fur coat with a matching hood and muff. It was something she would wear proudly for many years. She smiled as she held it to her face. Suddenly, she wanted to rip off her wedding ring and rush upstairs into his arms. Instead she cried again.

Mary came into the room and took her in her arms.

"Oh, Mom. Why couldn't Sheldon be like Rod?" Annabelle moaned. Mary tried to distract her. Finally, she subsided.

"What a lovely, thoughtful gift. But that's just like Rod," she said. In spite of her disapproval of Rod's and Melissa's past relationship, she wondered why everything Rod touched became something special to others, except that which was dearest to his own heart.

Sheldon came banging on the door. "Annabelle, we must get going. Hurry up."

"Go away." Annabelle called. Sheldon would hear that order often in the following year. He went back up the stairs and paced the floor.

Rod lifted Claudette into the front seat of the sleigh and tucked a blanket around her. Mark did the same with Melissa. He grinned happily at Claudette when he looked back to see Mark kissing his bride. She seemed to be returning his kisses with fervor.

His dear Melissa was now part of the family and would not be rushing off to marry a stranger. He winked at Claudette. She smiled and made a funny face. That funny face. It reminded Rod once again of someone from the past. The one he remembered had freckles and a plump body and loved chess . . . Laughing, they raced off in the swirling, sparkling snow, sleigh bells jingling. The twins, Joe and the boys waved from the porch and threw snowballs. Rod had promised them a ride later after he finished chauffeuring the brides and grooms.

Mary looked at Annabelle as she changed into a brown wool traveling suit with a soft melon colored sweater showing at the neck of the jacket. She's so lovely, Mary thought. How hard it is to let my children go. Moving to Deadwood had been to keep them near her. Now she must let them go to strange lands anyway. For the first time she understood her own mother's tears when they parted. She tried not to think of Claudette's parents who never returned from the sea. The girl had become like a daughter to her. Someday, she might marry a stranger and leave as well. She sighed.

"Tell me what I'm doing is right, Mom."

"Only you know your heart, Annabelle."

"I used to think life followed love and it all fit together like a lovely puzzle. Now it's mostly a painful puzzle. Why does everything have to be so complicated?"

"Sorry, I sound like a spoiled child, again." She squared her shoulders. "It will be lovely in Paris. Sheldon knows all the exciting places and people. We do make a good team. I'll just keep looking forward, not backward," like Rod says.

"The now is usually good, if not; better re-look at your life."

"I remember," she said looking off in a distance.

"Now?" Mary said and they both laughed.

Sheldon knocked again. "They're here. Your Dad says tell you he'll see you at the stage."

Mary and Annabelle clung to each other and cried. "Come back as soon as you can. I've always wanted to see Paris," she confided. "Enjoy it for me."

As she gave the twins a hug they said, "Can we have Rod now, Annabelle. Can we?"

She blushed and glanced at Sheldon. "It looks as though Claudette has already beaten you to him," she said with a tinge of envy in her voice. Rod was holding the door for them while Sheldon carried a few of Annabelle's bags.

"I thank you for the compliment. See you later, Mary. We'll be back to take everyone for a ride in the sleigh. You're invited. He leaned over impulsively, hugged her and kissed her cheek. Rod knew this was a hard moment for Mary. Both Dan and Annabelle leaving the same day.

They stood on the porch; tears ran down her cheeks, the twins stood on each side of her with an arm around her waist, their arms intertwined behind her back.

Suddenly snowballs came over the porch rails. Willie and Markie had been making a pile of them under the steps. The snow was not damp enough to hold together well so it was like being hit with a bundle of feathers. Laughing and sputtering, they climbed into the sleigh and rushed down the hill again.

Mary and the girls hurried into the silent house. "Girls, let's have a cup of coffee and a piece of that wedding cake. She kicked off her shoes and to their amazement, lay back on the couch. They brought her coffee and cake and followed her example, relieved to find they were in her good graces again and being treated like adults. Perhaps she'd have more time for them now and forgive them. When she closed her eyes they winked at one another.

Claudette sat contentedly under the warm robes in the sleigh. Rod had added hot coals to the foot warmers. With him at her side, she felt she could face the world. The snow and cozy warmth made her feel sleepy. Around them the world was like a beautiful fairyland. Maybe I'll wake up and this will all be a dream, she thought. She looked at Rod's smiling face and was glad that part of it was real.

Sheldon had clamored up into the sleigh and reached down to pull Annabelle up. Rod picked her up easily and sat her in the seat. She was wearing her beautiful coat and muff. "Thank you Rod for both lovely gifts," she whispered in his ear. Sheldon looked sharply at them as he stumbled through the sleigh and ducked when the boys threw more snowballs.

"Annabelle, sit back and let Rod get going," he said jealously. She put the muff to her face and smiled serenely. When Rod and Claudette glanced back at this couple, they were having a serious conversation. There were no passionate kisses for this bride.

The stage was ready and waiting. Joe and Dan stood beside it. "The next time I see you, I may be out your way campaigning, Rod." He lowered his voice. "Look after Claudette for me."

"I intend to," Rod said firmly. "Good Luck, Dan. May the sacrifice be worth the goal."

Dan walked to the sleigh, took Claudette's gloved hand and kissed it. He stumbled a bit as he walked back to the stage, shook hands with Joe and hugged him, and then climbed on his horse. He'd follow the stage out of town and then head east to the train near Rapid Creek. Sheldon had climbed aboard with a wave of his arm. Annabelle kissed her Dad and Rod. Before he could respond, she was on the stage and out of his life.

They stood for a long moment looking thoughtfully after the departing family members.

"Want a lift, Joe?"

"No thanks, son, I think I'll walk a bit and check the store. See you at the house for supper. He patted Claudette's hand as he walked by the buggy.

"Little lady, you know we're all fond of you and want you to stay with us, whether you marry Dan or not?"

She leaned over and kissed him." Thank you Mr. Bennett. You're the closest I've come to having a father since I was fourteen. I'll be down to help with the store tomorrow. Rod and I though we'd better help Mary clean up the house this evening."

He watched them drive off. "God moves in mysterious ways," he said to himself. "With the help of Mary."

Weddings & Surprises

In the sleigh Rod said, "Joe means it too."

"I know." There was a peaceful silence as the horses picked their way through the snow. The noisy town seemed subdued for a change. The sun was already low in the sky but its silver glow tried to peek through the fat swirling flakes.

"The first snow fall gives me a feeling that the past has been wiped out and I have a chance to begin again. Somehow, now that Dan's gone and the decision is finally made, I feel a little sad, but relaxed and almost relieved. Have you ever noticed, Dan and Annabelle always seemed to be keyed up?

"They're interesting and fun to be with, but after they leave, I feel I've been holding my breath," Claudette said with a sigh.

"What are you thinking Rod?" She asked and reached over, touching his hand with her gloved fingers. He took her hand in his before answering.

"Several things."

"Do you want to share them?"

"One, that Dan will come back to you sometime."

"No, Rod. He told me last night he and Miss Taylor will be married at Christmas. Her father wants them to campaign on one side of the territory while he campaigns on the other.

"He's a very foolish man."

"So is Annabelle." They were silent for awhile.

"What other things?"

"I've been wondering where we met and when. I feel as though I know you so well . . ."

"Really? If feel as though I've known you each time Annabelle or Dan talked about you. I've heard people speak of soul mates meeting . . ."

They looked at one another and laughed.

"Or are we just leftover souls," he said and every one knows they're better warmed up. Move over here and let's try it." He put his arm around her shoulders and they rode in silence, remembering. He let the horses find their way though the busy streets. Neither wanted to think of the people in the stagecoach riding out of their lives.

"Is that all you're thinking about, Rod?" she asked.

"I was thinking that I love my homestead. But I want a home and family. My parents were together a few short years. They had something special, like Joe and Mary. I suppose I'll never be completely satisfied until I find what they had."

"I know. My parents loved each other so much. When they left on acting jobs, I felt lost, left out and unloved. Maybe that's why I thought I wanted to act so much. It made me feel I was still part of that loving. When I went to live with the Bennett family, the acting seemed less important. I would gladly give up the stage to have a loving home." They rode on in silence.

"Rod," Claudette hesitated, until he looked at her fondly and smiled, "do you think we could make a good home together?"

Before Rod could answer, Willie, Markie, and the twins came racing out. "We're ready for a ride, Rod. What took you so long?" They jumped in the back with an armload of snow balls.

Someone threw a snowball. Mary was standing on the porch in her new coat and boots. Rod scooped her up in his arms and sat her in the front of the sleigh between him and Claudette. They went rushing off in the snow.

Somewhere along the way, they picked up Joseph. His deep mellow voice joined theirs as they sang Christmas Carols. People waved and joined them. When they pulled up at the house in the twilight, they could hear the gulches ringing in song. They trooped into the house shouting with laughter and happiness.

Mary made hot chocolate; they finished off the wedding sandwiches and cake. The twins played the piano, Claudette the guitar and Rod played the harmonica. He had brought a couple for the boys and they sounded off-key notes.

Mary became hoarse. Willie and Markie fell asleep on the couch and the twins began to yawn. Joe and Rod carried the boys to bed and slipped off their shoes and trousers.

When they came back upstairs Claudette turned to Joe and Mary giving them each a hug. "Thank you both for making me feel such a part of the family. If you'll all excuse me, I'm going to turn in."

She stood on her tiptoes and kissed Rod. "Good night and thanks so much. You were such a comfort," she murmured in his ear.

He felt a shock wave go through his body. "We'll talk tomorrow," he whispered. "I'll take you to work, if you'll make breakfast."

Mary raised her eyebrows and looked at Joe. He shook his head, no.

Claudette smiled. "Good night, Rod. See you at breakfast."

Rod returned the sleigh to the stable and went to bed. It still held Annabelle's scent, but it was not Annabelle he was thinking about. Had Claudette been serious? She excited him and was a lovely young lady. Could they have a relationship that was lasting, based on each of them loosing some one he or she loved?

Apparently, it wasn't slowing Mark and Melissa down and they were very thoughtful people whom he admired.

It would not be hard to love her. She was talented and lovely. Around her he felt content, like with Mary. With Annabelle, everything was bubbly surface, but when he was with Claudette, there was a sense of deeper understanding, of intimacy. That was the word. Mary and Joe did a lot of communicating without words. Perhaps that was more important than love's hot flash. Yet, when Claudette had kissed his lips or touched him, he had felt his body tingle with warmth.

Rod decided to take his own advice and imagine his ranch house with Claudette there. He could see her red hair shining in the light as she played the harp. It would be a joy to watch and listen to her deep melodic voice after a hard days work. He saw her with Fawn, holding a lamb, rocking a cradle. Rod remembered the smell of her and her femininity, even in her boyish outfit on the stage. His pulse quickened and he smiled at himself. The human heart is fickle, or, as I have proclaimed, it has room for many more people than we give it credit for having.

He thought of Melissa and of the special feelings they shared for one another. The male bond between Mark, Joe, Dan, and Willie, and of his special love for Mary and even the twins.

Ah, the twins. It was as though they lacked individuality, or a conscious; there was something alien about them. Rod sensed no one seemed to want to face up to their problem, because there didn't seem to be any solution. He pushed aside the thought of evil. Everyone loved Willie and Markie, but the twins had strangeness about them. Mary and Joe were worried about them. Maybe a visit to the ranch next summer would help. They were his family, too, so their problem was also his. At the thought of the ranch he felt a pang of longing. Were the animals in the barn out of the storm?

He fell asleep, only once remembering Annabelle and wondering where she was this night. Deliberately he turned back to Claudette and his image of her as a wife.

Mary was up when he arrived for breakfast. Joe had already left for the store. "You and Claudette have adjusted well to Dan's and Annabelle's leaving. You seem to be good for each other."

"Do you really think so, Mary?" She nodded and was silent because she sensed there was more to come.

"I knew when I came here Annabelle would not be marrying me. I had planned on asking you to help me find a wife and even considered proposing to Melissa, if I could drag her away to the country. It wasn't hard to see she was in love with Mark. Most of the women on the prairies are spoken for," Rod continued with a touch of humor.

There was a pause. Mary thought about Melissa's and Rod's child. It seemed a shame he would not be told. He would be such a wonderful father and husband.

Mary felt he was waiting for words of encouragement. "Claudette has matured a great deal since she left Vermillion. If you and she could overcome your past loves, I think you'd make a wonderful couple. She's not as stage struck as Annabelle and seems to take a real interest in having a home."

Rod knew Mary. He laughed and asked, "Do you have our wedding planned?" Her laughter joined his as Claudette came in, dressed for work. She looked pale and tired. "Sit down and have some breakfast, child. You look worn out. Are you all right?"

"No, yes, thank you, Mary. I'm not hungry. Guess I ate too much last night. She sounded listless and glancing at Rod said, "The snow has stopped. I can walk to work. I need the exercise."

"I'm afraid the drifts are over your boot tops. I'll hitch up your buggy, if you don't mind, Mary."

"Of course not. I may decide to use it later so leave it by the porch when you return. If you don't feel well, Claudette, have Joe drive you home, promise?" Mary kissed her and looked closely at her. Then nodded as though making up her mind about something.

Rod helped Claudette into the buggy and climbed in beside her, she turned to him, "About last night, will you forget what I said. I guess I was a bit groggy from the wine and all the emotions flying about. A sentimental, envious mood."

He turned to her. "Claudette, will you marry me?"

Mary had paused in the door when she saw they had not moved. She heard the proposal and felt her heart do a flip-flop while she waited for the answer. Then, caught her-self and stepped back inside, pausing long enough to hear the answer. It came as a shock.

Tears ran down Claudette's cheeks. "I can't. Rod. I was sick again this morning and my monthly cycle has not begun. I . . . I think I may be carrying Dan's child. So, you see, I'm not good enough for you."

He laughed in delight. She peered at him through her fingers. He took her hands gently away from her face and wiped her tears.

"Don't you see, Claudette? I love Dan. I love all the Bennetts. They've been a family to me. Indirectly, I could pay them back for some of their caring. Having Dan's child would be like having a bit of them with us always. Just as Markie will be a bit of Sylvia. Children are for loving; so are adults.

"I know you don't love me in the same way as you did Dan, or I Annabelle, but there are many kinds of love that might be deeper and longer lasting. I feel we have the capacity for a growing one, perhaps one as deep as our parents had, or Mary and Joe have."

"Do you really think so, Rod?" She needed reassurance.

"In countries where parents choose the mates for their children, they often grow to love each other deeply.

"I know the ranch may sound lonely to you, but Fawn is there with Newly, Sky, Witty, Mike, and Hannah. Now that Hannah and Mike are married, there will be company and several children for little Dan to play with. Anytime you wanted to come and spend time in town, you could. The train will soon pass by the place to Deadwood. It goes back east or Denver. You wouldn't feel so isolated. I'll be here for a few days longer. Think about it. I need a wife. You need a husband."

"Will you slow down, Rod?" She laid her fingers against his lips. "I would be delighted to have you for a husband, Rod."

"And I would be delighted to have you for a wife, Claudette." They laughed together and the paleness of her cheeks turned a lovely pink under the freckles.

He loved the way she wrinkled her nose when she laughed. Suddenly, he remembered. The girl on the boat, his first love. "Claudia. Claudia, do you remember an awkward boy on a ship crossing to England about ten years ago?"

"You? Rod? The same one? I don't believe it. How wonderful!" She hugged him to her.

"May I kiss the bride?" She lifted her lips in answer.

Mary wasn't the only ones listening. The twins had slipped away from their rooms and stood listening behind the lower porch. She didn't see the twins as they put their fingers to their lips, looked at one another and smiled knowingly.

Mary heard a door close downstairs close as the buggy left for town. She sat down in the kitchen, sighed, poured herself a cup of coffee and began planning another wedding.

"After that, we'll decide what to do about the twins . . . "

Rod and Claudette were married two days later. They wrote their own ceremony and spoke these words to one another:

Avonelle Kelsey

Love Is

Between two people
Growing in the same direction
With diverse yet common goals.
I will strive to:
Love without possession,
Allow you the freedom to
Become your best self.
Contribute to your growth and your needs
Without losing sight of my own identity.
Accept your no as well as your yes,
Your pain and sorrow, as well as
Your happiness and joy.
Support you when in need.
Accept both the high's and the low's
Of our relationship,
And give us time . . .
For lives must ebb and flow
In order to become
The very best person of which each of us is capable.

Reverend Rout spoke, "I now pronounce you man and wife. You
may kiss the bride."

The End

Printed in the United States
203578BV00001B/1-62/P

9 780981 611600